PENGUIN BOOKS

THE HISTORY OF A DIFFICULT CHILD

MIHRET SIBHAT was born and raised in a small town in western Ethiopia before moving to California when she was seventeen. A graduate of California State University, Northridge, and the University of Minnesota's MFA program, she was a 2019 A Public Space Fellow and a 2019 Minnesota State Arts Board Artist Initiative grantee. In a previous life, she was a waitress, a nanny, an occasional shoe shiner, a propagandist, and a terrible gospel singer.

Praise for *The History of a Difficult Child*

"An endearing coming-of-age story set in post-revolutionary Ethiopia . . . Sharp and witty . . . Like other child narrators—see Giovanna in Elena Ferrante's *The Lying Life of Adults*; Esch in Jesmyn Ward's *Salvage the Bones*—Selam is curious and obsessive about the truth. . . . A wily and operatic novel about a former aristocratic family's adjustment to post-revolutionary Ethiopia. . . . [Sibhat] has built a portrait of Ethiopia's history while giving us a compelling family drama anchored by a distinctive heroine. . . . Sibhat's ability to find humor in even the darkest situations keeps *The History of a Difficult Child* nimble and propulsive."　　　—Lovia Gyarkye, *The Washington Post*

"Sibhat . . . has created a memorable character in Selam, who entertains us—and her family of siblings and extended relatives—with her smarts, humor, and wily charm. . . . Sometimes heady, often rowdy . . . [the novel] delivers its message with humor and brio."　　　—*Star Tribune*

"A remarkable family saga . . . Sibhat wonderfully distills the political and historical context into a personal story, and centers Selam's emotional turmoil with inventive narration. This is a standout."

—*Publishers Weekly* (starred review)

"Sibhat's vivid narrative is captivating, particularly for its emotional depth, even as some of the events she depicts are shocking. She has achieved any fiction writer's first goal—transporting the reader into another world—and has set the bar high for what promises to be a brilliant career."

—Thane Tierney, *BookPage* (starred review)

"Sibhat tells Selam's tale with verve, offering a vibrant panorama of Ethiopian society in all its complexity with an unforgettable protagonist at the center."

—*Booklist* (starred review)

"[B]eautifully rendered . . . as rich and complicated as they come—a novel that delves fearlessly, with so much grace and compassion, into the most essential corners of our lives, the ones where family, politics, culture, and love are inextricably intertwined."

—Dinaw Mengestu, MacArthur "Genius Grant"–winning author of *All Our Names* and *The Beautiful Things That Heaven Bears*

"An exhilarating novel by a powerful new writer."

—Elif Batuman, author of Pulitzer Prize finalist *The Idiot* and *Either/Or*

"An extraordinary novel. It is at once a story of a sharp-witted young girl trying to hold herself together during political upheaval, and an achingly tender tale of community, family, grief, and forgiveness. Its most striking achievement, however, rests in young Selam's insistence that rebelliousness and nonconformity might, after all, be the greatest expressions of love."

—Maaza Mengiste, Booker Prize–shortlisted author of *The Shadow King*

"Mihret Sibhat's *The History of a Difficult Child* signals the emergence of a major new writing talent. Not only does the novel confront history, masculinity, and gender in refreshing but uncompromising ways, it also has a remarkably original voice, fresh and irreverent. This, combined with the unexpected reimagining of the novel form, her elegant and accessible language, and her deft hand at tragicomedy, ensures Sibhat will soon be one of the most influential voices in the literature of Africa. I am sure this is only the first of many important books that will come from this gifted writer."

—Chris Abani, author of *GraceLand* and *The Secret History of Las Vegas*

"Selam, Mihret Sibhat's ferociously witty young narrator, depicts her family's religious and political struggles in Ethiopia in extraordinarily rich and original prose. *The History of a Difficult Child* is deeply moving as well as hilarious. This is a one-of-a-kind *must-read* debut."

—Julie Schumacher, Thurber Prize–winning author of *Dear Committee Members* and *The Shakespeare Requirement*

"[A] debut novel about a precocious little girl and her family trying to survive against the backdrop of political upheaval in Ethiopia. Themes of religion, loss, community, and independence run through this unexpected and singular work."

—Karla Strand, *Ms.* magazine

"Mihret Sibhat wields the child narrator voice with rare finesse and brave conviction. A brilliant powerhouse of a novel, an incandescent read from an electrifying writer."

—Patricia Hampl, author of *The Art of the Wasted Day*

"A moving evocation of life in a time of terror, as seen through innocent eyes."

—*Kirkus Reviews*

"An unexpected and hilarious voice with a velocity all its own. You won't soon forget brutally frank Selam, or Mihret Sibhat's razor-sharp wit. *The History of a Difficulty Child* is tender and merciless, full of human and political insight. I couldn't stop turning the pages."

—V. V. Ganeshananthan, author of *Brotherless Night*

"A family story, a community story, a political critique, and a very funny rollicking novel . . . Mihret Sibhat's command of language, her sense of humor, and her love for Ethiopia combine to stir the memories of any who have encountered this culture and people. . . . A magnificent guide to this ancient and enduring culture."

—Richard Crepeau, *New York Journal of Books*

Penguin Reading Group Discussion Guide
available online at penguinrandomhouse.com

The History *of*
a Difficult Child

MIHRET SIBHAT

PENGUIN BOOKS

PENGUIN BOOKS
An imprint of Penguin Random House LLC
penguinrandomhouse.com

First published in the United States of America by Viking,
an imprint of Penguin Random House LLC, 2023
Published in Penguin Books 2024

ISBN 9780593298633 (paperback)

THE LIBRARY OF CONGRESS HAS CATALOGED THE
HARDCOVER EDITION AS FOLLOWS:
Names: Sibhat, Mihret, author.
Title: The history of a difficult child : a novel / Mihret Sibhat.
Description: [New York] : Viking, [2023]
Identifiers: LCCN 2022029967 | ISBN 9780593298619 (hardcover) |
ISBN 9780593298626 (ebook) Subjects: LCGFT: Novels.
Classification: LCC PS3619.I236 H57 2023 | DDC 813/.6—dc23/eng/20220819
LC record available at https://lccn.loc.gov/2022029967

Printed in the United States of America
1st Printing

Designed by Alexis Farabaugh

To Mulatwa, Tedla, Dawit, and Melesse:

How are you? I am fine, thank you.

They sang out their celebratory anthems of life gone right; they sang out their woeful but still danceable laments of things gone wrong.

◇

PETINA GAPPAH,
"THE MUPANDAWANA DANCING CHAMPION"

The Beginning

At the beginning is God, and for some reason God is trying to get rid of all the water in His possession, so He grabs His containers and turns them upside down, hurling down the water with all His might, as though He were mad at somebody. The water lands on a small town in southwestern Ethiopia, where this phenomenon is known as bokkaa or zinab, depending on which language your family speaks. It comes down with such violence that, if you're the type of girl who loves to disobey her father and run around in the rain, you'd mistake the liquid blanketing your face for a kind of punishment. When the thunder starts GOU-GOU-GOU-GOU-ing as if God Himself is chasing someone across the floor of the sky, and the lightning cuts through the thick black cloud like it's trying to open the sky for the Return, you do not disobey your father anymore—you run up the front stair into the house.

Your father is pacing around the living room muttering something, but you can't hear what he's saying because of the pounding on the corrugated tin roof, so you get very close to him and find out that he's praying,

Egzio mahrene, Egzio mahrene, Egzio mahrene, begging God for forgiveness because, clearly, He's got to be mad at somebody if He's sending all
this water at once even though He does it quite often. Your father turns
around and sees that you're wet, so he takes off his gabi and covers you
with it without even thinking that he was mad at you just a moment ago
for the running around. He gets rid of the wet gabi and grabs a fresh
one, which he wraps around himself. He opens a side of the wrap like a
big bird extending its wing, and you enter through it. It's a little game
you like to play, until you start accusing each other of hogging the gabi.
You both go sit on one of the two benches on the veranda to watch the
rain.

It rains like this every year in August. Even in the year of the Great
Famine when severe drought in the north caused a world-famous famine that led Bob Geldof and his friends to pen a song called "Do They
Know It's Christmas?" (*They* being Ethiopian children, half of whom
are Muslims or followers of Indigenous religions who, drought or not,
don't give a qub about anybody's Christmas, whereas the other half
are Orthodox Christians whose ancestors were so well acquainted with
the Virgin Mother and Her Son for at least a century longer than Bob
Geldof's and celebrated Christmas on January 7, Jesus's real actual fac-
tual birthday.)

What children in the north may not know is rain like this. Here in the
southwest, water flows and flows down so much that the government
brought farmers from drier parts of the country and resettled them in the
villages around the Small Town and others like it. Here is a small plot of
land; here's some cash for an ox; I know what's best for you; you live here
now. That's one of the reasons why, on any given Saturday at the farmers' market near the edge of town, one would hear six or more languages
spoken.

But today is not Saturday, and nobody has to leave the house for anything, so you and your father sit on the veranda watching the rain gather into a small flood rushing through the gutters on both sides of the asphalt road the Italians built during World War II, when they came to civilize Ethiopia by deploying poison gas against resistance fighters who survived their guns, by disemboweling pregnant women and burning up entire families in Addis Ababa, by mass murdering priests in a monastery, and more. You know this because you listen to the radio with your father every day, but now is not radio time, and you're on the veranda watching the rain erode the grassless surface of your sloping front yard, bringing more of the red out.

Out of the corner of your left eye, you see the flood coming from your backyard, carrying a big piece of paper with a familiar blue on one side. You're sure it's the blue of the poster you buried under the guava tree in the farthest part of your backyard a few days ago, beyond the turmeric and ginger sprouts filling the spaces between orange and coffee and mango trees, right before you reach the eucalyptus grove marking the end of the property. How the poster got out of its grave and made it past all those plants to end up in the front yard is a mystery—it's as if someone dug it out and purposely set it off on its current path—and you feel petrified briefly because you're afraid your father is going to see it. For a moment you consider leaving your father's gabi to go ensure the poster disappears in the flood, but you don't want to call his attention to it. Sometimes you can't believe the words that come out of this man who's supposed to love you—if he finds out what you did to the poster, he might even call you cursed: what have you done, you cursed child, are you trying to get us killed?

You just sit there instead, wrapped in your father's gabi, wishing and wishing for enough water to wash the poster into the gutter at the edge of the road, and it doesn't even take a minute for that to happen. Here in the southwest, there's enough water to wash away a whole country's transgressions. You pray in your heart for the poster not to appear somewhere it shouldn't and get your family in trouble. You pray for even more: you hope the blue you just saw isn't the blue of the poster; that the poster remains buried in the backyard. You can't wait for the rain to subside so that you can go check the grave.

You watch the flood in the gutter take everything on its way—more pieces of paper, plastic bags, somebody's rubber shoe, eroded soil, orange-tree leaves, small balls made of old socks stuffed with pieces of fabric and sponges—and rush past Zinash Hotel, past the offices of the Workers' Party of Ethiopia, past the police station, past the only high school in town and a line of shops selling sugar and lentils and frankincense, and past the big billboard of Marx, Engels, and Lenin welcoming visitors to town, to turn everything over to a small river some five kilometers away, like a dutiful boy who's been running errands for his mother.

The Small River takes all those things and more—a broken plastic doll, tree branches, a third-grade math book, a dead animal's carcass, more eroded soil—and runs along at the feet of densely forested mountains, to the Medium River some thirty-two kilometers away. The Medium River does the same: it takes everything from the Small River and adds bigger things—tree trunks, a portion of someone's house, a human body that had slipped through the cracks of one of the many shaky bridges in the area—and goes to give it to the Big River some two hundred kilometers away, like a middleman collecting bribes on behalf of an important official. The Big River takes what all the small and medium rivers of the region deposit in it—except for many of the corpses that wash up along the way—and starts cutting northwest through valleys, like the river is a blade and the land under it a holiday sheep being skinned, eventually passing over everything to the Blue Nile.

Finally, the Blue Nile takes it all and more—tons and tons of eroded soil containing invaluable minerals; all the lyrics farmers of its home province had sung for it for centuries; a photograph of a family gathered at the back of their house, staring at the camera's eye—and heads west, like a lover rushing to meet his mistress before a day's end. Or maybe like a deserter headed to the border on a horse, to defect to foreign invaders like the Sudanese, the Egyptians, the Turks, the Italians, and many others who have given this land so much grief throughout history. The Blue Nile leaves its home and meets the White Nile in the Sudan, where the two conspire every day to take Ethiopia's things and turn them over to the fucking Egyptians.

That's what the radio said.

MEANWHILE, back in the Small Town on this rainy afternoon, women are gathered at their neighbors' homes for coffee, completely unaware that the flood in the gutters in front of their homes is transforming itself into a treacherous geopolitical weapon. Inside a house across from a mosque, women sit in a circle, hands hovering above a charcoal stove the host keeps alive with a straw fan, discussing the latest pressing issues. A woman whose floral dress brushes the floor as she leans forward on her small wooden stool wonders out loud if it's true that so-and-so's daughter had lost her virginity to that new chemistry teacher who's been going through the town's virgins as if he were a contingent of soldiers all by himself. Or maybe he's like a troop of monkeys who, upon discovering an unprotected corn farm on a windy day, start running against the wind with their arms stretched, flattening the stalks in the process, because it's so much fun. That they're decimating someone's livelihood with their games is of no concern to them, just like this chemistry teacher man who will be transferred to a bigger town after a few years and won't have to deal with the damage he's caused here.

Another woman twists her lips like the seasoned gossipmonger that she is and states coolly that one needs to have one's virginity intact in the first place in order to lose it. Ha ha. What about Eteyé Zinash, says the lip-twister, referring to the owner of Zinash Hotel, which is really a mo-tel (slash restaurant slash brothel). Zinash was recently seen slapping the chemistry teacher's ass. Wey guud! says the lip-twister. That woman is a bottomless pit of promiscuity. Palms cover smirking faces. The man is young enough, the Women say, to be her son.

Nobody asks the lip-twister how she knows about what took place at a brothel. In this town of interconnected lives, possession of true infor-mation about the lives of others is taken for granted: the woman with the floral dress is a floating maid who goes from house to house bak-ing injera or washing clothes for people who are temporarily unable to take care of their own affairs; and the lip-twister has a son known for spending a considerable amount of time at Zinash Hotel. At another cof-fee ceremony, a woman whose daughter works the registration desk at the town's only clinic is present.

Of course there are occasions when a claim made is too outrageous, or a person's reputation has been tarnished by repeated cases of complete inaccuracy. On those occasions, the speaker may be questioned or even silenced by skeptical voices. In most other cases, it is assumed that every-one knows everything—like the radio and God.

———

AFTER THE RAIN subsides, your father leaves the veranda for his room, and you put on your rubber shoes to go to the guava tree in the backyard and see if what you saw in the flood earlier was the blue poster that you had buried days ago. You rush off through the mud lake that pools into the naked part of your backyard at this time of year.

You run past the barn, past the outhouse, and follow the narrow trail between orange, mango, and coffee trees. You must do this quickly as it is beginning to get dark. Very soon, the hyenas in the forest behind your house will start laughing. Foxes have snuck in through gaps in your fence a few times to appear in the open yard by the kitchen. You shudder when you see the hollow tree that your father said was home to poisonous snakes.

You part wet ginger leaves on your way to the guava tree. You pray in your heart: May that cursed poster be in its grave. That cursed big blue poster. That picture of the Comrade Chairman.

Part I

1.

The Real Beginning

On a rainy morning in August, a month ahead of the tenth anniversary celebrations of the revolution, a group of women gather at a house in the center of town to drink coffee, eat bread, and marvel at a thing that's been growing inside the troubled belly of Eteyé Degitu Galata, the former feudal landlady who lives in the green house next door but is clearly too good to join her neighbors for coffee.

"It can't be a child, can it?" they whisper amongst one another.

"No, it can't be. She has that disease that's been making her bleed for over a year now."

"You don't get pregnant while bleeding."

"No, you don't," they say. "No, you don't."

There has been confusion in town over the question of how to deal with Degitu's situation. Ever since the news of her abnormal bleeding got out—there was an incident involving a soiled habesha qemis at a wedding—women of the neighborhood have been sympathetic, her sickness having sucked the vigor out of their revulsion for that aristocratic louse. The revolution has spent the last decade teaching people how to hate the former landed gentry: sometimes, farmers marching through town would pause in front of Degitu's house, chanting "Death to bloodsuckers!" and forcing her and her husband to lock up their doors in fear. The revolution has offered no instructions on how to behave when former bloodsuckers start bleeding themselves. Women of the town don't know what to do, and it isn't just a matter of figuring out one's moral stance; there is also confusion over whether expressing sympathy for people like Degitu amounted to a counterrevolutionary act.

Degitu and her family are not entirely isolated from the community—she has been to the same funerals, weddings, and baptisms as the Women. She's also a member of the town's Mahber, an association of Christian women, where she is known for her dedication to service, inserting her imperialist face at every event, arriving at functions ahead of everyone else, taking on cooking duties never even assigned to her. *That* is sometimes more annoying than her past as a landlady who made her tenant farmers cough up the last cup of grain she was owed. It is more annoying than the fact that, despite losing her large tracts of land, her coffee farms, her businesses, and two homes, she lives in a house with an elevated concrete foundation, multiple rooms, and cement floors. At least that house isn't what it used to be: the exterior is the kind of green you would get if trees could shit and had diarrhea. It hasn't been green in the truest sense since Degitu spent what must have been the last of her monies on a sewing machine. (Or maybe that is what she wants people to think: those former feudal lords might sometimes wear pilling sweaters with missing buttons, but they could be hiding a stash of gold bought at a discount from people who have fallen on hard times.)

The point is: despite not joining her neighbors for coffee, Degitu is very much part of the community. The problem is: everyone knows the list of counterrevolutionary acts is a living list, so although it has been mostly safe to interact with Degitu so far, things might change tomorrow. Even seemingly upstanding citizens who have always been poor might turn out to be members of some counterrevolutionary movement. So much happens in secret, which is strange because in a town as big as a bull's forehead you think you would know everyone. You only get a full picture of your neighbors when they get arrested or, in the case of those who haven't been seen since the Red Terror, completely disappeared. You have to always be alert and ready to abandon people, for anything that's good today might turn out to be counterrevolutionary tomorrow.

This is a list of activities currently known to be counterrevolutionary:

1. Joining or cooperating with counterrevolutionary groups backed by Western imperialists, Egypt, Sudan, Somalia, and other historical enemies

2. Grieving for and or attending the funerals of those eliminated by the revolution

3. Possessing reading materials produced by counterrevolutionary elements

4. Listening to foreign radio stations backed by imperialists

5. Refusing to carry out revolutionary duties assigned to one by the people

6. Refusing to hoist the beautiful flag of the beautiful
Ethiopia during national holidays

7. Defecting to a foreign country

This list is subject to modifications, and ultimately, your imagination is your only protection—you must always try to imagine how anything you do might be deemed counterrevolutionary after the fact. It doesn't matter how small and benign the act is. Like that time an old man who had had one too many glasses of tej asked if the Commission for Organizing the Party of the Working People of Ethiopia was a man or a woman. He was summoned to the police station by the comrades to explain himself. Or like the group of kindergartners who threw stones at the home of a big comrade and ended up being detained by the police for several hours. Compared to these transgressions, coming to the aid of a former landlady appears egregious.

This is especially so considering that reporting a former aristocrat or anyone who partakes in forbidden activities—or activities that seem forbidden—is the easiest path to getting on the good sides of the comrades. Everyone knows the revolutionary government doesn't care much for due process, because the urgency the revolution demands leaves no time for courtroom debates. Nobody wants to be a jealous neighbor's breakfast, and for what—to be nice to the woman who lives in a house with several rooms and cement floors? Eree! It is her own business!

On the other hand, the Women feel that having a chronic illness that makes one bleed so much should result in a person's removal from the counterrevolutionary category, because their own body is countering them and there's no point in wasting more punishment. But in a Revolutionary

State that detains kindergartners, asking for common sense is like hoping for a mule to give birth.

All these unresolved concerns have made things awkward, and people don't know how to behave around Degitu, especially since this once seemingly indestructible giant no longer appears to be a worthy personal opponent. It was better when it was easy to just hate her. She's nearly defeated, although one should always be cautious: she may be sick with a mysterious thing eating her insides; her attempts to find a cure having resulted in none; and it may look like that imperialist cow is finally, finally going down; but you can never be sure with that woman. One moment she's being chased up and down the street by a mob, being properly shamed like the feudal thief that she was; the next she's opening the most successful tej bét in the wereda, her honey wine famous in town and in surrounding villages. Why is she working, anyway? Why isn't she bedridden like a normal sick person? How is she getting out of bed every morning with all that bleeding, going to work at the tailors' collective all day, and taking night classes at the high school before returning home to spend hours making tej for the bar? What is going to stop her? Maybe the government should have disappeared her like what's-his-name's father.

"No, it shouldn't have, what's wrong with you?"

"She has children."

"That poor boy, it wasn't his fault that his father was counterrevolutionary."

"You're right. Forgive me, Emeyé Maryam."

"Ayadris," the Women say. "Ayadris."

May God spare us her fate.

The past is gone, they say, look at Degitu now: she has lost so much weight, and her once intimidating muscular shoulders, which used to make

her look like a fat bull, are drooping. She even appears to avoid eye contact when you talk to her sometimes, as though she's ashamed of her situation.

Ashamed, she surely is. The Women learned of this at that wedding
when Degitu got up from a chair and touched the back of her white habesha dress. As soon as she felt the dampness, she turned to yell at her eldest
daughter, as if the poor teenager were responsible for that red map of
God-knows-what-country (maybe it's the impending map of Ethiopia after the civil war!) on her mother's dress. Poor Wederyelesh started sobbing and Degitu followed suit because she knew it was nobody's fault,
that this was just the Creator doing His work. That was also why, instead
of pointing and saying, look whose blood is being sucked out now, imperialist cow!, the Women briefly forgot all about their revolutionary
aspirations of rejecting bloodsuckers and rushed instead to Degitu's aid,
competing to cover her shame by wrapping their netelas around her
waist.

Some fourteen years later, a random preacher will come to town and
ask: do you know why so many poor people turn out for the funerals of
rich and famous people? Nobody says anything. Because they're equal
now! Ha!

It appears that the Women have come to a consensus to take the risk of
magnanimity toward Degitu. Her bleeding is reminding everyone of their
own fragility. They didn't come to her aid when chanting mobs gathered
in front of her house, or when she was chased about town like a thief, because they couldn't imagine that problem of being a former-landowner-
in-trouble. Most of the Women are of the hand-to-mouth classes and can
never imagine themselves becoming owners of vast farmlands with tenant farmers and servants doing the work—not even during the feudal
era, much less after the revolution nationalized all land, allowing each

family to cultivate a few hectares. But the bleeding, the bleeding is a different story because everyone's got blood and a vagina.

ABOUT A WEEK LATER, the Women stand by the door inside the same house at the center of town, craning their necks over one another's shoulders to get a better view of Degitu as she grips the metal rail along the steps of a white-striped dark-blue bus headed to the Medium Town. Degitu's daughters, Wederyelesh and Beza, wave good-bye at their mother as the bus begins to move.

Eteyé Khadija, who remained seated at the head of a half circle of wooden stools, pokes a stove with a stick, turning up the bottom charcoal to let in air and keep the fire awake. "She must be going to the hospital again," she says.

The Women return to their seats.

"What did the doctor say when she last went there?"

"I heard she was given medications."

"No, she was told there's no cure for it."

Khadija's eldest daughter goes around the room offering pieces of bread on a tray.

"Of course there's no cure for it," says a woman with a cross tattoo on her forehead. "Not at the hospital."

Khadija begins pouring coffee into small white cups. She moves the jebena in a circle, pouring nonstop as each cup fills up, drenching the rekebot with excess coffee.

"It sounds like satanic pregnancy." The tattooed woman crosses herself. "You all know what's-her-name's daughter. The one who was pregnant for fifteen months several years ago and wouldn't give birth."

"Besme Ab wa Weld wa Menfes Qidus." All the Christians in the room evoke the Trinity and cross themselves.

"Bismillah," says Khadija.

"She was impregnated by spirits."

"And not the good ones."

"Astagfirullah."

"I heard they took her to St. Gabriel's for holy water."

"The bump began diminishing right away."

"Somebody should tell Degitu to go to St. Gabriel's."

"Somebody should."

The woman with the cross tattoo leans forward to get her cup from Khadija. Silent chewing of bread and sipping of coffee ensue. Of all the homes they gather at for coffee, the Women like Khadija's the most because there's always proper bread on offer. Her husband works at the state-owned bakery and brings home a bag of bread every day.

"I have a cursed goat," says a woman.

Her goat ate a batch of malt she had prepared for the tela she was supposed to brew for the tenth anniversary celebrations of the revolution in just a few weeks.

"I think that goat is possessed," says the woman. "Maybe I should contribute her meat for the celebrations instead of tela."

"Maybe you should," says another woman. "How are you going to make a new batch of biqil in such a short time? And with no sunshine in sight."

"Who has time for any of it, eski?"

"Who has the energy?"

"I have to cook for my family for the New Year."

"And the day after we cook for the government."

"No break."

"Am I a horse?"

"Please keep your voices down."

"You're going to get us finished."

The Women have been ordered by the comrades to bake bread or cook or contribute household items needed for the festivities. The Provisional Military Government of Socialist Ethiopia is expected to make such a great announcement during the anniversary celebrations that everyone will hopefully, at least briefly, forget about the famine in the north. But the Women are not interested in that announcement or the ones before or after it.

The Women will attend the anniversary celebrations because it is counterrevolutionary to refuse when the Revolutionary State knocks on your door to say you're in the cooking committee, your daughter in the drama club, your son in the band, and don't forget to hoist your flag. It's just that they don't care for the announcements because there's only one truth that needs to be known in Revolutionary Ethiopia: maybe you will live or maybe you will die; maybe you'll live inside a prison or maybe you'll live outside, until you die. In other words, *whether you ride a horse on the left or on the right, the destination is the saddle.* Former aristocrat or not, man or woman, young or old, in the end, everyone is a bleeder. That is the fucking problem, not the goat who feasted on that batch of malt.

2.

A Nail in a Tree

On her way to the Medium Town, Degitu passes time reading a pamphlet—"On Good Parenting"—that she obtained through correspondence with an organization in Addis Ababa.

The bus is headed to the southwest border, with a stop in the Medium Town, where Degitu is from and where her half sister and mother live. Degitu sits next to a man who's been reading the state-owned daily *Addis Zemen* since she boarded. She keeps feeling her bosom for the roll of cash and watch she'd hidden there. She's heard all about the thievery that's become rampant in big cities, especially in Addis Ababa, where this bus originated.

Her hand glides down to her expanding belly. She rubs it tenderly as if she were pregnant with a child. She was done having children when she had her youngest, Little Yonas, eleven years ago. She would take an unplanned pregnancy over this mysterious growth in her belly. "A tumor," said her eldest daughter, Weder, recently. "That's what people are saying."

Degitu puts her pamphlet aside to take a peek at the man's paper. The newspapers are printed in Addis Ababa and only make it to the Small

Town on rare occasions. The man has his copy open to an article titled "The Problem Has to Be Solved Through Cooperation":

> More than any time before, the masses are intensifying the struggle
> being waged in all directions to ensure the successful formation
> of the Workers' Party of Ethiopia by nurturing the gains made
> through the bitter struggles of the past decade and by making all
> the necessary sacrifices.

Degitu reads that sentence—more like a sentence that swallowed other sentences—over several times and shakes her head.

One of her favorite features of the daily is the "Letters." Nothing gets past the censor's desk, and voluntary bootlicking is abundant, but the "Letters" are the closest one comes to reading sincere concerns from citizens. Degitu herself has considered writing to the paper numerous times, calling attention to the pervasion of bribery and arbitrary arrests in the Small Town. She doesn't think the national government would do anything to fix these problems. She just wants local officials to read her complaints and feel exposed. She would tear up her drafts when her husband, Asmelash, reminds her that they have enough enemies. Even when she proposed to write anonymously, Asmelash said that the postal officer might open the mail and report her. When she considered having the letters sent from the Medium Town, he said, you crazy woman, they will know it's you, are you trying to get us all killed?

She has since resorted to sifting through other people's letters, in search of something that reflects her views. Sometimes the letters leave her feeling alarmed at how closely people seem to be watching one another. A woman complained about security guards who have been selling coats they were given by the government to keep warm during night shifts.

Don't people know the guards do that because their salaries aren't good enough? Degitu has read letters in which people demand that the government do something about the low quality of music, and about young people who waste time playing on the streets instead of applying themselves to something useful. She sometimes fears someone might write complaining about her. She can't think of what they might say, beyond her being a former landlady, for which she feels she has already been punished enough. Who knows what people think she deserves.

Perhaps that love-fear relationship she has with the "Letters" feature is what makes it most interesting to her, because if she were only after uncensored words, she would have been into the "Estate Notices," which are right in front of her:

Since Ato Gizachew Yilma and Eteyé Achamyelesh Dagnachew have passed away, Eteyé Alemash Berhanu has requested to be the legal guardian of—

The man suddenly closes his newspaper and Degitu pretends like she's minding her business. He folds up the paper neatly and hands it to her. He must be some big shot with a sizable salary. A slogan on the upper-left corner of the front page declares: We shall build and protect Revolutionary Ethiopia!

IN THE EVENING, Degitu sits for a meal at her sister Haregua's house, where she will be staying while visiting the regional hospital. Their mother, Zeritu, sits between the sisters, her walking stick leaning against the back of her chair. On a table before them is a large tray of doro wat, tibs, cabbage, and carrot dishes on a bed of injera. Haregua spent the whole day making the stew, cutting up the chicken at the joints, careful not to break a bone at the wrong spot, soaking the meat in lemon juice for hours as she stewed half a pot of finely chopped shallots in myriad spices.

"You're not touching the food," says Haregua, looking at Degitu.

None of them are touching the food.

"It's my fault," says Zeritu. She's looking at a picture on the wall across—a haloed Virgin Mary with a hand of benediction.

"What is?" says Degitu.

Haregua scoops up chicken stew with a piece of injera and reaches across the table to feed her sister. "Just this one, for me." Degitu accepts the gursha and cuts a piece of injera to feed her sister in return.

Zeritu does not answer Degitu.

Aside from the clanking of pots and pans in the scullery, where the maid is on cleaning duty, the rest of the house is quiet. Haregua's daughters are away at her restaurant-bar, tending to evening customers. The restaurant-bar, popular in town for offering the best tej and tibs, technically belongs to Zeritu. The old woman has put Haregua, her eldest child, in charge of managing it. The revolution only went after big companies and the landed gentry. Small businesses like Zeritu's were not touched. Her restaurant-bar has continued to dispense hundreds of bottles of tej per day, allowing her and Haregua to lead a comfortable life of eating as much meat as they like and employing two maids—one for the house and one for the restaurant-bar.

Zeritu picks up her walking stick and grips it with both hands. Unlike the hands holding it, the wooden cane has gotten smoother with age.

"This doro wat," says Degitu, "is the best I've ever had."

"How are the children?" says Haregua. "And how is Asmelash?"

"That drunk," says Zeritu. "I don't care how he is."

Haregua scoops up tibs with a piece of injera. Earlier in the evening, she rubbed ground kororima, salt, and spiced butter onto fresh cubes of beef in a large bowl. She added minced garlic, chopped onions, and pepper, and left the mixture alone for a while. Haregua insists on doing all the cooking herself whenever her sister visits. She transferred the beef mixture onto a sizzling skillet and, about twenty minutes later, dinner was ready.

"He's the father of my children," says Degitu.

A neighbor's dog barks in the distance.

Zeritu doesn't understand this daughter of hers: years ago, when Haregua's husband, an engineer who had come to town to work on the construction of the regional hospital, turned out to be a drunk who abused her sister, Degitu would threaten to beat him up and had to be restrained by multiple men. In the end, Zeritu—known for walking about town in the evenings using a spear as a cane—threatened Haregua's husband into fleeing town, because who knew what was going to happen to him if he stayed, and who was going to believe a respected Christian woman would bribe a maid to poison a drunkard like him? Degitu, married to Asmelash and living in a faraway village, was furious that her mother didn't invite her to that party. Now that she has a drunkard of her own, she is willing neither to let him go nor to let Zeritu take care of the problem. It's not as if she needs him to provide; it is she who has carried him and her children from the beginning.

"What does that even mean?" asks Zeritu. "'Father of my children'?"

"He might teach them something I might not be able to," says Degitu.

Haregua tries to feed her mother, but she waves her away.

"What is a wife-beating drunkard going to teach his children?"

Zeritu was married to Haregua's late father, another drunk, for a few years. Why are so many men such drunks, she would often wonder, despite owning a popular honey-wine bar herself. She used to beat up her husband and scream for help whenever he came home drunk and belligerent. When neighbors rushed over, the man would be too embarrassed to say that he had been beaten by his wife. He could not take it anymore—it was one thing to be beaten but also to be denied protest. When she took Haregua and moved in with her mother, he did not resist.

"What is it to you?" says Degitu. "I am the one making the sacrifices."

"What was it to you," says Zeritu, "when you were threatening to beat up your sister's husband?"

"Please you women," says Haregua, "the food is getting cold."

Zeritu never married again after leaving Haregua's father.

"I want my children to have what I wished I had," says Degitu, taking a sip of birz.

The clanking of pots in the scullery has stopped. The neighbor's dog is silent for now.

Zeritu grips the edge of the dining table and rises to leave the room. She walks past black-and-white pictures of her late mother, Haregua's late father, and other bygone members of the extended family, hanging above the buffet cabinet. Degitu and her two brothers didn't know their fathers very well as the men had to shift their focus to raising their own families once they discovered Zeritu wasn't the marrying kind. Degitu's father went back to live in his home province of Wollega, and when she was in sixth grade, a letter came from his young wife announcing his death in a car accident. She didn't grieve his death any more than she already grieved his absence.

Zeritu doesn't look back as she disappears into the hallway.

———

LATER IN THE EVENING, Haregua lights a lantern and follows Degitu to an outhouse built of corrugated tin walls and roof.

"Remember the pestle?" says Haregua.

"As the saying goes, the stabber might forget, the one with the scar won't," says Degitu.

It happened some twenty-eight years ago, when Degitu was fourteen and had just been told about her impending engagement to Asmelash. Degitu didn't want to get married because she didn't know that man Asmelash and whether he would support her dream of becoming a teacher. She tried to run away. Zeritu caught and beat her with a big pestle her maids used for grinding corn and dry coffee cherries. You will not run away from me, said Zeritu, wherever you go, I will find you, kill you, and turn myself in to the police.

"She thinks that beating gave you the illness."

"Why that beating in particular?"

Haregua gives the lantern to her sister and waits outside the outhouse. Degitu is grateful for the wooden seat that's been built above the toilet hole to make life easy for Zeritu, who struggles to squat because her legs aren't what they used to be. Degitu hangs the lantern on a hook by the door and pulls up her nightgown.

"She feels it was the harshest beating she ever gave you," says Haregua. "The angriest she was at you. You didn't just disobey that time, you were going to run away and leave her, deny her a future with you and your children. She was saying she would rather kill you than lose you."

"Our mother is insane," says Degitu.

"You both are."

Zeritu believes that every event has a clear cause, every question a straightforward answer, and every illness an antidote. Once, when a doctor told her that she had high blood pressure, she asked him if he's sure that it's *high* and not *low*. The doctor told her he's sure, and she got up to leave his office. "Don't worry," she told him. "I'm going to suck seven lemons; it will take care of it in no time." Degitu's illness too has a clear cause and answer.

If a childhood beating, committed alongside the sins of selfishness and bitterness and unspoken curses, is the cause for Degitu's mysterious illness, the answer is clear: Zeritu must fast and beg the Blessed Mother to shift the curse to her.

Degitu hovers over the toilet before pushing down her underwear. Her homemade pad of layers of cotton cloth is thoroughly red and covered in clots. She sits down, bends over, and notices how she can no longer easily touch her toes like she was able to five months ago when she was last here. Whatever weight she lost due to the bleeding, she seems to have regained most of it because of the thing in her belly, which might be a tumor or a curse or an evil spirit's child.

AT THE HOSPITAL at dawn, there are already tens of people in line, and the gates aren't officially open for nonemergency business. Haregua wastes no time: she walks past everyone, goes to a guard, and shakes his hand with a fifth of his monthly salary. She tells him her sister can't stand for too long. The man walks over to his colleague, who sits inside a box by the gate, a tip of his rifle visible through the glass window. The guards whisper to each other, and the one with the money signals for Haregua. The sisters quickly enter the gate and hurry off to get ahead of the line at the registration office, the angry murmur of the crowd trailing off behind them.

Roughly three hours later, Degitu sits on the hallway floor of the women's health wing, waiting to be called into the doctor's office. Haregua has gone to the cafeteria to fetch breakfast. All the seats along the walls have been taken by those who arrived before Degitu or those who spent the night. She prays quietly, hoping the bribes she paid were good enough to keep her from spending the night before seeing a doctor.

A big clock on the wall says it's 1:30. Degitu doesn't believe it. She looks at her Omega watch, one of the few remnants of the days of money, and quickly covers it with her netela. The thieves in the Medium Town pretend to be novices from the countryside looking for directions; or devout Christians who've come from a different parish in search of a more powerful holy water; or sick people seeking medical attention.

No one is going to take my watch, Degitu promises herself. It was a wedding gift from her late father-in-law, who spent a small fortune on it. Degitu had known and adored Baba Gebre, a loyal patron of her mother's tej bét, for years before the arrangement of her marriage to his son. The old man, who walked with a limp due to injuries he sustained while fighting the Italians, used to come bearing gifts of honey, coffee, and eggs from his farm whenever he traveled to the Medium Town. He would also bring newspaper clippings and pretend he couldn't read, just so she would read to him. Memories of Baba Gebre were more reason for Degitu to cherish her expensive watch, which is telling her that the hospital clock is behind by about an hour.

THE WAIT HERE isn't as bad as those Degitu endured at the referral hospitals in Addis Ababa, where patients flock from all over the country.

Those hospitals are supposed to have the best doctors and equipment. She only got painkillers and medicine the doctors said should stop the bleeding.

About a year ago, Degitu was seen by a member of a traveling group of Swedish missionary doctors who spent two weeks at the regional hospital treating patients with severe cases. She had been bleeding for months by then. A burly man with brown-rimmed glasses, the doctor who examined Degitu told her that there was nothing he could do for her except to advise that she stop taking birth control pills. He didn't explain why, and there was no time to argue with him considering the number of people who were waiting to see him. She took his advice anyway because she believed in people of science. The bleeding didn't stop.

Degitu feels more hopeful at hospitals than she does at the clinic in the Small Town. She visited the health officer at that clinic numerous times over a few months when the irregular bleeding began.

"You woman, I think you think I'm a Waa Himaa," Ato Girma said to her during one of her visits. "A miracle worker, a prophet, maybe? Teller of futures, reader of unwritten things?"

Girma was a tenth-grade dropout who was trained in dressing wounds, prescribing malaria medicine, and dealing with minor ailments in between. He's one of thousands of high schoolers who were trained by the government to staff a slew of new clinics built after the revolution.

"All I know is that you women are supposed to bleed every month," said Girma. "Yours doesn't want to stop. Clearly, something is broken."

She wondered why she kept going back to him knowing that he would have no answers. Perhaps it was because she was addicted to asking questions. It was like a sickness: she often quizzed priests on Scripture, and Asmelash teased her that none of them would come to their house if it weren't for the free food and tej. The organization that produces Degitu's favorite pamphlets on family matters has a section for readers' questions. She has written in several times, asking such questions as whether having sex during pregnancy is safe and how divorce might affect children.

Perhaps Degitu kept visiting Ato Girma because she knew he wouldn't have an answer—maybe this is the one question for which she didn't want a correct answer. Maybe whatever is boring into her insides, making her bleed endlessly, is something that threatens her basic identity. She is a person who moves forward constantly, despite what stands in her way. She'd moved forward despite forced marriage; despite being saddled with a husband who is more of a burden than a helper; despite the scare of infertility early in her marriage; and despite the revolution and all the financial hardships and animosity it brought with it. All that power, all that moving forward, might be put to an end by this mysterious infection or imperfection or God knows what. She didn't want to know what was wrong with her at first; she just wanted her children to see that she was trying to fix it.

She would have loved to find a cure. She believed in the power of medicine; it was how she was cured of her infertility: a few shots of penicillin for her and Asmelash, and there she was, pregnant with Ezra. What she feared was learning about the true source of the bleeding and what that might reveal about the state of her body. She doesn't know anyone who has bled so much for so long. Most women she knows wouldn't tell anyone or seek medical attention for such an illness out of shame.

In the end, concern for her children overrode the false peace of avoidance. She sought a referral to the regional hospital and from there to the hospitals in Addis Ababa. There has been no solution, and with the emergence of *the thing*, the problem has reached new heights.

A BEARDED GYNECOLOGIST takes his time reading Degitu's file. It's been several hours since she and her sister came to the hospital. They sit in front of the doctor feeling lucky to have been called in this early. Degitu decides right away that she likes this man because he looks like one of those young men who hate the government.

"All right, my lady, you've seen the people waiting outside," says the doctor, leaning forward against his desk. "Tell me about this bleeding."

It's almost as if Degitu has never told her story before. She becomes a broken dam of words as she describes her troubles. It comes and goes, she says, sometimes lasting up to twenty days, and it's got nothing to do with her normal cycle, which has been lost in the barrage. There's also the matter of the stabbing pain in the pelvic area. Sometimes she gets dizzy and has to hold on to something for balance. The endless fatigue has resulted in low productivity and her family can't afford it, especially considering her husband is a no-good drunk who's better at wasting money than gaining it. None of the painkillers she has been given thus far have helped with the pain, the frequent headaches, and the dizziness.

The doctor writes all this down. Haregua is surprised—he should have cut off Degitu long ago. Nobody here has that kind of time with all those patients waiting.

The most humiliating thing about the bleeding is that it has kept Degitu out of God's house. For most of the past year and a half, she has been forced to pray outside the fence of St. Mary's, along with other women dealing with their Monthly Flowers. Every Sunday, the women who stand outside with her keep changing, but Degitu is always there. That's how everyone in town learns of your personal business, not to mention the clerk at the clinic—your diagnosis is out there in town before you even collect your prescription. Every loose woman in town knows Degitu is unclean and not giving her no-good drunk husband what he needs. It's not like she and her husband haven't been together at all since the bleeding began, but that's what all the women perceive.

The bearded gynecologist keeps listening, and Haregua is thinking, he's got to be drunk. That's her explanation for every odd behavior. The man is just tired. He's been at the hospital for just over three hours today, but yesterday he saw far more people than he should be seeing in a day. Especially not on this salary. Even Jesus Christ wouldn't take this job. He's thinking about how he doesn't want to see all those people in the hallway; how he wants to get away from this hospital, this town, this province, this country, this continent, and go to Sweden, where his cousin, also a physician, keeps sending pictures from. Pictures of himself standing by his Volvo; pictures of him and his pampered kids by a Christmas tree; pictures of him walking down streets cleaner than this hospital. How to get a passport and an exit visa, that's the question. He's got some serious counterrevolutionary thoughts swirling in his head.

That's not all, says Degitu. A priest said she's being punished for taking birth control pills—for countering the order of nature, for trying to put a brake on God's wheel.

Counter counter, the doctor is thinking. Counterrevolutionary. How to take free education given to you by the poor farmers of this country and go to Uppsala, Sweden, that's the real question. "That priest doesn't know what he's talking about."

"I know that, doctor," she says. "I'm not illiterate. But that priest is a man of influence. If he's going around telling people that—"

"Tell me," he says, "for how long were you taking contraception?"

"Since I gave birth to my youngest," she says. "Eleven years ago."

He writes this down.

"I stopped almost a year ago after a missionary doctor told me to. A nurse explained later that that should stop the bleeding, but it hasn't."

The bleeding won't stop until somebody stops socialism, he's thinking.

"What should I do, doctor? Where should I go?"

Sweden, he's thinking. "Were your monthly cycles regular before the bleeding started?"

The sisters look at each other. No, her periods weren't regular. Sometimes, they were three months apart, other times up to six.

"There's your answer," he says. "Possible answer. Your body is making up for lost time."

This isn't the first time Degitu has heard this explanation. She's tempted to believe it because it means there's nothing seriously wrong.

"If that's the case, the bleeding should stop on its own."

The sisters look at each other in cautious delight.

"What about the thing?" Degitu asks. "The growth in my stomach."

He puts his pen on the notebook and straightens up. "The symptoms you describe to me, including your long exposure to an estrogen-based contraception, suggest you might have an endometrial cancer."

The sisters search his face for more explanation.

"Neqersa," he says. "Of the uterus."

Degitu takes Haregua's hand. She grips the edge of her chair with the free hand.

"We need more tests to know for sure," he says. "I don't think we even have the technology for figuring that out in this country at the moment."

Neqersa, Degitu's thinking, and she's feeling dizzy.

"Do you have family members abroad? America, Sweden, West Germany?"

Degitu doesn't know much about neqersa, although she's heard it mentioned occasionally.

"Or the means to go abroad on your own?"

Out of all those instances when she had heard neqersa mentioned, one of them floats up to the surface of her memory: well over a decade ago, before the revolution, she had woken at dawn as usual to go to one of her farms to see if the laborers were at work. The servant who always accompanied her on her early morning tours was behind her. He was a perpetual blabbermouth who talked like a radio—so much so that the servants named him Tultula. That morning, he went on and on about one thing or another, but the thing she remembers is the only one that stuck: "If you drive a nail into a tree," he'd said, "it becomes like a neqersa." She remembers him pointing at a tree. "The course of the tree's life will change; it will either become stunted or die." She doesn't know if what he said was a scientific fact, but she's thinking there's a nail inside me there's a nail inside me there's a nail inside me and it's going to change the course of my life until I become stunted or die so she's feeling agitated and hot and dizzy and like she's going to die today and maybe the thing inside her is feeling the upheaval or maybe it's tired of the exchange and is feeling bored so it starts moving and kicking and kicking very hard and making its presence and aliveness known.

3.

Like a Flash Flood

The news of Degitu's pregnancy is everywhere like the smell of spiced butter and berbere during a major holiday. As soon as tests at the regional hospital confirmed that she's carrying a child, Degitu called the operator of the call center in the Small Town and asked to be transferred to her friend Zinash, because there's no telephone at her own home. Degitu related the news to her friend and the operator listened in. That's why you may learn of the pregnancy by the onion stands at the Saturday market. You'd also hear about it if you stopped at a tej bét for a birille of honey wine on your way back from the market. At the mosque on Fridays and at St. Mary's on Sundays. People are even talking about it on Meskerem Hulet, during the anniversary celebrations of the revolution.

A day after New Year, thousands of people from surrounding villages are streaming into town for the celebrations. They had to contend with up to fifteen kilometers of muddy trails on their way. Members of farmers' collectives march down the main street in soldierly formations, their leaders yelling, Gira-qegn! Gira-qegn! in rhythmic coordination with their movements. They're headed to the sports arena where the festivities will take place. When the women marchers kick up their legs left-right left-right, their dresses blow up in the air, and one can see their inner thighs. Onlookers wonder if they're here in their country where nakedness is a taboo or somewhere in the Soviet Union or wherever this tradition of making respectable mothers kick up their legs like a horny donkey came from.

The front porches of all houses in town are adorned with the national flag. Big banners with slogans hang above the main street, tied to poles on either side: ETHIOPIA FIRST! ONWARD WITH THE LEADERSHIP OF GENUINE REVOLUTIONARIES! The marchers go past Sheikh Hassan's bakery, past rows of two-room wattle-and-daub houses on either side of the street, past the police station, past Sheikh Shawara's store, past the offices of the town's registrar, and disappear into a crowd of people swarming the site of the Saturday market, adjacent to the sports arena.

At the edge of the arena where the fences are falling apart, women are gathered in groups around temporary firepits, cooking ground meat and eggs for sandwiches, frying sambusas, boiling spiced tea in pots large enough to fit a scrawny teenager, making time for gossip in between tasks. Degitu has been allowed to stay home this year because of her illness, which comes and goes even with the pregnancy. Asmelash and the children have been assigned work.

Asmelash is part of a team of men responsible for setting up a stage at the arena. Weder is to help with washing dishes and pots and pans after the celebrations. Beza wanted a part in a play. The director, a high school English teacher she's been in love with ever since he got transferred to this town a few years ago, told her she's too young for all the parts. It was like a double rejection. That's why she's helping deliver plates to the arena. Little Yonas is a messenger boy for the cooks. If the oldest two—

Ezra and Melkamu—were home, Ezra, a primary-school teacher in a nearby town, would be in the dance troupe or helping organize the march of the local branch of the Revolutionary Ethiopia Youth Association. As a kirar player for the town's band, Melkamu, who is away working on a two-year diploma in Geography, would have spent the previous few weeks driving the family mad with his nonstop rehearsals.

Comrade Kebede, the boss of all the comrades in town, is onstage speaking over a megaphone, leaning forward slightly because his massive gut is getting between him and the top of the pulpit where his written speech is. The big announcement that's been talked about for months is that today, after five years of preparations, the Workers' Party of Ethiopia has been formed, and the Derg, the junta that's been caring for this motherland of mankind since the overthrow of the emperor ten years ago, has been dissolved. A big applause rings around the arena. Pass me the salt, says one of the women making lamb tibs. As of today, the Comrade Chairman, along with other members of the Derg who have been serving their country honorably, have retired from their duties in the military to serve their people in new roles. More salt, says the woman, this meat is like a rock, nothing seems to improve it. Thanks to the struggles of the masses and the hard work of the Comrade Chairman and honorable members of the Derg, the mission of the Commission for Organizing the Party of the Working People of Ethiopia has been completed successfully! Applause! Applause! It's time to add pepper. The long-awaited Workers' Party of Ethiopia, the party of the masses, will work with the goal of establishing the People's Democratic Republic of Ethiopia! Ululation! Applause! I've got the peppers, you get the qibe.

Say it after me: KeEthiopia Wezaderoch Party Gar Wedefit! *Onward with the Workers' Party of Ethiopia!* That's too much qibe. YeEthiopia Wezaderoch Party ye tamagn abyotegnoch meswatinet wutet naw! *The*

Workers' Party of Ethiopia is a result of sacrifices made by genuine revolutionaries! A woman pulls back a ladle she's using to spoon spiced butter onto sizzling cubes of lamb and onions and freshly chopped peppers on a frying pan so large that it would accommodate a grown man in a fetal position. KeEthiopia Wezaderoch Party amerar gar yeEthiopia hizbawi demokrasiyawi republikin engenebalen! *We will build the People's Democratic Republic of Ethiopia with the leadership of the Workers' Party of Ethiopia!* Did you hear that that crazy wife of Asmelash Gebre Egziabher is pregnant? Mot le imperializm! *Death to imperialism!* Pregnant with what?

That is the question.

"What about the bleeding?"

"How could her husband go near her in that state?"

"Did he?"

"Was she not taking that medicine that blocks the uterus?"

"It can't be a child."

Others weren't so extreme.

"It's definitely a baby if it's moving."

"A crippled one probably."

"Or missing a limb or two."

"Whichever. It can't be normal."

"Has anyone told her to go to St. Gabriel's yet?"

She doesn't need to be told that: Degitu has already been to St. Gabriel's on her way back from St. Michael's in the Medium Town. To Medhanealem in another town. Numerous times to St. Mary's in town. She's been bringing back bottles of holy water after each visit. She's been praying, studying the Bible more often than normal. She no longer has doubts that the thing in her womb is a baby. The reason for her increased devotion is her concern for the child. The bleeding hasn't stopped. What kind of a child could possibly come out of a severely wounded uterus?

Degitu's cautious excitement has been contagious inside the green house. Everyone is delighted that the thing has been identified as a fetus. It is kicking more often and with more vigor. Beza, the youngest daughter, has taken to joking that it's triplets and they're always having a football match in there. Asmelash is often heard saying, what can you do if that's what the Creator wants. When he thinks nobody is listening, he'd mutter, Egzio mahrene, Egzio mahrene. Forgive us God, indeed. Imagine a child with one eye, a horn, and three legs. Imagine a child with one eye, a horn, and three legs, but also something of you.

THE PHYSICAL APPEARANCE of the Coming Child isn't the only thing Asmelash is worried about.

He left the anniversary celebrations as soon as the official functions ended. The town is festive and busier than normal, but not as busy as it is going to be when the thousands at the arena spill out later. Holding on to his closed walking umbrella, Asmelash takes careful steps across the market on his way to the main road. It's easy to identify him from tens of meters away just by the way he walks and by his aging black Italian trench coat.

The rainy season won't be over for another month, so the pregnant sky continues to terrorize those beneath it, perpetually threatening to break more water and drench everything. There are puddles on the asphalt road and everywhere else is muddy. Those with rubber boots use them; those without walk around with their mud-smeared shoes or bare feet, sometimes painted up to their calves and beyond with that brown stew of soil and water. Asmelash often turns up from a rainy season walk outside in shiny leather boots, the cuffs of his pants neatly tucked in. People marvel at his capacity for staying clean. His wife would tell you that it's because he's never in a rush to get anywhere. He can afford to spend as much time as he needs looking for the driest spots, rocks, or fallen branches. There's no point in rushing, he'd say—either he'll get the thing he's after or he won't. Even if he gets it, a revolution or something else might take it.

Asmelash is fine with others rushing toward whatever it is they want. Like the rebels in the north. In fact he wants them to rush toward overthrowing this government, toward bringing back saner days. Maybe give him back his lands. Lands were the best, the most reliable possessions, until they weren't. Maybe a new government would restore his faith in fixed properties. Let Degitu rush too, rush endlessly toward her myriad business endeavors. What drives him to the edge of madness is when she wants to bend him to her will. She doesn't ever seem to understand the idea of slowing down for a minute.

"May God give you good health, Ato Asmelash," says a passing man.

Asmelash tips his hat. "Tena yistilign, Ato Alemu."

His first year of marriage to Degitu was blissful. He hadn't expected that kind of happiness from married life, especially considering their initial resistance against the arranged union. When his father told him he was going to marry Degitu, Asmelash wasn't impressed: he had seen her a few times when he went to her mother's restaurant-bar. He thought she was awkward, too tall for a girl, and not good-looking enough. There was also the problem of her superior education—she had completed eighth grade with distinction, whereas he'd only managed to finish third grade before his father pulled him out of boarding school.

Asmelash couldn't refuse his father, a widower whose mobility was limited due to war injuries. His sisters were already married. The old man always said: daughters were born to be lost to someone else; sons stay and bring more people to the family. Asmelash was Baba Gebre's only surviving son. His stepson, Mesfin, was a violent alcoholic the old man didn't trust with his affairs. When Asmelash asked why he should marry this girl whose mother had no land to her name and sold honey wine for a living, Baba Gebre said he knew the girl and he knew what was best for him.

Asmelash gave in, expecting his relationship with Degitu to become the object upon which he projected all his resentments. In the course of numerous meetings and exchanges of letters during their three years of engagement, he grew fond of Degitu. She was bold, like no other girl he had ever met, often making him blush with her expressions of affection. It didn't seem as though she were going to use her superior education to make him feel lesser; as they got closer to their wedding, she seemed to worship him.

Degitu was satisfied with supervising the servants, keeping busy with small work around the house early in their marriage. In the evenings, they sat by the fire outside, and he played the kirar while she sang. Their first miscarriage was the turning point. Instead of getting closer to him for consolation, Degitu became withdrawn, seeking comfort in more work instead. After the second child arrived stillborn, it was as if she were repulsed by him.

Degitu was no longer content with what they had. She came up with a catalog of ideas. Within years of their marriage, they were buying more land, running the first coffee-processing plant in the region, the only flour mill, and the only proper restaurant-bar within an eight-kilometer radius of their village. They bought cowhide from farmers and sold them to wholesalers in Addis Ababa. They made a fortune. Where's any of it now? Why can't she see that it's all pointless? Why can't she slow down

or at least let Asmelash walk at his own pace? That woman won't rest; a
few years ago, she taught herself how to make clothes and joined the tailors' collective.

The only thing Asmelash considers to be reliable is a government job.
The government is the biggest robber around, and in order to be effective
at robbing, it needs to feed its own. He can't get a proper government job
because he never finished school. That's another thing his wife won't let
him rest about: Why won't you enroll in night school? Where have you
been? Who is that woman? Why are you wasting money? His head is
buzzing with replays of their fights, driving up his blood pressure. He
must return to his more pressing worries.

Worry number one: there's not enough money for another child. The
revolution took almost everything, but mistakes have been made since
then. He can't stand himself when he remembers all the disastrous moves
he's made. It irks him even more that he made those choices against his
wife's advice. He hates how she's always being proven right—city girl
who thinks she's better than everyone. He would have been smarter than
her had he been allowed to finish school.

Asmelash is pulled out of his thoughts by Eteyé Kebebush, who stands
before her tej bét wearing a tattered dress, her waist tied with a scarf.
"When am I getting the honey?" she shouts.

He wonders how she got back from the celebrations fast enough to get
into her work attire. "No later than a week." He keeps walking.

"You said that last time."

"I'm sure this time." He picks up his pace.

Back to worry number one: the family's main source of income, the tej
bét, requires considerable labor to run. As Degitu grows increasingly ill,
not only is her labor lost, all the income from the business is having to go
toward her trips to the hospitals. It's his fault that they have a labor-

intensive business like a honey-wine bar instead of a clothing boutique, which Degitu had wanted. It's also his fault that the family's savings disappeared after the revolution. Everything is his fault. All fingers point to him. Back to worry number one—

After the revolution stripped them of their possessions, each of the former landowners was allowed to cultivate up to ten hectares of land like everyone else. Even that was taken away from Asmelash and Degitu when envious comrades saw how the couple transformed their plot into a beautiful orchard and coffee farm. These bloodsuckers are prospering again right beneath our eyes, officials said.

For the past few years, Asmelash has been buying honey from local farmers and selling it to other tej bét owners. Honey producers are too small and unreliable. Asmelash makes just enough profits to cover some expenses for the household as well as expenses related to the maintenance of his sanity.

All this thinking he's been doing about the past and about the Coming Child has been making his head spin, so he decides to take a detour. He's too sober to go home. Home is where Degitu is, large in her personality, large in her sense of righteousness, even larger in her new fragility—how dare he upset an ill and pregnant woman. Standing up to her has always been easy when he's drunk. It used to be easier before the oldest boys became adults. All the children side with her, except for Beza, who seems to feel sorry for him, but she is powerless against everyone else.

He takes a right when he gets to the offices of the Workers' Party. If he keeps following the main road, he would have to walk past his house, and Degitu might see him. He looks for loose rocks on the muddy gravel road. The closed umbrella tucked under his arm, he skips from one rock to another. He will have to take a left when he gets to Ato Addisu's house, where the fence is lined with false banana trees. There are no loose rocks there; a block from the main street, you're in the forest. He will open his umbrella for protection against drips from trees as he skips from one patch of grass to another. Another left and another right later, he will be able to see the light-blue exterior of Mamitu's Bar, where his friend Shimelis and others will join him later.

THE BAR IS DARK. It won't get any brighter when the sole low-wattage bulb hanging from the ceiling turns on. It's better that way anyhow; there's enough light to see what you need to see.

Mamitu brings a bottle of Meta beer to Asmelash and sits next to him. He looks like he could use some company. He's looked like he could use company for all of the three decades she has known him. He's been coming to her since he was a teenager, the handsome son of a nearby landowner. He would come in to her bar with a mopey face and take up a seat at a corner just like tonight. He complained over the years about how his father wouldn't let him return to school in Addis Ababa; how he was being forced to marry some boyish city girl he didn't like; how he was saving money to run away and go back to school; and so on. Mamitu comforted him in all the ways a man could be comforted. He wasn't the only man she did that for, but he was one of the very few—and at times the only one—she felt particularly drawn to. He often dressed like a statesman, especially before the revolution—tailored suits, sweater vests, ties, and shiny oxfords. He knew how to pick clothes for a woman too. She sometimes gave him money when he traveled to Addis Ababa, and she's never disliked anything he brought back. What she likes the most about him is how, even when the alcohol made him cantankerous, he kissed her with a sort of gentleness that she believes is his truest self.

At some point, Mamitu entertained the thought that she would be the one he would run away with when he was ready. She wasn't deterred when Asmelash married the woman he said he didn't like. He resumed his visits to Mamitu's Bar after disappearing for about a year following his wedding. Mamitu's hopes were rekindled and stayed lit even as he kept having child upon child with that woman. She still had hopes a decade ago when Asmelash moved to town for good after the revolution stripped him of everything. It didn't matter that he no longer had money or that he was descending into a new kind of grief. He would come to the bar to complain, to be comforted by Mamitu's cooking, by her body, to drink himself into a state of near complete alteration. And to leave. He left every night, no matter how late, cursing, staggering, swearing that tonight was the night he was going to settle scores with that woman whose arrival in his life marked the crushing of his dreams, the woman who made him feel as though he were beneath her.

FOUR BEERS LATER, worry number two: Asmelash is not sure if it's good for this child to be born.

"Do you remember the time I went to the Waa Himaa?" Asmelash asks Mamitu. "Back when I lived in the countryside."

Mamitu touches the edges of her black head wrap as she stares past him at the corner of the room, trying to remember. She always wears that head wrap and, with her youthful face, it makes it difficult to guess just how old she is. Asmelash doesn't need to see her hair to guess how old she is. He keeps coming despite the presence of younger women at similar establishments. "I don't remember," she says.

It was over two decades ago. Asmelash came to the Small Town from the countryside where his family and the rest of the landed gentry lived, on his way to a village to see a famous fortune teller. He wanted to inquire about the future of his family, whether he and Degitu would have children. His father had insisted that he visit the Waa Himaa, saying that something needed to be done after three years of marriage resulted in no children. Asmelash didn't care that he wasn't having children with that mule; maybe that was his chance to get rid of her and marry someone more obedient, better looking. Degitu got it in his head that it was his fault she couldn't conceive, that he might have given her some disease that was interfering with her reproductive system. He had to prove her wrong before word of that got out.

After listening to some of the things the fortune teller said to him, Asmelash remembers thinking the man was just a charlatan. Some of the prophecies have come true since then. Asmelash has been remembering lately that the Waa Himaa had told him about a surprise child that was going to come out of nowhere, arriving like a derash wuha, like a flash flood that comes out of nowhere to turn a creek into a raging river. A river gives life and takes life, and Asmelash is distressed because he doesn't know which one the Coming Child is going to be.

Shimelis, Asmelash's closest friend, and a few other men enter the bar singing a farewell song to a bride:

> Atishegnuatim woy ahaha
> Atishegnuatim woy
> Mehedua aydelem woy!

The men face each other and shake their shoulders in eskista. Asmelash and Mamitu chuckle in understanding. It's a false good-bye to the military junta that everyone knows isn't going anywhere, just like a bride who might leave her parents' home on her wedding day but will probably be living within walking distance.

Mamitu leaves Asmelash to tend to the new patrons. Very soon, Shimelis will join Asmelash at his table and four beers will turn into seven and nine. Past midnight, Asmelash will go home a different man—not the soft-spoken one who listens to the radio in isolation every morning when the family gathers for coffee, letting the children bicker with one another. He will stagger into his house with shoes covered in mud, whistling and cursing, looking to pick a fight with Degitu. If there's no ready reason for a fight, he will open the windows and accuse her of leaving them so.

Worry number three to ninety-nine: people die during childbirth all the time. Degitu is his one true umbrella in a rainstorm.

4.

A Boy with a Vagina

Two days after Christmas, Degitu feels the unmistakable pangs of an impending labor. She is experienced enough to know it isn't just the spicy meals of the holidays causing this discomfort. She tells her youngest, Little Yonas, to go fetch the midwife, and he bolts out the door as if he's been expecting this command all his life.

Haregua runs around making sure there are enough towels, blankets, and extra pillows. She and Zeritu have been here for almost two weeks, waiting for the baby's arrival. Zeritu sits next to Degitu in the bedroom, murmuring prayers to Emeyé Maryam, who will understand this family's predicament more than anyone else. God's mother has been through labor herself; she knows what it is like to give birth to a much-anticipated being.

Zinash, Degitu's closest friend, sits on the other side, rubbing her friend's back. "How are you feeling, Degé?"

Degitu glares at her as if to say, why ask me such a stupid question.

Weder and Beza sit by Degitu's feet. Beza, who has a beauty mark the shape of a coffee bean on her right cheek like her mother, is thinking that maybe she shouldn't have been a disobedient child. She prays in her heart: Emeyé Maryam, if you help Emayé give birth in peace, I will stop being so difficult.

Weder rubs Degitu's feet. When she came out second in her class last year, she was mainly upset because she failed to match Degitu's perfect score on the eighth-grade national exam. To get the same score as her mother would have been the ultimate proof that Weder is the one who is truly like her mother, not Beza or anyone else. She will have other opportunities to make her mother proud between now and medical school, but her mother has to survive this labor. Emeyé Maryam, if you help my mother today, I'll buy a parasol for St. Mary's Church with my first doctor's salary.

Degitu grips the edge of the bed, her face projecting uncertainty.

Weder has memories of Little Yonas's birth. Degitu exuded confidence then; she was experienced enough to know that the pain was temporary. Weder has always felt reassured by her mother's physical appearance— her rectangular upper body and thick shoulder muscles—and the confident demeanor it lent her.

There's a treasured family story about a time Degitu attacked a policeman. The police had rounded up wives of former landowners to be beaten and chased about town "like proper thieves." The women were followed by a policeman and children who alternated between a song for common thieves (You thief, you thief! I'll kill you and flee!) and another one for former feudal lords (Bloodsucker, what will you do!). After chasing them the whole length of the main street, which cuts through the heart of town, the policeman brought the women back to the station. He singled out Degitu and took her to a nearby barn for being "a difficult cow." As soon as they entered the barn, Degitu struck his crotch and went for his gun. When other policemen came over in response to the commotion, there was a hostage situation in progress. They brought the other women prisoners to negotiate with Degitu. She agreed to let the hostage go in exchange for the formation of a committee consisting of the women prisoners to deliberate on the issue. The chief of police agreed, and at that meeting, Degitu argued her hostage was trying to rape her, that she was merely defending her dignity. The women sided with her as did the police chief. The family considered her subsequent release a miracle because, in this Revolutionary State, too many people have been disappeared for far lesser transgressions.

This day is not like those other days when the children felt their mother could defy anything. This isn't like any other labor. The woman who carried her family through the turbulence of the revolution is about to be torn apart by God knows what.

Asmelash stands leaning against the bedroom doorjamb, perturbed by what's about to befall his wife of twenty-five years. He's remembering what the Waa Himaa had told him, about a house full of children—I hear children's laughter and the noise of a playground, he'd said—but also about the one who was going to come like a flash flood that turns a creek into a raging river. Egzio mahrene, Egzio mahrene. Forgive us, God.

THE MIDWIFE ISN'T PREPARED to help deliver a regular baby, let alone a special *thing*. She was in her kitchen baking injera when Little Yonas found her. She's here wearing a tattered dark-green dress smeared with dough and soot. Asmelash moves out of the way to let her in. The children leave to make room for the midwife and other women arriving slowly: Eteyé Khadija from next door, Eteyé Tirunesh from across the street, and others are all coming wearing netelas, heads covered in floral wraps, eager to see the strange creature.

As the children make their way out, Degitu's contractions become more frequent. She moans louder and louder. Weder had led away the last of the customers at the tej bét as soon as Degitu began her labor, so the family has the biggest room in the house to themselves. Monday through Saturday, from noon to late evening, the living room turns into a tej bét, dispensing homemade honey wine to tens of customers daily. Weder wipes down tables, returns chairs to their places. She tells Beza and Little Yonas to help. Beza sits at a corner with arms crossed, frowning at no one in particular.

Little Yonas bites his fingernails, wishing none of this was happening. He's no longer so little but that's what everyone calls him to distinguish him from Big Yonas, an older cousin. Big Yonas, who was conscripted to join the national army, hasn't been home for years to necessitate the differentiation, but the names stuck. As the youngest child, Little Yonas often feels like an outsider looking in. Even as they take sides fighting one another, the older siblings seem like a unified entity, as though in the years before he was born they had formed a bond he may never become a part of. He was excited when he learned of the Coming Child because that means he is no longer going to be the outsider, but he's worried about his mother. He's happy when his father calls out to him.

"It's time for radio," says Asmelash.

Little Yonas steps outside to look around the house. A few years after the revolution, Asmelash was briefly detained and questioned by police after his niece reported him for possessing forbidden magazines. Someone has to go outside to make sure no tattletale is nearby before turning on forbidden radio stations. Little Yonas comes back and grabs the old red Philips radio always kept atop the buffet cabinet and turns the tuning knob in search of the Foreign Radio Service.

Shameless man, Weder thinks of her father. He wants to listen to the radio as if everything is normal. He doesn't know how to have a proper relationship with a woman, she's thinking. It's a regurgitation of the things Degitu had said to her in an attempt to explain him away: "His mother died too early and his nanny was hardly a role model."

After a few minutes of static noise and voices in languages no one recognizes, Little Yonas hits the target. This is why he's the minister of radio in this house.

"Keep it down," says Asmelash, looking over his shoulder in case any of the neighbors step out of the bedroom.

A woman's voice comes on the radio:

> This is the Foreign Radio Service, broadcasting in Amharic from Washington, D.C., every evening from two to three o'clock Ethiopian Time. We begin our program—

Degitu screams and Asmelash winces. He wants to know if the rebels in the north are making any progress, but more importantly, he's trying to forget about what's happening in the bedroom. A man on the radio says that even a year after the capture of the town of Tessenai by the Eritrean People's Liberation Front, the Ethiopian government refuses to acknowledge its significance or even concede that the event has taken place.

Someone knocks on the door. Asmelash slaps the radio's power button shut. Weder walks into the hallway to find out what's happening in the bedroom. Little Yonas gets the door and Shimelis walks in. He's holding up a bottle of Black Label that he must have paid a fortune for on the black market.

"My friend," says Shimelis, "I have come to congratulate you." His slightly slurred speech and shimmering face suggest his evening is already well under way.

"There's no birth yet." Asmelash turns on the radio but keeps the volume low.

"There will be one very soon."

Asmelash points to the chair across from him.

The two have been friends since Shimelis arrived in town nearly a decade ago to open the town's first private pharmacy. Shimelis had heard that Asmelash's father is a northerner from his home province, which presented sufficient grounds for friendship. Despite being one of those northerners who had never been to the north, Asmelash welcomed all who came from his father's home province. The two realized later they had something else in common—alcohol.

When Degitu kept insisting that Asmelash enroll in night school, it was Shimelis who advised his friend to agree to her demands just to stop her nagging. Asmelash had given up on his dreams of education after the revolution. Nothing mattered anymore, and his head no longer had the space for learning in a classroom. Shimelis told Degitu he would go to school with Asmelash. She promised to wait for them at home with fresh plates of qurt and whichever beverage they fancied. As promised, the two men left their homes the first night carrying exercise books and a spoonful of salt wrapped in paper. Instead of school, they headed for the back room of Mamitu's Bar, where they salted their beers, believing it was going to prevent intoxication. Asmelash came home late at night staggering and cursing, singing and dancing, to engage in his nightly ritual of opening the shuttered living room windows and accusing Degitu of leaving them open.

"I have sent my boy to the butcher," says Shimelis.

"They must be closed by now."

"They will open for good business."

Degitu screams. Asmelash turns up the volume on the radio.

Shimelis calls out to Beza. "Bring us glasses."

Asmelash shushes everyone. His favorite program, *Eset-Ageba*, has just started on the radio. It's a biweekly debate between Andargachew Nega, an Ethiopian professor of African history at Howard University, and Dawit Diriba, Ethiopia's deputy ambassador to the United States. The professor is calling the ambassador a hypocrite for showing up at their debates religiously while his embassy can rarely be reached by journalists seeking comments on major events in Ethiopia.

Degitu's screaming is intensifying, and Asmelash can't focus.

Beza hands Shimelis two glasses and returns to her seat to put her anxiety into her bouncing legs. When she was younger, Beza would run away whenever she got in trouble. She would find Asmelash at a bar and sit on the floor beneath his chair until nighttime, when he came home staggering. On those days, he had more reasons, in addition to the usual case of the open windows, to be belligerent. Don't you touch my child, he'd say. You touch my child and I'll break you. The chaos he caused would become a bigger issue than whatever it was that Beza had done, so she usually got away with her crimes. She's filled with regret now; she's hoping and praying for another chance to show her mother that she can be a better child.

Little Yonas has left for the backyard. Weder paces around the room, wishing she was a doctor already.

Degitu tears the house apart with a loud shriek. Asmelash can no longer sustain his denial. He shuts off the radio and goes out to the veranda. Shimelis follows him with their glasses of whiskey. They sit on one of the benches outside.

"Don't worry," says Shimelis. "This right here," he says, raising his glass, "this water of God will make all your worries go away."

Asmelash is thinking that maybe he should try to reach Ezra and Melkamu. Ezra lives in a town some eighteen kilometers away. He had to return to his teaching job yesterday after spending Christmas with the family. Melkamu refused to come home, not wanting to burden his mother with travel expenses. Maybe they should come home and see her now. Asmelash can persuade the operator of the call center to open up shop and let him phone his sons. He decides against this idea. Asking the boys to come home would be acknowledging that Degitu might be in danger tonight, thereby summoning a bad omen.

A FEW MINUTES past midnight, most of the women in the bedroom with Degitu hold up kerosene lanterns and flashlights. The town's power generator had gone off two hours earlier, as usual. The living room is lit by a stick candle on the dining table between Asmelash and Shimelis.

A loud ululation breaks out from the bedroom. "Elelelelelele!" One time! "Elelelelelele!" Two! "Elelelelelele!" Three! Asmelash and Shimelis are alert. "Elelelelelele!" Four! Hearts are racing. "Elelelelelele!" Five!

"It's a boy!" Shimelis springs up from his seat.

"Esey, esey, esey!" says Asmelash, rising up to embrace his friend.

Weder runs to the bedroom. Beza follows her.

Asmelash follows them but he stays in the hallway.

"Enkuan Maryam marechish," the women say one after another. To give birth and be alive is a sign that the Blessed Mother has forgiven you all your sins.

"Is anybody looking?" the midwife wonders out loud. "It's not done yet."

"What do you mean?" asks Degitu. "What just came out?"

The women lean over one another to look again. Eteyé Khadija is particularly eager. The next morning, the entire town will have a complete account of *the thing's* birth, and she is expected to be the primary source.

"It's just the head."

"Am I giving birth to conjoined twins?"

"No, it's the head of what appears to be a very fat baby boy."

Everyone cackles. Degitu is relieved.

"Push hard now," says the midwife.

Beza leaves the room to give Asmelash the news. He's pacing in the corridor.

"It's not done yet," says Beza.

"What do you mean it's not done yet? Why did they ululate?"

Degitu lets out a loud shriek.

"They were just too eager."

A loud ululation breaks out again, followed by a long pause.

"Go inside and look." Asmelash is impatient, feeling tempted to go in himself.

Beza goes back into the bedroom. She sneaks in between the women surrounding her mother like a fence to investigate what transpired after she left. It crosses her mind for a moment that perhaps *the thing* only has a head and a neck and nothing else. To her disappointment, what caused the collective sigh was the revelation that the boy has a vagina.

"Go on and ululate then; what are you waiting for?" says Degitu.

"Elelelelele!" One! "Elelelelele!" Two! "Elelelelele!" Three! "Elelelelele!" Four!

Beza goes out to the corridor.

"It's a girl?" asks Asmelash.

"Yes," she says. "But she has a boy's head."

"Is your mother fine? Is the baby missing anything?"

"The baby has a very large, abnormally sized head, and you should worry about that. I don't think anything is missing."

"Close your mouth; what's wrong with a big head?"

"You'll see," she says. "And congratulations, you've got another problem."

Asmelash chuckles. Beza is his weakness. Degitu blames him for encouraging the girl's insolence. Beza's insistence on referring to her father by his name used to be a subject of constant irritation for Degitu. Asmelash said that's how friends referred to one another. She's just jealous, said Beza, and the two snickered like little children, inviting a sidelong glance from Degitu.

Asmelash prays in his heart: may the new child be as free as Beza. He regrets never praying for Beza's freedom. She has made it this far by her own strength.

Shimelis comes over and embraces Asmelash. "Congratulations, my brother!" he says. "Even though it isn't a boy."

Just like that, about two months after Bob Geldof and his friends asked at an international concert whether children in Ethiopia knew that it was Christmas, Degitu rid her uterus of the thing that turned out to be me. I am the little terrorist who managed to fuck with an entire town's head before I was even born, and this is my story.

Part II

5.

Welcome to Me

It's six days before my baptism and I'm being watched like a difficult situation.

The wind is whooshing and whooshing outside, irritating Asmelash because he's trying to listen to the Foreign Radio Service. He sits by a small table in the parents' bedroom, ears stuck to the old red Philips radio. It's been hard to locate the exact frequency tonight, and the rustling leaves outside make it even harder to hear the woman in Washington, D.C., whose voice comes in and out of range as he turns the knob.

Evening coffee is over and the family is gathered, chitchatting about this and that with lowered voices, careful not to anger Asmelash. I'm not chitchatting because I don't have language even though I am ten weeks old.

Little Yonas takes over the radio's tuning knob.

On evenings like this, we gather in the parents' bedroom, our makeshift living room, and wait for the man who runs the town's power generator to dim the lights, signaling that he will be closing shop ten minutes later. After the power goes off, we light lanterns and candles and keep talking, sometimes until midnight, unless Degitu has work at the restaurant-bar. The school-aged children are expected to stay up and study or, in the case of Beza, pretend to study.

Degitu sits on the bed talking to Weder about preparations for my baptism feast. Weder, our future doctor, has me on her lap next to our mother, staring at me like I'm a bug she's examining through an invisible microscope. Beza sits on an old pillow on the floor near Asmelash, pretending to read a science book. The wind is knocking things over outside.

The woman in Washington, D.C., comes on and says something famine something Comrade Chairman and disappears again. Asmelash swears he'll break the radio. Everyone knows he'll break a person before he ever breaks that radio.

I wish I could tell Weder to stop staring at me like this.

There's a consensus in this house that I'm something dangerous who's also in danger, which makes me sound like a quandary, a puzzle that needs to be solved. That's why I'm afraid of aspiring problem solvers like Weder—I do not want to be solved. In addition to emerging alive out of a bloody uterus fighting its own battles against God knows what, I managed to come out fat, looking like two babies smooshed into one, in a famine year that's been taking babies in the north while causing shortages elsewhere. Degitu wasn't even eating as much as she should have when she was pregnant with me. Where did this ass the size of a deep-dish bread come from? Some things, only the Father knows.

The matter of my fatness has made the family's desire to show me off an obscene exercise. People are going to say, this family has too much food, where are they getting it from?

"It's all that gold they hid when they were landowners."

"And the cows they got to keep."

"They've got a lot of milk."

"They drink it every day."

You know who else is fat? Our neighbor Eteyé Khadija. Her husband works at the state-owned bakery, so he's always taking home lots and lots of yesterday's bread. She and her children are starting to resemble bread rolls themselves—smooth and round cheeks that make you want to take a bite. Every time Khadija comes into our house to see me (that's what she claims), she says, muchiguchiwuchibuchi, over and over, and I think, this woman is an idiot, why does she think I understand whatever language that is? When she picks me up, I calculate: any minute she will hold me close to her, and I'm going to take a bite out of that cheek. Degitu always knows my thoughts as if by magic. She takes me away from Khadija before I get my chance. I can't wait to grow muscles and put an end to this business of being passed around against my will.

Degitu is caught between two desires: she wants all the lice-infested gossipers who said her uterus was going to take her down to see that not only is she alive, she's also, by some miracle, no longer bleeding, and the life that came out of that uterus is a chubby life that's doing much better than most of them. On the other hand, you don't want to show off your good fortune too much because some people might give you the evil eye, summoning the selabi that disappears your things: your food storage will deplete fast; your clothes will start falling apart; you will eat and eat but never feel full. The crows hovering above your backyard waiting to steal your chicks will suddenly multiply. You may also fall ill, depending on how potent the evil eye in question is.

Illnesses are already a concern when it comes to me. Is it possible to come out of a wounded uterus without catching some of its illness? I may be fat and look as if I were made of bread rolls of many shapes and sizes put together, but what do I look like on the inside?

———

FAMINE. SOMETHING. Relief organizations. The government. Gone again.

Despite the grimness of the news, that radio station is Asmelash's instrument of hope. Any day now, this damned old red Philips radio is going to bring the news that the dictatorship has kissed the dust, that a new government is returning his vast coffee farms and his coffee-processing plant, which was supposed to revolutionize coffee exports from this region, making him the richest of all the minimally educated lower-nobility bastards who ever mistook him for an equal.

Little Yonas keeps turning the knob.

The rebel groups fighting to depose this government are just another bunch of Marxist lunatics. Maybe the God of Israel, if He's on His throne, will strike them with confusion, causing them to give us our lands back.

Degitu is thinking, Asmelash is crazy and needs a bucket of holy water to bathe in. She doesn't believe these days of "Land to the tiller!" will ever be reversed. Even if that were to happen, she doesn't want to waste time waiting for it. She is eager about smaller things, like recovering completely from the illnesses of the past year and the unexpected birth. She's grateful that the bleeding stopped shortly after I was born. She remains worried about safety and well-being for herself and her children, especially for me. She's holding on to the bed's metal frame, gazing at me.

Do you know what my mother did a week after my birth? She gathered my siblings and announced that she had written her will to instruct that, should anything happen to her, all her possessions, including our house, what's left of her jewelry, and cattle shall belong to me. Yes, me, the blood-stopping peace bringer she has named Selam. I am already taking things from people who have been around for years. There's been so much grumbling about this. First of all, why is our mother summoning a bad omen by writing her will? Secondly, why is this new child getting everything when the rest of us have not finished growing up?

Little Yonas has finally found the correct frequency. Asmelash shushes everyone and it's all quiet as death except for the wind outside. The newsman comes on:

> Human Rights International has released a statement disputing the widespread claim that the catastrophic event currently known as the Great Famine was caused by drought. Mr. David Brown, head of the Africa Division at Human Rights International, has told the Foreign Radio Service that famine was already under way for months when drought struck much of northern Ethiopia. According to Mr. Brown, the real cause of the famine is widespread human rights abuses undertaken by the government of Chairman Mengistu Hailemariam, whom Mr. Brown refers to as a dictator responsible for the deaths of hundreds of thousands of innocent Ethiopians. At the moment, various relief organizations have put the estimates for casualties between four and five hundred thousand people.

"Egzio mahrene," says Asmelash. "Egzio mahrene."
"What's new?" says Degitu.

> Our efforts to reach the Ethiopian embassy in Washington, D.C., for comments were not successful. However, according to the government-owned daily *Addis Zemen*, attempts to blame the Provisional Military Government of Socialist Ethiopia for the famine are nothing but Western imperialist orchestrations to undermine the progress that has been made since the revolution—

The radio says bulumbubumbum. Asmelash slaps it angrily because that sometimes makes it work. It doesn't this time. He gives up and turns away from the speaker.

I'm still cradled on Weder's lap and I know what my sister is doing: Degitu's gaze is often directed at me, so if somebody wants our mother's attention, the trick is to be nice to me like I'm some kind of an intermediary. Who gave you all this power, you ask? Nobody. I took it.

The siblings consider me strange and destabilizing. This feeling is made even worse by the bitterness of having to help care for a helpless little person who has only arrived to steal their inheritance and a considerable amount of the respective shares of parental attention they have worked to secure over the years. Weder stands to lose the most because through a combination of tactics—frequently falling ill or being on the verge of illness, always obeying her mother, and succeeding at school—she'd earned the position of Degitu's confidant. I am vying for the top ministerial position right in front of her.

One way to stop a person's unfair rise to power is by showing her unfitness. My siblings don't know yet that they are gathering evidence against me. That's why this constant surveillance bothers me: everything a person does or doesn't do throughout her life is a potential exhibit for some future trial. Many minds in this house have even been collecting evidence since my conception. Exhibit A: conceived under strange circumstances. Exhibit B: probably decimated an already wounded uterus for own survival (also file under: destroying our mother from within in order to clear the way for household domination).

"Do you think she's going to be normal when she grows up?" asks Weder.

Cow.

(Exhibit C: possibly demented.)

"Ha! If she's going to be normal, I'm going to be the ruler of Ethiopia," says Beza.

I told you she isn't reading anything important.

"Shut your mouth, my child," says Asmelash coolly, as if that's a lovely thing to say. I like him for it.

"I'm joking," she says.

He responds by slapping her head.

I ask myself, can I make people do things just by wishing?

Asmelash is thinking, if Beza doesn't understand at the age of fourteen that there's no such thing as just joking in this Revolutionary State, words won't help her get it. Better a slap at home than at the police station. "Ruler of Ethiopia" is a joke best left to the rebels in the radio.

Beza is upset because Asmelash rarely hits his children. When he does, even a small slap on the head feels like a slap on the heart. He's supposed to be her friend, her refuge from Degitu's repressive regime, the parent she refers to by name. She's twisting her face as if it were clothes being wrung. I am wishing I had arms long enough to reach and slap the one holding me. *Do you think she's normal?* I'll tell you what's normal—my palm on your cheeks. I like this slapping business.

I'm lost in fantasies of revenge against Weder, and so is Degitu against the Women. She's thinking about all the dishes she'll be serving at the feast of my baptism next week when my soul is to be officially placed in God's hands.

"This child stares back at me as if she can really see me," says Weder.

"Of course she can see you," says Little Yonas.

There has to be raw beef, Degitu is thinking. A whole limb of a fat bull hanging in the middle of the living room. There will be beef tibs, lamb tibs, doro wat, and two types of lamb stew—spicy and mild. There will be three vegetable dishes and cheese. The tej is already fermenting, and she's going to order crates of beer and soft drinks from Zinash Hotel. No less than fifty people will attend.

"I know she has eyes, but she can't see me like an adult would," says Weder.

"Have you spoken to the butcher?" Degitu turns to Asmelash. "The beef is to be delivered on Sunday morning, and it must be fresh."

"I will speak to him tomorrow," he says.

Asmelash doesn't think they should spend all this money to feed people who aren't even their real friends.

Degitu doesn't think he has the standing to offer advice on money. She's wishing he'd open his mouth to say something disagreeable so she could spit fire at him.

Asmelash has hit Degitu so many times in the twenty-five years they've been married because he didn't know of a proper way to deal with the overwhelming sense of inadequacy he felt in the face of her relentless independence and superior intelligence. She let him hit her on most of those occasions and went into hiding the rest of the time. She doesn't want her children to grow up like her, carrying a bottomless pit in their chest, the pit of wondering what it would have been like to have a father in the house.

She's growing weary and impatient. The past two years of bleeding have reminded her of the temporariness of her body. Someone has to ensure this new child has a proper upbringing. Asmelash cannot be relied upon if he continues wasting money at Mamitu's Bar. By this calculation, what of Degitu's own decision to spend so much money on the baptism feast? She would answer your question with a question: is it so bad for a mother to throw her infant child a big baptism party if she's not sure she'll make it to her wedding?

Degitu and Asmelash exchange fire with their eyes. Nobody else sees it.

6

The Flag and the Comrade

Three days before my baptism, Asmelash has been assigned to care for me. Everyone else is busy mixing injera dough, cutting firewood, fetching water. Asmelash is a bit of an aristocrat to cut firewood or fetch water; too much of a man to help in the kitchen. The revolution said women can do what men do, so women have been saying, I can be a pilot or a doctor or an engineer just like you. Men have been making fun in response, saying that women need them to dig graves and bury the dead. No one is laughing in this house where one look at Degitu makes you feel like she can dig your grave three times over and put you in it too.

Asmelash has been doing a decent job caring for me, although he's been taking every chance to leave whenever a relative or neighbor walks into the bedroom to visit me. He hands me over and exits promptly to go to the backyard where all the feast preparations are taking place, to give out instructions to my siblings and pretend like he's the rooster running this compound. He takes me with him once in a while, and when we pass by the kitchen, I see the Real Rooster standing by barrels of fermenting tej, her waist tightly belted with a scarf to keep all the flabby skin from the recent birth in place. She tells Weder and Beza to put all their muscles into mixing teff dough; she shouts at the women outside not to add too much minced garlic into the giant pot of spiced butter they're about to make; she gathers my brothers to help her add half a steel drum of boiling gesho and sugar into one of the tej barrels.

Asmelash is not entirely begrudging the task of caring for me. He thinks I'm a wonderful surprise he's delighted to have at forty-eight. His feelings are suspended between desires, like what happens when you want to keep something pretty on top of a dresser in your bedroom but don't want to dust it all the time.

He has many nicknames for me: Chumaté, Mikirkipo, Hiywete, and others. Some of them belong to mischievous folktale characters; others are meaningless, whereas one means something about me being his life. Whenever he leaves me, I want to say, if this kind of wishy-washiness is how you treat *your life*, I don't know what your life is like, you man.

"Do you know that you have my forehead, Mikirkipo?" he says.

I didn't know that.

"You have my eyes too."

I accept.

"You have your mother's nose." He looks over his shoulder. "Unfortunately."

I'm laughing inside.

"I'm only joking; she's beautiful."

Let's say so for now.

"You want to see pictures of younger me?"

Asmelash takes out an album from the shelf under the nightstand. He lies down next to me and starts producing black-and-white pictures.

"Look," he says. "This is me, and this is your mother. See my fore-head? You have it too."

That's a lot of forehead. I don't think I need it all.

"You see those eyes?"

I *cannot* not see those eyes. I'm afraid they're going to fall out if he keeps holding the picture upside down like that.

"And this one," he says, holding up a group photo. It's my parents and siblings. "We were all gathered in the backyard; you would've been in it if you'd existed."

I don't want to be in it. They were all ashy like they worked at a flour mill.

"It was a few years after we lost everything," he says.

Including their lotions.

"And this one," he says of an old man wrapped in a gabi, a hesitant smile crossing his wrinkled face. "This is your grandfather Gebre Egzi-abher." He says nothing for a while as if something is the matter. "I wish he were here to see you. He was a hero."

Something bad is in the air because my eyes are stinging a little.

My father shows me a picture of Ezra and Melkamu standing next to each other in a photo studio with a fake forest background, wearing bell-bottom denim pants and big Afros, Melkamu towering over our old-est brother. The stinging is making water in my eyes, but I see another picture—one of Weder and Beza among the trees in our backyard—and I smile. The clip on Beza's head couldn't keep her unruly hair together.

He takes out another picture. "This is your mother on our wedding day." She's wearing a white dress with a net over her face as if she had to be trapped to attend her own wedding.

My father is silent. He's thinking about their wedding day. Or about the time before their wedding day. Or even maybe about the time before the engagement. About the beginning, the real real beginning, when Baba Gebre came home from a trip to the Medium Town on a sunny November afternoon, to break his promise of sending my father back to school by announcing the arrangement of his marriage to my mother.

He has summoned the spirit of sadness, which is holding us both down, making my eyes sting. I start crying and my father asks what's wrong, as if I'm the only one seeing what's happening.

MY MOTHER HAS ARRIVED on the scene as if she can sense when I am in distress.

"When was the last time you fed her?"

She walks past us into the bedroom and we follow her. She undresses, untying the scarf around her waist first. When she lifts her light pink slip dress, I see that where I used to live, the skin is drooping and purposeless. She gets underneath a wide floral dress she took out of a wooden trunk and lets the fabric fall around her round body. Sitting on the bed, she takes me from Asmelash and places her breast in my mouth. I'm quiet.

"Ah!" says Asmelash. "Just like that."

I'm biting and sucking.

"This is our sixth child," she says.

There's a party inside my mouth.

"Heh heh!" says Asmelash.

I'm so happy I want to stop time.

"Did you talk to the butcher?"

This milk in Degitu's breast is the answer to sadness.

"I did," he says.

She doesn't believe him. Years ago Degitu sent Asmelash to the Medium Town to get a business license for a clothing boutique. She had made a deal with a supplier, a distant family member in Addis Ababa. It was the perfect business plan—she could run the store with minimal effort, the children taking turns to help her. She would finally be able to focus on finishing high school, and the children would have more time to study. All Asmelash had to do was turn in an application, pay the fees, and pick up the business license.

"What did you tell the butcher?" she asks.

"I told him what you told me."

He came back from that trip to the Medium Town with a license for a tej bét. Look at so-and-so, he'd said, she's making so much money selling tej. Degitu was stunned. And so-and-so, and so-and-so, he said. They're all making a fortune; we could do the same. As if it was a good idea to open the kind of business everyone already had running. Like this spoiled child of the aristocracy was going to help with making honey wine.

When my father says he's already spoken to the butcher, something in my mother is stirring. It's almost as if she doesn't care if he has actually done it; she wants him to know that she doesn't trust him.

"If I go talk to the butcher, would he say you've put in the right order?"

"You woman, why would I lie to you?" He sits down next to us.

"Why should I trust you?"

"Do you want to go talk to him?"

"I think I'll do that."

She gets up with me sucking her breast. She bends down with only one hand around me, opens a trunk, grabs a netela. She struggles to wrap it around us with one hand. Asmelash comes over to help. He places the netela on her back and brings the ends to the front. He's smiling because he sometimes finds her anger and stubbornness amusing and because this moment is reminding him of the day he lifted the veil on her bridal gown to claim her as his. Degitu is thinking how annoying it is that his teeth are so white and straight like a freshly built fence.

Degitu's initial resistance to marrying Asmelash began eroding when she saw his gap-toothed smile. The erosion accelerated when she discovered that he was amenable. He had shown up to their first meeting looking shabby. Perhaps his standards were deteriorating due to the low expectations of the countryside. Or he was looking for ways to sabotage their marriage. Degitu told him he looked terrible and gave him precise instructions on how to dress up for his official introduction to her family. He accepted the challenge. It was a sign that marriage to him wasn't going to be the death of her independence.

His gap tooth is gone now. Sometimes thinking about how much she misses it makes her forget how disappointed she is in him. Not today; she's determined to stay angry.

WE'RE WRAPPED IN netela on our way to the butcher. Degitu takes big steps like she's attacking the ground. She walks down the front stair between the two sour orange trees before marching across the front yard to the street.

We go past Sheikh Hassan's bakery, and almost pass the offices of the Workers' Party when I hear a man wish my mother good health. She stops.

I stop sucking her breast.

"May God give you good health, comrade Sisay." Degitu tucks back her breast.

It's a chubby man whose ears look like they're about to be swallowed up by his bulging cheeks. "I hear you're preparing a feast," he says. His head would be a perfect rectangle if it weren't for the bulging cheeks.

"Yes yes, this one is getting baptized."

"Congratulations," he says, smiling. All his upper teeth are of the same size, like somebody took a tiny chain saw to even things out.

"I'm on my way to the butcher," she says.

"Eshi eshi," he says, looking down. "I won't keep you. I was just wondering earlier when I passed by your house, what happened to your flag."

"What?"

"I know it's been weeks since Adwa celebrations, but people leave their flags out—"

"What are you saying, comrade Sisay?"

He tells us that our flag wasn't on our front porch yesterday and the day before. I'm thinking, who's this man who's always watching us when we're not watching him back? Degitu doesn't know what to say. Comrade Sisay is smiling, as if he's trying to say something is the matter, but it's not a big deal although it is kind of a big deal.

"We didn't remove it."

"I'm sure you didn't. The wind was strong a few days ago. And you're busy."

Degitu's heart is beating fast.

"I would check those trees," he says. "They're tall and green and the flag just blends in." He grins like Satan as he tells us that it isn't nice to let the flag live on a tree, as if it is a monkey or something. He says our family is respected in this town whether Degitu believes it or not. I can feel her tightening her grip around me as if I'm some kind of arrow she wants to fire at him.

"People look up to you."

"I'm sorry, comrade Sisay, I'm embarrassed."

He's not moving and we're not moving.

"Ah," says Degitu finally. "Has Asmelash not invited you to the baptism?"

"I'm sure he's very busy. And it's not necessary."

"I don't know what to do with that man. Please come. And bring Eteyé Hibist. It would be an honor to have you."

"It's not necessary, Eteyé Degitu."

"I beg you. The celebrations won't be complete without all our friends there."

"Eshi eshi. We will be there if you say so. May God give you."

"May God give you too."

Rectangle-Head finally says his good-byes. Degitu takes a few steps forward before turning around. Forget that fresh beef; she has a bigger problem. Since the revolution, people like comrade Sisay have been hovering over her life, looking for the smallest excuse to detain her and Asmelash, which they have done numerous times.

She steps onto the stair leading up to our house—one two three—and cocks her head this way and that. It's true, the flag is near the top of the orange tree above our roof, out of sight and entangled with a branch. Maybe it was trying to run away too. Degitu marches into the house and calls out for Asmelash. He's in the backyard giving instructions to the boys who are cutting firewood. "Do you know where the flag is?"

"What?"

"Do you know where our flag is?"

"What is this woman talking about now?" He searches the boys' faces as if to say, come to my rescue, please.

"The flag. Green-yellow-red!"

"Where it's always been, on the veranda. Why are you berating me? I'm not a flag guard."

"The flag has been gone for three days and you don't notice it?"

"Where did it go? And why should I be the only one to notice it?"

"I'm always in the kitchen or at work breaking my back. You're always out there doing God knows what!"

"What do you want me to do?"

"Nothing, you're useless." Degitu turns away from Asmelash. She orders Little Yonas to climb the tree and take the rogue flag down.

IN THE EVENING, my father and I wait for *Eset-Ageba* on the Foreign Radio Service. The debate is broadcast every other Tuesday, but when it goes over time, they transmit the remaining portions over subsequent days. Asmelash notices a picture that had fallen out of the album he was showing me earlier and picks it up.

"Look at her," he says to me, "she's your grandfather's aunt, the mother of General Wondyirad." He takes out the album again and finds a picture of the general, a handsome man with an angular jawline and slick hair. "He was very accomplished in the air force," he says. "I wish he were around to meet you."

The general cannot meet me because he was executed by the revolution over ten years ago. He was the one who took my father away from home when he was twelve years old to enroll him in boarding school near Addis Ababa. Baba Gebre, my grandfather, was upset because the general had already taken his oldest son to send him to school too and that son became an air force pilot, showing no signs of ever returning to the countryside.

Education elevates a man, the general used to say every time the two met, and Baba Gebre couldn't say anything to counter that. He knew the general had done so well because he was educated. Baba himself had gained so much because he was literate. When Baba Gebre's oldest son died in a plane crash during a military exercise, my grandfather finally had his response: education does elevate a man, he said, until it brings him crashing down. Nobody was going to crash again. Baba Gebre pulled Asmelash out of school.

The radio man says, here comes the second part of this week's debate between Andargachew Nega, professor of African history at Howard University, and Dawit Diriba, Ethiopia's deputy ambassador to the United States.

PROFESSOR ANDARGACHEW: I fear that depriving citizens of information is causing them to rely on ridiculous conspiracy theories. It is infantilizing to keep people in the dark. People cannot grow properly unless they know the truth of their conditions.

DEPUTY AMBASSADOR DAWIT: My dear professor, my government has always informed citizens of what they need to know. The rest is state secret.

PROFESSOR: You know I am not talking about state secrets.

AMBASSADOR: Most of our people are Christians, and in the book of Genesis, Adam and Eve learn that it is not good for them to know everything—

PROFESSOR: You are appealing to religion while representing a revolutionary Marxist government?

AMBASSADOR: Let me ask you, professor: God forbid, if some-one you know dies, do you go straight to his mother and say, your son has died? No, you don't. You make sure she's sitting down. You drive her to her son's house, perhaps, all the while keeping the se-cret. And finally, you don't say her son has died. You say: your son has gone to rest. Some things are best kept secrets. This has always been our culture.

PROFESSOR: You are appealing to our culture. I thought yours was a revolutionary government who sought to change the way—

AMBASSADOR: Ours is a very communal society. Socialism is merely a return to that core of what makes us—

PROFESSOR: Excuse me, ambassador, let me finish—

Asmelash laughs whenever the debate gets to this point. The modera-tor intervenes to redirect the conversation.

The men in the radio are the sort of people my father wanted to be like when he was young. I promise I'll not become a pilot, he'd said, when Baba Gebre pulled him out of school. The general told me he would send me to Europe to study medicine, he'd said. When that didn't work, Asmelash told his father about conversations he had overheard at the general's house—that the emperor was planning to open the country's first university soon, and he could become one of the first teachers there. Or like the men who argued with one another in the newspapers. He wanted to receive a medal from the emperor for being the first Ethiopian to do something. There were so many opportunities in those days to be the first this and first that. My father wanted to be elevated like his uncle and like the fathers of his classmates, who came to the boarding school every weekend to pick up their sons, looking like ambassadors in their tailored suits and shiny shoes and European watches. He didn't understand why his father couldn't see that times were changing: that being a literate landowner was no longer enough to rise and be respected among fellow aristocrats.

Baba Gebre made a promise then. "I'll send you to school close to home," he said. "Come help me with the farms for a bit now."

Sometimes, when you break a promise, you break the heart that's holding it too. When you break the heart that's holding the promise, you break the person holding the heart too. When you break a person, you break the hearts of all the people who hold that person in their hearts. My father is in my heart.

7

A Child of Love and Discord

I've been brought to St. Mary's for the baptism torture. My father is missing. Yesterday, as Degitu sat in the backyard cleaning chickens she was going to cook for the feast, Asmelash approached nervously to suggest that they buy whiskey for their guests.

"This feast was your idea," he said. "But my friends are coming. People have come to expect such things from us."

Degitu threw a whole chicken at him.

In the past, when he came home drunk out of his mind and falsely accused Degitu of leaving the windows open, she didn't defend herself because she understood she couldn't reason with his madness. It appears she has had enough of his aristocratic nonsense; she's gotten tired of waiting for him to become a man, of handing him her savings so he might feel like he was in charge.

In the middle of a room full of chanting deacons bearing giant silver crosses atop long wooden stems, my mother sits on a carved stool holding me close to her chest, as the deacon swinging the chains of a censer full of burning frankincense circles us. In front of her, our family's spiritual father, Meri Geta, hovers his cross over a green plastic bucket holding ordinary water that he must turn holy. The chanting continues until the priest decides it's time, and my mother strips down my clothes. A deacon takes me from her and circles in place a few times because if he doesn't, there is no telling whether my soul will be saved. Someone brings a bigger bucket close to the deacon and he holds me over it; another monster picks up the water in the green bucket and pours it over me. It's very cold and I'm feeling shock and anger and wishing I had muscles and long arms to make all these criminals pay, but everyone else is delighted and the chant grows louder.

Boys are saved much earlier than girls—at the age of forty days—because maybe there aren't enough of them in heaven. God must have said to send the girls at a slower pace as a measure of population control. That was one among numerous issues that never made sense to Degitu, who asked questions of priests from St. Mary's every opportunity she got, always taking care not to sound disrespectful because, while many of them came to her bar to drink themselves into a state of utter insensibility, they wore turbans, embroidered vestments, and stoles; they were men of God. She found times of drunkenness to be the best for asking questions, because the priests were too relaxed and at the mercy of her supplies to accuse her of mutiny.

Our nefs abat, Meri Geta, is the most frequent visitor of all the priests. As the man assigned to shepherd our household, he is like a family doctor who takes the initiative to make preemptive visits. A spiritual disease rarely causes you to wake up early in the morning sweating and shivering while running a high fever; instead, like the slickest of snakes, you never see it entering your house, and by the time it convinces you to eat that apple, it would have been too late to call your nefs abat. That's why Meri Geta visits frequently, mostly uninvited.

"Father," Degitu once said to Meri Geta after handing him a birille of tej. "Do you know Matthew six by heart?"

"Tadiyas," said the old man, holding the birille's neck between his fingers. "I'm a priest."

The subsequent throat clearing, the shifting in his seat, and the evasion of eye contact made Degitu suspicious. She brought a Bible from the bedroom and opened it to Matthew 6:

> Be careful not to practice your righteousness in front of others to
> be seen by them. If you do, you will have no reward from your
> Father in heaven.

She kept reading until verse 18, where Jesus commands His followers not to advertise their fasts. The priest nodded, pulling at his beard, looking up at the ceiling.

Degitu closed the Bible. "Why is the fasting season announced publicly? Why do we go to church wrapped in white during Lent, announcing to the world that we have been fasting?"

Meri Geta took a sip of tej. "My child," he said, "it's how our forefathers did it."

The ways of the forefathers were the answer to most of Degitu's questions. This morning of my baptism, Degitu remembers other questions she's had for a long time: Why do we baptize boys much earlier than girls? Why do we baptize them this young when Jesus Himself wasn't baptized until thirty? She knows she is not going to get answers. For now, she is better off celebrating that this miracle who came out of her wounded uterus twelve years after she thought she was done having children has made it to eighty days.

THE FRESH BEEF that Degitu ordered hangs on a rack in the middle of our living room. Women of her Mahber are here to help serve guests. The men drink bottles of honey wine. They go back to the beef rack for seconds and thirds. The lamb and beef tibs are already gone, the doro wat is nearly out. Degitu joins some of the women dancing eskista to the songs playing on the stereo. Guests, including Rectangle-Head and his wife, come and go. One of my family's former servants, Tultula, has brought me a live goat as a gift. My mother told him it was too much, and he said he didn't want to hear it. Nothing is too much for a grandchild of Baba Gebre.

My father is nowhere to be seen.

It's embarrassing that he is missing the feast of his own child's baptism. As soon as Rectangle-Head walked in, Degitu wished my father were here to entertain and keep the man in check. Who knows what a dedicated cadre can dig up. The comrade has to be watched, and most importantly, someone has to shake his hand with some cash to thank him for bringing the family's attention to the runaway flag.

LATE IN THE EVENING, the last of our guests spot Asmelash at the front stair on their way out. He struggles to make his way up. Tultula and Ezra help him.

My father is in the house, saying, I'm tired of things being taken all the time everything is going and nothing is coming back and we're just standing around I want to say good-bye to my uncle the general but he's so far away. My father turns to where I'm cradled on Weder's lap and begins to move toward me, looking like a garment hanging on a clothesline on a windy day, bending this and that way. Give her to me, he says, and Degitu appears next to me as if by magic and says, away from that child or more things are going to be lost tonight. She's my child, you untamed mule of a woman, remember always that you're the wife. Back away, she says, there has to be a husband for there to be a wife. A few guests have stayed behind to watch this. She's my child, says Asmelash, she's my child, give her to me, over and over, and I'm sitting here with my eyes stinging and thinking that it's true: I'm a child of a drinker who is sad because he can't say good-bye to his uncle the air force general who was executed over a decade ago and I'm a child of storm and of a captain trying to steady the ship, a child of give and take and trust and betray, of forced marriage and love and discord, of war and famine and bleeding uterus. I'm like revolution.

My father turns around to go open the windows so wide that, through them, I can see all the way back to another beginning.

8.

A Window to the Past

THE COUNTRYSIDE, 1963-1976

We rose before dawn as always, rubbing sleep out of our eyes as we peeled our bodies off hay mattresses, to start our daily chores before the new lady of the house came by to check on us. We only called her new because she was the latest outsider to join Lord Gebre Egziabher's family—that taskmistress had in fact been there for three years. She hadn't shown up the previous three days, and it was no more peaceful than usual for us; we kept expecting her all day. She had only missed that many days in a row while at home twice before. It would have been foolish of us to assume she wasn't going to show up for a fourth day, so we were up washing our faces, waking the fire, measuring corn flour for instant bread.

She ran that place as if it were some kind of factory making lifesaving potion for children. We pleaded with God to grant her twenty-eight children in a year thinking that might be the only thing that could exhaust her enough to stay in bed till sunrise like a normal person, instead of walking around the servants' quarters at dawn, nagging us. She came to us those mornings wearing her husband's long coat and rubber boots. She knew he was too much of a human being to need those things that early, snoring and dreaming of all the women he'd rather be with. Women shorter than him like a proper wife. Women who could give him children.

There was no time to sit around thinking about her husband's dreams: if she didn't find the women getting a head start on the workers' breakfast; if she didn't see the men headed out to weed the coffee farms; if the younger ones weren't fetching water from the well, that woman would sit you down and ask you difficult questions: do you know how many people would fast and pray for days to get a chance to live here and eat for free and get paid two birr a month? We never responded to her questions. We thought about how, where we came from in the north, there was nobody left for us. Or how, where we came from in the east, our widowed mothers were waiting for us to come back when those two birr a month reached sixty, so that we could buy oxen for the farm. As for some of us from the south, we had scars the shape of thick vines running up our backs and legs, imitating the ropes our fathers took to our bodies when we failed as shepherds.

We were waiting, but there was no smell of her.

When she didn't feel like asking difficult questions, she would tell you a story. Say you had been lagging behind at work: you didn't pick enough coffee, you took too much time churning butter, or your supervisors complained that you took too many breaks during harvest. She would have you called up to the main house where she would be making yarn or mending clothes. You sat down on a stool or on the floor to make sure you were lower than her, and when she asked if you knew the tale of the donkey and the ox, you lied and said no because you knew it was about letting her make a point.

"Once upon a time," she'd say, not even looking at you, "there was an ox who went to a donkey to complain about how tired he was from working all the time. The donkey gave him advice: 'Tomorrow morning, you should fall on your back moaning and saying that you've got a stomachache and can't do anything.' The ox thanked the donkey, went back to his barn, and did as he was told the next day. He was allowed to stay home, but someone had to pull the plow, so the farmer took the donkey to work. The donkey came home exhausted."

She'd pause then. "Would you pass me that basket?" she'd ask, and you'd deliver a basket of cotton fibers or spools of thread to her in no time.

"The ox was happy he had a day off. He wanted advice on how to get more, so he went to the donkey. 'I don't think you should take another day off,' said the donkey. 'I've heard the farmer say he's going to slaughter you if you keep on being sick.' The ox realized how fragile his place was and decided to stop deceiving his owner." She'd look at you then, smiling. "Return my tale, wipe my mouth with bread."

We wanted to wipe the history of her marriage to that family—we wanted to reverse time and send her back to whichever section of hell she had come from. Before her arrival, we slept till sunrise; nobody cared about how long or how hard we worked. Lords Gebre and Asmelash didn't press us. Lord Gebre's daughters rarely came by the servants' quarters before they got married and moved away. We only had the unpredictable tempers of that mad Mesfin, Lord Gebre's stepson, to fear until he built himself a house a quarter of a day's walk away.

We waited and waited that morning. Our mistress was nowhere.

Only that house servant of hers, the one we called Tultula because he never stopped blabbering, showed up at our doorsteps. He was always with our mistress on her morning terror missions. The way he walked behind her (like a rooster who was also a landowner) and his endless bragging (about how she was teaching him reading and writing) made us question whether our mistress should be the most hated person in that compound. Tultula came over and said he needed to get the mule ready, and we were thinking, which mule? Nobody dared say it out loud. We only said it to one another later over morning coffee.

Tultula said he didn't know why our lady wasn't here. It was one thing to be absent for four days, but to also send for the mule? Our minds raced. There were a hundred possibilities as to why that was happening. We settled on one that made us happy: the curse had finally crippled her.

By sunrise, we saw that we were wrong. We weren't surprised; we couldn't remember the last time our wishes came true. From our kitchen door, we could see across a field of grass to the front yard of the main house, and the devil was slower than usual as she walked toward the saddled mule, followed by Lord Asmelash, holding on to his closed walking umbrella, and Tultula, carrying a bag on his shoulder. We had seen her mount that mule before, putting her left leg on the stirrup before sweeping her right across the back of the animal with no trouble, like some kind of a warrior in disguise. The husband had to help her that morning. For the sake of Lord Asmelash (and for our sake!), we hoped she hadn't lost another child. We couldn't wait for Tayitu, the housemaid, to come by our quarters in search of the supervisor of the day laborers, who had been giving it to her almost every afternoon since her last man left. Lord Asmelash grabbed the mule's cheekpiece, Lady Degitu took the reins, and with Tultula following proudly in his role as a glorified pack animal, off the three of them went, down the main path and out the front gate.

THREE DAYS AFTER our masters left, we collected a few coins from everyone, added a small sack of coffee and grain we skimmed from the main house, and traded them for the fattest sheep we had seen since that shiny ram Degitu bought for Lord Gebre about two years earlier. The main house was empty except for the old man, who couldn't even go outside for morning sun on his own anymore. The leg he damaged at war had been getting worse.

We dipped into the flour sacks at the main house and baked ourselves teff injera, having been desperate for a break from eating corn injera every single day. We sent the children away to fetch us a dozen bottles of tela. We ate like kings, drank like queens, and referred to our mistress by her name.

We learned about the lost child the same day the masters left for town with Degitu on the back of the mule. Tayitu came for her man in the afternoon like a hungry chicken in the rainy season. We were beginning to think that maybe the curse was working against Degitu, even though she had been losing children before the curse was put on her by that old nanny. Anyone who had looked the old nanny in the eyes could feel death looking back at them. We didn't feel too sorry for the nanny when she was thrown out the previous year. That old cow loved to sit on her round bottom, which had no business belonging to a servant, and ordered us around as if she were our mistress. We couldn't refuse her because we had all seen Lord Asmelash going in and out of her chambers at odd hours.

That nanny was the one who taught Lord Asmelash the ways of manhood. The oldest of us had been around since he was a boy, before he went to school for a few years in Addis Ababa. The nanny had a spell over him that only those of us who had seen her carry him to her bed as a boy understood. She had him tied up in her waist scarf like her savings. Everything she asked, he did. Even after he came back from Addis Ababa all grown, even after he got married, all she had to do was signal for him to follow her and he went to her room like a calf following its mother. If she saw him looking at another servant twice, God help that woman, because the nanny would threaten to set her up for theft unless she left immediately.

Degitu was as bothered about it as sorghum on a hot skillet when she figured it out at first. She was dropping plates, Tayitu told us, knocking stools over, staring out the window, and being irritable with everyone. Degitu and Asmelash were mad in love when they first got married. It ended when she lost her first child and became sullen, sending her husband in search of his old addiction.

Degitu didn't like the old nanny from the start. She demanded to know why that old nanny was living in the compound and eating for free when she was doing nothing. Crazy city girl, Lord Asmelash had said. That was what he said whenever Degitu did something he didn't like—crazy city girl—even though he was the one who couldn't be kept away from the city. You expect me to get rid of the woman who raised me? he said.

Degitu yelled at Asmelash when he came back from one of his nightly visits to the old nanny. We heard about how Asmelash called Degitu an untamed mule, telling her he had never done anything any man wouldn't do. About the slap across the face that could have turned into a thorough beating had she not run across the house toward Lord Gebre's room, threatening to tell.

Degitu began biding her time. She knew old man Gebre would let her do whatever she wanted. The two often sat on the front porch at sunset, Degitu reading the Bible to him and the old man smiling as if Medhanealem Himself were giving a sermon. None of his children, besides Asmelash, could read to him, so sometimes, when Asmelash's eldest sister came to visit, you could see a plan to poison Degitu written all over her face. No one understood the spell Degitu had on Lord Gebre. If you were to believe Mesfin, his younger brother's wife had visited a powerful tenquay. She was trying to use her spell to lock Mesfin and his sisters out of their inheritance.

Degitu waited for Lord Asmelash to go on one of his trips and told the nanny to pack her things. We came out of our quarters that day when we heard the screaming—the nanny wailed as if somebody had died. Tayitu told us later that the wailing came second—first was disbelief, followed by defiance. The nanny had asked Degitu who she thought she was. Degitu told Tultula and another house servant to drag her out. That was when we came out to hear the curse:

MAY THE FRUITS OF YOUR WOMB ROT

MAY YOUR CROPS TURN INTO HAY

MAY YOUR HARVEST CATCH FIRE

MAY YOUR DRINKING WATER TURN INTO BLOOD

MAY YOUR LEGS LOSE THEIR STRENGTH

MAY YOUR HOUSE DROWN IN SORROW

Eyes red like the heart of a sleeping fire, shouting curses at Degitu, her fat hips shifted below a makeshift sack made of a tattered netela as the nanny walked out the main gate, flanked by Tultula and another house servant. We turned around to see Tayitu collecting the parting money Degitu had offered the nanny before she slapped it out of her hand. We wondered then: how much do you have saved in your waist scarf to leave twenty birr scattered on the ground?

A FAT RAM could be fat all it wants, but in the hands of thirty-three people, it was hardly enough for a single lunch. In the evening, some of us sat around a wood fire in the kitchen, drinking coffee with our legs stretched out on the floor, savoring the comfort of knowing that our masters weren't due back for a few more days. Degitu had gone to a Greek doctor in her hometown to see if he could tell her why no child would stick to her womb. Had she bothered to ask us, we would have told her it was because she was a man in disguise.

Our children made their own fire. They roasted the poor ram's seed sack on a stake and howled and laughed when it exploded, exposing its fatty insides. Some of them dug into the boiled head of the ram, scooping out the brain and cutting up the tongue to share amongst one another. The rest of us wanted none of that. It was all we got when our masters slaughtered animals: the head, the intestine, and everything else they didn't want. We had already feasted on tibs fried in spiced butter and herbs and onions that special day. We didn't want to think about how we had saved every piece of bone from that lamb to slip into the watery ground pea stews we would be eating until God gave us some meat again.

We drank coffee, laughed loudly, and talked about whatever we wanted that evening. Coffee was the one thing we could drink all day and all night long and nobody, not even that devil, bothered us about it. We asked Tayitu about our mistress. Tayitu was supposed to govern the household in the absence of our masters. There she was, telling us about how Degitu wanted to visit the Greek doctor who had been healing people in her hometown of all kinds of ailments. City girl, Asmelash had said. You just want to go to the city. After she lost a child the third time, he gave in.

Tayitu told us that Lord Gebre had been grieving all over again, wishing there was a doctor like the one Degitu wanted to visit when his wife was lying in her deathbed many years ago, sick from a weak heart. Asmelash must have been a boy of ten or so when his mother died. Lord Gebre didn't stop wearing black until three years ago, when Asmelash married Degitu. The old man wouldn't listen even when his children sought the intercession of elders, begging him to stop grieving, to consider remarriage. When Asmelash resisted marriage to Degitu, old man Gebre saw an opportunity: if you bring that girl to my home, he'd said, if you make her my child, I will wear white to your wedding.

About a year after Asmelash married Degitu, Lord Gebre summoned his stepson, Mesfin, and asked him to buy him a good sheep. Mesfin, as unlucky as he is, starting with his ugly face, went out and came back with the scrawniest little lamb we had ever seen, the scrawniest little lamb that also looked like it had taken a bath in its own shit. Lord Gebre told us to take that mess of a thing out of his sight. He called in Degitu and asked her to buy him a sheep. We swear on our mothers' lives: all that woman had to do was step outside the gate and there was a farmer, dragging the fattest and shiniest ram we'd ever seen in our lives.

THE GREEK DOCTOR'S potion proved too strong for the old nanny's curse to stand. Years after Degitu went to visit him, there were four children running around the compound, with a fifth on the way. If you counted the students who had been attending the school Degitu opened three years ago, there were sixteen.

We learned from Tultula that the week Degitu stayed in her hometown visiting the Greek doctor, Lord Asmelash stayed in the Small Town, coming in and out of his mistress's home, looking for a black rooster and a brown goat with a white forehead, to fulfill the commands of a Waa Himaa who had insisted that our lord's future was written all over such a rooster's gizzard and the goat's caul fat. As our ancestors would say, a fortune teller doesn't know his own business but loves to blabber about the lives of others. If that Waa Himaa had asked some of us what his business was, we would have told him that he was only after the rooster's legs and the goat's ribs. Nobody ever asked us these things; we were only good for skinning somebody else's lambs, milking cows, and, before Degitu opened a flour mill, grinding flour with pestle and mortar until our palms blistered.

That flour mill never seemed to stop running. Every farmer's wife from nearby villages flocked to it as if it were St. Gabriel's on Tahsas 19. Lines of women carrying grain in sacks and plaited palm bags stood around the fence, gossiping about the "crazy wife of Asmelash Gebre," who had been bringing things they had never seen to the village ever since her husband built that bridge to town.

Degitu had been traveling to town more frequently by then—even to Addis Ababa a few times—coming back with machinery: a meat grinder for her restaurant; a metal stick she heated and curled her hair with; a thing that milked her breasts and that, according to her, could tell how many coffee cherries a tree would produce. She took that breast pump around to terrorize her tenant farmers, pointing it at coffee trees, telling them how many cherries that tree was going to yield that year. It was known everywhere she owned lands that the crazy wife of Asmelash Gebre Egziabher had a machine that counted coffee beans before they even showed up on the tree, so no one should steal from her.

Whether that breast pump could really count nonexistent coffee cherries or not, we weren't surprised that she could tell the future because, two weeks before Lord Gebre Egziabher went to his eternal rest, Degitu made us prepare a feast for his wake. She told us she had a dream that he was going to die on St. Michael's feast day. We woke up on St. Michael's day; the old man didn't. We couldn't even speculate that she had strangled him in his sleep, because he died surrounded by his children. People returning from the funeral were welcomed by a feast. Where did all this food come from, people asked. The crazy wife of Asmelash Gebre Egziabher, it was said.

That was what the farmers said when she opened a school too—the crazy wife of Asmelash Gebre Egziabher wants us to send our children to her. They were suspicious about this place that wanted to keep their children away from fetching water and gathering firewood. Some of them gave in eventually. Three years after the school's opening, twelve of the farmers' children were running around the compound, coming by our quarters to ask for bread and water during recess.

At first we thought having children would exhaust Degitu into leaving us alone. The woman didn't know how to stop, as if she were related to that flour mill. She opened a restaurant-bar, like her mother in the city, making us work like horses to help her run it. All the farmers passing through the village to use the bridge Lord Asmelash had built began stopping at the restaurant for sustenance. Tayitu began raising her chin at us after being promoted to governess of the restaurant. We gave her sidelong glances, reminded her that she needed the men on our side of the compound to relieve the eternal itch between her legs. The flour mill came after the restaurant. Someone had to sweep spillover flour daily and feed it to the cows.

When Ezra turned six, instead of sending him away to a school in the city like some of the landowners do for their boys, Degitu built rooms at the edge of the compound, hired a teacher, bought books, and said here was a school for everyone. We were no longer just washing clothes, digging wells, harvesting corn; we also had to tend to the desires of all these children.

Did our wages increase? No. We couldn't complain because Degitu would have asked us her questions: Have you ever been asked to grind corn since the flour mill opened? Did I ask to reduce your wages after that? Would you like to go work at Dejazmach Morada's farm instead, where you would get nothing for your work besides food and shelter? We had no answers.

SOMETIMES WE FORGOT how angry we were at our ever growing responsibilities when we saw Ezra, Degitu's eldest, who seemed to love spending more time with us than he did with his mother. He used to sneak into our kitchen in the mornings to ask for whatever hodgepodge breakfast we were making for ourselves. He didn't seem to be interested in the scrambled eggs or the firfir or the chechebsa soaked in spiced butter waiting for him at his mother's table. He returned to the main house with his mouth smeared in corn dough, to get a condemnation or sometimes a whipping. The next day, he was back with us.

Ezra refused to go to school until the children of the servants were made to go with him. Our kids went to learn with him how to read and write signs we couldn't decipher. When our masters went on trips together, Ezra would bring their radio to us and let us listen to music, his face bursting in giggles as he joined us in dancing eskista. Those were the only times we listened to the radio. No one ever dared touch that thing.

Ezra's tenderness reminded us of old man Gebre, who used to cry with his tenant farmers as they recounted their troubles to him, begging for their debts to be forgiven. Ezra was the only child we knew who cried for the donkey in the tale of the donkey and the dog. He would ask for that story occasionally, nagging us until we obeyed.

"Teret teret," we would say.

"Yelam beret."

"Once upon a time, a donkey went to a dog to complain about how tired he was all the time, carrying people, hauling loads, traveling long roads. 'Me too,' said the dog, 'I'm so tired of barking so much, staying on guard all the time.' Together, they decided to leave their master's house in search of a better one. After walking a long way, they took a break in a field where there was plenty of grass for the donkey. The donkey ate too much and announced that he needed to bray. 'Please don't,' said the dog. 'You're going to alert the hyenas.' The donkey said he couldn't help himself; he was too full. He brayed once. 'You bray once and you alert the hyenas,' said the dog, 'you do it twice, they will be able to locate us.' The donkey said he felt like he was going to explode unless he did it one more time.

"As the dog predicted, a hyena came and killed the donkey. The dog sat there watching. The hyena ate some of his kill and looked up to ask the dog what he was doing there. The dog explained that he and the donkey were on a journey to find a better master. 'And you have found a better master,' said the hyena, laughing. The hyena asked the dog to guard the dead donkey for him as he went down to the river for a drink.

The dog agreed. A while later, the hyena came back and counted the body parts he had left behind. He noticed that the heart was missing.

"'Where's the heart?' the hyena asked.

"'What heart?' said the dog.

"'The donkey's heart.'

"'My lord,' said the dog, 'if that donkey had a heart, he would've had the wisdom not to bray and alert you to his presence.'"

Everyone in the room would cackle at that point.

Except Ezra, who would cry like the dead donkey was his blood relative.

A FEW MONTHS after Ezra's tenth birthday, it seemed the city girl finally got her biggest wish. A number of our men were told to round up the cattle and deliver them to the barn at the new house she had built in the Small Town.

She gathered her personal belongings along with the children and left the village, with Tultula and another house servant helping her herd pack animals carrying bags and trunks. She was in a hurry; she didn't even throw a feast for Christmas the week before. We didn't know what to tell farmers who had gotten used to coming by for bread and tela during the holidays.

Tayitu said the departure had to do with the latest fights between our masters, over Degitu's dreams and what people in the radio had been saying about change in government. Some of us had been alive since before the days of Talian, but we only knew His Majesty's government. We didn't know what a change in government was and didn't understand what it had to do with our masters. Tayitu said that Degitu had had a dream about soldiers setting the compound on fire, so she wanted to move the family to town before that happened. Asmelash said no bedwetting soldier was going to come near his property.

Asmelash had left town on business the day before Degitu ordered our men to round up the cattle. There was a lot of fighting over the new house. City girl, he'd said, you just want an excuse to go back to the city. She started building the house when he went on a long trip to Addis Ababa with the first shipment of coffee from his new coffee-washing plant, which had been buzzing with laborers. There was a big row when Asmelash came back to see a house under construction. Degitu had sold a truck full of corn without his permission to buy the construction materials. The event almost tore them apart: Degitu was deemed "ofiin bultuu"—an independent woman, a woman who disobeys her husband and does whatever she wants. Elders were involved. She promised to behave herself going forward. Ha! The husband agreed to the completion of the house since she had already poured money into it. The men who delivered the cattle told us that the house was nothing like the homes in this village. It was big and green, they said, with cement floors, a tall concrete foundation, a compound big enough to build many more houses.

One thing they said stood out to us: a hundred steps or so away from the house, there was a big mound sitting in the middle of the trees as if somebody had put it there. That reminded us of what Tultula told us about Lord Asmelash's visit to that Waa Himaa eleven years ago. I hear the laughter of many children, the fortune teller had said, in a house by a mound. We thought the man was mad at the time because there was not a single mound in sight in this village. One of us asked the men who delivered the cattle if there was a fallen tree near the house. That was another thing the Waa Himaa had said. We realized immediately how foolish that question was; trees were always falling. The man could have been talking about the future, a future in which a tree near the new house falls, a future in which another child comes out of nowhere.

THERE WERE TWENTY-NINE of us left in this compound, not counting the new workers at the coffee-washing plant, who lived on the farthest side of the compound. The place felt so empty without the children running around making life harder for us through their endless demands.

Ezra was inconsolable about leaving us. He refused to heed his mother's orders to come with her, despite threats of whipping, hiding in our quarters with our children, begging them not to let him go. His younger brother, Melkamu, came by to tell Ezra that if he stayed behind, he would be missing his siblings and who was going to protect them if something were to happen? How clever—Melkamu knew how to move Ezra. The younger one had always been that shrewd: when he wanted some toy or food or clothes that Ezra had, Melkamu would disparage it; he would say it was rotten or ugly or bound to make him sick. Ezra would dispose of it. The next day, you would see the thing in Melkamu's possession.

I promise I'll come back, Ezra said to us when they left. He went around kissing as many of us as he could. We couldn't believe we had grown so fond of a child that came out of Degitu.

THREE WEEKS BEFORE Easter, there were strangers living in the main house. They called themselves zemachoch, nineteen city boys and girls who looked like they had taken the wrong road to end up here. They claimed that they were sent to our village by a new government, that they were among thousands of students who had been sent to villages around the country to educate farmers and people like us about a new Ethiopia, about a new order.

We didn't understand most of what the strangers had been saying to us. When they opened their blasphemous mouths to say that His Majesty the emperor Haile Selassie was no longer our ruler, that he had been dead for months, some of our men picked up woodcutters and spades and machetes and told those cursed children to get out of our masters' compound or we would do to them what we did to holiday sheep. One of them fired a pistol to the sky. Our men dropped their tools and shut their mouths.

The leader of the zemachoch had called us for a gathering a few times by then. He told us that the compound was ours, that the land surrounding it was to be divided among us, that the tenant farmers who used to give half of their harvests to our masters no longer needed to do so. None of that made sense to us. All we wanted was for our masters to pay the salaries they owed us.

Easter was coming soon. We didn't know if we should start brewing tela, grinding sun-dried red peppers for berbere, keeping a lookout for fat rams or goats. Our masters hadn't come back since they left a week after Christmas. Strangers were living in their house. The confusion was enough to rob us of our sanity. Our anger at our masters' disappearance kept us focused.

We understood why our masters wouldn't want to come back to the village if they had heard what the zemachoch did to landowners like them. Lord Asmelash's brother, Mesfin, and other landlords who stayed in the countryside were force-fed the raw, unclean intestines of oxen slaughtered by a Muslim butcher before being expelled from their homes with nothing but the clothes they were wearing.

We prayed to the Blessed Mother, begging her to move our masters to send us our salaries even if they didn't want to return to the village soon. We gave Tultula some coffee and honey for Degitu and told him over and over to stress to her that we were in disarray without our masters; that we needed money for salt; that we were almost out of food because we were feeding nineteen zemachoch who had taken over the place like a plague of locusts; that we had not been given instructions on what to do about the coming rain and seed and oxen for pulling the plows.

Tultula left our quarters carrying a silicha full of honey and a sack of coffee beans. The leader of the zemachoch stopped him before he was even halfway to the main gate, leading Tultula to the main house. Tultula came by shivering after a while to tell us that the man had confiscated his bags. He had been ordered to deliver a different message to our masters: you must come back and collect personal items, like family photographs, that you left behind. We wanted to tell Tultula not to make the masters come here—to tell them about what had been done to the others—but we saw that he was already trembling from something and that he would know what to tell the masters. We wished him luck and sent him on his way.

We told the leader of the zemachoch that Degitu was the only landowner who paid her servants. People like Lord Asmelash were friendly to us. They sat down and talked to us as equals when we worked. People like him—born into landed families, into comfort, shoes, good food—didn't pay us wages. They gave us food and a place to live in exchange for our labor. Degitu gave us those things in addition to a monthly salary. The leader of the zemachoch scolded us, saying we didn't know anything and needed an education in something called hibretesebawinet. He said two birr a month was as good as nothing. Degitu was a bloodsucking trickster who paid us to keep us from moving onto other farms, for us to be desperate and work for her forever. We didn't understand him because we were desperate before we came to work here too. It was better to be desperate with sixteen, twenty-eight, forty-four birr rolled up in our waist scarves.

The leader of the zemachoch asked us why we would want our masters back when we could have their things—when we could divide the compound amongst us. Tayitu, who had taken it up with that man soon after he arrived, declared that Degitu's restaurant belonged to her. We no longer trusted her at that point. The rest of us didn't know what fantasyland those children from the city lived in. We knew that it wasn't going to be long before Asmelash and his landowner friends stormed in with their guns to expel those strangers. When we looked at the zemachoch, merely boys and girls—except for their leader, who might have been as old as Lord Asmelash—whose hands looked like they had never held a pestle once in their lives, we couldn't see them standing up to people like Lord Asmelash, who grew up hunting animals for fun. We didn't see that compound and surrounding farms becoming ours or that of tenant farmers, so we prayed and waited for our masters to pay us what we were owed.

WHEN TULTULA RETURNED from town, we wanted to take him to our quarters and keep the news of our masters to ourselves. The zemachoch got to him first.

Tultula came by later to tell us things we never thought we would hear. We heard that ugly man, Mesfin, gathered his family and went to Degitu's house, thinking she would take them in. She turned them away, as she did Lord Asmelash's older sister. Mesfin didn't waste any time going to the zemachoch in town to report Lord Asmelash for grieving for his uncle, a general who had been executed in Addis Ababa months ago. Asmelash was taken to the police station for a warning, to be told that it was against the new government to mourn for people like his uncle.

Tultula had managed to escape the leader of the zemachoch with the money Degitu gave him sewed into the inside of his pant leg. We took the money and counted it. There was only twenty birr. We held it up, wondering if that woman was serious. We thought that maybe she wanted us to harm one another fighting over it. What was twenty birr, ten people's monthly wage, going to do for twenty-nine people who hadn't been paid in three months?

There's no money, said Tultula. Asmelash looked like he was starving, thinning down to the size of his oldest boy. We reminded Tultula that our masters walked out of this place with so many cows; all that woman had to do to pay our salaries was sell three of them. There's no money, said Tultula, as if he'd been born to be her attorney. Our mistress was crying, he said. Lord Asmelash had taken money she'd put aside for the finishing works on the new house. He used it to buy land on the edge of town, only to have that land taken by the new government weeks later. What's there to finish, we said to Tultula, didn't you tell us that house was already tall and grand? For the windows, said Tultula, she was going to put glass in the windows and a cement floor in one of the bedrooms with an earthen floor. Listen to yourself, you dumb child, we told him. We walk and sleep on dirt, what's wrong with dirt? Why does she need glass in the windows? Why do you believe everything that woman tells you, we asked.

There's really no money, said Tultula, the lord's last shipment of coffee is stuck in Addis Ababa because the people who were going to buy it from him refused after the change of government, preferring to hold on to their money instead. Our masters are really poor now, he said, Lady Degitu swore to me. Just a little better than the lord's siblings, who don't even have anywhere to live. These twenty birr she sent us, he said, are for salt and soap and incidental needs. Until better days come around.

We didn't believe a word that woman said.

WE NEVER IMAGINED we would live to see a time like that.

Two Christmases after our masters left, it seemed the zemachoch were right about almost everything—that the laws of the land had changed, that we would no longer give our labor to anyone else, that we would all have a piece of land to call ours. The compound was no more—the fences had been broken down—and we were members of a farmers' collective that included tens of others. The closest thing we had to masters was the people telling us to register for this and that, to march for this and that, to gather for this and that.

Tayitu had managed to run the restaurant to the ground before leaving town with the leader of the zemachoch. The coffee-washing plant had to be shut down since nobody knew how to run it. Local officials took over Degitu's school and the flour mill.

We sent Tultula to our old masters to see how everyone was doing. Degitu complained about being chased about town like a thief, being shamed by farmers who occasionally gathered in front of her house. Lord Asmelash had been detained a few times on charges of conspiring to harm the new government. One of his friends, a former landowner like him, had disappeared. Degitu complained about how Asmelash wasted

all her savings on his relatives in Addis Ababa, who had also lost everything to the Change. There we were, thinking: what savings—didn't that
cow say she had nothing when we sent for our salaries?

We wondered if Tultula would ever figure out her ways. He was one
of the boys who arrived at Lord Gebre's house carrying wounds inflicted
upon them by their fathers. His mother had been a servant like us in Lord
Gebre's compound before she suddenly disappeared decades ago. We
didn't know what became of her until Tultula came to us. She had married a farmer in a faraway village, given birth to three children, before
disappearing with her youngest two, leaving Tultula behind with his
cruel father.

Tultula's wounds were covered in flies. Lord Gebre made him take
his clothes off and put medicinal herbs on his wounds, covering them up
with heated caul fat. The old man tended to that boy for weeks, as if he
were his own child. Tultula latched on to whatever and whoever Lord
Gebre loved after that. Unfortunately for him, one of those things was a
bloodsucking trickster called Degitu.

We should be celebrating Degitu's downfall. We should be joining those
farmers to go chant threats at her house. All we think about is Ezra, our
child, and how we have our own things to worry about.

The only things holding us together are memories of that old compound we shared as Degitu's servants. That compound is gone, Degitu
is gone, and we are merely neighbors. We have occasional disputes over
whose goat is overrunning whose garden and whose oxen are vandalizing whose corn farm. Very soon, our children may no longer speak
as one.

We believe one thing to be true: we do not know what other miracles
and sufferings tomorrow will bring, but we are happy to be living.

9.

Bring Milk

Comrade Rectangle-Head came by our house yesterday to tell us who's singing and marching and cooking and running errands for the ninetieth anniversary celebrations of the Battle of Adwa. I'm not singing or marching or cooking or running errands because I've only been here for thirteen months and babies are free. The radio man is saying that Yekatit is a very important month in Ethiopian history. I don't think it's going to be an important month in the history of my mobility; I've made no attempts to walk or even crawl. Degitu is worried I might be a cripple. Our ancestors say that an egg should start walking slowly, but this egg is refusing.

We're gathered for morning coffee in the living room. Ezra and Melkamu are home for the weekend. Melkamu has graduated with a diploma in Geography, and he's a teacher at a high school in a nearby town. My father sits by a table next to his radio as always, occasionally holding up his empty coffee cup and calling out to my siblings. Teshager, our new tenant and the only owner of a camera in town, gets up to leave after two cups of coffee. He is the new accountant at the local branch of the Coffee & Tea Authority. We rented what used to be our dining room at the back end of the house to him to make extra money and send my mother to a missionary doctor in Wollega because her bleeding is back.

Asmelash shushes everyone. The radio man says that Yekatit is when, forty-nine years ago, the Italians massacred tens of thousands of Ethiopians in Addis Ababa, including babies like me. I am thinking that they would have murdered me without any trouble. I spend most of my waking hours sitting, making no attempts to learn how to run away from anything, eyebrows raised to the maximum as if my enormous eyes aren't big enough to see all the nonsense around me.

Asmelash makes little moaning sounds like he's in pain. He likes the state-owned radio when it talks about parts of the past that he cares about. I can see the spirit of sadness descending upon him. He's thinking about Baba Gebre, whose friends abandoned him in the battlefield, thinking he was dead, after the Italians shot him. My father is not thinking about how Baba Gebre survived the war to return to the southwest and deposit him in Emama Debritu's womb. That when the Italians were killing babies in Addis Ababa, my father was safely tucked in his mother's bed hundreds of kilometers away. Last year, when famine was taking children in the north, I was a fat new baby tucked in Degitu's arms, here in the fertile land of my mother's ancestors. Maybe my father is moaning because he knows surviving is just another name for waiting to die.

THIS SATURDAY MORNING, we've eaten eggs from our chickens, drunk milk from our cows. We're not rich landowners with servants and endless land beyond what we can see, but we eat like kings and drink like queens. We have a mother, a kind of father, and there's six of us. We can fight anybody.

Degitu will leave us in a little while to start her shift at the tailors' collective. When she takes me to the Libs Sefi Bét with her, I sit on a blanket on the floor, watching her work. Instead of making the same dresses repeatedly like most of her colleagues, she uses different designs. Sometimes she adds laces, fabric flowers, and beads, combines different patterns, or instead of just dresses, she makes jackets and skirts. When some of her customers find a picture of a dress in a rare magazine that contains images other than those of Workers' Party comrades in their khaki uniforms, they bring them to Degitu, who can copy any design just by looking at a picture.

At the end of a workday, my mother packs the small round pillow she sits on in a plastic bag. It's bloody and needs to be washed. She began bleeding again months after my baptism, and no number of her homemade pads can contain the deluge.

I want to tell Degitu to sit with me more instead of always running. In this life, you think you're running away from one trouble when you're only running toward another. I can't tell her any of these things since I only have two words so far. Right now, she has me cradled on her lap, touching my legs, searching my toes for any sign of trouble, raising me by the armpits, trying to make me stand. Walking is not for me at this time. I'm more interested in objects lying around the house, waiting for oral examination. I have some teeth and I bite everything that comes close.

The radio man says Yekatit is also a month of triumph for Ethiopia. Ninety years ago, when the Italians came the first time, we beat them so good at the Battle of Adwa that they went home with a bitter grudge. I'm wishing I were alive then; I would have bitten them so hard to keep them from coming back forty years later to shoot my Baba Gebre. There are no Italians here, so I've been biting paper, blankets, and cups. Degitu has caught me examining a bar of soap, a sock, and a hair clip. Every time she catches me, she yells at my siblings for leaving me alone. My mother is at the Libs Sefi Bét all day, my father often chasing honey farmers when he is not at a bar with his friends.

Beza is my usual babysitter. She's not good at other chores. She is not very good at this chore either; that's why I get so much freedom to do my oral examinations. Degitu knows this, so sometimes she comes home from work unannounced. When she rushes over to get things out of my mouth, I grab her hand and start examining her too. I want to know what things and people are made of, and based on initial results, I can say that a big chunk of Degitu is made of worries. Right now, failing to make me stand, this is it, she's telling herself, this is what we've all been waiting for. My mother has confided in Weder that the delay in my mobility could have been caused by a disease Asmelash might have given her and me when I was conceived. She's been giving my father more sidelong glances than usual.

As for the Women, they think the strange circumstances surrounding my birth are finally manifesting themselves.

"The thing is crippled."

"Don't call her a thing; she's a beautiful baby."

"Beautiful in what country?"

"Don't let that enormous head distract you."

"She's got her father's features."

"Can you imagine if that poor thing had taken after her mother?"

"God never does that to you."

"He takes one thing, He gives you something else."

"About the legs—"

"Degitu better take that child to St. Gabriel's."

"But it isn't just the legs."

They all nod.

"That child's head. It's like her neck can't carry it."

The demons say these things in front of me too. Eteyé Khadija and her friends visit our house occasionally to pass me around, saying how adorable I am. As soon as Degitu leaves the room to make them tea, they start their whispering.

"See how the head looks like a ball sitting atop a small flagpole?"

"And she's chubby, definitely not a flagpole."

"Imagine the head if she were skinny."

I want to tell them to shut their face openings for the rest of time, but I only have two words. When I first said those two words—amta aannan!—Degitu couldn't believe it, as if she were also expecting me to be mute. She kept telling people that my first words were a command to bring milk, in a mix of two languages. My child has untied her tongue in two languages at once, she kept bragging. She told every neighbor she ran into; my oldest brothers who weren't home for the event; even our nefs abat, Meri Geta, who feigned excitement because that priest loves my mother's cooking. All this excitement is good for me. I tell the adults to bring milk all the time and they do it and milk is always flowing down the corners of my mouth and my bottom is as fat as ever, making it very comfortable to sit and sit and refuse to stand up.

ASMELASH SITS on the veranda waiting for farmers headed to the marketplace to sell their produce. He doesn't like going to the marketplace, where a cattle stampede might break out or where the dust might spoil his shiny shoes. He waits in ambush instead, looking for the chunkiest sheep or goat for us and a few family friends, scanning the crowd for those transporting honey in leather sacks piled on the backs of pack animals. We can't justify slaughtering a whole sheep when it's not a holiday, so a few households pool money and divide it up among them.

The streets are full of donkeys carrying produce; farmers with their wives and children, who rarely get to see the town with the asphalt road; cars; and stores with magnificent new clothes or tailors who can make them for you with a strange machine. The youngest visitors flee the street like a pack of birds, sensing danger when a car passes by.

Little Yonas begins sweeping the floor and burning frankincense to ready the tej bét for business. Beza takes me to the parents' bedroom, where we sit on the bouncy spring bed by a window looking out to the main street. Saturdays are the busiest at our tej bét. At noon our house will begin shaking with the noise of tens of customers coming in to spend monies they earned at the market. The patrons will fight one another play-fully for speaking time.

"Listen to me now," one of them will say, pointing a finger as if he's about to deliver a warning. "Listen to me; I have something to say." The others ignore him and keep talking over one another. "Do you know what happens when an elephant goes downhill to a river?"

On Sundays, my mother hangs a weekly calendar with everyone's daily tasks. My siblings are responsible for knowing if they're fetching water, washing clothes, helping make tej, or cutting firewood. On the days when the floors are due for mopping, Degitu comes home from work unannounced and goes to the backyard to bend at an angle and see if the floor in the hallway is shining. If it isn't shining, the floor mopper has to do it again.

Ezra is going to get in trouble today. He's by the roadside talking to our new tenant, Teshager, instead of making lunch. He loves cooking. He gets impatient watching other people chop onions. He takes the cutting board away, saying, is your hand broken?

When my mother walks around the living room running her fingers across furniture to see if it's been dusted properly, you must stand at a corner praying to all the saints. The punishment won't be harsh; you can dust furniture again anytime of day. What you can't do anytime is fetch water from the government pump because the water woman only comes by for a few hours midmornings. That's why, in the dry season, if the barrels in the backyard aren't full by the time Degitu comes home for lunch, you are going to want to run as fast as a gazelle who's seen a leopard. Degitu will yell that she'll catch you eventually, kill you, and turn herself in to the police. You want neither to die nor to cause your mother's imprisonment, so you turn yourself in.

Unless you are Beza.

My grandmother Zeritu says Beza inherited Degitu's spirit of rebellion. She was sent here by God to make our mother pay. My mother disagrees. She feels her rebellions always had a cause, whereas Beza, who can continue school for as long as she wants and will never be subjected to arranged marriage, is a rebel for the sake of rebellion.

Little Yonas lays out tens of clean glasses on top of the buffet cabinet. Melkamu had been excused to go practice with the town's band for the upcoming anniversary celebrations of the Battle of Adwa. He's been making us melancholic playing Kassa Tessema's "Fano," about all the heroes who perished in the wilderness of the Ogaden while fighting the Italians. The Ogaden front was where Baba Gebre fought. My father's eyes fill with tears whenever Melkamu sings, tickling his kirar, that the hero's mother should tie her waist with rope for strength because her son is to be buried by crows.

BEZA HOLDS ME against her chest, pushes the curtain aside, and scans the street. She is hoping to catch sight of Yohannes, or Johnny, her high school English teacher and the head of the town's drama club, as he comes into Tana Hotel next door. Beza has been a member of the drama club for a long time. Johnny wouldn't give her parts; she's always either too young or too old for the roles. She sees his refusals as his failure to notice her the way she's been noticing him.

Beza doesn't care for boys her age. She wants stylish men from places like Addis Ababa. She is determined to make Johnny notice her by acquiring a pair of fancy shoes she had seen people wearing in the Medium Town. She's been working for Degitu at the Libs Sefi Bét for pay. She would have made enough to buy those shoes already had our mother not been getting in the way. Degitu tried to teach all my siblings how to make clothes. Only Beza picked it up. Degitu made a deal with her: for every dress she made, Beza would earn fifty cents. But she could only work after school.

Beza became impatient; she wanted to buy those shoes before they sold out. One afternoon, she decided to cut school and go to the Libs Sefi Bét.

"Why are you here?"

"They let my class out early," said Beza. "The teacher is sick."

"That's unfortunate," said Degitu. "Go clean the barn until school hours are over."

Beza spent the next few hours shoveling cow dung.

There's no sight of Johnny. All we see beyond the leaves of our orange trees is Ezra and Teshager talking and laughing; farmers carrying bunched up—chickens upside down; women wearing babies on their backs while carrying bags of produce on their heads; donkeys hauling sacks of teff and corn. A man drags a goat, its tail pointed to the sky. Somewhere in the thick forest surrounding our town, a gazelle or its ghost is saying, here I thought I was alive but my skin is already at the market.

WE SEE ASMELASH running down the front steps. He calls out to a farmer pulling a beautiful ram with a rope. The trick is catching the sellers before they get to the marketplace where they might get multiple competing offers. The farmer comes up to Asmelash, who lifts the ram's tail to see how fat it is. He sees that it's very fat. He's reminded of shepherds who make holes in the tails of fat rams, pour salt into the hole, and suck out the fat with wooden straws.

"How much?"

"Forty."

"Akakaka!" Asmelash takes a handkerchief out of his chest pocket and wipes his hand. "Is this daylight robbery?"

The farmer turns back to the sheep and lifts the tail. "Look at how fat it is."

"There's nothing much there. I saw a sheep twice as big for the same price earlier."

"I don't believe that."

"Are you saying I am a liar?"

"No, my lord."

"Just go to the market and see your competition."

"Thirty-eight."

"May God give you. I'm going to keep looking." Asmelash turns around.

"Thirty-five."

Asmelash keeps walking away. "I'll give you twenty-five and that's it."

"Thirty. Please, my lord."

Up the stairs.

"Twenty-eight."

Asmelash stops.

"Please, my lord."

"Eshi eshi, what can I do, please stop pleading."

Asmelash pays the farmer. Little Yonas takes the sheep through the back gate.

In the backyard, the two of them tie the sheep's legs and flip it over. Little Yonas hands Asmelash a sharp knife and holds down the head. Asmelash invokes the name of the Trinity and cuts the sheep's throat. Blood flows out and the poor animal writhes and writhes. It should never have entered our house silently.

10.

The Meaning of Politics

Our new tenant, Teshager, says Jesus Christ died and came back three days later, and I am thinking, what a cruel prank to play on your mother. I cannot play such a prank on my mother because I'm already a worrisome child. I've been refusing to walk despite being here fifteen months, and some two weeks ago my body broke out in mysterious wounds. Degitu, who had just returned from a visit to the missionary doctor, rushed me to the clinic.

The health officer couldn't say where the wounds came from. He wanted to dress them all, to cover my whole body in gauze and bandages and send me home looking like I'm ready to be buried. Degitu begged him to refer us to the regional hospital instead. The wounds began healing before we left for the Medium Town, drying up as mysteriously as they appeared the day after we got there. Degitu took me to the doctor anyway. She wanted to know if my inability to walk and the mysterious wounds were caused by a disease that entered my bloodstream when I was in her womb because of Asmelash.

My father told me the scars the wounds left behind are evidence that I am secretly a leopard finally getting my spots. I like this diagnosis.

After our visit to the clinic in town, my mother was furious. She came home ready to spit fire at my father for bringing endless hardship upon our family. When she couldn't find him at home, she took a bottle of whiskey from a locked cabinet in the scullery, a bottle my aunt Etabeba Haregua had brought us to celebrate my first birthday. Degitu marched to Mamitu's Bar with me perched on her hip and the bottle in hand. Inside the dark bar, all the men sitting by the tables along the walls turned to stare at us. We saw my father sitting at the bar, talking to a woman who stood behind the counter wearing a black headdress. My mother was incoherent at first as she yelled at my father. Something something about him wasting money when he could have whiskey at home. She held up the bottle.

My father was in shock. He walked over to us. "Have you lost your mind, you woman?"

"I lost it long time ago," said my mother. "You took it from me."

She shattered the bottle at his feet. My father's jaw dropped as shards of glass flew all around him. When Degitu turned around to march out of the place, I saw the patrons stare at the whiskey rushing across the floor.

The doctor at the regional hospital tested us and said we didn't have that disease my mother feared Asmelash had given us. She cried from relief, briefly forgetting that I was immobile.

THE NEIGHBORHOOD SMELLS of smoke and spices the day before Easter. Our backyard is bustling, everyone busy with chores. Degitu sits on a stool, two dead chickens in a plastic tub before her. The missionary doctor sent a sample of her blood to Germany for testing. She was told to rest while she waits for the results.

Our new tenant, Teshager, has been assigned a task: cutting firewood. He's taking a break right now, sitting on a wooden stool chatting with Degitu. The two have become friends, talking about the Bible every chance they get. Degitu has been challenging him with her questions, and she said she liked how his answers were rooted in the Word, unlike those of the priests from St. Mary's, who appealed to tradition to silence her.

My mother thinks Teshager might become a positive influence on Ezra. She worries about Ezra because of what she calls his misguided sense of charity. As a child, he used to roll on the floor crying until she gave out free beverages to customers at her restaurant. She had hoped becoming a teacher would give him a proper outlet for his generosity, but he's been giving away his salary and borrowing money to sustain himself. As a stand-up professional—and clearly a man of God—that Ezra seems to be drawn to, Teshager might nudge Ezra toward responsibility. She's been allowing Ezra to invite Teshager to family activities, and our tenant has been eating most meals with us.

Sometimes Teshager takes me from my mother, and I stare into his eyes. They look like they want to step out of him and become their own entity. He has full brows just like my father.

When Degitu and I returned from the hospital in the Medium Town, Teshager told my mother that prayer was what was needed—for the wounds, for my walking problems, and for any other disease that might be buried inside me. Degitu agreed, and the two have been getting together some evenings over the past few weeks, reading the Bible to each other and praying for me to Jesus Christ directly, without the intercession of the Virgin Mother.

They often read from the Gospels:

Heal the sick, raise the dead, cleanse those who have leprosy, drive out demons. Freely you have received; freely give.

Teshager puts his hand on my head and says, in Jesus's name, I order all sicknesses to leave this child.

We will see if this Jesus man will make me walk.

Teshager stands before us on those evenings, an open Bible in hand, talking about how Jesus Christ came back from the dead three days later, how sinners don't like the light, and so on. Ezra listens, smiling, to whatever his new friend has to say. Weder is alarmed by Teshager's strange ways—like his love of saying Jesus repeatedly as if Jesus Christ is a friend we met on a playground, instead of the respectfully distant Medhanealem, Savior of the World—but she doesn't want to openly oppose anything our mother supports. Melkamu doesn't like the man's obsession with the Bible and prayer; he'd rather drive everyone mad practicing the kirar. Beza and Little Yonas attend because our mother demands it. My father doesn't like the sound of Teshager's teachings—he smells like a heretic—but there's not enough evidence to accuse him of such things so far, especially since he has only been reading from the Bible, our own book.

After an early morning visit to church on Easter Sunday, we sit around a messob of doro wat and cheese on a bed of injera. Asmelash blesses the meal and crosses over it. Eight right hands begin cutting injera.

One of the hands belongs to Tultula, my family's former servant. He joins us on holidays because he doesn't have a family of his own. He brought me a young cow for my first birthday, saying that I should be spoiled like my father was when he was young. He's always visiting us on market days with fruits and vegetables from his farm even after my mother told him to stop. She makes him free clothes, including a handsome suit that he won't stop talking about.

Ezra's hand is missing this morning. He's sulking in the boys' room because of a fight he had with our mother yesterday. He came home from the market and asked her to give a chicken to a widow with two small children. He had run into the woman on his way back from the market and learned that she couldn't afford meat this Easter. My mother told him that we couldn't afford to give whole chickens to everyone in that woman's position. Ezra dropped the bag of fresh butter he brought from the market, kicked a water jug in front of Degitu, and disappeared into the ginger and turmeric sprouts in the farther part of our backyard.

The rest of my siblings carried on with their chores as if Ezra were just a child throwing a tantrum. Melkamu says Ezra is broken in the head, that madness is the only explanation for a twenty-two-year-old who thinks he can help every poor person he meets. Degitu tells him to stop saying such things, that Ezra is only suffering from a condition he must have inherited from Baba Gebre, who used to lend people money and forget all about it.

When Ezra disappeared into the backyard, Teshager dropped his wood-cutter and followed him. Later in the afternoon, we saw the two of them go to the market to buy chicken for the widow. Teshager, who didn't fast the past two months or go to church early in the morning, is eating with us this morning.

Degitu feeds me injera soaked in the sauce of the mild lamb stew the rest of them will be having for lunch and dinner. My father chews the lamb meat to soften it for me. When he leans over to feed me, I open my mouth, close my eyes, and gnomgnomgnom—my mother is the best cook and my father the best chewer in the world.

After devouring the best of what my mother stayed up making most of the night, difo dabo is cut into squares and passed around the room as Weder presides over coffee. This feast is only the beginning. Later, we will visit friends and friends will visit us. Lamb and vegetable dishes and raw beef and doro wat will be served along with tej and tela and difo dabo. All of us, like many Christians in town, are going to be sick from overeating by tomorrow morning.

Weder puts half a teaspoon of spiced butter in each cup. When she pours hot coffee into the cups, the butter melts instantly and rises to the top, making our favorite dark-brown beverage shimmer in the morning light.

NOT TOO LONG after that Easter feast, comrade Rectangle-Head came to our house to tell us to attend a public gathering to discuss the draft constitution. The town announcer had already gone about the street a few days earlier, advertising the mandatory meeting through a megaphone. The comrade wanted to remind us that he can come into our homes anytime he wanted. That man should be afraid of the day I start walking because I might go to his house too.

All of us go to the secondary school to discuss the draft constitution on a Sunday afternoon. My mother carried me and walked with her friend Zinash. The two have been friends since my family moved to town after the revolution. Like us, Zinash has a house made of concrete, separated from her neighbors by a backyard fence and a stair leading up to her front door. There are only a handful of houses like that in town, and the owners tend to befriend one another.

There's almost no room to sit when we arrive at the auditorium. My father, who sits with his friend Shimelis, signals for us and a few people near him to move over to make space for the sick lady with the crippled baby. The Women are scattered throughout, giving us quick glances.

"Who is going to carry her around when she gets older?"

"That poor child."

"At least she survived that recent disease."

"The spots have disappeared from her neck."

"Who knows what's coming next?"

What's coming next is that the spots are on the inside and I'm a leopard in disguise, with a list of all the people I'm going to eat in this town.

Abba Lemma, a day laborer who makes a living working on construction sites, building fences, and clearing backyards of mud lakes after the rainy season, is sitting on the bench in front of us, drunk as a honey-wine cask.

"Tell me," he says, turning around, "what's this constitution? Is it food? Is it a job?"

My father and his friends shake in their seats, hands covering faces.

"Is the draft constitution going to hire me to build its house at the end of this meeting?"

Abba Lemma can get away with saying these things because he is always either drunk or behaving like a madman. A madman who just happens to be good at making the tightest fence or mixing cement and sand to pour into a concrete foundation. Years ago, older men like him were forced by the government to attend political science classes. Most of them resented those sessions because they'd rather be at work or drinking. No one else would say so openly. Abba Lemma had had enough of those lessons, and as someone with no family or a home of his own, he had the least to lose. When the instructor asked the class once what they thought politics was, Abba Lemma was the only one who stood up to answer. His answer made him a legend, but that he got away with it was even more impressive. People were disappearing for far lesser crimes in the early days of the revolution. That sort of unpredictability is what gives the revolution most of its power.

The comrades are sitting in a panel onstage. Comrade Kebede, the boss of all the comrades, speaks first. He says into a megaphone that this draft constitution is the second ever in the history of our ancient nation. It's the fruit of our revolution, our struggle to free ourselves from backward systems, to build a Marxist-Leninist Ethiopia that puts all her citizens first. We're here to take part in the making of history.

"I don't want to make history; I want to build fences."

Comrade Kebede explains how the discussion is going to proceed. Comrade Tesema, sitting to his left, will read each article of the constitution. Unless we have a comment, we will approve the articles with applause. If we have comments, we are to raise our hands.

Comrade Tesema begins reading the articles into a megaphone. Everyone applauds after each article. Some members of the Revolutionary Ethiopia Youth Association and the Revolutionary Ethiopia Women's Association raise their hands to express enthusiastic support. Some people are falling asleep, but none of those within earshot of Abba Lemma.

"Article forty-three. Number one: Ethiopians are guaranteed inviolability of the person. Number two: Ethiopians are guaranteed inviolability of the home. No one may enter the home of another against his will, except as prescribed by law."

Abba Lemma raises his hand.

The auditorium is quiet. The comrades look at each other. Comrade Tesema tells Abba Lemma to speak.

"Does it include comrade Sisay?"

"What?"

"You said no one can enter the home of another against his will. I've never heard of anyone who likes it when comrade Sisay goes to their house."

People everywhere lower their eyes. Women cover their mouths with their netelas. The men in our area shake in their seats.

"First of all," says comrade Kebede, "this shouldn't be a concern to you since you don't have a home."

Fuck comrade Kebede.

Some people laugh. Fuck them too.

"Comrade Sisay is not above the law," says comrade Kebede. "If anybody feels comrade Sisay has entered their home illegally, you can report him to the police like you would anyone else."

The crowd applauds.

Comrade Tesema continues. "Article forty-four. Number two: any arrested person shall be produced in court within forty-eight hours."

Abba Lemma raises his hand. "Our friend was arrested eleven years ago." A murmur breaks out in our area of the auditorium. "He hasn't been produced at court or in life. He's never been seen again. That's thousands of forty-eight hours—"

Comrade Kebede interjects. "Abba Lemma, this is a serious meeting."

Maybe Abba Lemma wants to be finished today. "I am a serious man," he says. "The disappearance of a man is a serious matter."

"It is true that many reactionaries have been lost during our bitter struggle to save the revolution. We are here today at a historic moment because our fight to preserve the gains of our revolution—"

"All right all right," says Abba Lemma, raising his right fist. "Onward with the Workers' Party of Ethiopia!"

"In socialist Ethiopia, we raise our left fists," says comrade Kebede.

The crowd applauds. A bunch of bootlicking motherfuckers.

A couple of men sitting next to Abba Lemma get up to change places, feeling it necessary to display their cowardice to the comrades. Their self-preservation instincts are strong. As soon as comrade Tesema tells us about Article 49, which guarantees the right to secrecy of correspondence, Abba Lemma himself bursts out laughing. He starts saying things that make everyone, including my father and Shimelis, get up to leave. I am disappointed.

Zinash tugs at my mother's dress, wanting to leave. The comrades will be getting a detailed report from someone of what Abba Lemma was saying. Nobody wants to be seen laughing. My mother refuses to leave. When a policeman comes over to escort Abba Lemma out, she intercedes. She tells the policeman that Abba Lemma is just drunk, that she will take him home with her and give him a place to sleep for the night. Abba Lemma is homeless and sleeps on the veranda or back porches of the people he does day jobs for. She tells the policeman that she is not feeling well and has to leave anyway. He believes her because everyone knows about her fluctuating health. My mother puts on her stern face and tells Abba Lemma to follow us.

ON THE WAY HOME, children follow Abba Lemma and yell, kur kur kur kur, as if they're calling on a donkey, and they immediately go on my list of people to eat when I get big. Abba Lemma says, do you want me to box you, you little rascals? Do you want to lose your tiny pretty teeth? They laugh and keep following him. He swings both his arms at them and sways. My mother turns around and glares at the children; they disperse immediately.

At home, Abba Lemma is loud and cantankerous. Little Yonas brings a jug of water and a bucket for Abba Lemma to wash his hands. Degitu places a plate of food before the old man, injera topped with split pea stew and cabbage and yogurt. He refuses to eat. He's transforming before us, from a mere drunk to a madman. He looks at the plate and tells it, very loudly, "Fuck your mother's vagina!"

Little Yonas leads Abba Lemma to the old maid's room. It is the rainy season, too cold for the old man to sleep on the back porch.

IN THE EVENING, we gather in the living room for coffee. The tej bét is closed on Sundays. Teshager has taken the place of a fourth son in just five months. Even my father sometimes forgets all about Teshager's suspicious Christianity because he is good at talking politics. They often disagree, with Teshager supporting socialism and my father believing that Marx is the devil. Teshager has also been putting a face to all the horrific stories my family has heard of through the Foreign Radio Service, about the violence that happened in Addis Ababa during the Red Terror. Teshager lost an older brother, whose body was displayed on the street as a warning to others. He was sent to the countryside to live with his aunt for a few years.

Teshager found the frequency for the FRS faster than Little Yonas normally does. The newsman comes on and says something about the rebels and their endless advances.

"Get here already," says my father.

"You can't believe everything this radio station tells you," says Teshager.

"Why not?"

"I don't support this government, but not everything it says is a lie. It's true that these foreign radio stations are funded by imperialists."

"What's wrong with that?"

The generator man sends his signal and Weder leaves the room to fetch a lantern.

"The West doesn't have our best interest at heart. Have you forgotten about the Italians?"

"That was a long time ago, and this is America, not Italy," says my father.

"How many of our people died when the Somalis invaded us less than a decade ago?" says Teshager. "Aided by the Americans."

Weder brings in a lit lantern and places it on the buffet cabinet.

"The Americans were after these Marxist idiots," says my father. "Not our country."

"They were doing it for their benefits."

"What's wrong with that if their benefit is also our benefit?" says Degitu.

"It is not," says Teshager. "We need socialism."

"To run things to the ground?" says Degitu.

"That is not socialism," says Teshager.

"It is," says Weder. "Do you know what they did to our coffee-washing plant?"

Degitu looks at Weder and smiles.

"Please don't bring that up," says my father.

"What this regime is doing is not what socialism is supposed to be like."

"We don't care," says Beza. "We hate socialism in this house and if you want your food to keep coming, you should hate it too."

Everyone laughs.

Weder begins collecting coffee cups.

We hear Abba Lemma cursing in the distance and something is

knocked over in the hallway. The old man stumbles into the living room shouting, fuck your mother's vagina, and swinging both his arms at imaginary children taunting him. He marches around the living room cursing. Teshager and my father get up to try to calm him down. They grab him by the arms and guide him to a chair, where he slumps down.

Years ago in that political science class that Abba Lemma and other elderly men were forced to attend, he was the only one who raised his hand to answer the teacher's question about the meaning of politics. All the men looked at him when he stood up to answer, curious and worried.

"Politics is," he said, poking the air with his index finger. "Politics is a lie."

He sat down. Everyone else shrank in place. He was summoned by the comrades to explain himself. He went to them drunk out of his mind. They detained him at the police station until he was sober. When they questioned him again, he swore he didn't remember ever saying such a thing in class. My head isn't all there, he told them. They sent him back to detention and only let him go because he didn't have anyone to bring him food and they didn't want a mere day laborer to die at the police station from starvation.

He is sitting by the dining table, looking like he's carrying three lifetimes' worth of sadness. The friend he was talking about earlier, the one who was arrested eleven years ago, was also my father's friend. His name was Ato Shibiru and he was seen at the police station once, naked and shivering in the morning cold. He was never seen again and no one ever found out what his crime was except that he was branded counterrevolutionary. Men like my father and Abba Lemma, men who have been branded counterrevolutionary at one time or another, have been walking around ever since waiting for their turn.

I want to touch Abba Lemma's face. I wriggle out of my mother's arms and hit the ground. I march across the room like a drunken soldier, sway-ing left and right like a blanket on a clothesline on a windy day, like my drunken father the day of my baptism, all the way to Abba Lemma. I fall right beneath him when the room erupts in screams. I get back up and, holding on to Abba Lemma's knee with my left hand, I touch his nose with my right.

"Heh." He smiles. "My flower."

I hear ululations and thumping behind me and turn around to see ev-eryone standing and my mother jumping up and down like a madwoman. She's pointing and crying, shouting that I just stood up and walked as if everyone else isn't seeing it too. God has answered my prayers, she says. God has answered me! I don't think so, lady. Unless I am the god you're talking about.

11.

The People's Democratic Republic of Degitu

I've been running and running and some people in this house are wishing they never prayed for my mobility. Sit down now, you child! they say. I get under a table one side and come out the other like a miracle because I'm small and fast and they have to be two to catch me. You know who else is running around? Comrade Rectangle-Head, wearing his sky-blue khaki uniform for Party members, pestering everyone about taking part in the upcoming referendum on the new constitution. They are not going to let me vote because I'm only about to turn two, but the constitution is already affecting my life since it says no more polygamy. I had plans to marry Teshager and Little Yonas. I don't know what I'll do about husbands, but I have more pressing issues to deal with.

My first concern is the protection of my possessions. This is the year of owning things and Degitu has given me a wooden trunk to keep them in. I don't have the muscles to open it, so I ask whoever is around to do it. I have many words and this morning I told Sheikh Hassan's goat to stop eating the leaves of our orange trees. I don't think he speaks Amharic or Afan Oromo.

I ask Little Yonas to open the trunk for me to see if my things are there. Little Yonas isn't so little anymore. His voice can't decide whether it wants to stay small or go big—he sounds as if some animal is trapped in his throat. I love him, but I don't like being left alone with him that much anymore because I'm thinking, what if the animal comes out of his throat? He doesn't have to go to school until the afternoon shift, so he's at home watching me.

Little Yonas opens the trunk, which is kept in a corner in the parents' room. I see all the dresses, trousers, shirts, and hats Degitu made for me are almost filling the trunk, except for a small corner where my book and doll are. Teshager went to Addis Ababa to visit his family a few months ago and brought me a book called *Bible in Pictures*. It has a cover image of Jesus on shepherd duty, standing amidst a flock of sheep, carrying His staff and a lost lamb. Teshager sits next to me sometimes to describe the images inside the book: Adam and Eve standing with hands covering the places between their legs; Abraham with a knife extended over Isaac's neck; pairs of animals entering Noah's ark; Elijah being taken to heaven on a chariot of fire; and pages and pages more. I'm obsessed with the colors in this book. I want to befriend some of the people in the stories.

My other possession is a pink plastic doll with scary corn-silk-looking white hair and even scarier green eyes. Zinash brought her for me from Addis Ababa. The doll would have been a nice friend but her green eyes scare me so much that I can only play with her face turned away from me and that gets boring quickly. Everything is safe, so I tell Little Yonas to close the trunk.

Those aren't my only possessions: Ezra bought me a Ge'ez alphabet board that's hanging low in the girls' room. I think the letters are petrified living beings that are going to start walking at some point. I have seen those letters in books before—including in my *Bible in Pictures*—but they're very big and worrisome on the alphabet board. Little Yonas would squat next to the board and make me watch as he points at each one, telling me their names. I can't pay full attention to him, expecting the letters to move. I don't want to be there alone the day they decide to walk, so most of the time I choose the noise and drama outside our house, where donkeys smell and blow in one another's noses, children chase balls, roosters stretch out their wings as they dance around hens.

I'M ON THE VERANDA NOW. I'm not allowed to go beyond here on my own. I'm glad because the front stair is so high that I keep imagining myself rolling down like a ball, and I say to myself, I'm not a ball and don't wish to be a ball. Whenever I see comrade Rectangle-Head running up and down our front stair so effortlessly, I burn with envy: if an ugly man like him can do it, why not me? I can ask Little Yonas to take me to my mother at the Libs Sefi Bét now, but I would rather wait here for my father in case he shows up for radio.

These days he's been disappearing more and more, even for radio time. Maybe it's to avoid my mother's ever escalating Bible talk and prayer with Teshager and the new people who have been coming to our house to pray with them. Or maybe to get away from her illness, which comes and goes and makes my father feel useless. She came back from her second visit to the missionary doctor without her uterus. She doesn't bleed anymore but she gets terrible stomachaches and constipation all the time. That's my other concern. When I catch her sitting by herself moaning and clutching her belly, it hurts me in the chest. She tells me that I make her feel better, that I am her medicine, so I sit with her until she starts smiling again. Maybe I should go to the Libs Sefi Bét and be her medicine instead of waiting for that slippery father of mine. The problem is that I always know where she is, whereas if I miss my father this afternoon, I might not see him until the next morning, which is another pain in the chest.

I can't wait on the veranda forever. Little Yonas is going to come take me inside when morning-shift students from the primary school start throwing stones at our orange trees on their way home. The oranges fall and roll down our sloping front yard; the kids grab them and run like the criminals they are. Sometimes the rocks pass through the branches and land on the veranda. I am afraid that someday they're going to break me into three.

I see Sheikh Hassan's goat approaching one of our orange trees and I want to tell him that Asmelash said eating all the leaves is going to make the branches naked and the trees dry up. I know he won't listen to me. He gets on his hind legs and begins chewing the leaves. I think about telling Little Yonas, but my brother is going to chase him away without trying to talk to him. I don't want that because sometimes, when children are at school and adults at work, the street gets quiet and boring, as if half the men have been conscripted by the army and the rest have gone into hiding or have stayed home grieving with the women.

Where is that Asmelash now? His disappearances are my biggest concern. Sometimes I call him Abayé and other times I call him Asmelash. Melkamu said I am rude for referring to my parents with their names, that I am learning bad behavior from Beza, who also calls our father by his name. Asmelash told my brother to shut up, that I am his friend and that's how friends refer to one another. I don't care what name I use for that man; I just want him to hear me.

You know how cows make their babies come to them? They say, moo moo moo. I want to say, moo, Asmelash, moo, you bastard, come to me.

IN THE EVENING, Teshager talks nonstop about some potato stew Ezra made him once. When he's home on the weekends, Ezra has sometimes been cooking special meals on a charcoal stove in Teshager's room. The two eat there by themselves and miss meals with us. I went into Teshager's room with my *Bible in Pictures* once. I wanted him to explain an image. I saw the two of them playing a game that I have only seen among the pigeons who congregate on the telephone wires on our front yard: sucking each other's mouths.

"I used to hate potato stew," says Teshager. "I couldn't stop eating the one Ezra made. I wanted to lick the bottom of the pot." He tells my mother how remarkable it is that she taught her sons how to cook.

My mother tells him a story about people of a faraway province where women run into the kitchen when their husbands threaten them because they know they won't be followed.

Teshager throws his head back and laughs.

"The kitchen is like a foreign embassy where you can take refuge if you're a woman," she says. "Melkamu would be ashamed to tell you that he knows how to bake injera."

I tell them to shut up. *Eset-Ageba* just came on the FRS. The professor and the deputy ambassador are about to go at each other. Asmelash is not here, so I have to listen to it for him. I don't always understand everything they say, but I do my best to summarize for him.

PROFESSOR ANDARGACHEW: I worry that we are raising a generation that's a stranger to debates. Children in our country are not watching their elders debating and resolving issues peacefully.

DEPUTY AMBASSADOR DAWIT: You and I are debating peacefully.

PROFESSOR: How many people have access to the radio? And those with access are afraid of listening to it because your government has banned radio stations like this. Are you not ashamed of yourself, Mr. Deputy Ambassador, when you sit here and speak as if this debate of ours can be accessed by a significant number of the population?

AMBASSADOR: Calm down, professor. The kind of debate that you speak of, to begin with, is foreign. In our culture, we raise our children to listen more and speak less. We raise them to listen to their elders, to take instruction from them. We do not have to debate each other harshly outside the courtroom in order to survive as a society. We didn't get here because of debates, but because children listened to their elders. And there will come a day, when they grow up and become elders themselves, when they become the ones who speak. As the Holy Book says, direct your children onto the right path, and when they are older, they will not leave it.

My mother is laughing. "It's as if he keeps quoting the Bible to irritate the professor."

The men—whom I call Professor "I Worry" and Ambassador "Calm

Down"—are now arguing over whether a representative of a Marxist government should be quoting the Bible.

> AMBASSADOR: This is the problem with you educated people, you're so dogmatic. A person can only be one thing or another.

> PROFESSOR: Dogma isn't the problem of the educated, ambassador. But going back to what you said: Are you admitting that we are raising submissive children who don't know how to ask questions? And that the project begins at home? The parents get together and break—

I give my mother a sidelong glance. Nobody is breaking me.

I wish my father was here. These are too many words to remember. Someday, I am going to figure out how to transport myself to Mamitu's Bar on my own, and Mamitu better pray to God and His mother because I am going there.

A DAY BEFORE my second birthday, my mother sits outside the Libs Sefi Bét on a chair next to the door during a slow hour. I came here with her after lunch, wearing my pink overalls over a white T-shirt, white canvas shoes, and a big pinkish floral hat, looking like it's my wedding day. On our way here earlier, I saw Kamila, one of Eteyé Khadija's daughters, and Fetiya, from two houses down, playing on our front yard. They were barefooted, wearing tattered dresses that have lost their original meanings. I looked at the girls and they looked back at me. We said nothing to one another, and Degitu picked me up to cross the street. It has been like this ever since I first noticed the girls—we stare at one another and that's it.

I am playing a game I invented: I leap from the stoop of the Libs Sefi Bét door and land on the floor, delighted that I can fly, and after each leap, I bury my face in my mother's lap. Good job, my child, she says. I feel encouraged. I do it repeatedly. Leap, bury face, giggle. Every time, she says, good job, my child. I am too caught up in this bliss to notice that she needed to lean her head against the wall and that her words are increasingly slurred.

A teenage boy comes running. "Eteyé Zinash said—" he starts. He pauses to stare at Degitu's face and I look up too. Degitu is looking into a faraway place, away from the boy and away from me, to a place that's maybe not here on earth. I imagine the boy has come to say to her what all the other messengers from Zinash come here to tell Degitu: that Zinash isn't feeling well and needs to see her friend. Degitu would often run over immediately, and according to my siblings, the illness is a ruse—Zinash wants to gossip about her boyfriends. Degitu is not responding to the messenger boy today; instead, she slides to her right, slowly at first but faster as soon as more than half of her body leaves the chair. She is on the floor and the boy screams.

MY MOTHER HAS MADE the day special by fainting, so my father stayed home in the evening. Even Ezra and Melkamu have come home. My parents had a fight earlier. My father is angry that Degitu keeps going to work. Between what we make from the tej bét and his honey business, we have enough to eat, he said. She said she wants to recover the money spent on her trips to hospitals, especially the time she stayed at the missionary clinic having her uterus taken out. She was gone for so long that I almost forgot her. Who is going to pay for Weder's transportation to the university when she eventually leaves? she asked. What about Little Yonas? What is going to happen to Beza? And the little one?

We're all gathered around Degitu in the parents' bedroom. She told Weder to close the tej bét early because the customers' chatters would get in the way of prayer. She has been doing this more often lately. Teshager is talking about the Bible. I sit next to Degitu, trying to keep her attention by kissing her ear, sleeping on her breasts, and touching her face. She plays with me with her hands but she's focused on her Bible talk with Teshager, which no one else is taking part in.

More and more prayers have been taking place in our house. Some strangers that Teshager invited have been visiting us from Addis Ababa. One of the men from Addis Ababa told my mother to consider shutting down her tej bét because alcohol leads people to sin. Teshager has been inviting a few locals, some of whom are his coworkers, to join our evening prayers.

My father doesn't like these prayer sessions. My mother says people like Asmelash are Christian in name alone: they go to church during major holidays, they gift a liturgical parasol to the church and think their work is done. My father says the God of Orthodox Christianity is good enough for him. He considers himself a patriot, and to be a patriot is to be an Orthodox Christian, because all those who came to invade us throughout history came in the name of their respective religions. Other religions are the weapons of invaders. What invader could be behind this brand of Christianity Teshager is pushing on our family?

Teshager and the men he invited from Addis Ababa sound like Protestants. My father is confused. He's heard Protestantism belongs to the Americans. Teshager, a socialist, believes the Americans have been against our interests. My father likes that the Americans hate our government, but he doesn't want their religion. Two and two aren't adding up to four in this house. One thing is clear: our family has been infiltrated by an agent of a foreign religion.

My mother likes that Teshager studies the Bible rigorously. The two have discussed her questions: Why do we baptize children when Jesus was baptized at thirty? Why do we pour water over their heads instead of immersion? Why does the Orthodox Church announce fasting seasons in public when Jesus had commanded us in the Gospels not to do so? She learned that Teshager's brand of Christianity rejects all those and more: drunkenness, adultery, secular singing.

This evening, after listening for so long to what sometimes seems like an incomprehensible back-and-forth between my mother and Teshager, my father gathered enough courage to say something. "What's all this nonsense?"

"It's not nonsense," says my mother. "We're studying the Bible."

"I already go to church. Why should I listen to this?"

"Standing in a barn doesn't make you an ox, does it?" says my mother. "Going to church on Sundays doesn't make you a Christian."

It's a fire exchange now.

"What Eteyé Degitu means is—" Teshager begins.

"I don't need you to explain what my own wife is saying."

"I don't mean to be disrespectful. I just want to clarify that this is about accepting our Lord Jesus Christ as your personal savior, and building a relationship with Him."

Most of us don't know what the fuck Teshager is talking about. Everyone but Ezra, who is already in this infiltrator's chest pocket, and my mother, stares at him like the foreign creature that he is. The people who visited us from Addis Ababa talked about this personal savior and relationship business. Most of us don't understand it. My father doesn't bother to ask for clarifications; he gets up without saying a word, walks into the living room and out the door.

I start crying. I hope the rebels in the north get here soon, and when they do, I hope they blow up Mamitu's Bar with their tanks.

SHORTLY AFTER MY father's departure, our nefs abat, Meri Geta, knocks on the door. He must have heard about my mother's fainting. All my siblings but Ezra have left the room. As soon as he sat down, the priest made the mistake of mentioning prayer to the Mother of Light in front of Teshager.

"Why do we need to pray to Her?" says Teshager.

The priest is silent for a moment. "What do you mean, my son?"

"Doesn't the sacrifice Jesus made for us mean that we no longer need an intermediary?"

The priest looks at Teshager and at my mother. She says nothing.

"Do you not read the Bible, Abba?" asks Teshager.

"Teshager!" My mother speaks up this time. "This is our father; have some respect."

I'm stunned by all this. Ezra keeps smiling like he's witnessing a completely different event on another planet.

"Is this the young man who has been trying to lead you astray?"

Teshager laughs. He walks over to the priest and extends a hand.

The priest takes out a cross from the inner pocket of his coat to bless him. Teshager remains upright instead of bowing to take the blessing.

"I don't need that," says Teshager. "None of this ritual is rooted in the Word."

Meri Geta puts the cross back. "Eteyé Degitu," he says, rising to leave, "I don't know what you are doing with a heretic in your house."

Degitu knew a debate between the two was inevitable. She is caught off guard by Teshager's brazenness.

The priest wishes us well on his way out.

MY SIBLINGS THOUGHT it was going to be the end of Teshager after the way he behaved with the priest. Degitu decreed, without consulting anyone, that Teshager is to lead a Bible study three nights a week and everyone must attend.

My father was the first to resist. He announced that he was going to restart paying tithe to the Orthodox Church. My mother told him it was fine, that he can nurture his Christianity at Mamitu's Bar. Melkamu said he has dreams of becoming a musician in a band, and he's heard that Teshager's religion doesn't approve of secular songs. My mother told him that he can keep his music, and nobody said anything about converting to anything. He can do whatever he wants as long as he attends the Bible studies when he's home. He agreed reluctantly.

Teshager has been teaching us songs I'd never heard on the radio.

Wede Egziabher bet enihid silugn des alegn
Qalun enisma enihid silugn des alegn

I know this song is a lie. I've never been delighted to go to God's house—the only times I went, I did so because I was made to.

Tonight, Teshager tells us that God is merciful, so if we pray hard, He will heal our mother. He has our attention. We are prepared to do what he wants so that God will heal my mother. At the same time I'm wishing for this Bible study to be over soon and for my father to come home for radio time.

SOMEBODY HAS GRANTED my wish. Maybe God or His mother or Satan. I sit on my father's lap listening to the radio.

The radio man says today is a new day. Following the wishes of the Ethiopian people, who came out by the millions to adopt the new constitution, the People's Democratic Republic of Ethiopia has been inaugurated.

"What were we before today?" asks Little Yonas.

The radio man says the Comrade Chairman has called our attention to the wide range of freedoms the new constitution grants citizens—from freedom of speech to a free press and freedom of this and that.

"Liar," I say.

My father throws his head back and laughs so hard that I worry he might drop me.

12.

An Increased Marxist-
Leninist Consciousness

I am sick with malaria. Do you know who isn't sick? Comrade Rectangle-Head. He has been coming by our house more frequently to tell us that our Marxist-Leninist consciousness is in need of raising. Degitu and her Bible friends keep saying, God is just, God is just. If He were truly just, how is it that my mother and I have been sick many times since I first saw Rectangle-Head over three years ago while that definition of ugliness is always running up and down our stair as if he's got a brand-new car engine in his legs?

Ezra has been summoned to the offices of Revolutionary Ethiopia Youth Association twice recently because my cousin Hirut, an enthusiastic member of the association, reported him, saying that he needed more education in Marxism-Leninism. Hirut is the same person who reported my father years ago for possessing forbidden magazines. She's the eldest child of my uncle Mesfin, who lives in a thatched-roof hut in the countryside, resenting my father for being better off. Hirut is right below comrade Rectangle-Head on the list of people I am going to eat when I grow into full leopard.

Ever since Teshager had that debate with the priest and a group of strangers began gathering at our house in the evenings to sing songs and pray to Jesus Christ, people have been giving us more sidelong glances than before, whispering all the time.

"That crazy woman has denied the Virgin Mother."

"How much American money do you think she is getting?"

My mother closed down our tej bét because selling alcohol is unchristian. My parents have been fighting almost every day since. The closing of the bar was confusing for all of us. My mother was the one who refused to rest even when she was bleeding, always wanting to make money. Ever since Teshager's Jesus Christ came into her life, her thinking has been upside down and we don't know what's what. Her best friend, Zinash, whom my mother tried and failed to convert, is alarmed. Zinash told my mother that she's been making extra trips to church to pray for her mental health. She brought a bottle of holy water and told Degitu to drink it; my mother laughed in her face.

When my father threatened to run the bar himself, Degitu told him that he couldn't even run a chicken coop. He said he'll do it with the help of my siblings, but my siblings would never do anything against her wishes. Number one: our mother is terrifying; number two: she's always ill; number three: we love her so much that we would let her suffocate us to death. Melkamu, who's been afraid of losing his music to Teshager's Jesus Christ, recently refused to attend Bible study. When my mother asked him why, he lied and said he wanted to raise his Marxist-Leninist consciousness and this Western religion was getting in the way.

"Oh, you want to raise your Marxist-Leninist consciousness?" She got into her fighting posture, fists on her hips. "You want to raise it on me? Is that what you kids do when you go to those meetings? Agitate people against us, former landowners? You want to go work against me?"

Melkamu didn't like where she was going with that. She had beaten him as an adult, right before he went to college. He was trying to trick Ezra out of a suitcase Degitu had bought for him. She knew he had tricked Ezra out of things all his life. When she tried to interfere, Melkamu made the error of telling her that the matter was between him and Ezra. She had to remind him that there was no business in this house that was not hers, so she bent him over like a baby and slapped his buttocks repeatedly. He didn't fight back.

I'M LYING DOWN on my parents' bed, my father next to me with the back of his palm on my forehead, asking if I want Coca-Cola. The malaria medicine I have been taking doesn't seem to be working. Comrade Rectangle-Head is running up our front stair. The mention of Coca-Cola would normally excite me, but everything is disgusting when I get malaria. The comrade knocks on the door and my father leaves to go answer him. Milk is also disgusting; eggs smell like something I have never smelled before; even my mother, lying next to me worried more than ever, smells different. The only thing that hasn't changed is my hatred for comrade Rectangle-Head. We can hear him talking to my father in the living room, something something about comrade Kebede, the boss of all the comrades, wanting my father to appear in his office. The revolution is always summoning us and making us vote and gather and bake and dance and sing and hoist the flag. None of it is ever going to make this nosy cadre evaporate.

My father comes back with his nostrils flaring. "Look what you're doing to our family," he says to my mother.

"What now?"

"The head of the hyenas wants to talk to me. I'm sure it has to do with your new religion."

"Matthew ten, twenty-two," she says. "You will be hated by everyone because of me, but the one who stands firm to the end will be saved."

"You woman," he says. "You can do whatever you want with your life, don't let the children get killed."

"Proverbs twenty-two, six," she says. "Train up a child in the way he should go; even when he is old he will not depart from it."

You can see my father's veins trying to get out through his forehead. "I swear on my mother's life, if you were not sick, I would give you a good whipping with my cane."

I think my parents are worse than malaria because my head is leaving—

I LIE ON MY BACK on a clinic bed, eyes upside down. Ato Girma, the health officer, closes my eyelids and exits the room to go tell my parents about a dead leopard. The angels from my *Bible in Pictures* book are sitting with me. There's a long white stair with no end in sight. I am three and a half and can walk on stairs, but this one is too high. The angels look at each other and grab each of my arms. They fly above the stair with me between them, terrified.

We land in a colorless place where everything is white. The ground is white, the clothes the people are wearing are white, the houses are white, the sky is white. At a distance, a large gathering of people is singing a song I recognize, before an exceptionally tall throne I only notice due to the shadow it's casting. The angels take me to an empty house and everything in it is so white that it is hard to distinguish the chairs from the walls at first. They lead me into a hallway, where we enter a room with a big fluffy bed in the middle.

"This is your parents' room," says one of them.

They search my face for a response, but I say nothing. One of them grabs me by the armpits and puts me on the bed. It's like sitting on air.

"See how comfortable it is?"

I touch the blanket and I barely feel it against my fingers.

"Your mother will like it here."

They keep staring at me, waiting for me to say something.

"We brought you here to ask your permission."

Permission for what?

"We want to bring your mother here."

They haven't told me where here is, but from the large gathering of people singing in front of a throne, I think it is heaven, because I have seen it in *Bible in Pictures*.

"Do you permit us to bring your mother here?"

"What about my father?"

"It is not his time."

The whole house starts shaking suddenly. A white empty frame on the wall drops. We hear a muffled scream. One of the angels reaches for the bed to steady himself and the other one stands in the middle of the room swaying. The muffled scream gets louder. I realize it's my mother.

"Think about it," yells the swaying angel.

I wake up on the clinic bed with my mother on top of me screaming so I scream too, and she sees that I am screaming and she screams again and I scream more and she is covered in tears when she picks me up to say, my child my child, let me go in your place let me die in your place come to me my child let me die in your place my child my child my child—

THREE DAYS AFTER the resurrection of a leopard, comrade Rectangle-Head comes to the door of the green house with the head of the Revolutionary Ethiopia Youth Association and two policemen. He has come to take Teshager and all the leopard's siblings. The leopard's father can't get up from his chair because he feels paralyzed.

The mother turns to her children. "Listen to me," she says. "Matthew ten, thirty-three. Whoever denies me before men, I also will deny before my Father who is in heaven."

Baby leopard hugs the leg of the dining table, for objects feel more permanent than people.

THE GREEN HOUSE is scary when empty.

My mother is at work since making clothes is not unchristian. One of the men who visited us from Addis Ababa praised her decision to close the tej bét and told her about a bookkeeping diploma she can obtain through distance education. When she's not making clothes, praying, or cooking, she studies and does homework.

My father is in the house talking to a group of elders about mediation. He told me to play outside. People often come to my father for their mediation needs because he is known as the man with a horse's tongue. A horse has a smooth tongue but can break you with a kick, unlike a cow, which has a rough tongue but is meek. Despite his losses to the revolution, people think he is influential. Professor "I Worry" said on the FRS that the revolution spent fourteen years trying to destroy the image of the aristocratic man without providing an alternative idea of manhood. People still look up to men like my father, the handsome former landowner who resembles a statesman in his old but quality suits and shiny leather shoes.

My father never turns down mediation requests. Being asked means he is respected in the community. That's one of the reasons why he is upset with my mother's new religion: he doesn't think people will respect those who turn their backs on the Virgin Maryam, no matter the depth of their experience in diplomacy.

It is my father who needed the elders this time. "My wife is sick," he was saying, right before he told me to go outside. "The children don't want to have anything to do with this religion." He wants the elders to plead with comrade Kebede for him. He's going to give them one of our cows as a gift for the boss of the comrades.

I TAKE MY *Bible in Pictures* outside because kids don't always let me play with them. Kamila and Fetiya push me sometimes. Once, my mother and I were on our way home from the Libs Sefi Bét. I was dressed in khaki pants, a white shirt with embroideries on the chest, and a matching hat. All the children stopped what they were doing to stare at me. Kamila and Fetiya, who are always barefooted, were wearing the same dirty dresses they always wore.

Degitu told me to play and left me. The children and I stared at one another some more until Kamila extended a hand. We went to the stoop in front of her house. I sat between her and Fetiya. The rest of the children went back to chasing balls, throwing marbles in holes, skipping inside boxes drawn on the ground with chalk.

"I always see you jump up and down next to your mother," said Kamila. "Is that all you know how to play?"

I had no answer.

"Don't you know how to play dimo, fursh, eqa-eqa, akukulu?" says Fetiya.

I asked myself how do I not know any of the things they're saying when I know so much about the rebels in the north, the Italians, God, and Comrade Chairman. I see that my father and the radio haven't been telling me everything.

Come with me, said Kamila. Fetiya and I followed her into her house. Half of the living room was covered in mattresses. The other half had earthen benches built into the wall, with a couple of beaten tables in front of them. In the back room, an old shelf with plastic plates and cups stood at one corner, with pots and pans covered in soot lying in disarray beneath it. The other side of the back room had piles of sacks and clothes.

The backyard was a little wider than the standalone kitchen. I saw two ropes tied to our fence. There was a pile of cow dung that Eteyé Khadija was going to dry and use as firewood—sometimes the smell of burning cow dung wafted toward our house. I thought to myself that I needed to keep away from that pile when we passed it because I don't want to get my white sneakers dirty, but right away I realized we were never meant to go past it. Kamila let go of my hand, grabbed my shoulders, and pushed me onto the pile of dung, and one minute I was wearing khaki and white, the next I was smeared in dark green, screaming.

"You're ugly now," said Kamila.

I only stopped crying that night when my father came home for radio. Since then, Kamila and her friends sometimes throw stones at me and call me maté, outsider, and penté, short for Pentecostal. I keep going outside to see if they will let me play because sometimes they do. Unpredictability is their source of power. My source of hope.

I SIT ON THE BOTTOM step of our front stair, looking at my *Bible in Pictures,* hoping to be invited to play. Little Yonas has been trying to teach me how to read. I only know some of the letters so far.

I open the page to Elijah being taken to heaven on a chariot of fire. It's one of my favorite stories, along with that of Joseph, son of Jacob. I get angry thinking about how Joseph's brothers threw him into a ditch and soaked his coat in animal blood to deceive their father into believing that Joseph was attacked by an animal. I want to get inside the book to tell Jacob they were lying. I'm glad that Joseph became prosperous in Egypt, that his ugly brothers ended up seeking his help.

Teshager said my mother is like the prophet Elijah. She is not afraid to stand amidst people who do not worship the Lord and to declare the Truth.

There is a sudden silence on the front yard and I look up from my book to see what's got the children's attention.

It's my siblings! I see Weder and Ezra and Melkamu and Little Yonas and Beza. I even see Teshager and the people who have been coming to our house for prayers in the evenings. They're walking down the road carrying machetes and spades. I bounce up and down, pointing and yelling my siblings' names. They are near our house. I cannot contain my excitement, thinking about being picked up, spun around, kissed, and getting my belly tickled. They only wave at me, smile, and keep walking. I am confused, because when our cows come from foraging, they take a turn when they reach our house, entering through the backyard door.

My siblings didn't turn, as if they have forgotten their home. As if they no longer want me.

MY MOTHER IS PACKING food to take to my siblings at the police station. I ask her why they are not coming home. She says comrade Rectangle-Head has them. He sends them to work in the countryside in the mornings, weeding farmlands or digging water wells for hours. When they return exhausted, he tries to raise their Marxist-Leninist consciousness.

She writes notes on small pieces of paper. We have to send them words of encouragement, she tells me. We have to send them Scripture reminding them not to give up their faith. She places the notes at the bottom of lunch containers and covers them with injera. She adds cabbage, potato, and lentil stews, topped with another layer of injera.

At the police station, she tells me to wait outside. I tell her I want to see my siblings. She says I am not allowed to, and that, if I cry, they will get in more trouble. I sit outside shaking, trying to keep my sadness in.

THE NEXT AFTERNOON, my mother and I go to the police station with food. We're bringing fresh fruit Tultula brought from his farm. My mother has converted Tultula to Protestantism, and he's been joining us for Sunday sermons. After he brought us the fruit in the morning, he stayed awhile helping my mother with chores. He brought water from the government pump and filled our barrels. He cut a pile of firewood, enough for a week, and stored it in the chicken coop. He even began chopping onions, but he cut himself while doing so. My mother cleaned his cut with alcohol and covered it. She sat there staring at his hand. I went over and snatched her hands away. "She's my mother," I said to Tultula. "Give her back." They both laughed at me as if I were joking.

At the police station, my mother tells me to wait outside, but I wander away. I follow the edge of the building to the back of the station and look through the gaps in the fence. I don't believe what I am seeing. I also believe it because here are my eyes that I always use to see everything and there are my siblings, standing against the back wall of the station, looking at the ground. A man whose face I can't see paces in front of them. I want to call their names. I can't make my mouth work. I want to go back to where my mother left me but my feet are stuck.

Beza is wearing a ruffled blue dress she made herself at the Libs Sefi Bét. She has become an expert at making clothes, covering for our mother whenever she is unable to work. Beza no longer takes payment from my mother because we are too poor after the tej bét was closed.

I wish I could go touch Beza's face but there is a fence, so many comrades, and their guns between us.

13.

Children Who Talk to God

There's an uprising against my mother's Protestant regime.

My siblings have been released after two weeks of imprisonment. The head of the Youth Association said that my mother's imperialist religion controls young people's minds and keeps them from working for our Revolutionary State. Look at how it made her close her tej bét, he said, that means less taxes for the state. My father sent a group of elders and a gift of a cow to the comrades, begging them to release my siblings, promising they will no longer have anything to do with their mother's religion. At the same time our mother was sending threats to my siblings along with Bible verses, saying that they won't be welcome at her house if they deny Jesus Christ. The comrades decided to let my siblings go with a warning: if they don't behave themselves and fail to exhibit an increased Marxist-Leninist consciousness, they will be taken back.

Judging by the rebellion in this house tonight, the raising of their Marxist-Leninist consciousness has made a difference. Melkamu and Beza are leading the resistance. Even after my mother told him that he could keep his secular music, Melkamu doesn't think that will last, as

Teshager has continued listing secular singing alongside sinful activities good Christians should avoid. Beza never cared for this or that Jesus Christ; she just doesn't like what she recently heard Teshager say: that Protestants are only to marry other Protestants. It is written, he'd said: "Do not be yoked together with unbelievers. For what do righteousness and wickedness have in common? Or what fellowship can light have with darkness?"

My father is encouraging them, agitating the others, trying to get them to leave tonight's Bible study. Teshager's Marxist-Leninist consciousness hasn't been raised at all. He is standing before us holding a black Bible with a golden cross on the front. Teshager has been offered a job in Addis Ababa by the people who have been visiting us, to be an evangelist who goes around the country spreading Jesus Christ. Ezra is not happy about this.

The day my siblings came home from detention, I tried to play with Melkamu the pigeon game that I have seen Teshager and Ezra playing. I was so happy that I went around kissing and biting everyone's cheeks. I sat on Melkamu's lap and tried to suck his mouth. He pushed me away and hissed. He told me that's a disgusting thing I should never do with anyone. I was upset and asked why Teshager and Ezra do it then.

Melkamu dragged me to our parents' room to become a witness in a secret trial. He brought our mother into the room and told me to recount what I saw.

"I knew it," said Melkamu. "I knew there was something wrong with him."

"Wrong with whom?"

"Both of them!" said Melkamu, pacing around the room. "You know it, Emayé," he said, in a voice that was whispering but sounded like yelling. "Why are you trying to make me say it?"

"You boy, say what you are trying to say clearly."

"I saw him do this with one of the servant boys when we were kids. I thought it was just a game." He held his head with both hands. He reminded our mother of a time when she let a woman spend a night in the same room as Ezra because she knew *this thing* about him.

I wanted to know why the pigeon game was bad. I was too scared of my brother to ask.

"Keep your mouth shut," said my mother. "Answer me this: Have you been trying to extort your brother with this? Is this why he borrows all that money?"

"I can't believe you're trying to turn the table on me."

"Listen to me carefully: you speak of this to anyone, I will be charging you the price."

"I will tell everyone if you continue letting that charlatan teach us the Bible," said Melkamu. "He's not a man of God. You have to kick him out."

"Does a person stop being a man of God because he's a sinner? Read John eight, seven: he that is without sin among you, let him first cast a stone."

"It is not the same."

"That a person is struggling with sin doesn't make what they are saying wrong," said my mother. "Our job is to pray for sinners. This just means we have more praying to do."

Melkamu was in disbelief. "I am going to tell Abayé."

My mother told him she was going to kill him and repent her sins if he told anybody. "Do I look like I am afraid of going to prison?" she asked. "What is the government going to do to me that my own body isn't already doing?"

Melkamu gave up, out of words. I have been watching him watch Ezra and Teshager since then. He looks like a cat who's tracking a bird, biding his time. I worry about the pigeons that gather on the telephone lines outside our house, blissfully sucking each other's beaks and climbing each other, oblivious to the predator near them.

IN THE DAYS AFTER the initial rebellion and her argument with Melkamu, we watched our mother suffer in pain. It's the stomachache that no pain-killer could get rid of. On a few occasions, we watched her drop what she was carrying to reach for something solid to hold on to. It's just light-headedness, she would say. Nothing to worry about. We worry because our mother is our first planet, the first ground we ever stood on, and her stumbles are the earthquakes of our hearts.

Tonight, Teshager stands before us carrying his black Bible with the golden cross. My mother is less threatening and more melancholic.

"We have to pray for me," she says. "I cannot stand the pain anymore. We have to beg God for forgiveness and healing."

Silence falls upon us. Mother and country, mother and music, mother and love interests, are being compared in every head. The foundations of faith are being shaken.

"Will God get rid of her illness?" asks Weder.

"Teshager has witnessed miraculous healings in Addis Ababa," says Degitu.

"It is written," says Teshager. "If the Orthodox Church had done its job of teaching you the Bible, you would know too."

"What is this written written business you keep repeating?" asks Melkamu.

Teshager thumbs through the Bible. "I will read from Mark sixteen, verse seventeen." He assumes a solemn look. "And these signs will accompany those who believe: In my name they will drive out demons; they will speak in new tongues; they will pick up snakes with their hands; and when they drink deadly poison, it will not hurt them at all; they will place their hands on sick people, and they will get well."

We all shut our mouths and keep our heads down because we know we cannot argue with the Word. My father is not falling for this; he can spot a cross-eyed fruit fly let alone see through a foreign infiltrator's agendas. My mother looks on as my father gets up and walks into the bedroom.

Teshager instructs us to close our eyes and follow him in prayer. Sitting on a stool next to my mother, I watch my siblings bow their heads to do as Teshager commands, taking a big step toward becoming what the rest of the town calls maté. Outsiders. Western imports.

My father emerges from the bedroom sliding his arms into the sleeves of his jacket. On his way to Mamitu's Bar.

I've had enough of watching him walk out night after night. I go to a corner and start wailing, holding my head with both hands. "Wayoo, wayoo, wayoo!" It is something I had seen people in funeral processions do.

My mother yells at me. She calls me muartegna, accusing me of summoning death.

MY MOTHER IS about to leave for a hospital in Addis Ababa. She wanted to be home when Weder gets her school-leaving exam results in a few weeks, but the stomachaches have become unbearable.

Days ago I followed my father to the backyard in the evening after he left their bedroom to escape my mother's moaning. I saw him shaking, trying to keep in his tears. He is taking her to the hospital today.

Degitu doesn't think there is a cure for her illness. The missionary doctor that took out her uterus had told her that her disease was going to eat her intestines too. When I overheard her and Weder talk about that, I remembered a story I heard somewhere about elephants: When an elephant goes downhill to a river, its anus opens up widely. So wide that a clever animal whose name I don't recall jumps in and cuts up its insides. The elephant won't feel this at first because it is too big. The clever one jumps out. Once the elephant starts back uphill after drinking from the river, the anus closes up. The clever one sits in ambush waiting for the elephant to fall down. I think something like that is happening to my mother.

She and I were sitting in bed recently, looking out to the street. She's been too sick to work for weeks. Beza has been covering for her at the Libs Sefi Bét but she doesn't make clothes as fast as my mother, and without the bar, our money is running out. We haven't eaten meat in a while.

As we looked out the window, a funeral procession came to pass on the street.

"Do you know why those people are crying?" asked Degitu.

I nodded. "They took their mother away."

"Who did?"

"The same people who have been asking me if they can take you."

She yelped. Weder and Little Yonas came running in. "I told you," said my mother. "Children talk to God." She told them what I said and Weder snatched me away.

"Don't ever say such things," said Weder. "You're too young to know about death."

She says that to me all the time. That I am too young to know things. A while ago I asked her to examine my hands to see if I am my father's child.

"What are you talking about?" said Weder.

I told her that I overheard my mother telling her to examine Tultula's hands because his hands are a carbon copy of my father's hands, suggesting he might be my father's son. "I want my hands to be a carbon copy of my father's hands," I said.

Weder told me that I was too young to be talking about such things, shame on me for spying on my elders. I wanted to tell her that I was not spying, I was sitting right there when my mother said that to her and Ezra. People in my family are always whispering things to one another in front of me as if I am deaf or don't understand their language. Weder said I should not mention what I heard to anyone, especially to our father. I nodded in agreement because I didn't want to get pinched. My siblings have taken to pinching me whenever I disobey them or say something bad. But no amount of pinching can make me forget the things I have heard.

DEGITU IS LEAVING for Addis Ababa today and I do not agree with it. I am tired of her coming and going. Someday when I am big, I am going to go to the Medium Town and Addis Ababa and Uppsala and Washington, D.C., and she will see what she has been doing to me and hopefully cry. She doesn't even want to take me with her; only Ezra and my father are going.

She has gathered the rest of my siblings to give them instructions. They are to make new wooden spoons for cooking; wash all the curtains, tablecloths, bed linens, clothes; clean every inch of the house, making sure the floor is shining every day.

"Every day," she says.

Earlier in the morning, when they told me my father was going to Addis Ababa, I fell on the floor, held my head, and wailed, wayoo wayoo!

"Please stop it, you child," he begged me. He promised he was coming back immediately. "As soon as I get your mother to the hospital."

Degitu sat there watching. When she told me she was going away too, I said nothing.

She is wearing a wide black dress and a gray cardigan under a netela, her hair wrapped in a black headdress. "Come to me," she says. "Won't you kiss me good-bye?"

I shrug. She begs me.

She turns to my siblings. "I told you," she says. "Children know."

The woman makes me angry.

"My mother always says children talk to God. And they know the things He knows because they are innocent," says Degitu.

I know you're an infuriating woman, I'm thinking.

Ezra forcefully takes me to her. She tries to kiss my face, my neck, and my hands, but I fight her away. I wipe my cheeks and run out to the backyard to hide until she's gone.

At night, I wake up crying, asking for water. I find Weder lying next to me instead of my mother. My sister wakes up and points a flashlight at the ceiling. I ask when my mother is coming back, and Weder tells me tomorrow. I tell myself tomorrow isn't too far away. I go back to sleep without drinking the water I had asked for.

14.

Tomorrow

The day after New Year, during the fourteenth anniversary celebrations of the revolution, Little Yonas jumps through a ring of fire and my heart drops to new depths. He had joined the circus team. I hide my face in Weder's chest.

Weder is heartbroken because her school-leaving exam results came back, and she didn't get the score needed for admission to medical school. She'll attend Addis Ababa University for a year, and the school will decide what she studies. The Women are burning with envy. A child of former bloodsuckers who turned her back on the Virgin Maryam is one of only two people from our town to be admitted to university this year.

Melkamu played kirar with the band as usual. Beza finally made it into a play. She played the mistress of a man who wrote embarrassing poems. The actor, Yeneneh, is the new biology teacher at the high school. In the play, his wife kicks down the door and catches Yeneneh on one knee, reading a love poem to Beza. He and my sister spring up, but Beza can't get away because the wife has the door. That's what happens to people who betray the revolution.

Ezra and our parents are at the hospital in Addis Ababa. My sisters made doro wat and difo dabo for New Year's Day. The floor isn't shining as my mother had instructed. There were plates with bread crumbs on dirty tablecloths, unmade beds, and chairs out of place when we left the house.

I see comrade Rectangle-Head with his boss, comrade Kebede, sitting in the front row to the left of the stage. They look as healthy as always. Comrade Kebede's belly has gotten even bigger, like he's pregnant with a wine cask.

THE DAY AFTER, my siblings and I have gathered around a nameless dish we have been eating a lot lately: injera tossed in a mixture of berbere and buttermilk. We finished the chicken stew from New Year's in two days. I'm sick of this buttermilk dish, so I only take a few gurshas and go outside where there's a drizzle in the sun. I stand at the bottom of our front stair hoping to be invited to play by the kids. A little boy who wears nothing but a dirty white T-shirt runs up to me and says, a hyena has given birth. He runs away as fast as he appeared.

Whenever I leave our house to join the children, I feel like a solo traveler trying to navigate a vast darkness with a small candle. Learning something new is being handed another candle to expand the frontiers of what I can see. I don't always understand what the children say, and I don't follow up with questions. My mind gives its own meaning to some of the things I hear. The first time I heard about the city of Jimma, I decided it meant a giant block of the color blue.

This talk of a hyena giving birth is too intriguing to pass without a follow-up question. I already know that the hyena, also known to me as amugnu, is a fearsome beast that sometimes hides under your bed to punish you for disobedience. Sometimes, we can hear the laughter of hyenas from the forest behind our house. My father has also told me stories about hyenas. Once upon a time, a hyena ate a donkey's ears and the latter said, here I was praying for horns but I just lost my ears. Ha!

I track the boy down to ask him what he meant.

"When it drizzles in the sun, it means a hyena has given birth," he says.

I am astounded by this new knowledge, by the ever expanding powers of the hyena, which apparently include a Godlike capacity for affecting weather.

I feel a tug on my shoulder. It's Kamila and Fetiya.

"When is your mother coming back?" asks Kamila.

"Tomorrow," I say.

They want to know when my mother is coming because I had bragged that she is bringing me candies and cake. They've made me swear that I will give them some.

"But you said that yesterday," says Kamila.

"And the day before yesterday," adds Fetiya.

"Every day, you say tomorrow."

They look at each other.

I run back into the house.

"When is Emayé coming back?"

"Tomorrow," says Weder. "Today is not tomorrow."

I am confused because this is also true.

My siblings talk about how they need to complete their assignments before our mother comes back. They know they would all be beaten if she saw this floor.

"Who was supposed to make the wooden spoons?" asks Weder.

Then we hear a woman's muffled wailing outside.

"What's that?"

Now it's a group of women wailing. "Wayoo! Wayoo! Wayoo!"

"Did a car hit somebody?"

We all go outside to see.

A white minibus has stopped in front of our house, but it hasn't hit anybody. Out of it come my aunt Haregua, my cousins, my grandmother Zeritu, and other women I haven't seen before. They wail, arms flailing, as they yell things I don't understand. Behind me, Beza screams. Weder flies down the front stair. Melkamu follows her screaming, ouououou! Weder falls near the bottom of the stair. Etabeba Haregua comes running to her. Beza screams again, and when I turn around to look at her, I see Little Yonas tearing off his shirt.

OUR HOUSE IS UPSIDE DOWN. The living room and corridor are full of women who flail their arms and wail, waists tightly belted with netelas. Eteyé Zinash, my mother's best friend, tore the crowd into two earlier when she came in screaming louder than everyone else. Visitors have spilled over to our front yard and backyard. People have been staring at me and clicking their tongues.

Nobody would talk to me, but I find Weder in a corner of the living room, where she sits on the floor being tended to by a woman who presses a wet handkerchief to her forehead. I ask why everybody is crying, why she is crying, and she tells me that a stranger died on the bus and our family has agreed to host his wake. The corpse is arriving later.

I go outside when I get tired of the screaming. Kamila and Fetiya find me again. They want to know what is going on in our house. I tell them what Weder told me. They look at each other and leave me.

A RED-AND-WHITE-STRIPED old Italian bus stops in front of our house. All the wailing women spill out to the front yard. I stick my fingers in my ears to keep out some of the noise. I see my father, Ezra, and Teshager coming out of the bus. I don't see my mother. I am happy my father is back, but I am not running to him. I am angry that he left me in the first place, and when he comes to me later, I am going to punch him in the chest.

Gash Nesro, our neighbor, and Gash Shimelis, my father's friend, get inside the bus along with other men and bring out a big wooden box. They get on either side of the box and carry it into our house. When I ease my fingers off my ears just a little, I hear the screaming has intensified. I notice that Emama Zeritu is missing from this crowd. Etabeba Haregua and my cousins throw their hands in the air like a group of dancers at one of the anniversary celebrations.

I find my grandmother Zeritu on our back porch. She's sitting on a bench staring at nothing in particular. She stares like the way my mother was staring the day she collapsed on the veranda of the Libs Sefi Bét, and I worry Emama Zeritu is also going to collapse. I decide to sit with her to make sure that doesn't happen.

Where is she, I wonder, that Degitu? My father came to greet me earlier and I slapped him in the face. I wanted to ask him where he left my mother but I couldn't stand to talk to him.

I stand between Emama Zeritu's legs, staring into space just like her. She has her hands around me. The wailing has continued around us. My grandmother is the only quiet place. I turn around to look at her face, but she doesn't return my gaze.

15.

The Fallen Tree

When the village crier went around blowing his horn and announcing the death, we were grinding coffee and baking instant bread for our husbands, who had risen before sunrise to inspect the cornfields. Plates and pots were dropped, heads were held, and wails were let out. We called out to one another across fences, sent our children to fetch their fathers, and hurried to get out of our work clothes. As we descend the side of the mountain overlooking the Small Town, the loud wailing would have you thinking that that evil king from the Holy Book had visited this place to kill all the babies in sight.

We arrived in the Small Town just as the funeral procession was starting, and we cannot see the beginning or end of the crowd, as if this were a celebration of Epiphany or Meskel. We hold our heads and start wailing again. Some among us want to jump around and writhe, as if they were possessed, to show that they are the saddest of us all. We want to tell them to calm down, that no family member can see them, but who has the time as we are all struggling to reach the center.

We have reached St. Mary's, where priests burn incense and chant. We cannot hear a word of what they are saying since we are too far away from the front row. We can guess they are praying for Eteyé Degitu's soul, and we wonder: didn't they say she will never be buried at St. Mary's for turning her back on the Virgin Maryam? We ourselves are here wailing for our former mistress, so maybe death changes the meaning of things.

We finally reach the front of the crowd at the graveyard, and we see all female relatives covered in black from head to toe, having already shaved their heads. As the men lower the coffin into the grave, the screaming reaches the heavens, and we have to cover our ears. Degitu's sister, Eteyé Haregua, is restrained by multiple men because she wants to be buried with her sister. The mother just stands staring into the grave, holding on to her cane with one hand, her free fist planted on her waist as if she wants to fight somebody, something.

Back at the green house, the men of the town's edir have already erected a tent covering the whole of the front yard, and several benches and tables have been arranged inside it. Most people can't find a seat; the place looks as though it is under siege. We push through the crowd into the house and we see a disheveled Gash Asmelash sitting on a mattress on the veranda with his sons and other men, the little child on his lap, her face buried in his chest. All the other children, female relatives, and family friends sit on mattresses and plaited palm rugs laid out on the living-room floor. As we make our way to the back, we cannot believe our eyes, because we see Tayitu, the old housemaid, sitting on a rug in the living room, as if she were a family member. There's no time to stop and marvel at things in this chaos, so we keep moving.

In the backyard, women have set up firepits to brew coffee and tea in large pots. We put away our netelas and offer help. Our husbands return to the village in the evening. We spend the night on empty coffee sacks laid out on the back veranda. We barely fall asleep when we are awakened at dawn by loud wailing. In the living room, Eteyé Haregua and Eteyé Zinash move in circles, beating their chests, yelling Degitu's name. Everyone joins in, and it's like the end of the world, as if there had been total destruction, the earth beneath our feet gone. At that point, we cannot help ourselves but begin sobbing. We see Tayitu throwing her hands in the air and screaming, wayoo wayoo, and we want to know how she has wormed her way back into this family after taking over their restaurant during the revolution, ransacking their home, running away with the leader of the zemachoch.

We help the women of the town's edir serve breakfast before returning to our village to bring back coffee and food. A week later, we are in and out of the green house, sometimes spending the night. Tultula has been here for days, wrapped in his gabi, eyes bloodshot, crying with the wailing women every time they start. He missed the funeral because he has chosen to build himself a house on his coffee farm in the woods instead of living with us in the village, so nobody remembered to tell him the news in time.

Everyone but Degitu's mother sits on mattresses during the day, feet under blankets, backs lined against walls. They talk to one another in hushed tones, rising only to go to the outhouse or to greet newly arriving relatives. Degitu's mother has been sitting on eucalyptus leaves on the bare cement floor. She has been refusing to eat or talk to anyone. When she's not with her father, Degitu's little one goes to her grandmother to sit between her legs. The old woman would sit in silence for hours and suddenly begin wailing: Moo, my child! Moo, my child! Won't you come back to me. The little one would turn to her grandmother and say that her mother is coming back, that she has only gone to the hospital in Addis Ababa. She would hold the old woman's face with her tiny hands and say,

I am telling you the truth, Emama, my father told me so. The old woman begins groaning like a wounded animal at that point, and somebody has to come snatch the little one away. The whole house breaks down in wails again.

Ezra has come to the back to talk to us a few times. We look at Degitu's boys and ask ourselves: why are they all here when most of us have lost our oldest boys to conscription? We know the answer, of course. Money. Money for bribes. Money for letting the children continue school while ours had to stay home to help their fathers farm. Even those of us with enough hands to work the farms can't let our children go beyond eighth grade because high schools only exist in towns and cities. And finally: money for the buses that transport the children to teachers' training colleges so that they are completely safe from conscription, busy helping the country in the war against illiteracy, as the comrades keep telling us.

We are not angry at our Ezra, who has visited us in the countryside a number of times since he became old enough to get out of his mother's grip. He always came bearing gifts: exercise books and pencils for the little ones; rubber shoes, netelas, and painkillers for the mothers. He reminds us of Lord Gebre Egziabher, who used to work for the governor of the province as a tax collector before he was granted land upon his return from the war with the Italians. Lord Gebre used to travel the countryside forgiving the debts of many tenant farmers. The governor would be furious, but he couldn't replace him. There weren't many people at the time who could read and add numbers. Here's his grandson now, trying to help us wash the dishes, mocking us and saying, is your hand broken, you missed a spot, give it to me. We slap his hand and tell him it is not his job.

Tayitu leaves the living room to wash and go to the outhouse. She doesn't help in the back like the rest of us who are busy cutting firewood, milking the cows, receiving the endless stream of visitors who have been bringing injera and jebenas full of coffee. We heard many years ago that the head of the zemachoch abandoned Tayitu in the Medium Town. We didn't think we would hear of her again until someone ran into her at the Saturday market. She lives in a village near the Small Town after marrying the son of Girazmach Morada, the biggest landowner in the region before the revolution. Her husband is a farmer who lives in a hut like the rest of us, like all former landowners who weren't shrewd enough to build a proper home in town before the revolution, like our former mistress. Tayitu wants to raise her chin at us even higher than she used to, telling everyone she meets that her kids are the grandchildren of a girazmach who used to own all the land between here and Tiji, more land than Gash Asmelash, as if we didn't already know that, as if her children are going to cook the nonexistent status of their dead grandfather and eat it.

16

Chariots of Fire

Weeks after the stranger's funeral, the crying women have left our house. I had to live through all that noise again when it was Emama Zeritu's turn to be carried out in a coffin. My grandmother stopped eating food the day of the stranger's funeral. She left us for the Medium Town when she got tired of people nagging her to eat and to stop sitting on eucalyptus leaves on the cold cement floor. Weeks later, Emama's body stopped working, so we went to the Medium Town to bury her. I saw Degitu the same day Emama left us. Had my grandmother stayed a little longer, she would have seen my mother being taken on chariots of fire to go speak to God.

I have heard many stories about my grandmother. "Mengistu Hailemariam needs to be up front with us," she once said loudly of our dictator. It was at a government store where people were in line to buy their rations of essentials. Everyone shrank in place, afraid of what might befall them as a result of what that crazy woman was about to say. She was holding up a new product—a black bar of soap the government stores had just rolled out. "He needs to tell us whether this is really soap or his shit in a package!"

Some of the customers hurried out. My grandmother walked out like it was any other Saturday, with a bag full of goods in one hand and a walking stick in the other. Sometimes she pointed her walking stick at random men to say, "You know I know how to use this." She also did that with the spear she carried about town in the evenings.

Emama Zeritu was also known for refusing to get out of the way for cars. She believed that people were here before cars and the roads belonged to them, so the machines should show some respect and let people pass.

I am going to miss her very much. Maybe when I grow up, I will honor my Emama Zeritu by walking about town in the evenings carrying a spear, striking fear into every man who passed me saying: "You know I know how to use this."

We are back at home but smaller in number. Weder left us for the university. She woke up early one morning and didn't say good-bye to me. I will never speak to her again. Ezra and Melkamu are back at their jobs. The day the angels took her on the chariot, Degitu told me she was returning soon from heaven. It's been a long time.

It's just me, my father, Beza, and Little Yonas. In the evenings, we hold hands and pray. I tell Jesus Christ to return my mother to me immediately. My father prays with us now. He hasn't been to Mamitu's Bar in a long time. Last night we sang one of the songs Teshager taught us: they said let's go to God's house and I was happy; they said let's go listen to His words and I was happy. Teshager left a few days after the stranger's funeral. He has taken a new job as an evangelist. He will be traveling all over the country from his base in Addis Ababa.

The power generator is not working tonight. The living room is lit by a lantern. My father washed my feet and is searching them for mujele with a flashlight. When you spend a lot of time playing outside in the dust, some parasites enter your toes. Your parents have to search your feet every evening, and if they find something, they take it out with a needle.

Beza and Little Yonas are making noise in the parents' bedroom. I tell my father that I want to go play with them. He says they are not playing. I free my feet from his hand and hit the ground. One second, two seconds, three, four, I'm in the bedroom.

I don't understand.

My siblings have taken my mother's clothes out of the wardrobe and the trunk. They have laid out some of her dresses on the bed. Others have been stuffed into plastic bags on the floor.

"What are you doing?" I ask.

They don't say anything.

"Emayé will need her clothes when she comes back."

They stand as if somebody nailed their feet to the ground.

I'm angry in this house. I'm angry that people are always leaving. I'm angry that God is keeping my mother for so long.

"Put it all back," I say. "Put my mother's clothes back in the trunk or I'm going to burn you in your sleep, you bad children."

They start shaking. They are scared of me because I think maybe the leopard is coming out. They both drop the dresses and run out of the room.

I start picking up my mother's clothes. I pull together all the ones on the bed but they are too big for my arms. I trip on one and start crying. My father comes into the room and tries to pick me up but I slap his hands

away and storm out to the living room where I go to a dark corner to sit
and keep my leopard from coming out to eat everyone in this house.

I'm angry that Weder woke up so early in the morning to avoid seeing
me before she left for the university. I'm angry at God, sitting up there
like a coward, always making loud thunder and sending too much water
or too little, snatching people's mothers away and keeping them for too
long. Maybe somebody took His mother and never gave her back. Most
of all, I'm angry at Asmelash. Maybe he's the reason Degitu hasn't come
back as soon as she said she would. All his drinking and money wasting
and anger at her new religion.

I should have promised that I would love her more the day the angels
took her. That I would get more excited when she comes home than I do
when Asmelash comes home. That I would cry more when she goes to
Addis Ababa. That I would be a good student and a good child when I
grow up. I tried to speak to her that day, I wanted to tell her more things
than I was able to say but the angels and their chariots were too fast.

I had gone outside to see off Emama Zeritu when I saw Degitu coming
out of the bus. I couldn't even alert my grandmother because she was
already on the bus and it was moving and my mother was walking away
from me. Emayé Emayé, I yelled! I had forgotten how angry I was at her
for being away for so long. She had a big smile when she saw me. "You
can kiss me now, Emayé," I yelled. I was thinking that, any minute now,
I am going to be in her arms being searched for signs of illness, being
called ema-gela—her mother, her body. The angels swooped in and
pulled her onto chariots of fire, like the ones that took the prophet Elijah.
I yelled at the angels to leave my mother alone. Degitu yelled back and
said this was temporary, that she was only going to talk to God, that she
will come back to me soon.

She was wearing her nicest habesha qemis with the colorful embroidery at the chest and lower edges, which she only wore on special occasions. I chased the chariot as it took off.

"You can kiss me when you come back," I yelled again. "You can kiss me all the time!"

I'M SITTING IN my dark corner, shaking a little and feeling hot. I know my father is shaking in the bedroom too, but his is from sadness like it has been since the stranger's funeral.

For weeks after the red-and-white-striped bus arrived with the stranger's coffin, there was so much frightening noise at our house that I often hid my face in my father's chest. That was why I started talking to him again. I asked him where he left my mother, and he said she was in Addis Ababa, and he began shaking as he does whenever he tries to hold in tears. I thought that maybe she refused to come with him. He said she was being treated and would return soon. I began going outside every afternoon after that to wait for the bus from Addis Ababa.

Everyone looked at me as though I were some rare, delicate object that needed careful handling. Every woman I passed by in the house would click her tongue and say, ooh, she's so young! Whenever the wailing began, the women would yell: How dare you leave without me? How will I live without you? Oouu oouu oouu! It was confusing at times because the criers kept yelling my mother's name. When I asked Weder why they were doing that, she said they were confused. They were confusing me too, until the day I saw my mother with the angels.

My father was mostly silent in those days. He was surrounded by his friends but didn't appear to listen to their conversations. I sat with him often, and whenever the wailing began, I could feel little tremors in his chest and legs.

MY FATHER HAS BEEN in the bedroom a long time. I can hear the little moaning sounds he makes when he is in pain. Maybe he is also angry at himself for beating and cursing her, for angering her all the time by going to Mamitu's Bar, for wasting her savings. For calling her a horse and a cow as if she weren't the horse that carried him and the cow that fed him.

One part of me wants to go in there and say, shushushu, Abayé, let me be sad in your place, shushushu. Another part of me wants to stay angry at him. I know he would like to know if the rebels in the north are coming and I also want to know that, so I shout out that it's radio time. Nobody says anything. I slip on my shoes and go to the boys' room to look for Little Yonas. I see that he and Beza are sleeping on a mattress on their bellies. I ask Little Yonas to come turn on the radio, but he says he is not feeling well. I tell him he can get back to sleep after turning on the radio. He says to leave him alone. I slam the door and leave.

I drag a chair to the buffet cabinet where the radio is kept. I climb up the chair very easily. I am almost four and very strong. I reach for the radio, which is far away, close to the wall. I can only touch it with my fingertips. I decide the best way is to push and push it to the edge of the cabinet so that I can take the chair over to the other side and climb up again to get to the radio. I push and push and push. I'm thinking at the same time that I can't wait for my mother to come back because I have so much to tell her. I push and grunt and push.

My father hears me and comes out. "What are you doing?" he says, and I panic because I don't think he wants me to be pushing his radio. "I want to know if the rebels are coming," I say, but maybe I already pushed too much because the radio is flying and on the floor in three different places, and I scream because my father will never forgive me for this he is going to be so mad at me that he is going to go to Mamitu's Bar and never come back and I see he's flying to me like a chicken whose chick is being taken by a crow and grabs me by the armpits and I think I am dead today and when he holds me tight to his chest I am thinking it is going to be by suffocation but, my child my child my child, enen enen enen, let me cry in your place, that ugly radio making my child cry, I am glad it is broken, horrible radio, go away. I am confused and crying and my father is holding me and saying, enen enen enen.

"Tomorrow we will go to Sheikh Shawara's store and get a new radio," he says. "This one is too old and too ugly. Let's kick it."

He puts me down next to the fallen radio's pieces. Enen, he says. Let me take your pain, he says. He kicks one piece of the old red Philips radio and tells me to do the same, and I kick the other piece and the other piece and I kick them all again and again and again and again and again and again and again and again

Part III

17

Forbidden Songs

A beetle buzzes above my head like a tiny helicopter, one of its hind legs tied to a string I'm holding. I let it lead me this and that way on our front yard as I try to ignore my number one bully, Kamila Nesro, who stands under one of our orange trees leaning against the concrete foundation of my house, making a monkey face at me as if to say that I'm one. The leopard in me feels insulted. If I go near Kamila now, she would tell me that I can't walk this way because it belongs to Orthodox Christians or that way because it belongs to Muslims. The leopard says all the ways can be mine if I just let him out to eat Kamila, the comrade chairman of the neighborhood. I tell him I don't want to get banished to the wild just yet.

Little Yonas suddenly appears next to me like the Holy Spirit to sweep me off my feet. It's learning time, he says. I drop my string and the beetle flies away. My brother has been teaching me the alphabets and the Bible. I can write lots of words, including my name: ሰላም ክለሞካኽ፡፡ He says if I continue like this, I will be able to write my first letter soon.

Whenever I refuse to learn the alphabets, Little Yonas would say, don't you want to write a letter to Weder? To Ezra? To Melkamu? I say yes because I want to tell my siblings how upset I am that they're always going away. Weder is in college in Addis Ababa; she can only visit us during breaks. Ezra and Melkamu don't visit us every weekend like they used to after being transferred to schools in towns too many kilometers away.

When I refuse to learn the Bible, Little Yonas would say, don't you want to go to Degitu? I ask him, who is Degitu? He would sit still as if nailed in place, staring at me for a while before leaving. Later, he would ask, don't you remember our mother? I tell him I don't. If she were our mother, why isn't she here making us food, washing our clothes, giving me a bath like the other mothers do for their children? I once saw our neighbor Eteyé Khadija washing Kamila inside a big plastic tub. I was looking into their backyard through our fence. That Piece of Satan would have killed me if she knew that I saw her naked because nakedness is embarrassing for girls. I learned this when Weder came to visit us for Christmas break and brought me my first pair of panties as a birthday gift. I put on the panties and walked into a room full of people in our living room to lift up my dress and show off. Everybody laughed at me. Boys in my neighborhood always run around wearing nothing but T-shirts. Weder pulled me aside to say that I shouldn't be naked like that.

I've asked Little Yonas why that Degitu woman isn't here if she was our mother. He told me she couldn't; she's in heaven. I once overheard my siblings talking, huddled together in the girls' bedroom, Ezra crying and telling the others about how Degitu was in so much pain at a hospital in Addis Ababa that she asked the nurses to give her medicine that kills. I burst into their midst like the thunder of God and demanded to know: is this Degitu woman dead in Addis Ababa or alive in heaven? Dead is what happened to Kamila's beetle last week, when it fell on the ground and stopped moving because it got tired of flying all the time and never getting anywhere. Dead is also what my leopard wants to make happen to Kamila, comrade Rectangle-Head, the Women, and all others who make me so angry that I shake and feel very hot and red.

My siblings didn't answer me. Everybody keeps quiet when I ask questions these days. They stop talking in Amharic and Afan Oromo if I am around. They speak instead in the secret language they call gilbitosh—Afan Oromo backward—which I haven't learned yet. I only know one sentence in gilbitosh: "The little one is coming." Someday I am going to learn all the languages and everything. In the meantime I have been trying to be stealthy and obtain as much information as possible. I am tired of people in this house not telling me whether this Degitu woman is in heaven or in Addis Ababa. Sometimes I wonder if Addis Ababa is on the way to heaven. Other times I think Addis Ababa is another name for heaven. Weder brought me pastries that were so delicious that I refused to share them with anybody. If that city has such sweet things, beautiful clothes, tall buildings, and cars I have only seen in pictures, and if our Comrade Chairman, who has become our president, chooses to live there, Addis Ababa itself must be the real heaven.

This Degitu woman, whose picture hangs above the buffet cabinet, has chosen to live in Addis Ababa too. Or heaven. Instead of being here to be my mother. My siblings claim that she made the dress I wore for my fourth birthday many weeks ago, that she made the pants I am wearing now, and more dresses for my fifth and sixth birthdays. Maybe she did or maybe they are lying. All the confusing information, the whispers, and the silences make me doubt my siblings.

I sometimes wonder if Weder is keeping Degitu to herself in Addis Ababa. I heard my siblings talk about how Degitu was tired from working all the time, caring for and worrying about *the little one*. "That's what made her ill," said Melkamu. Maybe Degitu is away taking a break because it was exhausting to be my mother since I am always running and running and demanding milk. Other times I think about what that prophet who came to our house a long time ago said: that Degitu was taken away by God because she is righteous.

No matter the reason for Degitu's absence, despite hearing her name repeated, despite seeing her picture on the wall every day, I don't remember that woman and what it felt like to be her child. I know what it feels like to be Asmelash's child because I sleep in his bed, and every morning I kiss his cheeks and smell his head. I don't know what that woman smells like.

MY SIBLINGS WANT to go to heaven to be with that Degitu woman. The way to heaven is to worship Jesus Christ with all your heart, to stand as a witness for Him, to be free of sin.

My father has joined my siblings. I think he wants to go to Degitu too. I once heard him say before a congregation that when Degitu was at the hospital in Addis Ababa, her pain went away for long periods of time whenever a group of Pentecostals came to pray for her. He said that was when he saw God's healing power.

I have never seen God healing anybody but I love my father. I would like to go wherever my father and siblings are going, so I have been praying with them. The only problem is that this new Jesus Christ doesn't like songs in the radio. My siblings turn the volume down every time a song comes on. They say secular songs are full of sinful ideas. I can hear songs from Tana Hotel next door. I am worried Jesus Christ is going to take away my new favorite.

The café inside the hotel next door plays loud music all day. That's how I heard Neway Debebe sing Aya-ya-ya-ya! and thought I was going to forget myself from happiness. I couldn't hear everything he was saying but his voice, flowing down like a river and rising and leaping and twisting through the turns in melody like something I don't know, without pause for breath, made him my secret Jesus Christ. I have been singing it a lot since then. I would make up the rest of the words, which aren't really words, to the tune of the song: Aya-ya-ya-ya, chuki chikubu, chiki chiki chiki . . .

I was doing that on our veranda when the Sister-Stealer saw me. His name is Yeneneh, a high school biology teacher and a member of the town's drama club. Ever since he and Beza did a play together at the last anniversary celebrations of the revolution, when she played his mistress and he read embarrassing love poems, she has been sneaking out of the house to go to rehearsals at odd hours. Nobody believes her. Everyone knows Yeneneh is her secret boyfriend. My siblings don't like it because the man isn't born-again. Melkamu, now a scary preacher who has been busy spreading the Word, says that if Beza continues to be with Yeneneh, she won't go to heaven with us.

Yeneneh comes to our house all the time under the guise of visiting his friend Kiros, a new tenant who has taken Teshager's old room. Beza would sneak into Kiros's room whenever she thought nobody was watching, and God knows what she and Yeneneh do in there. I made a scary face at Yeneneh. He walked up to me grinning like the devil and kissed my cheeks. I slapped his hands away and wiped my cheeks.

"I'm going to teach you a song," he said.

Who asked him to?

Right then, members of a farmers' collective came marching down the street.

"See those people?" The Sister-Stealer pointed at the marchers. "They're bad dancers. Don't be like them. I'm going to teach you a song and a dance."

I should have left him immediately. Once he began snapping his fingers as he twisted his feet on the floor, gliding from one side to another, it was too late. "Aya-ya-ya-ya-ya-ya!" he sang.

I'm ashamed to admit that I forgot the man was an aggressor against my family. I was too afraid to attempt his sorcery of gliding across the floor. I did a version of it. I picked up some lines of the song after he repeated them to me many times.

> Meteqatun atiyi fiqrish eyerabew
> Anchin anchin yilal tey liben qirebiw

People have been stopping me in the neighborhood to ask that I perform "Ayaya" for them. I shift my hips, snap my fingers, twist my feet as I attempt to glide across floors while singing. Kamila and Fetiya have been burning with envy at my increasing popularity among the grown-ups.

I use my new talents to entertain Asmelash, who hasn't been entirely healthy for months. He would throw his head back and laugh when I perform for him. For me that is the meaning of happiness.

OUR LIVING ROOM has been converted into a makeshift church tonight. The dining table has been taken out to the back to make way for benches. Three nights a week, strangers gather in our living room to yell the name of Jesus Christ, sing, and speak in a foreign language.

Little Yonas stands before us leading tonight's worship. If Melkamu were here, he would have been the one. After a prophet from Addis Ababa visited us months ago, Melkamu has declared himself the spiritual leader of our family.

The prophet spoke of a curse Degitu had told him about when he had gone to pray for her in Addis Ababa. He read from the book of Isaiah, something about how no weapon fashioned against us shall succeed. I was imagining a very long spear flying in the air toward our house. God placed His massive hand in the way to block it.

"But this weapon against your family has succeeded, hasn't it?"

The spear went through God's palms, straight into our living room.

My father, who was sitting in a corner wrapped in his gabi, moaned as if he were in pain.

"Is God a liar then?" asked the prophet.

I would say incompetent.

The prophet said the protection promised in the book of Isaiah was conditional: it only applies to those who serve God. He recited other Scripture about how continuous sin might lead to the loss of God's protection.

"Eteyé Degitu is worshipping God with angels," said the prophet. "It is written in the book of Isaiah that all will be well with the righteous."

My father covered his face with his gabi. I knew he was sobbing.

"She told me that some of you struggled with sin," said the prophet.

My siblings looked at the ground.

"When one of you sins, you open the door for the devil to divide you." Prayer only works if we are all in agreement. We needed to stop sinning for our prayers against the curse to succeed.

The prophet told us afterward that Melkamu had been chosen by God to be a leader. Did we elect him? No. Did he fight for this power like the rebels in the north? No. Even the old monarchs who said they were chosen by God had victorious armies behind them. This was an unjust usurpation of power.

"God shows me the spirit of Saul of Tarsus in you," said the prophet, looking at Melkamu. He told us about the zealous persecutor of Christians who became the apostle Paul. "You resisted the Lord at first, didn't you?" he said. "You wanted to persecute those who embraced Him." He paced before us. "Despite that strength of character, you feel lost in the absence of your mother." He smirked like he knew a secret. "That is exactly how Saul of Tarsus felt when the Lord blinded him on his way to Damascus to arrest Christians." The prophet told Melkamu that he needed to embrace his calling—spreading the Word—if he wanted to end his moment of blindness.

My brother has been insufferable since then. After Teshager sent him some albums, he announced that spreading the Gospel wasn't enough: he was going to pursue a career in gospel music.

Melkamu led the effort to persuade Beza to give up her nonbeliever boyfriend. "You need to stop harming your spiritual life," he said to her. "You will not enter the kingdom of God if you continue behaving this way."

"Aren't you the same man who was resisting all this just a year ago?" asked Beza.

"I have been saved."

"So anything is possible."

Ezra was quiet, covering a grin with his right palm. When Melkamu's tone rose with each sentence, making Beza flinch, Ezra interfered. "She's just a teenager," he said.

"Nobody needs your advice," said Melkamu.

"He's the oldest," said Beza.

"Seniority is not decided by coming out of the womb first, but through anointing," said Melkamu. "Haven't you read the story of Esau and Jacob?"

Ezra left the room.

"He knows why he's no longer the firstborn in God's eyes," said Melkamu.

Ezra had had to deal with his younger brother being shrewd and taller than him all his life. My siblings joke that Ezra is shorter due to the malnourishment of eating with servants when he was a child. Ezra could not challenge Melkamu's claim to seniority. The same Jesus Christ that he helped bring to our house by embracing Teshager was the one who anointed Melkamu.

LITTLE YONAS TELLS US to repent our sins. Ever since Weder left for university, he has become a better student. He studies inside the old maid's room, which he remodeled and moved into because it's quiet. He carries a Bible around with his textbooks and spies on our sinful sister.

He tried to rebuke Beza about her nonbeliever boyfriend. He told her she shouldn't be putting our family to shame so soon after what had happened to Degitu. That woman's absence is being used to make people do things in this house. Beza smiled at Little Yonas and patted his head in a way that said, you're two years younger than me. She kept running around with Yeneneh.

I can't disobey him like Beza because I am afraid of being pinched.

I once had questions for him when he was teaching me the book of Genesis. "Where did Abayé come from?"

"From our grandparents."

"Where did they come from?"

"From their parents."

"Who were the first parents?"

"I just told you. Adam and Eve."

"Where did they come from?"

"God created them."

"Who created God?"

He got very close to my face in a threatening way to tell me never to ask that again.

I SIT ON THE FLOOR beneath my father's chair, listening to Little Yonas list the reasons why we should repent: for our sinful utterances, for lustful thoughts, for the lies we've told, for our addictions. I pretend like my eyes are covered while looking through my fingers.

Murmurs and quiet sobs fill the room.

The number of attendees has been rising fast. My oldest brothers go out to convert people whenever they visit. If you are an unmarried woman who has been shamed and isolated by friends and family for doing bad things with men, you must come to us because our Jesus offers second chances. If you're a grieving widow, you will find comfort in our Lord because He was once a dead man Himself. If you feel unmoored and need something to hold you in place with love and rules, our Jesus is for you. When Melkamu approached an isolated community of potters to deliver the Good News, my family's new religion won the lottery. Potters, like most artisans, are disliked by the larger community. They were delighted to hear that our Jesus loves everybody, that they can come sit with us because of Him.

After repentance, there is singing and speaking in foreign languages. That's when our neighbors start throwing stones at our house. I do not speak the foreign language my brothers and the new converts speak. Little Yonas says it is for people who have been filled with the Holy Spirit. Maybe the Holy Spirit doesn't want to enter my heart because of my mean thoughts about God and my love of sinful songs from the radio. I just watch in terror as the grown-ups shake like they've got seizures and say, shalabalalababa.

The first time I heard stones land on our roof, I thought, here come those criminal kids to steal our oranges. I tugged at my father's pant leg to tell him what was happening. He said it's not for oranges; it's because people don't like our new religion. It is written, Little Yonas said later, that in His name, we shall be hated. That's how we know we are on the Right Path.

We don't know who exactly has been throwing stones at our house. The Women have been whispering about us.

"They have been punished for turning their backs on the Virgin Maryam."

"But they're not turning back from their Wrong Path."

"It's all that American money."

"And American wheat."

I want American money very badly.

Asmelash gives me ten cents every time I ask him for candy. That only buys me one Desta Keremela or two Nanaye mint candies. I want more because Kamila and Fetiya come to me for candy. That's why I look through my fingers during prayer instead of closing my eyes—Kamila and Fetiya said American money comes out of our ceiling when we pray; that's why so many people are converting. I've been waiting since then, ready to pounce as soon as the money starts raining.

The Women, the priests, and comrade Rectangle-Head have been saying that we have turned our backs on our forefathers and on our country. Recently, comrade Rectangle-Head stopped on his way to Tana Hotel next door; he leaned against the ledge separating the hotel from our property and said to my father that he needed to stop my brothers from spreading an imperialist religion. My father nodded and said nothing.

My brothers appear to have forgotten about their arrest. The oldest two have been busy spreading the Good News in their respective towns. Melkamu's Bible study grew too big for his room, so the meetings had to be moved to the living room of a new convert. Melkamu has become intoxicated by his new power: the power to approach a stranger and convince him to take up a religion that may result in his arrest and isolation.

AFTER WORSHIP, it is radio time. Our new radio is gray and ugly like everyone else's. An episode of *Eset-Ageba* will be airing tonight. We are eager to hear the history professor and the deputy ambassador argue with each other. I sit on my father's lap, looking for the frequency. I am glad our Jesus Christ has cut Mamitu's Bar out of our lives.

Asmelash says I am going to unseat Little Yonas as the minister of radio very soon, although he gets impatient with me when he is eager not to miss a program like today.

"Turn it back, turn it back, you almost found it."

"Quiet, Abayé, I am trying to focus."

I like it when we argue because he's not ignoring me like he does when he prays. In the evenings, he kneels down to pray: forgive me Jesus, for everything. Sometimes he forgets I am next to him and whispers: what have I done, what have I done, what have I done.

He confessed at an evening prayer session about the last time he went to Mamitu's Bar. Everyone surrounded him; Melkamu placed his hand on my father's head to pray for him. Asmelash said he went to the bar and ordered a beer. Mamitu and the rest of his friends smiled, thinking he was back. He said it felt good to make them happy until the beer gave him a stomachache that caused him to throw up.

He is home most of the time now, leaving only to go to court and to travel. He's been going to court to argue for his old flour mill back. After the revolution, he was entitled to keep one of his businesses. Local officials took everything and he was too afraid to ask for one back. Desperation for money has made him fearless now. He has also been traveling to Jimma on church business. When he is not sitting on the veranda or away, he shutters his bedroom window to sleep in the dark. Sometimes it's because he's sick; other times he doesn't say why.

The radio says the government has continued killing innocent people in retaliation for a defeat by the Eritrean People's Liberation Front in a big battle. My father says the killings are a sign that the dictator is feeling weak. We don't like that the Front wants to separate Eritrea from us. We just think anything is better than living under this bloodthirsty regime. I want the government to lose so that I'm free to finish comrade Rectangle-Head and his like.

It's time for *Eset-Ageba*. The moderator says the two men should stay clear of personal attacks. Asmelash and I laugh every time he says that.

PROFESSOR ANDARGACHEW: This war against separatists has gone too far. The government is bombing its own citizens.

When does the love of Ethiopia become poison for Ethiopia? Where is the red line?

DEPUTY AMBASSADOR DAWIT: The government is trying to keep the country together. That's its basic responsibility.

PROFESSOR: And in trying to do so, it is ripping the country apart.

AMBASSADOR: I disagree. It is more like trying to keep a child from jumping over a cliff. Whatever force is used to that end is better than the jump.

PROFESSOR: Outrageous. We are not talking about a child but millions of people.

AMBASSADOR: Millions of people who are being misled by power-thirsty men like you.

My father and I laugh. We feel sorry for the moderator.

"Please never bomb me," I say to my father. He puts me down to throw his head back and shake from laughter. He calls out Little Yonas to say, come listen to what this one said to me. My brother chuckles and says that I talk like I am possessed sometimes.

MY FATHER HAS gone to Jimma again. Little Yonas says four is the number of times our father has traveled to Jimma to beg the administrators of our province to grant us land for a church. One of the preachers visiting from Addis Ababa said it was possible to persuade officials to respect freedom of religion through persistence and prayer, that Protestants in other parts of the country have been increasingly successful in obtaining land. Members of our church decided to send my father to try. They chose to begin their efforts in Jimma because local officials who know and hate my father might block the request.

My father brings me pastries or new clothes whenever he returns from his trips. I don't forget that he left, so I slap his hands away when he tries to hug me. I refuse to talk to him for hours until he tricks me by telling me a story or something.

He is gone again. I want to sing "Ayaya" and make myself feel better. My father likes my performances. He hasn't become a scary preacher yet. I am always careful not to sing "Ayaya" around Little Yonas and Melkamu. I don't see anybody now—it's just me and that Degitu woman above the buffet cabinet. I get under the dining table. I shift my hips and snap my fingers.

> Meteqatun atiyi fiqrish eyerabew
> Anchin anchin yilal tey liben qirebiw

"Stop it!"

I'm petrified. I think it's the Holy Ghost.

I see the shoes approaching. It's not the Holy Ghost—it's worse. Little Yonas squats and tells me to come out. I want to start running.

"No pinching," he says. "I just want to teach you something."

I think it best to turn myself in. He'll get me eventually. I come out slowly and stand next to him. What the fuck does this budding tyrant want?

"You need to choose," he says, "between Jesus and 'Ayaya'!"

I am dead today. Maybe that's better than living in this house.

He grabs me by the shoulders. "Choose, Selam. Today is the day of salvation."

"'Ayaya,'" I say.

"What?"

"I choose 'Ayaya.'"

Fuck you, you man.

"That is the wrong choice," he says. "No more 'Ayaya' or God will punish you."

Why the fuck did he ask me to choose if the only alternative is the wrong choice?

Fuck this house. Fuck everything in this house.

18.

Forbidden Games

Most of my father's friends have abandoned him because of our new Jesus Christ. His closest friend, Gash Shimelis the pharmacist, no longer speaks to my father, and he hasn't been to our house in a long time. One of my family's former servants, Tultula, is among the very few people close to us who have converted. My siblings are not allowed to call him Tultula. I get away with it because I am small.

Tultula visits us on market days, bringing honey and fresh fruits. My father says Tultula is a resourceful farmer who uses the space between his coffee trees for keeping bees and growing spices. He also has many cows and chickens, grows fruits and vegetables in his backyard. He makes a lot of money, and unlike most people who keep their savings under their mattresses, Tultula keeps his in a bank account my father helped him open in the Medium Town. Every Saturday, he brings a portion of the money he earns from selling his produce. My father deposits it for him when he travels to the Medium Town. Tultula becomes upset when my father tries to update him on his balance. He thinks that means my father doesn't think Tultula trusts him.

My father has succeeded in converting other people from the country-side. Another former servant, Tayitu, almost converted. Her husband, a drunk who beats her, forbade her, because conversion would mean she would have to stop brewing tela at home. Beza says Tayitu wanted to convert not because she understood the difference between our Christianity and that of the Orthodox Church, but because our Jesus has been fixing men who drink and beat their wives. Men like Asmelash Gebre Egziabher.

Abba Lemma, the day laborer, has not abandoned us. He comes over sometimes to do work for us or to eat food. My father told him about our Jesus Christ.

"Why are you sharing this Good News with me for free?" asked Abba Lemma.

"Because you are my friend; I want you to be saved."

"How about giving me one of those rooms in your backyard along with your leftovers?"

Another time, Abba Lemma wanted to know who wrote the Bible. My father told him he should already know from being an Orthodox Christian that it was written by men who were inspired by God.

"Why should I believe them?" asked Abba Lemma. "I don't know those men. I don't think they would tell me if the devil inspired them."

Abba Lemma offered to convert in exchange for some of that American money we have been receiving. He said he didn't believe anyone would subject themselves to isolation and imprisonment for nothing.

———

KAMILA AND FETIYA don't believe us either. They have been demanding that I share the American money they say rains out of our ceiling. They have been accusing me of greed. I used to think of our ceiling, cotton cloth supported by wooden frames, as a mice haven filled with darkness. I am beginning to think it's bright and clean, with a network of tubes through which money is transported and large openings that release coins and birr. I wonder who's been sneaking in there on prayer nights to push the buttons that make the money rain. I wonder why I can't see any of it. Maybe it's because God doesn't bless sinners who love secular songs.

I circle our living room, looking up at all corners of the ceiling in search of an opening. Kamila and Fetiya have increased their nagging. All I can afford is to share half the candy I buy from Sheikh Abdullah's souk with the ten cents my father gives me almost every day. I saw the two eating candies of their own once and nervously approached to ask for some. I thought, if I share mine, they should do the same. They refused. I tried refusing the next time I had candy, but Kamila invoked the name of God and I obeyed out of fear. I did the same thing the next time I saw Kamila eating candy.

"Safu," she said.

"What is safu?"

"It means the name of God doesn't work once I say safu."

"Don't you know anything?" said the foot soldier.

I wasn't allowed to use that excuse next time. I don't know what the rules are and it makes me fear leaving the house. I leave anyway because sometimes I forget what they did to me the previous day and other times

I do it because of hope. Maybe the mouse who attended a cat's funeral isn't arrogant or stupid but stubbornly hopeful.

Yesterday Kamila saw me wearing a pair of green flip-flops Etabeba Haregua had sent me. "Your shoes are ugly," she said.

No amount of prayer seems to work against that demon.

Obtaining a large amount of candies is the only way to improve my status in this neighborhood.

MELKAMU AND LITTLE Yonas talk in hushed tones in the girls' room. I sit near them playing, trying to make a paper plane, humming a Jesus song: mihret'n yemiwed yeserawit geta, mmmmm, mmmm. I'm spying. I want to understand what they're saying in that secret gilbitosh language. The older tyrant tells me to go outside before I decipher anything. "We want to talk about something," he says. I walk into the hallway and begin pacing, thinking about how I am going to defeat all the tyrannies around me.

Beza enters the room and closes the door. She has taken her school-leaving exam. She has been talking about moving to Dembi Dollo to work for a distant relative who owns a hair salon.

One step, two step, three step. Ear to the door. They're talking in Afan Oromo this time. Melkamu says he has found out that Beza's boy-friend, Yeneneh, has been transferred to Dembi Dollo for work. He knows that's why she's moving to Dembi Dollo. No, she says. She's only moving because she won't find other job opportunities soon; she's sure she has failed the national exam. He tells her she needs to cut all contact with Yeneneh or he won't let her move. "I'm old enough to run away," she says.

One step, two step, three step, I go away. I'm pacing. One step, two step, three step, I'm back to the door. Something hot is washing over my body. Maybe the leopard is tired of people in this house doing what they want whenever they want without asking me. Coming and going all the time. I'm hot and trembling. I kick in the door and enter. Hot and red. Beza sits on a chair and my brothers stand before her.

"This woman." I point. "You think she's going to listen to you? You think she's going to change her ways? There's no hope for her! She's useless!" I storm out of the room.

I'm going to a corner in my father's room now. I'm afraid of this leopard myself.

TESHAGER HAS COME to visit us. Our excitement about his arrival has been spoiled by the news that he won't be visiting us much anymore. He has been promoted to a trainer of evangelists and will spend almost all his time in Addis Ababa. He said the church elders want him to settle down and raise a family. They have even found him a wife.

Ezra is unhappy with this development. He told our family gathering, in the absence of Teshager, that he had met the fiancée at a Bible study the last time he went to Addis Ababa. The two weren't engaged yet. Had Ezra known she was preying on his friend, he would have stopped her. She is ugly, dumb, and just not good enough. He said the elders were rushing Teshager.

"You need to keep your mouth shut," said Melkamu. "This is none of your business."

Ezra told us he had persuaded Teshager to flee the country with him through the Sudan. They were going to move to America or West Germany to find better-paying jobs.

"Why won't you go by yourself then?" asked Melkamu.

"Teshager speaks good English. He was supposed to be my guide."

"He can flee if he wants," said Melkamu. "Nobody is forcing him to get married. You must have overestimated his desire to leave with you."

Ezra stormed out of the room.

Later, Ezra and Melkamu had a fight in the boys' room. I went to the door to spy as usual and heard Ezra demanding to know what Melkamu told the church elders. Melkamu left the room. Ezra locked himself in for a long time. The next day, I followed Ezra and Teshager to the farthest part of our backyard and saw them playing the pigeon game, sucking each other's mouths, leaning against a tree trunk in the eucalyptus grove. I ran back quickly because that part of our backyard is too close to the forest where hyenas laugh at night.

Teshager stands before our evening congregation with his black Bible in hand. "Our people always beg God to keep the worst thing away," he says. "Do the worst things stay away?"

People laugh.

I want to tell him: God won't keep the worst things away because He Himself is the worst thing around.

"Do you know why our people are always praying like that?" asks Teshager.

Nobody says anything.

I don't think God will ever answer any of my prayers with such mean thoughts about Him popping into my head all the time. I am repenting: Forgive me, Jesus. Wash me in a tub of your blood. I need it.

"Because they have been through so much, better things are hard to imagine," says Teshager. He paces back and forth in silence as if to give us time to think about what he'd just said. I imagine myself splashing in a tub of the Lord's blood. I am doomed.

"What does the Word say? I can do all things through Christ who strengthens me—Philippians four, thirteen."

Shouts of Amen and hallelujah around the room.

My mind jumps to the pigeon game. There's a memory teasing the back of my mind.

"We all must stop obsessing over the worst things and start reaching for the best things."

The pigeon game is forbidden. I raise my hand. "I have a question."

Everybody laughs.

"Why is the pigeon game forbidden?"

"What?"

Melkamu arrives next to me with the speed of the Holy Ghost. He snatches and takes me to the boys' room before I even open my mouth. He orders me never to mention the pigeon game again. He is frightening, so I don't even ask him why. "You tell Abayé about this and it is going to kill him," he says.

After prayer, when my father asks what all that pigeon game business was about, I keep my mouth shut.

"You know her," says Melkamu, "she was talking about nonsense she saw on the street."

I don't know if telling my father the truth would kill him but I don't want to experiment with his life. And yet the curiosity is building up in me to unbearable levels. This is not the same as the question of who created God. I would like to know the answer to that question, but it is not pressing since I have never even met the man. This is about two men who are active in my life.

Everyone is drinking coffee and chatting. Little Yonas signals for me to follow him to the boys' room. He assures me he won't tell anybody if I tell him what the pigeon game is. A crack has formed in the Jesus tyranny in our house due to individual nosiness. This is my opportunity to exploit it. I explain what I saw Ezra and Teshager doing and ask why it is forbidden. Little Yonas says the pigeon game is a very bad sin, far worse than listening to secular music, having a nonbeliever boyfriend, lying, and stealing. Ezra plays it because our family is cursed.

I pray in my heart. For Ezra, for Teshager, and for the pigeons. Forgive us, Jesus. Let us swim in the lake of your blood. We need it.

THE RADIO SAYS change is coming. A former American president named Jimmy Carter is going to lead negotiations between our government and the Eritrean People's Liberation Front. Not long ago, the Cubans withdrew their troops from our country.

Change is happening in our house too. Beza left for Dembi Dollo despite Melkamu's threats. My brother tried to have my father stop her. My father said if Beza's decision to move to Dembi Dollo is a bad one, let her find out on her own. Our job is to pray for her and leave our doors open if she wants to come back.

I found myself in Beza's bed the morning of the day before she left. "What is this? Why am I here?" I shook her awake.

"I stole you," she said.

"Why?"

"Because I love you."

What nonsense. I left to go find my father and demand answers. Beza followed me to his bedroom nervously. She thought God was speaking through me, like He did through the talking donkey in the book of Numbers, the day I stormed into the girls' room and told her she was useless.

"Asmelash!"

"What is it?" He was groggy.

"Why did you let her steal me?"

He propped himself up on his elbow. "You are grown now," he said. "You have to learn how to sleep without me."

The nonsense in this house.

Beza approached me slowly. "I'm leaving for Dembi Dollo tomorrow."

"Fuck you," I said.

Asmelash flinched. Beza covered her mouth.

"You child!" said Asmelash.

"Where did you hear that?" asked Beza.

"I said, tenefeshi, fly away." I flailed my arms to demonstrate what flying away looks like.

"You've been playing around street children, haven't you?"

I ran out of the room trembling. Hot and red and mad.

My cousin Tariku came to live with us after Beza's departure. My father asked one of his older sisters, who lives in the countryside, to send us someone to help out around the house. She sent us Tariku since her daughters were all married. People in the countryside are always eager to send their children to relatives in town, where schools are easily accessible.

I tried to make Tariku my friend by telling him stories. I told him one about how I used to be in the third grade before my father pulled me out of school for no reason. He laughed at me and called me a liar. He has a narrow face, high cheekbones, and teeth that look like they're too big for his face and are yellowing at the gum. I told him I wasn't lying. He said that I'm mixing my dreams with reality or I have taken my father's story. He makes monkey faces at me, like my bully Kamila, when no one is looking. When the generator stops working and most of our house is dark in the evenings, Tariku hides behind doors to scare me.

I ask myself why, despite so many changes in the world, I remain sur-rounded by such demons. I ask myself if I am cursed.

LITTLE YONAS SAYS if I do homework, he will make me a ball. The home-work is writing a letter to Weder. She had come to visit us during kiremt season. She finished her first year of university with good grades and has been assigned to study Physics. She complained of nonstop headaches that have been going on for months. The doctors would only give her painkillers.

"It's because you're crying all the time," said Little Yonas. "You're losing too much water."

Weder said she's not stupid; that she'd been drinking lots of water.

I went to her later when she was alone and asked why she cried a lot. I also wanted to know if she was living with Degitu in Addis Ababa. My questions only made her cry more. She told me later that she hadn't seen Degitu, that she suspected Degitu didn't want to be found for some rea-son. I also learned that Addis Ababa was neither heaven nor on the way to heaven; that it was just a city like any other but much bigger. I asked why my other siblings said Degitu was in Addis Ababa and in heaven. She said that was because Degitu was last seen in Addis Ababa, and talk of her being in heaven was just speculation.

I no longer think people are lying to me about Degitu's relationship to me. My aunt Etabeba Haregua recently came to our house to give us money that she said my grandmother Emama Zeritu left me. The money came from the sale of a property next to Etabeba Haregua's restaurant-bar. It was initially supposed to go to Degitu, but in her absence, Emama

Zeritu instructed my aunt to give it to me. I don't think people would put so much money behind a lie.

The problem is that I don't remember the feeling of being Degitu's child.

I AM ALREADY DONE with my homework. Little Yonas is busy reading his biology book. I study his face. People say he is a carbon copy of Baba Gebre. He has a straight nose, whereas my nose is round and looks as though it stopped before it was done being made—you can almost see inside it while across from me. My father, who has a straight one like Little Yonas, sometimes calls me afincha-gorada, and I think, call me half-nose one more time, you criminal, and I'll eat yours in your sleep. Little Yonas has a slightly lopsided hairline just like me and my father. That's how we know he's ours. He has some hair on his face, but it is not big and scary like Sheikh Abdullah's beard.

Sheikh Abdullah is the owner of the souk I buy candies from. His store is next to Zinash Hotel across the street from us. He calls me "Asmelash Gebre's flower." He asks how my father is doing; he hasn't abandoned us because of our new religion.

"Show me your homework," says Little Yonas. I push my exercise book to him.

ከመዓድ እነተ ወደር
እንደም ነሽ እኔ ዘበር ይመስ ደና ነኝ
ትናንትና ኞንዘዘዮ ምተ
ከህተሽ ሰላም ካስመላሽ ጃም ጃም

My brother's jaw drops. He's impressed and I'm embarrassed. I look down and play with my fingers. Too late to hide; he grabs and spins me in the air.

"'Yesterday my beetle died'! That's a good sentence! A very good sentence!" He kisses my neck. "I told you, you are going to be a genius!"

I can't wait to have my own ball. I also can't wait to be a genius like Weder and Little Yonas. I love my sister and my brother and even my other sister and my other brothers and my father. I love everybody.

I TAKE THE BALL Little Yonas made me to the front yard and start kicking it against the foundation of our house. The sponges stuffed in it make it bouncy. It's supposed to come back to me so I can kick it to the wall again, but it rebounds fast, flying past me into forbidden territory. I say to myself it's the last time I am going to see that ball.

I stand in despair, watching my ball on the other end of Kamila's front yard. I don't see her around, but she's good at emerging out of nowhere like Satan. I see Jamal, Kamila's little brother, running toward the ball and I think she sent him. He's only wearing a T-shirt that is torn at the stomach and too short for him. He grabs the ball and starts back—to his house, I think. But no. He's coming to me, the extra piece of meat that God couldn't find a place for dangling between his naked legs. He hands me the ball and stands there. He says nothing, doesn't even ask for candy. Do I hug him? Do I kiss him? Do I take off my clothes and give them to him? What happens in such circumstances?

"Do you want to play?" The words came out on their own.

He nods.

First thing is going to safety before Satan and her foot soldier come. I tell Jamal to follow me to my veranda. I go to one end of the veranda and kick the ball toward Jamal slowly. He kicks it back to me. I kick, he kicks. It is blissful. I get too excited and kick the ball too hard. It flies past him into the front yard. Jamal giggles and runs down the stairs. He's so much faster than me despite being a little younger. When he reaches the bottom, he runs like a new calf who's just escaped the barn. Does this mean I have a friend now? I am so excited when he comes back to the veranda that I want to give him something, but I don't know what, so I just hug him instead and Jamal giggles. He's so handsome when he giggles. I tickle his belly and Jamal giggles some more. I feel so intoxicated with this power that I bend over and tickle the dangling meat between his legs and Jamal almost chokes from giggling too much.

I only stop when my father calls out to say that lunch is ready. I take Jamal's hand and bring him inside with me.

JAMAL AND I HAVE become friends. We play with my bouncy ball. I share my candy with him, and whenever he brings back a runaway ball, I play with his dangling meat.

Today all the children of the neighborhood have gathered in groups on the front yards, playing football, dimo, fursh, and yelling, laughing, running around. Jamal and I have found a safe corner near Tana Hotel, as far away from Kamila as possible. Our ball flies into forbidden territory, landing in the midst of all the other kids. Jamal sprints after it. I get right to tickling his dangling meat as soon as he gets back. It's his reward. His giggling has a shyness to it whenever I do this.

I hear mocking laughter gathering on the playground. What is she doing, what is she doing. For some reason, I know it is about me. I stop tickling Jamal and look at them. Kamila is pointing, yelling, balege balege balege! The other kids follow her lead. Too much excitement is bad when you live on the same planet as people like Kamila and comrade Rectangle-Head.

I thought the word "balege" meant a big pestle, the kind people use to grind whole coffee beans, corn, and other tough cereals. Today I learned "balege" is something you say to someone who does something worth pointing, laughing, and gaping at. I see that tickling the dangling meat between a boy's legs is a forbidden game. I am never leaving my house again.

19

Candy Diplomacy

I ask so many questions and talk so much that people in this house are saying, this child is worse than the radio; we should get her a power button. They can't do that, and my power is always increasing because I drink milk from our cows and eat eggs from our chickens and I don't have a mother but I have legs and I run and dance and kneel and can count to sixty and, according to my brother, I am a future genius who will multiply and divide everything.

The first thing I am going to divide is comrade Rectangle-Head. He has continued to harass my family for spreading a Western religion. He comes by our house to say that we have a vast backyard that we are not using, a backyard that the lady next door, the owner of Tana Hotel, could put to use and generate taxes for the government. He reminds us that land is primarily the property of the government, and that if some lands are going to waste, the government can confiscate and redistribute them. I wish he would just take our land and arrest everybody, including me, because the fear of all that happening at some unexpected date is worse.

Every time Rectangle-Head runs up our front stair, I imagine how I am going to take him apart and make an inventory of his body parts like the hyena in the tale of the donkey and the dog. I am going to invite all the hyenas from the forest behind our house, make them sit quietly and orderly on our front stair, before handing them comrade Rectangle-Head's body parts one by one: one eye and a liver for you, one eye and two kidneys for you, a limb for the father, a limb for the mother, and so on. I just have to figure out how to make them not eat me too. I may be a leopard, but I'm only one.

In the meantime I ask questions: Why can't I catch the dark thing that follows me around when it is sunny outside? Why doesn't the sky get closer when Little Yonas raises me up? Why did God create nail polish if he didn't want us to wear it? What is the "rude thing" that children outside keep mentioning?

When not asking questions, I am reporting on everything I see outside our house because I'm watching most of the time instead of playing. I haven't been going to our front yard much, afraid of being taunted by children for what they saw me doing to Jamal. I have been spending a lot of time with Little Yonas, who wants me to count to one hundred. I have also been studying English. Do you know how to say endemn nesh in English? I do: how are you? Edmesh sint naw—how old are you? I'm going to be five in a few months.

When Little Yonas goes to school, I teach my father things like how to sing songs properly and how to pronounce words right. He does everything wrong. I make him practice the songs but it appears to me that something is fundamentally wrong with him. He can't seem to get the melodies right no matter how much he practices. There's always something to teach him. Once he asked me to get him a spoon and I could not believe the way he pronounced it.

"It is not manka," I said. "It is mankiya!"

"Manka."

It's exhausting.

I miss arguing with him when he's gone. He has been traveling to Jimma more. It isn't just for church business anymore. He's also been visiting the hospital there. He's been falling ill more often: sometimes it's his kidney, other times high blood pressure or something about his stomach burning. He went away again yesterday.

Today I am left with my cousin Tariku, who is in the morning shift at school. He is in the third grade at twelve years old. He seems to find pleasure in tormenting me. I heard my siblings say that Tariku's mother hated Degitu because Degitu was Baba Gebre's favorite. Maybe Tariku hates me too, thinking Degitu is my mother.

On days like this, I lie on my back on a bench in the living room, praying to God to please give me money. My father says I am not allowed to buy candy with the money my grandmother left me. He put it in the bank for my future. I would rather buy candy and gain influence in this neighborhood in the present. Tariku is somewhere in the back doing a chore. Dear God, I say, what is happening? Why aren't you responding to my prayers? Are you out of money? I understand if so. Would you at least lend it to me? All I want is the silver coins: one of the big ones and one of the medium ones. With those two, I can buy enough Nanaye mint candies from Sheikh Abdullah's souk for everyone in the neighborhood. I will pay you back when Ezra and Melkamu come to town. Thank you, amen.

I FELL ASLEEP while waiting for God to send money. I wake up thinking that I don't think He will ever answer my prayers. I would rather go to the window and watch the children play. I rub my eyes. One step, two step, three step, I'm by the dining table. I see something out of the corner of my eye. In the middle of the table.

I get close. I see at least one crumpled birr note. I do not believe this but I must believe it because here are my eyes that are good at seeing and there is the green of the money. I climb a chair fast. Closer and closer. God is real. I grab the birr and realize there's not just one, but two. I stuff them in my pants pocket. I am running now. Out the door. Down the steps. Past everybody and everything.

The counter at Sheikh Abdullah's souk is much taller than me. I have to tap the side to alert the sheikh to my presence. Sheikh Abdullah emerges from his hiding, his massive beard moving up and down as he chews khat. He leans over the counter to get a closer look.

"Aren't you Asmelash Gebre's flower?"

"I'm not a flower."

"What are you then?"

I don't have an answer. Maybe I'm a leopard, a person, a goddess. It's a question.

"I want Nanaye and Desta Keremela," I say. I hand him both the crumpled birr notes.

He looks at the notes and at me. "How many?"

"Twenty Nanaye and twenty Desta Keremelas."

He raises his brows. "You don't have enough money for that."

I don't think my math goes that far.

"You have enough for twenty Nanayes and ten Desta Keremelas." He stares at me intently. "Where did you get this money?"

"God gave it to me."

He squints his right eye. I don't think he believes me. I frown at him. He grabs a small plastic bag. "Ten cents for the bag," he says. "That means eighteen Nanayes, ten Desta Keremelas." He takes a bunch of candies out of a jar and counts them on the counter. I am salivating. He hands me a bag full of candies.

OUR FRONT YARD is bustling as always. As I get close with my bag of candies, I notice something unusual—Jamal and his friends are chanting and clapping, making fun of Kamila, who's wagging a finger at them. Kedir, Kedir, Kedir! They chant in her face.

Jamal sees me with my bag and comes running, as if he's not ashamed of being seen with me. He tells me that Kamila has done "balege neger" with Kedir. I have learned that "balege" means rude. What is the *rude thing*? Before I ask, Jamal reaches for my bag. "You sit down first!" I scream in his face as if he weren't my dearest friend once. It is my moment to be big and I don't want to share it with anyone.

He looks at me as if I'm possessed.

"Go tell the others!" I command. "Tell them to gather by the stair if they want candies!"

Jamal runs back to announce the Good News of the Candies. In no time, kids in my neighborhood gather at the bottom steps of my front stair, clamoring to be first in line.

"Keep quiet," I command. "If you don't behave yourselves, no candy for you!"

Today is the end of disorder, of shoving and pulling, needless screaming and lawlessness in this neighborhood. I demand that they sit in neat rows and keep quiet before I start handing out candies. They do what I say. Kamila is at the front, very quiet, and I want to laugh.

I open the bag and go from left to right, placing a candy in each hand.

They are happy and I am happy too because I am responsible for their happiness.

Little Yonas appears next to me before I finish handing out candies to everyone. I thought he was at school. He grabs me by the arm and lifts me up like I'm his pet monkey or something.

IT'S JUDGMENT DAY. Little Yonas doesn't believe me when I say that God gave me the money. He claims the money was left there for Tariku to buy cooking oil. You are a thief, he tells me. Theft is a sin—the kind that requires punishment both here on earth and in the afterlife, unless I repent and stop sinning. Let's pray, says Little Yonas. Repeat after me.

"My Lord and Savior Jesus Christ, today I have taken something that didn't belong to me. Please wash away my sins with your blood; I promise not to do it again."

Tariku has brought a switch for my earthly punishment. I have never known this kind of pain. Every contact the switch made with my arms, legs, and buttocks left a burning sensation and hurt my feelings deeply. I wish somebody were here to save me. I wish Asmelash were here. I even wish that Degitu were here.

"I won't do it again," I plead with my brother.

Little Yonas doesn't stop, and I don't want to be his sister anymore or be in this house. I ask him in between gasps to let me go free so that I can find Degitu in Addis Ababa and live with her. I want to scream as big as I can but the gasping gets in the way. Tariku stands at the corner smiling with his yellow teeth like the devil fashioned his heart out of cold stone.

Little Yonas finally stops whipping me. I tell him I'm leaving this house. He ties me up with a two-ply cordage made of tree bark that my father uses for mending burlap coffee sacks. As soon as my brother leaves me with my hands and feet bound, Tariku begins mocking me: "'God gave it to me! God gave it to me!' Ha ha ha!"

I taste my salty tears. I try to keep my snot from going into my mouth.

OUR FRONT YARD has become even more hostile than before. Kamila mocks me all the time. I can only sit at the top of the stair watching children play if my father or someone else is on the veranda to watch over me. My father is sitting behind me now, bundled in gabi, wearing glasses and reading a Bible. When he got back from Jimma, I told him that Little Yonas whipped me. He has yet to punish my brother for it.

Jamal and his friends are playing football. I have been watching the strikers, Sintayehu and Atinkut, who are very good at dribbling and getting past everybody to score goals. Girls don't play football, but I want to. When I finally start playing, I want to be a striker.

I know my father is going to leave me to lie down soon. He's been getting sick with kidney and gastric problems or high blood pressure and sadness. Sometimes I wait for him to wake up so that we can play or sit together. A while ago, I followed him to the backyard without his knowledge. I wasn't spying on him; I just wanted to play hide-and-seek. I hid between ginger sprouts, waiting for the best opportunity to yell, "Akukulu!"

He was supposed to say, "Endet walu!" and start looking for me.

I saw him squat down under the guava tree. He started digging with a stick. I had seen him do a few chores around the house before, but this was a strange one. He wasn't even dressed for it; he was wearing his proper dress pants. He took out a folded piece of paper from his pocket and placed it in the hole. I had forgotten all about the hide-and-seek game at that point.

"Abayé."

He jumped. "Shhhh." He signaled for me to go to him.

I approached him cautiously. I was thinking, this man has some worrisome secrets. I asked him what he was doing. He whispered that I should promise not to tell anybody. "Abayé is going to get in trouble with the government if you tell."

I know we're not supposed to trust anyone. My own cousin has reported us multiple times. There's a woman who comes around to wash our clothes sometimes. My father says, if that woman sees something in this house by breakfast, it will be at the other end of town by lunchtime.

"I'm burying Marx's picture," he said. He unfolded the piece of paper, revealing an image of the bearded man who appears in the billboards around town with his two friends. "I got it out of a magazine." He laughed quietly. "I want to come here once in a while to pee on it. I want his ideas to die, to leave this country, to leave us alone so that we can live the way we always did."

He'd told me about Marx before. He said Marx is an embodiment of the devil who, despite being dead, refuses to die. Marx is the reason we lost everything. I understood why my father would want to bury Marx's picture and pee on the grave. What I didn't know was that one could bury the images of people one hates and make them disappear.

IT'S JUST ME and my father in the house. He is sick and has been in bed for days. I am playing in his bedroom. Sometimes I tell him about all the things that are happening on the street. Other times we argue about pronunciations and songs. He's too sick for all that today.

I don't know if it's the ulcers, the kidneys, the blood pressure, or the sadness this time. He is getting darker and thinner. I want him to be better so that I don't have to worry about him all the time. I want us to go on walks, to sit on the veranda together. I am happy that he is here because that means we can eat breakfast together when he is in an eating mood, dipping bread in milk and coffee. There are worse things, like going to the big hospital in Addis Ababa and never coming back.

He is always asking me questions about alphabets and numbers, and when I answer, he says, correct, good child. I am proud of myself because my father is proud of me. Despite all the bullies who have made the front yard inhospitable for me, I stand on our veranda with hands in my pants pockets like I'm everybody's boss because my father is my father.

He is in his bed making little moaning sounds. I will be honest with you that I don't like looking at him when he moans. It makes me sadder than I can bear, even though I am very good at handling sadness. His bed is in the corner of the room. I'm sitting here throwing Coca-Cola bottle caps around, picking them up, pretending to be playing, ignoring him.

"Selamyé," he calls out.

I say nothing. I throw a bottle cap.

"Selamyé."

I go to get the bottle cap.

"Please come and give Abayé a hug."

I don't like this. I am saying no. People give you a hug when they're saying hello but also good-bye. How do you know which one is which?

He is moaning more. "Mikirkipo," he says. "Abayé wants a hug."

People shake hands, hug, and kiss when they go to Addis Ababa and when they come from Addis Ababa and when they go to Addis Ababa on their way to heaven. I refuse to say hello to my father when he comes back from Addis Ababa and Jimma and the Medium Town because I don't know if the coming is also the going and I cannot stand the going.

"Chumaté," he says. He extends his hands.

I'm thinking that maybe he can reach me from his bed and I get angry. "Don't you touch me!" I scream. I go to the corner opposite from him. "Don't you come near me!"

"What have I done?"

I am crying now. I am wanting for someone to come and hold my father in place and keep him from going away but there is nobody in the house. I am screaming and crying and yelling, no no no, no going away this time, Abayé, please don't go. Jesus Christ never listens to me but I am wanting to make a deal with Him so I say, if you let me keep my father this time I will worship You properly no more singing "Ayaya" Jesus Christ please no more being a bad child I will worship You forever please let me keep my father and I will be a very good child always please please please Jesus Christ hear me one time only

20

I Am Not a Monkey

My father doesn't open the windows at night anymore because Jesus Christ has changed him. He locks them and checks repeatedly to see if he's done it properly—five, seven, or eight times. I'm waiting for Little Yonas to turn on the radio while I count the number of times my father walks to the windows and the door, mumbling a butchered Jesus song. I have seen him do it three times so far. Each time, he turns the metal knob on the windows to get the clicking sound. The original lock on the door is broken, so he pushes in the makeshift latches. He thinks all this locking will save us from the threats the government, our neighbors, and the coming rebels pose. I am glad he's here to be his defective self. My deal with Jesus Christ to keep my father around has worked. I'm struggling to become a good Christian.

Little Yonas is working the radio's tuning knob. The FRS has been telling us about miraculous events that have been happening around the country and the rest of the world. Ever since the Soviet Union said no more military aid for our government, and ever since Communist regimes in

Eastern Europe began falling down one by one like oranges on a tree under attack by children with stones, our government has been claiming to have changed. Our ugly president says he has given up on socialism after murdering thousands of people and making many mothers pay for the bullets that killed their children in the name of his Marxist-Leninist pile of goat feces. We don't believe him.

First of all, comrade Rectangle-Head has continued wearing his sky-blue khaki uniform and nagging us about hoisting this and baking that. Rectangle-Head is trying to be my friend now. The last time he came to our house, he gave me a big signed poster of the Comrade Chairman with a blue background. He wrote on the back: from comrade Sisay Tegenu to child Selam Asmelash.

"I heard you can read," he said. "This is your reward, my flower."

His flower? I wished I could headbutt him.

"Keep it close. Hang it above your bed."

"Look at how ugly he is," said my father, pointing at the dictator's image as soon as comrade Rectangle-Head left our house. "How can we go from a handsome emperor to being ruled by this ugly shitter for sixteen years? Our country is cursed."

I agree. Both about the ugliness and the curse.

The second reason why we don't believe the dictator when he says socialism is over is that pictures of Marx, Lenin, and Engels are still on billboards at the edge of town and on the way to the elementary school, both of which I have seen as recently as this week when I passed by with Little Yonas on the way to our new "church." Third reason: my father says that even though the government is getting weaker, unable to stop the advances of the Eritrean People's Liberation Front and the Tigrayan People's Liberation Front, our dictator has twelve lives and he will keep coming back if they kill him. He says we should not celebrate anything openly yet, that we should keep our heads down. Except for when it comes to worshipping Jesus Christ.

Would you believe me if I tell you that the government has granted land to our anti-Maryam anti-Ethiopia treacherous imperialist Protestant church? Is up down now? Have Tuesday and Monday switched places? Is Kamila Nesro no longer the comrade chairman of our neighborhood? No, none of those other things have happened—fortunately or unfortunately, things don't go upside down all at once. Little Yonas said sixteen is the number of times my father traveled to the administrators of our province in Jimma to beg for land. Either because Jesus Christ works sometimes or because our government is trying to suck up to the Americans by saying economic reform this and free market that, they gave us a piece of land far away from town. St. Mary's is already at the edge of town; our land is farther away by at least a kilometer, off the main road, hidden in the forest where only monkeys live. I am not ready to walk that far despite turning five just a month ago. My father and Little Yonas have been carrying me some of the way.

The people of our town have turned the location of our church into an insult against us: look at those monkeys who worship in the forest, ha ha! We don't have the money for building a church, so Sunday services are being held out in the open. Some of our men made a clearing where they laid out fallen tree trunks like makeshift benches. Every Sunday morning we go to the forest to sing and speak in our foreign languages as loud as we want and to listen to a preacher share the Word from a makeshift pulpit. We are in good company: it is written that even the trees of the forest will sing for joy before the Lord!

Marta, an early convert who worked for the Coffee & Tea Authority with Teshager, has been telling prophecies, saying people should repent their sins and pray hard because the end is near! Very very near! It's terrifying. She has also been freeing people from their addictions to coffee and khat, and placing her hand on their stomachs to heal their ulcers. She tried to heal my father from his various illnesses and maybe that's why he recovered and not because of my deal with Jesus Christ. We will never find out. Marta says if we cleanse ourselves of sin and give ourselves completely to Jesus, even cripples will jump, the blind will see. It would be great if that happened, so I have been saying, amen, sister!

THE FRS'S INTRODUCTORY jingle is playing. My father has sat down after checking the door and the windows six times.

> This is the Foreign Radio Service, broadcasting in Amharic every
> evening from Washington, D.C., at three o'clock, Ethiopian Time.

The radio isn't the only one bringing news of the advancing rebels. People who recently traveled to towns near the border with the Sudan have been coming back with news of heavy weaponry fire exchanges. All these rumors are frightening people of our town because we are only a few hundred kilometers from the Sudanese border and we don't know who is going to protect us if the government collapses.

A member of the tailors' collective across the street was recently rushed to the clinic because of a gunshot wound. Little Yonas found out that the man had accidentally shot himself while cleaning his old rifle in preparation for What's Coming. My cousin Tariku also heard that a farmer had to be brought to the clinic in town for a similar injury. The day they told us these stories, my father said something to Little Yonas and Tariku in gilbitosh, and they all switched to talking in their secret language. I feel more frightened when I think there are worse things that I'm not being told. I said to my father that soldiers came to take him away from me, and he said it was just a nightmare. I keep peeing in bed at night.

Good evening, listeners, I am Tizita Alebachew with the news. Agence France-Presse reports today that the Eritrean People's Liberation Front has captured the city of Massawa after defeating the forces of the People's Democratic Republic of Ethiopia.

We all jump up from our seats. My father and Little Yonas get very close to the speakers as if to encourage more good news.

Our attempts to speak to the Ethiopian embassy in Washington, D.C., have not been fruitful. However, a United States–based representative of the EPLF has confirmed the capture of Massawa through a statement sent to our newsroom. The FRS has reached out to members of the Ethiopian community in the United States. Dr. Andargachew Nega, a historian at Howard University, told the FRS that victories by separatist groups are to be expected considering the government's fraudulent interpretation of socialism. Dr. Andargachew says the government's failure to deliver on its promises to the working masses of Ethiopia has led to the demoralization of the national army. We will shortly present an interview with—

Then it's all static.

We are dancing now—to the left, to the right, to the back, Jesus is Lord! My father is a bad dancer. I tell him and Little Yonas to sit down.

They obey and I start singing "I Am David, the Chosen One"—my new favorite. I try to shift my hips and glide on the floor and snap my fingers like I do with "Ayaya." I sing about killing Goliath with my slingshot, cutting his head, and taking my loot to Israel. My father and brother say, amen! I shall fight, I sing, I shall win! I sing and dance, my father and brother smile and clap. I am David, I sing, and Goliath is hurting.

ON EASTER DAY, our house is overflowing with Protestants from neighboring towns. It was decided that it would be encouraging for us to come together occasionally.

This morning, the visiting women are dressed in habesha qemis and the men in suits. We are all headed to our church in the forest. A woman carries a small liturgical drum with cloth suspenders hanging from her shoulder. As we pass the government store, the mosque, and the post office, we see women standing outside their homes, looking at us and whispering to one another.

Some of the guests brought their children, who walk along with their parents wearing their best outfits. I'm wearing a blue dress with layers of ruffles from the waist down, making me look like an upside-down flower. It's one of the dresses Degitu made, according to my siblings.

As we approach our church of fallen tree trunks, I see Melkamu standing near the front of the rows in a gray suit, towering over a couple of men setting up a podium. I nervously approach a row of children sitting on a trunk. Some of our new converts in town have children—potential friends!—but they all live in different parts of town, so we don't see one another on weekdays. I find a seat at the edge of the children's row. There is a foul smell but no one complains—when your church is in the forest, you don't get to choose what you smell.

Melkamu tells us he is ready to start. Everyone disperses to look for seats. My cousin Tariku sits on a trunk in front of me. Our benches are set up on a slope, with the podium at the lowest point, like a sports arena. Tariku plants his palms on the ground before me and leans back. The foul smell increases drastically. I scan the area but don't see anything until my eyes return to Tariku's hands, which appear to be planted in two piles of diarrhea covered in leaves. I don't know what to say. Why is he not feeling the wetness? Maybe the shit is warm. Melkamu is speaking up front. I see noses twitching.

A woman screams two rows behind us. Everyone turns to her. Tariku screams. Finally. He gets up and runs off, in search of wet leaves to wipe his hands on. Everybody begins looking at their shoes, covering their mouths. The stench is getting worse. I press my nostrils together. Murmurs and yelps everywhere.

It turns out there's shit all over the grounds, covered in leaves. Many attendants leave their seats to look for dry spots and rub their soles clean. There's nothing on my soles. Sometimes I think I'm cursed, other times I'm lucky.

Melkamu has been informed of what is going on. It doesn't seem to shake him at all that people in town have carried out a defecation campaign on our land.

"Let's go to Aba Faji," he announces.

Aba Faji is a river a short walk away.

Once at the river, as everyone takes off their shoes to clean the soles, we break into the fashionable Jesus song of the day. It has nothing to do with Easter, but any day is a good day to stand against the claim made by crazy scientists that humans were descended from monkeys.

Zinjero aydelehum yeEgziabher amsal negn

Keinsisat belay siltan yetesetegn

I am not a monkey, we sing, I was created in God's image, with authority over animals! Repeat, says Melkamu. I am not a monkey—

My leopard growls.

THE SHIT-ATTACK HAS energized the new converts. How could diarrhea
stop people who embraced a religion that could get them arrested and
subjected to forced labor?

The believers are feeling special and True. Jesus said His children will
be hated. If one isn't being hated, one can't be the Right Kind of Christian. The guests left behind all the monies they had with them, promising to send more. Close to five hundred birr was collected. Considering
these people make two and three hundred birr a month and have children
to feed, it was a lot.

The converts in town raised more funds and built a thatched-roof
gathering hall with plain wood for walls on the site of the shit-attack.
Everyone contributed labor; even some of Ezra's and Melkamu's out-of-
town converts came to help for a weekend. The women cooked and
young men dug holes and erected walls, whereas elders like my father
supervised. My brothers had blisters on their hands from all the digging.

Last Sunday, as Solomon the orphan, an early convert who has just
been made a full-time preacher, stood at the podium of our new church
talking about the scary fire that awaited those who don't accept Jesus
Christ in the exact way we do, I went to the wall and stared out through
the gaps in the fence-like structure, looking for birds or some pattern I

could make out of the trees to pass time. A woman pinched me, saying that I should get back to my seat and pay attention.

On one side are Jesus Christ and His comrades with their pinching fingers and fiery hell; on the other, stone-throwing crowds. I am trapped between pinches and rocks and eternal damnation. Fucked, whichever way I turn.

21

Radio Degitu

Our church was burned down a few months after it was built. We were drinking coffee in the morning when Solomon, the orphan preacher, who goes to church at odd hours to pray by himself, burst in to tell us about the fire. When my father went to survey the damages, he found half of the thatched-roof building in ashes.

Like in the aftermath of the shit-attack on our church grounds, the believers were defiant. Money was collected for the rebuilding effort. A guard was hired. To show whoever burned our church that we can't be stopped, a three-day revival conference has been planned and members of my brothers' churches in nearby towns have been invited.

My older brothers will no longer be teachers after the end of the year. Melkamu has accepted a job offer from the headquarters of our Protestant denomination, the same people who employ Teshager. His primary job will be looking after the spiritual lives of the new converts in his town. He will travel occasionally to spread the Gospel to other towns. Ezra has decided to leave his teaching job and move to Addis Ababa to open a shop. My father is going to lend Ezra the money my grandmother left me. Melkamu and Little Yonas don't think Ezra will pay back the money. Little Yonas told my father he was being irresponsible. Melkamu wanted the money to be lent to him so he could attend music school in Addis Ababa, with a plan to open a Christian recording studio. The number of Protestants is growing fast, he said, the demand for gospel music will increase. My father told Melkamu that he was worried about Ezra and wanted to help him become independent.

"One has to be irresponsible to get help in this house?" said Melkamu.

"Please don't damage your life to get my attention," said my father.

My oldest brothers have taken time off from their jobs to lead a weeklong prayer in preparation for the upcoming conference. They have been fasting and praying every day. We're gathered in our living room for spiritual cleansing, repenting our sins. Lust. Lies. Stealing. Excessive love of earthly things, maybe like my love of candies.

Melkamu is leading the program. When he found out about the burning of our church, he told me that my insolence, especially my disrespect for my father, is one of the reasons our church lost God's protection. I had gotten in trouble for punching my father on the nose sometime before the burning of the church.

It happened the day I discovered Degitu's radio station. I was searching for new stations as I sometimes do to pass time when I heard her reading the Bible. It was not like other stations; I could talk to her and she could hear me. I asked her why she was hiding, if it was because she did not love me. She said that was not true, that she loved me very much; she was hiding from my father in Addis Ababa. She said he used to chase her around the house, hit her with a cane. The static made her voice disappear before I could tell her that my father had changed, that he was a man of God, and that, even if he wasn't, I would protect her.

I was angry after that. Mad at the static, at my father, at everything. My father came to me asking what was wrong. I didn't say anything until he got very close to me. I swung my arm at him as hard as I could. I only ended up scratching him and hurting my fingers. He yelped and touched his nose, which started bleeding a little.

"This child is spoiled," said Melkamu. "She needs a good whipping."

"Leave her alone," said my father.

I told them what Degitu told me on her radio station.

Melkamu lifted me up so that our eyes are level. "There's no Radio Degitu," he said. "You are possessed."

I kicked him in the chest.

I was saved from a whipping by my father. I was sentenced to a more rigorous Bible study, focusing on verses about respect for parents.

"You're lucky you weren't born in the days of the Old Testament," said Melkamu. "According to Exodus twenty-one, fifteen, Whoever strikes his father or his mother shall be put to death."

I have been banned from calling my father by his name from this point on. "Your father is not your friend," said Melkamu.

I'm only obeying because I have yet to come up with a plan for overthrowing Melkamu.

EZRA IS KNEELING DOWN next to me, crying. I can only reach the edge of the chair when I kneel. Ezra cries like he's been hurt badly. I try to spy on his prayers to find out why he is crying. I can't make out anything he's saying.

"Let's rise," says Melkamu.

Ezra wipes his eyes with his sleeves.

"We're going to take turns confessing our sins before our Lord."

There's about to be drama.

"I'll start," says Melkamu. "I've been going through a spiritual trial because of a woman."

The High Priest has fallen. It isn't just the rest of us mortals who've been sinning.

"I have not *fallen in sin*. But I am guilty of the sin of lust."

How slick is that? Look at me, I am not just tall and scary, I have weaknesses. Yet my weaknesses aren't as terrible as yours, so you should feel like a pile of goat feces.

"I have lusted after a married woman," says Melkamu. "I am here standing before you with humility, asking God to forgive me."

I want to know who that woman is.

"Who is next?" asks Melkamu.

I open my eyes to see what everyone is up to. I catch my father with an eye open. Ha!

"I am going to call on you one by one."

Fuck.

When I was nagging everyone to tell me what the "rude thing" was that children in my neighborhood kept talking about, my cousin Tariku volunteered to show it to me. I have been playing with the button between my legs since then because it feels good. I don't know if it's a sin but it was shown to me in hiding and Tariku told me not to tell anyone. I assumed it is another forbidden game. I have already repented for it. I refuse to confess in front of everyone.

Ezra decides to turn himself in. He breaks down crying, talking about how he sinned gravely when he drank two bottles of beer after friends pressured him.

This house is full of cowards. Give me a real scandal. Who fathered a child with another man's wife? Who tried to murder comrade Rectangle-Head? Nobody? Nobody?

A woman from the Coffee & Tea Authority gets up crying, talking about lust. There have been rumors of a lost virginity while she was in Addis Ababa for work recently.

"Is there more you want to say?" asks Melkamu.

The woman beefs up her crying before storming out. Does she think Jesus Christ won't catch up with her outside?

My father and Little Yonas confess to not praying enough; they are too invested in life and school, respectively. If every evening and morning of prayers isn't enough, I don't know what more this Jesus Christ wants from my family. My cousin Tariku confesses that he stole fifty cents from the house and bought himself bread and tea at Sheikh Hassan's bakery. Is he going to get whipped for this? How is there justice if he doesn't?

More and more people get up to confess about useless things. I'm watching everyone.

"Selam?" says Melkamu.

I say nothing.

"You've been dancing to alemawi songs."

Nothing.

"You've also been rebelling against your elders."

I see Tariku smirking at me.

"Let's all ask God for forgiveness now," says Melkamu.

He leads us in prayer and we say, amen. I'm only saying amen because every amen is leading to the end of this nonsense.

A FEW DAYS ahead of the conference, the generator is not working and the living room is lit by a lantern. Solomon the orphan preacher and another man from our church sit at the dining table with my father, who is holding on to the rifle they bought for the new guard at our church. Conference guests will start arriving from nearby towns tomorrow. Our elders are concerned that people of our town might try to burn the church ahead of the event. That's why they bought the rifle.

My father takes the rifle from Solomon and makes it klank-klank. "This is how it's done."

"I disagree," says the third man. He takes the rifle and makes a klank-klank.

My heart drops with every klank-klank. I don't want my father to get shot accidentally.

Solomon takes the rifle and makes another klank-klank.

I want to grow wings, snatch the rifle, and fly as far away from our house as possible to drop it in the forest. The rifle keeps going from one man to another, klank-klanking. My father knows how to use a gun; he used to be a hunter. Where did these men get their expertise from? I want to jump out of the dark corner and yell, shut up and listen to my father. I fear I'll only scare them into firing it. I sit here trembling instead, angry and hot, peeing in my pants.

A CRIPPLED MAN who always sat by the main road begging came to our big conference looking to be healed. Two blind men from the countryside were also in attendance. My brothers had gone around town posting signs that said Cripples Will Walk and the Blind Will See. Comrade Rectangle-Head had the posters torn down, attracting more attention to the conference.

On the first day, a prophet who came from Addis Ababa called all those with ailments to come forward. Most attendants gathered near the podium inside our brand-new church of wattle-and-daub walls and corrugated tin roof.

"Shalabalala ribarabara!" The man summoned Jesus Christ in that secret language. Jesus responded by appearing through His Other Personality. "The Holy Ghost is amidst us! Do you feel His presence?"

Shouts of yes, amen, hallelujah, shalabalalala, echoed around the room.

The conference was peaceful. Our townspeople ignored us, making us suspicious.

The prophet commanded the crippled man to walk. In the name of Jesus, he told him. The cripple was bawling. Look at me, he said, I've been healed, I can walk, I can walk. He tried his very best to put his body behind his words, but all he could do was roll on the ground.

The blind men couldn't see either. They were all reminded that God worked in His own time. They should keep praying, attending church, staying clear of sin.

Most attendants appeared satisfied by the presence of the Holy Ghost. They jumped around all three days of the conference, singing, speaking in that secret language. The devil was in disarray. On the last day, a woman screamed and dropped to the floor. The evil spirits inside her couldn't take it anymore.

22

The Blue Poster

The spirit of sadness is trying to crush me but I'm refusing.

Four of my siblings woke up early this morning and left without saying good-bye to me. They always do that to avoid seeing me roll on the floor crying. I remind myself that I have been enrolled in first grade and that I might make friends when school starts soon. The sadness persists; the departure of my siblings is a reminder of all former and future departures.

Weder is deferring her last year of university because of her chronic headache. A doctor diagnosed her with something called migraine and has no cure. She decided to take a year off from university to see if the headache will subside. She has returned to Addis Ababa to work in Ezra's kiosk while she looks for a proper job. Everyone is surprised that Ezra's shop has lasted this long, although he is not making enough profits to pay back the loan my father gave him.

Little Yonas told my father recently that he was reckless for giving money that should have been used for my education to Ezra, whom he called a lost cause. My father was upset that Little Yonas spoke so disrespectfully of Ezra, saying Ezra should not be dismissed by his siblings just because he has different ideas about what he wants to do.

"We oppose his wastefulness," said Little Yonas. "We don't care that he wants to be a businessman."

Little Yonas told my father that he's not a good father unless he comes up with the money to send me to a better school. My father said there's no money. Little Yonas reminded him that he's getting his flour mill back soon; he should sell it and use the money for my education.

"What are you going to eat?" said my father. "How are you going to get to university?"

"I'll find a way to pay for my transportation. The rest is your job to figure out."

"The schools here are fine. You went to them."

"I would have done much better had I gone to a better school," said Little Yonas. "This child is too smart for the schools here."

It is true that my father doesn't have money. He doesn't know how to do anything either; he thinks everything will be taken away from him. By the government or by life. I don't even know where the money for our food is coming from. My father hasn't bought or sold honey in a long time. The income we earn from renting rooms pays for little more than our monthly supply of teff. Asmelash has sent me to Zinash a few times to borrow money. The last time I went, she asked me when he was going to pay what she lent him before that and I didn't know what to say. I'm only five and seven months and just because I know about the rebels in the north and how to break down or build up numbers doesn't mean I know the answer to such a question.

―――――

MY SIBLINGS LEFT ME ONE BIRR, and normally that would have made me the happiest child. One birr buys ten Desta Keremelas. Today, I feel it would have been better to have my siblings here than to have a hundred birr. We were all sitting around the charcoal stove yesterday morning, drinking coffee with milk, eating roasted corn on the cob. They announced that I was to start referring to each of them with a new name.

"You have to call me Etalem," said Weder. "I'm your sister and your world."

"But you are only my sister."

Everybody laughed at me.

"You have to listen to your elders," said Ezra. "You have to call me Wendimalem."

"Why?"

"I'm your brother and your world."

"I am Etabeba," said Beza.

"But that is Etabeba Haregua's name."

"That's because Degitu called her that. It means 'my sister my flower.'"

I have been thinking about Degitu. I have asked my father to take me to Addis Ababa to look for her.

"Little Yonas is Wendimabeba," I said. "He's my one true flower."

They laughed at me again.

Little Yonas reached over and kissed my cheek so hard it hurt.

I love him the most because he always stays. I know he too will go to the university eventually. He will be taking his school-leaving exam in less than a year. He will get excellent grades since he is a genius whose teachers often come to my father to praise him.

When I asked my father to take me to Addis Ababa to search for Degitu, he said it is expensive for us to travel that far. We made a compromise: if the dictatorship falls, my father will borrow money and take me to Addis Ababa with him to celebrate the occasion. According to the FRS, the rebels in the north have the upper hand. Judges in lower courts have also begun making decisions that upset the comrades. A judge in the Medium Town ordered local officials to return our old flour mill to us. The comrades are refusing to execute the order, saying they will appeal the decision. My father says all these events are signs of a fracture within the system.

I am impatient. Little Yonas says God does things in His own time. What's the point of believing that prayer will change anything then? Fear of hell and other punishments is the only reason I worship this Jesus Christ my family is crazy about. Like joining the Workers' Party to avoid harassment. God should allow other gods to compete with Him in a fair and democratic election like people in the FRS have said should happen in our country. I would vote for Neway Debebe and sing "Ayaya" till the day I die.

I don't understand how my family hates the government for always telling us what to do but loves Jesus Christ who's also saying don't sing this, don't wear this, don't love people like Beza's boyfriend, Yeneneh. I wouldn't say this out loud; Little Yonas would turn from a flower into a monster and make me pay in pinches. Sometimes I think Little Yonas and my father are the only true believers in our house. My father has accepted Jesus Christ because he is riddled with guilt and needs redemption. I don't know what drives Little Yonas besides the want of going to heaven to be with Degitu, which is sad because I don't even think that's real anymore—Degitu is clearly in Addis Ababa and that city is not heaven.

I am always confused by the way our Christianity works. Weeks ago Melkamu was leading an exorcism in the old storage room. A maid employed by a woman who owns a restaurant and has five children had been brought to our house after screaming and collapsing during a Sunday service. A number of men and women from our church came to offer prayer support but Melkamu was the leader, seconded by Solomon the orphan preacher.

Melkamu commanded the leader of the evil spirits to disclose why and where he entered the maid, what his name is, how many spirits lived inside her, and so on. The spirit responded by talking nonsense. The woman was locked up for six days because the spirits wouldn't leave. She was escorted to the outhouse a few times a day. The prayer went on nonstop all day and late into the evenings, only pausing for meal breaks. On the last day, I was sitting outside by the window, listening. Melkamu ordered the leader of the spirits to crow like a rooster five times and leave the woman.

The spirit obeyed that time. It crowed five times and announced, "I am dead."

All the people inside the room broke out in ululations. I went inside and saw them hugging one another and the woman in celebration of her freedom. I was wondering: if the saying is that a dead man can't even weep for himself, how is a spirit announcing its own death? I did not say anything out of fear.

I have learned not to trust people in my house to know better than me all the time. That's why I'm not leaving the matter of my trip to Addis Ababa to my father. When he said he'd take me to Addis Ababa when the dictator falls, I began thinking of ways to expedite that. A few days ago I took that big blue poster of the dictator that comrade Rectangle-Head had given me and buried it next to my father's grave for Marx. I made a bigger hole because the poster was big. I covered the grave with soil, dry leaves, and twigs. I squatted over it to pee and said, "May you die, may your ideas die and leave our country."

I hope the Comrade Chairman evaporates soon.

Just in case that plan fails, I have decided to start making my own money for the trip. When drivers of gasoline trucks passing through our town park near our house to go to one of the hotels for refreshments, children in our neighborhood gather around the trucks with jugs to collect oil from the old and leaky tanks. Their parents use it to power lanterns and stoves. I am going to collect gasoline like that and sell it when I fill a jerrican. I lied to Little Yonas about my plan, saying that it is to save money for private school. He's supporting me enthusiastically. He made me a jug by cutting the top off a small jerrican. I am waiting for the next oil truck to arrive.

I AM WET FROM running around in the rain. My father and I had been wrapped up in his gabi, watching the heavy rain flood our front yard. The rain has subsided, and it's beginning to get dark. I run to the guava tree in our backyard to check if the poster of the Comrade that I had buried days ago is there.

I wish I never spied on my father the day he buried Marx. You know what they say: one looking for fish sometimes pulls out a serpent. Does that mean one should stop fishing? I was only looking to play with my father the day I followed him to the backyard.

I'm by the guava tree. The leaves and soil covering the poster's grave have been washed away and the poster is missing. Did someone see me bury it? Is it the neighbors? Maybe the lady who's been coming by our house once in a while to wash our clothes? She might tell the rest of the Women or report me herself for favors from comrade Rectangle-Head. I'm hoping it was one of the animals lurking in the backyard at night that dug out the poster. What if the poster washes up in front of the offices of the Workers' Party? What if it turns up at the door of an enthusiastic member of the Youth Association? What if comrade Rectangle-Head himself finds it?

I'm trembling and want to pee. I lift up my dress and squat over Marx, whose grave seems intact. I pray to Jesus Christ—even if I don't always believe in Him—for the poster to reach the Small River, the Medium River, the Big River, the Blue Nile, and leave the country.

I hear my father calling out my name.

I jump up midpee and start running back to the house. I part the turmeric leaves and sprint through hopelessly like a rabbit. I imagine gossip about my burial of the poster traveling through town like flood in the gutters, going from one coffee ceremony to another until it reaches comrade Rectangle-Head. I yell that I'm here when I reach the outhouse, that I only wanted to pee.

"You little rascal," says my father. "I told you not to go too far by yourself."

I slip and fall in the mud beneath the papaya tree near the barn and my father yells, "Lijen!" He says that every time I fall or even stumble. *My child*. As if someone else is trying to claim me. He runs toward me.

Maybe nobody saw me bury the poster. Maybe the poster is on its way to Egypt, uninterrupted, driven by the abundant waters of my home province. But I am supposed to be afraid all the time. Here in the southwest where it rains a lot and in the north where it rains less and in the west and the east and the south, the clearest sign of knowledge and the best path to safety is to always be afraid. Afraid of my neighbors and cousins

and comrade Rectangle-Head and the government. Afraid of the curse.
Of life. Afraid of God, who can deny us water or send us too much of it.
It even says it in the Bible: God is love, but the fear of Him is the begin-
ning of wisdom.

My father lifts me up by the armpits. "Enen," he says. Let me fall in
your place.

23

A Brewing Trouble

It is the first day of school. Kamila and Fetiya have come to ask if I want to go to school with them. The Bible tells us to expect extraordinary events in End Times, but I was not prepared for a friendly gesture from the comrade chairman of our neighborhood and her foot soldier.

No one in my house prepared me for today. Little Yonas says the school here is garbage, so he doesn't care if I go or not. Even if I finish first grade here, he is taking me to Addis Ababa next year, when he goes to university, to make me start over at a private school. He's helping me collect gasoline from the oil trucks by protecting me from bullies. When one of the neighborhood boys recently kicked my gasoline jug, spilling the contents, Little Yonas chased him down and twisted his ear. The boy avoids me now.

My father tells my cousin Tariku to run to Sheikh Abdullah's souk for my school supplies while I put on proper clothes and shoes. My mind is spinning. Not only is it the first day of school, but for some strange reason, my biggest bullies are also waiting for me outside. Is this a trick or are they finally ready to be my friends? I put a shoe on the wrong foot. My father comes to help me.

Tariku returns with a pencil, a blue Bic pen, and a green exercise book with the logo of the Ministry of Education on the front and a multiplication table on the back. I jump off the chair and grab them all.

There are so many children on the street as if it's a market day just for us. Maybe Kamila and Fetiya are nervous about going to this new place with new people and comrade chairmen of other neighborhoods. Maybe Kamila needs as many soldiers of her own as possible to face this new world, and I am merely a recruit. I used to think that lions, kings of the jungle, were fearless and able to eat whoever they want whenever they want. My father told me that isn't true, that they too have their own fears, that other animals could get together and attack them. As our forefathers said, my lord has a lord too.

We turn left on the road across the street from the post office. I went to the post office days ago to mail a letter. I used the one birr my siblings left me to buy an envelope and a stamp. The postal officer looked at the front of the envelope and said I needed to write down the exact address of the recipient, that I couldn't just say Addis Ababa. I told him to tell the postal people in Addis Ababa to give the letter to a woman named Degitu Galata, that I am sure they will find her because the radio says the government knows everything about everyone. My siblings say she is very big and scary, like no one else they know; it should not be difficult for the government to locate her. He told me that is not how sending letters works. He said to have my father correct the address for me. I gave the letter to my father. He'll send it for me as soon as he figures out Degitu's exact address.

The noise from the playgrounds at the elementary school is dizzying. The football field is big enough for multiple matches and other games.

Children run around, yelling, kicking and chasing balls. I'm terrified of this new place full of new people. I follow Kamila and Fetiya quietly, hoping they let me stay with them.

The bell rings as soon as we reach the classroom buildings. We spot Zahara and Amina Hassan—they're daughters of Sheikh Hassan, owner of the bakery in our neighborhood. Zahara is repeating first grade. Our older siblings are friends. We follow Zahara, who knows her way around. Everyone gathers in front of the principal's office, next to the football field. The principal comes out and signals for us to shut up. The silence is amazing.

We stand before a stern-looking woman who says her name is teacher Felekech, and a soft-faced woman named teacher Gobané. Whoever calls our names will be our homeroom teacher. I want to be in Kamila and Fetiya's class. I feel overwhelmed by the number of new faces I see around me. I am among the youngest at five and eight months. You have to be at least six to enroll in first grade. I was able to enroll after submitting to a physical test to prove that I am old enough: I was asked to reach across the middle of my head with my right hand and touch my left ear. Teacher Gobané calls my name along with Zahara's and Amina's.

Teacher Gobané leads us to our classroom behind a big tree that covers much of the building with its shade. The exterior of the building is made of rough concrete walls like my house. We are told to form a line and enter our classroom in an orderly manner. One side of the classroom has wall-to-wall louvered windows looking out to a field lined by eucalyptus trees. Teacher Gobané announces that she is deciding our seating arrangement. I am disappointed when she separates me from Zahara and Amina. I am to sit with a Ribka Sisay near the middle of the row, closest to the windows. I hope she's not the daughter of comrade Sisay the Rectangle-Head.

Teacher Gobané is speaking but I keep stealing looks at Ribka Sisay in search of any resemblances with Rectangle-Head. Her round mouth juts out of her face. She has a smooth hair, unlike me, roughly braided into four rows. Her skin is of a much lighter shade than Rectangle-Head's. I don't see any resemblances so far, but I study her anyway. I hope she doesn't think I'm giving her the evil eye. She's wearing a pretty purple dress and white canvas shoes. Better than my rubber shoes. She's got a parent with a salary or access to bribes but not enough to afford leather shoes.

Teacher Gobané is going to be our life skills teacher in addition to our homeroom teacher. We have been asked to choose a class monitor to make sure we behave ourselves when teachers aren't around. A boy raises his hand and nominates Aselefech Hailu, probably the oldest student in the classroom. She looks like she's Tariku's age. Teacher Gobané says to raise our hands if we agree Aselefech Hailu should be our monitor. I don't raise a hand because I don't know this person. Most hands go up. Aselefech will be reporting us to teachers if we make trouble. God help us.

The teacher with the stern face, Felekech, is going to be our math teacher. She is trying to teach us a song. She tells us to repeat after her.

"Asir arenguade termusoch begidgida lay, dinget andu wedqo biseber zetegn yiqeralu!"

We repeat that if there were ten green bottles on the wall and one of them falls down and breaks, there will be nine left.

"Zetegn arenguade termusoch begidgida lay—"

Now there are eight bottles left.

I'm sorry for the owner of the bottles. I am also sorry for the boy who is about to get in trouble because he forgot he was supposed to sing with us and sang with the teacher.

"Jamil Yasin!" says teacher Felekech. "I know you're good at songs. I wish you were as good at math!"

Jamil looks down. He's a grade-repeater.

Teacher Felekech continues with the song until no bottles are left. She turns to her desk and takes a piece of paper out of a folder. "Selam Asmelash!"

I say nothing.

"Selam Asmelash!"

"Abét." I am going to pee.

"Come up here."

What did I do? I just got here.

"Jamil Yasin!"

"Abét!"

"Come up here and help your classmates practice the song until I get back."

Jamil runs to the front.

"Follow me," she tells me.

Has she discovered that I am not old enough to be in first grade? I follow her outside praying to Jesus, to His mother, to everybody.

"Is it true that you can read?"

Jesus is Lord. I nod.

She hands me the piece of paper. It's a complaint addressed to a court by someone who must have been a chicken; the handwriting is horrific. Thankfully, I have been reading my father's writing for a long time, so I read the letter like Tizita Alebachew reads the news on the Foreign Radio Service. I give it back to teacher Felekech. I don't know how to describe to you the face she's making except to say that I think she's stunned.

———————

TEACHERS HAVE BEEN coming in and out all afternoon, introducing themselves, giving us textbooks. We met our music, Amharic, general science, and drawing teachers. Whenever a bell rang and a new teacher came in, we rose up from our seats.

"Good afternoon, students."

"Good afternoon, teacher."

"You may sit down."

The school day is over now. We are in line outside the principal's office to salute the flag as it is taken down. Each class section has two lines, for boys and girls, the shortest students at the front, the tallest at the back, all of us facing the flag. I am near the middle.

Our Amharic teacher, Ato Teodros, orders: kenda! I learn by looking at upper-level students that that means to place your right hand on the right shoulder of the person in front of you. Awrid! We take our hands down. Wede fit! A few steps forward. Wede huala! A few steps back. Wede gira! A step to the left. Wede qegn! A step to the right. Tetenqeq! We stand upright, hands raised to our ears, saluting the flag. It is chaos in the first graders' section. The boy by the flagpole begins pulling down a rope and the flag begins its descent.

We sing the national anthem.

WE HAVE BEEN TOLD to go home, but I remain in place. I feel overwhelmed by the chaos and don't know with whom I'm walking home. An older boy walks up to me to ask if I'm Selam Asmelash. I confirm. He pinches my arm, tells me to go back to America. He slaps my head and runs away.

I feel a tug on my shoulder.

Zahara puts her arm around me. "We heard you know math and how to read."

I nod.

"Do you want to come to our house and help us study?" asks Amina.

This is what we have seen our older siblings do all our lives—getting together in the evenings to study. We must continue the tradition. I follow the sisters to their house.

By dusk, I'm still at Sheikh Hassan's house. Studying is harder than I thought. It's a struggle to focus and, even when we manage to focus, not everyone understands the material. We wasted time when we got here, eating snacks the girls' mother, Eteyé Zeytuna, gave us: fresh bread from the bakery with sweet tea. There was so much sugar in the tea that my lips got sticky. They can afford to put a lot of sugar in their tea in this house because they make money from their bakery.

I bowed to pray quietly before we began eating. Zahara and Amina didn't pray, but they waited for me to finish. Bread dipped in sweet tea is the most beautiful thing on earth—maybe next to pastries from Addis Ababa. I love it even more because it is my father's favorite. I ate and ate until my stomach turned into a small drum. Zahara asked if I wanted more; I said no out of shame.

Eteyé Zeytuna placed a kerosene lamp on the table for us because the generator isn't working. We have Zahara's math book before us. We go straight to the middle, and I am trying to make the sisters understand how 20 and 20 got married to become 40. Those aren't easy numbers to add since there aren't enough fingers to count. I show the sisters how to draw sticks on paper and count them. Amina doesn't know anything about numbers even though she's been to kindergarten. I don't think Zahara knows how to count to 40 despite repeating first grade. I don't understand why their older siblings haven't taught them anything.

Zahara keeps leaving the room. Amina takes out a coin from her pocket and rolls it down the table. She asks me to catch and return it the same way. I return the coin. Amina decides to remove the math book from the table so that we can play, but she knocks the kerosene lamp over instead and spills gasoline onto the book, which catches fire. We both scream.

HALF OF ZAHARA'S book is gone. Eteyé Zeytuna came in to put out the fire. We are trying to figure out if we can learn something from the remainder of the book.

Everything ends when Eteyé Zeytuna comes in to say that my brother is here looking for me. It is so late and I didn't tell anybody at home where I was going after school. I am going to die. I gather my books quickly and leave the room.

"What are you doing here?"

I can see the veins in Little Yonas's forehead. I'm praying for no pinches.

"Wey guud!" I say. "You didn't know?"

"Know what?"

"Let's go home first."

"Your trouble is brewing."

I know, brother.

We walk out of Sheikh Hassan's house.

"You will not believe it, Little Yonas."

"Shut your mouth."

"I came to help Zahara and Amina with math. Can you believe that they don't know anything? How is it possible?"

My brother grabs my shoulder and turns to me. He squats in front of me. "What did you do to the poster?"

"What poster?"

"The poster of Mengistu Hailemariam that comrade Sisay gave you?"

I want to pee right now.

Little Yonas squeezes my shoulder. "Where did you put it?"

Rectangle-Head had come to my house in my absence with a neatly folded but tattered poster. He unfolded it on the dining table before my father, pointed to the blue ink writing on the back—"from comrade Sisay Tegenu to child Selam Asmelash"—and demanded to know what "the idea" behind all that was. When my father asked him what he meant, Rectangle-Head said he wanted to know what message we were trying to communicate by defacing a picture of the president. My father told him that it was just a mistake, that someone must have accidentally thrown it away. Rectangle-Head was not satisfied by that explanation, so he ordered my father to appear at comrade Kebede's office tomorrow to explain himself properly.

We are home now, but I don't want to go inside. My shoes are drenched in pee.

24

The Klank-Klanking of Life

My father has been detained by the police after failing to convince local officials that the defacement of the Comrade Chairman's image was an innocent mistake.

The evening I came home from Sheikh Hassan's house drenched in pee, I confessed everything. I told my father that I had buried the poster like he buried Marx's image, hoping to cause the fall of the dictatorship. I said I was ready to die and extended both my hands to him so that he could tie me like my brothers tie sheep before flipping them over to cut their throats. My father started laughing like he was being tickled. Little Yonas and Tariku stood nearby fuming.

"She's going to get us all killed someday," said my father.

I offered to go to comrade Kebede's office to confess that I was the real criminal. My father said not to worry, that the government is weak and local officials were merely trying to appear strong. Little Yonas told me that if I even thought about going anywhere other than school, he would tie and lock me up in the storage room. I kept my mouth shut in the interest of keeping my physical freedom until I figure out the best course of action.

When my father came back from his first meeting with comrade Kebede, he said the conversation went like he expected: it was less about the poster than it was about him spreading an imperialist religion. About him suing local officials for the return of his old flour mill and winning. We had heard rumors that, recently, when the Comrade Chairman made a surprise appearance at a large gathering of cadres in Jimma, Rectangle-Head stood up to tell the president about how new changes in policy have been confusing at the local level. He cited the case of a former landlord who was given his old flour mill back by a lower court. "What are those of us who have loyally served the revolution to do when courts start undermining us?" he asked. The Comrade Chairman told Rectangle-Head that he couldn't be everywhere all the time to fix everything; loyal comrades like Rectangle-Head should stay vigilant against judges and other officials who want to use recent changes in policy as an excuse to return economic power to bloodsucking feudal lords.

After a second appearance at comrade Kebede's office, my father told us that the comrades were trying to squeeze money out of him. They would need it when the time came to flee town. The FRS has been telling us for months about the formation of the Ethiopian People's Revolutionary Democratic Front (EPRDF), a coalition of rebel groups that is close to deposing the government. My father, who had given comrade Kebede a cow to free my siblings from imprisonment years ago, said he was not going to give him a cent this time. Bribery is a sin, according to our Protestantism.

Little Yonas suggested that my father go away for a couple of weeks. Years before I was born, whenever my father got wind that he was about to be arrested on one charge or another, he would go to the Medium Town to bribe doctors and get admitted to the hospital. He would sneak out in the evenings to go to my aunt Etabeba Haregua's house to eat and drink. He would come home a week or two later. Bribing doctors is out of the question now. Even if it weren't, my father said he didn't want to go anywhere; he's tired of being afraid all the time.

When my father was ordered to report to the police station for the third time, we thought they were just going to hold him there for an afternoon to let him know that their threats were serious. A policeman came by to tell us to bring him a blanket and food. It has been three days.

Melkamu arrived today, and he's already told me that I am cursed. He asked why I buried the poster. I explained why except for the part about wanting to go to Addis Ababa to look for Degitu. He would tell me that I am possessed for thinking she's in Addis Ababa. He might lock me up in the storage room like that maid to get the evil spirits out of me. I said I wanted to make the government fall; I was tired of Rectangle-Head coming by to harass us all the time. I said that the people in the radio say the EPRDF will bring democracy; I want it so that we can vote against fear.

"What do you know about politics?" he said. "You're just a child."

He turned to Little Yonas and said the Waa Himaa was right about me. That I was truly a flood, a danger to the whole family. They both laughed as if to say that they didn't take what the Waa Himaa said seriously since fortune-telling is backward, whereas my brothers are educated modern men. In truth, they spend a lot of time during prayer rebuking the spirit of the Waa Himaa, the spirit of witchcraft. I fear the Waa Himaa and what he said about me.

Melkamu had recently asked my father to borrow money from the bank, using our house as collateral, so he could take guitar and piano lessons in Addis Ababa. He met a gospel singer who has been traveling around the country, singing at Protestant churches. They got along well and the singer told him that he would bring him along on his trips if he knew how to play the guitar or the synthesizer instead of the kirar. Melkamu now thinks the kirar is backward, whereas the guitar is more exciting and popular in the cities. He wants to accompany singers like his new friend, with the plan to eventually open a recording studio for gospel singers. He told my father that this was a good investment. He will pay him back from the studio fees he will be charging.

My father refused, saying that he did not want to risk losing the house. He told Melkamu that our house belonged to Degitu, who built it in spite of his protests. She had made it clear that she wanted me to have the house.

"You know our mother was done giving birth," Melkamu said to me later. "Why did you have to come and take everything?"

He apologized later when he saw me crying.

Melkamu is here in my father's absence. I know I am going to pee in bed tonight like I have been doing every day since my father was detained.

My father claims he's having a good time in prison. I have come to visit him. He's being held in a room the size of our old storage room with several men. There are two long benches along the walls, and the prisoners have given one to my father and the other to an elderly man. Everyone kept the food their families brought them in the same room.

One of the men in detention is a wife-beating farmer that my father once helped reconcile with his wife. He has been detained for breaking the leg of a cow that was vandalizing his cornfield. I once asked my father why he helps men like that get their wives back. He told me that sending the man to prison wouldn't be just, because there would be no one to help feed the family.

I sit next to my father on his bench. There are bite marks on the back of his hand. He says they are from bedbugs. He organized fellow prisoners the day after his arrival and made them clean the place. They swept the earthen floor with bunched-up twigs, and took their blankets outside to beat them with sticks and get the dust out.

My father has also been telling the prisoners about Jesus Christ. He regrets not paying attention when I tried to teach him how to sing properly. The men keep laughing at his terrible singing when he tries to teach them our Jesus songs. I remind him that's why the Bible says, today is the day of salvation, meaning today is the day of doing everything you must do because another day is not guaranteed. He should have learned how to sing when he had the chance.

"That's why I need you by my side," he says. "You're as wise as your mother."

I tell him I'm sorry that I caused him to be imprisoned. He whispers in my ear that I should remember what he told me: that the poster was just an excuse; the dictatorship was falling; his arrest was the comrades' attempt to reassert themselves.

I want to believe him but I remember what he had told me in the past: that our dictator has many lives and would keep coming back even if they killed him. I have also been thinking about all the times when things appeared to be getting better before they got worse: like how my sister Weder got into university but couldn't graduate because of headaches.

I have been remembering some things about my mother. I remember a time when I kept jumping from the door stoop at the tailors' collective to bury my face in her lap. Good job, she was saying. Right before fainting. Then recovering. That's what I remember the most: the coming and going, which made both coming and going meaningless to me. Look at all the other comings and goings in my house. I wish people would just go away or stay. Life is like the klank-klanking of the rifle my father and two men passed amongst one another that one evening after the burning of our church. The klank-klanking is more terror inducing than the firing of a bullet. Here is my father klank-klanking away, getting sick and recovering before getting sick again, being taken to prison but pretending like he hasn't been taken away from me, being alive but fragile, making me feel helpless.

Some weeks ago, Professor "I Worry" said to Ambassador "Calm Down" to stop quoting the Bible because there's no such thing as God and "you know it." My head was spinning about that for days: first of all, more than one person knew about it? I have heard what some crazy scientists said about humans descending from monkeys; I thought they meant God made those monkeys to begin with. I don't believe the professor. I refuse to accept that nature spontaneously created this disaster. There has to be some sick being behind it. And I suspect that being is God. My theory is that somebody took His mother and He's angry that she was taken, that nobody understands the severity of His pain, so He's making all this pain for everyone else as a measure of self-expression. I want to find Him, grab Him by the shoulders, and say, we get it, you fucking monster, we fucking get it, shut down this cruel experiment.

WEDER IS HOME from Addis Ababa. She came back from visiting my father in detention to tell me that it's time somebody began raising me *properly*. That my father was spoiling me too much. It was unacceptable that I continue to urinate in bed when I am almost six. She said Little Yonas stopped when he was barely nine months old because he was pinched midpee once.

Weder has decided to stay home for a while, to do the work of raising me properly. I kept my eyes down and said, yes yes, to everything she said. My leopard was growling the whole time. I told myself in that moment that the key to surviving in this house is to say, yes yes, and keep my head down as my siblings list their decrees, but to keep my leopard strong on the inside.

"I'm going to make a calendar for you," said my sister. "You can read now, so you're going to check it every day to see what your chores are."

My leopard said, let's run away now. How hard is it to go to Addis Ababa?

"If you don't do what the calendar says, you'll pay the price."

Everyone knows the price is whipping. I told my leopard to be patient, that Addis Ababa is full of thieves and violent people, that we needed a plan. Look at the rebels, I said, they have been trying for years to reach Addis Ababa. I told him that freeing my father was our best chance.

SHEIKH ABDULLAH AND ZINASH have been trying to help me free my father. They visited comrade Kebede to beg him to free my father on the grounds that he has a small child at home. The comrade told them that our family has been in rebellion against the government, that we needed to be put in our place. Zinash and the sheikh came to our house and suggested that Melkamu visit the comrade with a gift—one of our cows perhaps—and to assure him that we will behave ourselves.

Comrade Kebede needs more money than other comrades to maintain his elevated living standards. He has a white-haired pet dog that he named Tigist. She's foreign; no one has ever seen so much hair on a dog around here before. Tigist has a bed inside the house and is given a weekly bath.

The Women say the comrade is inviting a curse upon himself by wasting so much water on a dog. My father thinks the man is a joker for naming his dog "patience" when it's everyone else who's had to be patient watching him strut about town without being able to open his hanging gut to take back all the bribes they've given him.

Melkamu told Zinash and the sheikh that he was grateful for their help, but our Christianity forbade giving and receiving bribes. He told them that our father was in God's hands. God, whose hands are clearly broken. Sheikh Abdullah visited my father in detention to tell him the same thing, but my father said no bribes. Word of our stance against bribes is spreading through town; even Kamila and Fetiya asked me about it. When I went to Zinash to ask her to make a phone call to my aunt Etabeba Haregua, she said that this new religion of ours has made my family crazy. That's what I told my aunt when she picked up: that my father and brothers are insane; she needed to come bribe the comrade for me.

AT HOME, I TRY to avoid my sister Weder as much as possible. She is irritable because of her headache, because she has had to defer her last year of university, and because she can't find a job. She said she doesn't want to work for Ezra anymore. He's using her presence as an excuse to go missing for days.

Ezra and Weder lived in a single room behind his shop, where they also did their cooking. She slept on a small bed in one corner, he on a mattress across the room. The place was too small for the two of them to begin with; it got even smaller when Ezra came home some nights smelling of alcohol and in a terrible mood. He came home with bruises some days. He would get under his blanket and cry. When she asked him what was wrong, he would say that he was struggling with the sin of drinking. I wanted to say, let's bring our brother home, but she was telling all this to Melkamu and Little Yonas; I was not supposed to be listening. I went to the backyard to kick the wall until my toes began hurting.

I take refuge in the radio as usual. I wish my father were home for to-day's episode of *Eset-Ageba*. I listen for the both of us.

PROFESSOR ANDARGACHEW: Is it not odd to you, ambassador, how a government that came to exist through an insurrection is accusing others all the time of insurrection itself?

DEPUTY AMBASSADOR DAWIT: Come on, professor, you know better. If a woman upsets her parents by running away and marrying someone she loves, it is disingenuous to expect that woman not to be upset if her daughters do the same thing. What if the men her daughters run away with happen to be abusive drunkards? Should the mother keep her mouth shut simply because she too had married under the same circumstances? The mother's past rebellion does not justify her daughters' rebellion for the sake of rebellion. What matters is the substance of the issue in question. The revolution was just. The rebels have no cause.

PROFESSOR: According to you.

AMBASSADOR: That's redundant, professor. Obviously, we are on this program to express our respective opinions.

I laugh loudly, as if to compensate for my father's absence.

———

RIBKA SISAY IS BECOMING my friend. At recess, we sit under a tree or stand against a wall to watch other kids play. I avoid playing most of the time to lower the chances of being attacked by kids who hate Protestants. I also don't like most of the games except football. Boys in my neighborhood have been letting me play football occasionally. I'm the only girl who plays.

Ribka rarely talks. I don't know why she is hiding from the world. I haven't seen anybody attack her. She's not like one of those kids with scabies who everyone else stays away from. I wonder if she has a leopard inside her that she's trying to keep from eating some people. "Why don't you like playing?" I ask.

I don't know why I waited this long.

She says nothing. She stares into the distance that's full of children yelling and running.

"Are you comrade Sisay's daughter?"

She turns to me slightly as if to acknowledge my existence. I pray that she says no.

She nods yes.

I want to take off my rubber shoes and smack her head with them. That's all the damage I could do to Rectangle-Head at this time. I only restrain myself because her father has my father. My leopard, on the other hand, knows no reason: he's scratching my insides as if I were the enemy. I'm hot and red and shivery from madness.

25

A Child of Leaving and Staying

My father was freed by my aunt after two weeks of detention. Etabeba Haregua went to comrade Kebede's office as soon as she arrived in the Small Town. We didn't even know she was in town until she arrived at our doorstep followed by my father, who carried his blanket in a plastic bag and looked like a boy coming home from the market with his mother.

My aunt waited for my father to shower and shave and told all of us to gather. We sat around the dining table frightened of what was to come. Normally when she visits, she fusses over me and gives me treats. She didn't say much to any of us today; she just paced around our living room like an agitated cow whose calf had gone missing.

"This new religion of yours," she said. "It's nonsense."

She told us that if God has a problem with bribing officials to get justice in a place where one can't get anything done without bribing somebody, He should take it up with the government. She told my father that he is unfit to raise me if he thought spending weeks in prison was the right thing to do when he should be home caring for me.

"I'm taking this child with me," she announced.

"Heh heh," said my father.

"This is not funny, you man."

Etabeba Haregua planted her fists on her hips. She is round like Zinash and Eteyé Yeshi, owner of Tana Hotel, because of all the meat and honey she consumes.

"Do you also want to take my reading glasses and leave me blind?" said my father.

My aunt told us she gave comrade Kebede a hundred birr. We all became upset anew that our father was detained for so long for a third of a high school teacher's monthly salary.

"The money was to soften him," she said.

She told us that comrade Kebede, who is rumored to have impregnated half the wives of the lowly comrades in town, had punched up recently by impregnating the sixteen-year-old daughter of a much bigger comrade in the Medium Town. He met the girl while attending a dinner party at her father's house after a summit of big cadres. Etabeba Haregua told comrade Kebede that Mr. Much Bigger Comrade was a regular customer at her restaurant-bar, and unless Kebede freed my father immediately, the man will find out who damaged his daughter.

How did Etabeba Haregua know about all this?

"I don't know who impregnated the poor child."

Comrade Kebede denied it too. He swore by all the saints. Etabeba Haregua believed he might have been stating the fact. What mattered in the end wasn't the fact but the truth: comrade Kebede has a reputation for impregnating women who didn't belong to him. Etabeba Haregua is a respected Christian woman who isn't known for unjustly harming people. No one would believe she would lie about this.

"But this is unjust," said Weder.

"Are you stupid?" said my aunt. "Who raised you? Where are Degitu's children?"

Etabeba Haregua said comrade Kebede is a rapist and a fornicator; being accused of damaging someone's daughter, factually correct or not, was the least he deserved. "Case closed," she said, in English.

She went to spend the night at Zinash's house because she found our prayer sessions nauseating. Melkamu said later that the nausea was caused by the discomfort the evil spirits inside her felt whenever the name of Jesus was mentioned. All who resist his version of Jesus are possessed.

I spent the night with my aunt at Zinash's house. I told her about Radio Degitu. She said setting up a radio station that lets listeners talk to the host sounded like something her sister would do. She wasn't surprised my mother was hiding from my father. I told her my father has changed: he doesn't go to Mamitu's Bar anymore. I said she and I should go to Addis Ababa together and convince Degitu to come back. My aunt said it was better for Degitu to decide that on her own, that people have to travel on this earth at their own pace or it would disrupt the balance of things. What balance is that? What about my life that's been disrupted by my mother's absence?

My aunt asked if I wanted to live with her. I told her I couldn't because I loved the Small Town and my friends at school. It was a complete lie. Had I said that I couldn't leave my father, she would have said more mean things about him. She told me to call her if I changed my mind.

She told me stories about my mother until I fell asleep. Degitu had received a certificate from the emperor for winning a national playwriting contest when she was only a fifth grader. But this is the story that my leopard and I loved the most:

When Degitu was nine years old, she went to visit Etabeba Haregua, who was staying with her father and stepmother in another town over kiremt break. Degitu saw how the stepmother made Etabeba Haregua work nonstop, giving her no time to clean herself; how she beat her up for burning the onion while cooking or if the coffee was deemed watery. Emama Zeritu was a terrorist herself but she didn't beat up her children over small mistakes. Degitu decided Etabeba Haregua should no longer live with that woman. She grabbed her older sister by the hand and set off to the Medium Town, which was eighteen kilometers away, by foot. Etabeba Haregua never went to stay with her father after that.

My leopard was saying: you must see it now, it's our destiny. To run away is in our blood. Remember how our grandmother Emama Zeritu ran away from her drunkard husband? It is not in our nature to coexist with nonsense.

I said to my leopard: My mother stayed for decades when others said she had enough reasons to leave. I am as much a child of staying as I am of leaving. We cannot leave my father; he is a very sad man and my mother is not here to save him. More importantly, God Himself is the biggest source of nonsense in the universe. How can we escape Him?

My leopard kept growling at me until I fell asleep on Etabeba Haregua's bosoms.

I HAVE BEEN TRYING to avoid Ribka Sisay but it's impossible because we sit together in class.

I think about eating her, instead of her father, and sending comrade Rectangle-Head a letter saying, this is how it feels when you take our loved ones. My father told me about how people in Baba Gebre's birthplace settle disputes. If someone kills your father, you do not kill the killer; you kill his father instead so that the man may live and feel the pain you endured. If someone killed your father when you were in the womb or too little to know, your mother is supposed to raise you telling you about who killed your father, reminding you of your duty. When you come of age, she gives you an agelgil full of food and a weapon and sends you off. Your duty is to kill the father of your father's killer after telling him that you seek to return the blood that was taken from your family. Some people move to another province and change their names after completing their duty. Others become shiftas, bandits who wander the wilderness. Belay Zeleke, one of Ethiopia's biggest heroes in the resistance against Italians, was a man who grew up planning to return the blood of his father.

Ribka doesn't know that I'm contemplating her destruction. We're almost always quiet, so she can't pick up on changes in the tone of my voice. My face must always look angry from the bullying, the slaps, the pinches, the occasional whipping. I have been leaving the classroom quickly during recess to avoid sitting with her, but she usually finds me.

That's why I have decided to keep moving during recess. One day I went to the back of the classroom buildings, far from the big playgrounds. I walked quickly, looking over my shoulders for bullies and Ribka. I noticed that the place was mostly deserted, with a few kids sitting on the grass passing time in the sun or playing alone. I came up on Amir Bilal, a boy from my class, kicking a ball against a wall. I wondered what his Jesus Christ was, why he was playing alone. Amir's ball came my way and he just stood there looking, not even asking if I'd return it to him. I kicked it back.

"Do you want to play?" he asked.

We spent the whole of recess kicking the ball to each other in silence.

Amir didn't come to school the whole of last week and I'm upset.

School is boring and full of homework. I have nightmares about getting whipped for forgetting to do homework. I keep going to get into second grade, third, fourth, and eventually twelfth grade so that I can go to university to become a doctor or something like that. I want to make enough money for traveling to places like Addis Ababa to search for my mother if I haven't found her by then. Maybe I'll go to America afterward and get inside the radio to leak real news instead of what the government wants. Everyone will know what is going on instead of suffering in ignorance like me about what the rude thing is or if the rebels are coming or where all the missing mothers are.

I don't want to leave for recess today. Ribka is not my friend anymore; Amir is not here. I bury my face in my folded arms on the desk. I keep waiting for Ribka to move but she doesn't. I don't know how to tell this person that we are supposed to be enemies, that very soon she's going to be my food. I hear the crunching of a plastic bag on the desk; she's probably taking out her snack. I want to tell her to go away. I look up when I feel a tug on my shoulder. Ribka stares at me with her big brown eyes. She's holding a slice of difo dabo in her hand.

"My mother sent this for you," she says, handing me the bread.

I hate her more now. I also hate her mother.

Maybe I should eat them both and make comrade Rectangle-Head suffer.

GROUND PEA STEW and cabbage with injera is all we eat these days. After dinner, I try to teach my father one of the songs we were taught at school and that Little Yonas said was fine to sing because it is about our country, not a radio song about sinful ideas.

The last song I tried to teach my father only had one line; all he had to do was repeat: "Eritrea shall not secede!" while clapping. He butchered it.

Today's song is about our flag:

> Bandirachin arenguade bicha qey!
> Armachin naw, meleyachin!
> YeEthiopia yagerachin!
> Bandirachin arenguade bicha qey!

My father can't focus.

"I liked the flag better during the time of His Majesty," he says.

He's angry at the flag because the government is always forcing him to hoist it. I love this song. When we sing it in music class, my classmates and I compete for who can clap the hardest.

Our flag is green yellow red! Clap clap! It's our banner, our symbol! Of our Ethiopia, our country! Our flag is green yellow red! Clap clap clap!

People say Protestants are treacherous anti-Ethiopian infiltrators, but I love my country so much that, when I sing this song, even the leopard sings with me.

AMIR BILAL IS BACK at school and I cannot wait for recess. Teacher Gobané asks Amir why he missed so many days. He goes to her desk to whisper something. He unzips his pants to show her the dangling meat between his legs, which I have learned is called charé. Teacher Gobané whispers something and Amir zips his pants. I am more eager for recess now; I want to see what's happened to his charé.

I run after Amir Bilal at recess. I tell him I'm going to my house to use the outhouse and invite him to come with me. I hate the outhouse at school—the floor is full of feces and, even if you find a way to the toilet, the stench might kill you. We can run fast to my house, use the outhouse, and come back right when recess is over. Amir follows me.

When we reach my outhouse, I ask Amir to show me what he showed teacher Gobané. He unzips his pants, takes out his charé. The tip is grisly. He says he had been circumcised. I hold the healthy middle part of his charé with my fingers to observe the wound. Jamal, Kamila's younger brother, got circumcised a while back but I never got to see his wounded charé; he never left the house until it healed completely. When I saw him sometime later, wearing nothing but a T-shirt as usual, his charé was missing its hood.

Girls get circumcised too. I don't know what they cut since we don't have spare meat between our legs. I haven't been cut yet and I pray to Jesus Christ for it never to happen. They throw a small feast during circumcision; they make doro wat, difo dabo, and the like as if it's a holiday. The child gets some money and treats from the family and visiting friends. I don't want any of it; I don't want a blade near me for any amount of money.

Amir says his charé is healing but all I see is a battlefield.

ALL MY SIBLINGS, except Beza, are home for Christmas break.

Beza told my father on the phone that she couldn't afford the bus fare, that the woman who employs her, a distant relative, has not paid her in a while. Melkamu called her back, offering to pay her bus fare, but she refused, telling him to give the money to my father instead. My father said she should come home if she was not getting paid. She said she was not going to leave the job until she collects her back pay. And she would rather look for another job there than return to the Small Town. In our town, a person's success is measured by how far away they are from here.

Melkamu told the rest of my siblings that Beza must be hiding something from us, that it probably had to do with that boyfriend of hers, Yeneneh. He asked Ezra, who had also spoken to her recently on the phone, if she sounded abnormal. Ezra said she was fine, making jokes as usual, this time at the expense of his forehead. She told him that possession of a big forehead should replace the Ethiopian passport, and Ezra's should be used as a model.

I'm going to write Beza, saying that she's mean for not coming to see me, her little sister who feels pain in the heart from missing her so much.

To have so many siblings is to have as many opportunities for love. But where there is love, there's a greater chance of pain. My goal in life is to reduce the number of people I love in order to keep my heart from being destroyed. To look at this gathering of my siblings is to know that there's little difference between their presence and absence because, too many times, they have woken up early in the morning to disappear from my life for weeks and months. Their presence is a mere accident that will soon correct itself by transforming into an absence. The problem is that I always forget that my siblings are leaving soon and let myself be happier than my body can contain.

Ezra is lying on his back on a mattress in the living room. I sit on his stomach because being next to him isn't enough. I tell him everything that happened since he was here last. I consider bringing up what Weder told us about how he sometimes came home with bruises. I want to ask who harmed him. I want to add his enemies to my list of enemies. I am afraid of asking. I wasn't even supposed to know about the bruises; I found out by spying on my siblings.

I ask him about Teshager instead, why he no longer visits or writes. Ezra says Teshager is occupied because church leaders keep giving him more and more responsibilities. He hardly sees his pregnant wife. They are about to send him to America for training. "It's strange," says Ezra. "They wanted him to settle down in Addis Ababa to raise a family, but they are sending him away for months when his wife needs him the most."

"It's good for him," says Melkamu. "Scripture calls on us to immerse ourselves in our faith and in service of the Lord."

I'm sure Scripture also says, nininininininini. Somewhere in the Gospel of Matthew.

Everyone except me is drinking coffee with milk. Weder has banned me from drinking in the evenings because she says it makes me pee. My father is going to take some milk into his bedroom soon and sneak me in there to give it to me. I don't know why that man has to sneak around in his own house instead of telling my sister to leave me alone. He did tell her once to stop punishing me for peeing, that my bedsheets are his property and I can do whatever I want to them. She asked him if he was going to wash my bedsheets every day; the coward said nothing. He always pulls me aside after she whips me for one thing or another to say that she's unhappy because her life has stalled, that he hopes things will turn around for her soon, so I should be patient.

Ezra tells us that Teshager wants Weder to go to Addis Ababa and stay with his wife for the duration of his training in America.

"She won't," says Melkamu. "She's not his maid."

"She's his sister," says my father. "Teshager is one of us."

"It would be nice to get away from here for some time," says Weder.

The topic of discussion changes to what Little Yonas should study at the university next year. He's taking his school-leaving exam in less than six months and everyone is sure he will get 4.0. With that score, he can study the best majors: medicine, engineering, law.

"He has to go for medicine," says Weder.

"Civil engineering," says Melkamu. "This government won't stay in power very long. There will be real free market soon and he can start a construction company."

"Please keep your voice down," says my father.

Nobody asks Little Yonas what he wants.

My father grabs the radio from the buffet cabinet.

> Good evening, listeners. This is Tizita Alebachew with the news. The Foreign Radio Service has been able to confirm that the Ethiopian People's Revolutionary Democratic Front has defeated Ethiopian government forces and has captured the cities of Gondar, Bahir Dar, and Dessie. Our attempts to reach the Ethiopian ambassador in Washington, D.C.—

We are stunned. The rebels in the north are truly coming. Gondar, our ancient capital city, has been captured. Baba Gebre Egziabher's people are free. Very soon we will be too.

LIKE THE GOVERNMENT in the north, sadness is losing ground in our neighborhood. After letting me play football with them whenever they were a man short, boys in my neighborhood noticed that I could kick a ball properly. They began including me more. I have been practicing for

years with the balls Little Yonas made me as rewards for doing homework. I began dribbling and scoring goals. We want Selam, they say
now, and it makes me happy. Last week Sintayehu, one of the top players
in our neighborhood, picked me first for his team. I pass balls between
boys' legs, dribble past them, and pass to Sintayehu for him to score when
I'm not scoring myself.

People say football is for boys. I don't care if it is a boys' or hyenas'
game; I am addicted. Whenever I go to Sheikh Abdullah's souk to buy
candy, cooking oil, or sugar, I kick pebbles. If I come across a small rock
on my way to school, I dribble it past invisible players. I'm here now, I'm
there next. Goal! You lose, I win. I think that very soon, I will be one of
the top players in our neighborhood. Currently the number one player is
Atinkut, whom everyone calls Qimem because his dribbling skills are
the spice of our matches. Number two is Sintayehu, who has been nick-
named Qentu in admiration of his stylish passes. Merely scoring a goal
doesn't matter to Sintayehu—he would go out of his way to make movements that add to the beauty of the game, and instead of chastising him,
we love him for it and encourage him to do more.

Football in our neighborhood is pure happiness. There is as much a
place for beginners as there is for the likes of Atinkut and Sintayehu. The
rules are clear: the better you are, the more you get rewarded with applause and adoration. Nobody punishes you for being bad. As long as
you find a way to contribute to your team, you will always have a place.
Even if you never get selected by teams, you can either enjoy yourself as
a spectator or take your own ball and start a match for those at your level.
As long as you have a ball to play with, sadness will not touch you.

26.

A Time of Fear and Joy

There's an upside-down situation in the Small Town.

I go outside to find that the front yards of all the homes I can see are full of people who have come out to observe unusual movements on the street.

I run down the stair to get close to the crowds. Near Zinash Hotel on the street, I see comrade Kebede, the boss of all the comrades, and his underlings, except for Rectangle-Head, pacing in agitation, regrouping, whispering things to one another, and dispersing again. None of their usual way of walking around with chins pointed to the sky. I ask the nearest person what's going on. Whoever it is—I am too distracted by the restless comrades to pay attention—tells me that President Hailemariam, our Comrade Chairman, top murderer, ugliest man in the land, has fled the country.

I don't understand why I'm hearing this from some stranger. I have been listening to the radio since before I was even born.

The stranger says the comrades are looking for a car. "They're trying to leave town."

I sprint back to my house to look for my father. This news means he has to finally take me to Addis Ababa.

"Have you heard?" I ask him, breathless.

He's lying down in his bed as if this is any other day.

I yell that the dictator has run away.

He doesn't even look up at me. "Please lower your voice, my child."

I am confused.

"He's probably hiding somewhere to see who comes out to celebrate," he says. "Then he's going to have all of them shot."

My father wouldn't move.

"We'll celebrate when we know for sure," he says. "Keep your mouth shut for now."

I go outside to look at the crowds. No one is doing anything. Comrade Kebede is about to flee town with a gut full of bribes. No one is going to make him pay for all the indiscriminate arrests and beatings. For the years of being forced to bake and brew and dance and hoist flags. Despite months of rumors and radio reports that the rebels in the north have been advancing, capturing cities and entire provinces, people of my town refuse to believe that change is really coming.

In the evening, the Foreign Radio Service confirms that our dictator has fled to Zimbabwe. He claimed he was going to inspect troops at a base in southern Ethiopia and snuck out of the country into Kenya on his way to Harare with his family, like a proper coward who is only good at sending death to meet other people's children. The FRS says that the Ethiopian People's Revolutionary Democratic Front is advancing on the capital city from all sides.

We realize that, until the rebels get here, we are on our own.

———

OUR EXCITEMENT OVER the fall of the dictatorship has given way to anxieties. We don't have a proper government to protect us until our new masters arrive.

Days after the Comrade Chairman fled, the FRS reported the capture of Assab by the Eritrean People's Liberation Front. The EPLF formed a provisional government of Eritrea soon after. Over half a million people died in the fight for the liberation of Eritrea, and hundreds of thousands were displaced from their homes, most of them fleeing the country. In my family we are too excited about the evaporation of the dictatorship to be upset over Eritrea's secession.

Our favorite debate program on the FRS, *Eset-Ageba*, has been suspended indefinitely after Deputy Ambassador Dawit Diriba left his job to seek asylum in the United States. Professor Andargachew Nega called in to the station to congratulate the Ethiopian people on our freedom from the dictatorship. He said he is preparing to move back to Ethiopia to establish a human rights organization with other academics.

The big comrades have left town. Comrade Rectangle-Head has been left behind, with insufficient funds to flee. He has four children and didn't collect as many bribes as his bosses. The people with the most money in town often went above the heads of comrades like Rectangle-Head to impress his bosses.

My father has accepted the fall of the dictatorship. He says it is not wise to travel to Addis Ababa in a time of instability when anyone with a gun could be looking to take advantage of the power vacuum. There are bandits along the road to Addis Ababa, waiting to ambush buses and rob travelers. We must wait until it is safe.

We won't need to borrow money for our travels. My father has been given his old flour mill back. After ruling party officials like comrade Kebede fled town, the low-level cadres and administrators who stayed behind decided to execute the court order for the return of our flour mill out of fear of What's Coming. The fear of a power vacuum has made us all equal at least at this time. All the machinery of the flour mill was delivered to our house in a truck and I have never seen so much metal in one place like that. It took up half our veranda. My father sold it for twenty thousand birr a week later. He did not want to open a flour mill again. He will never trust any government with anything.

Some of the new money is being invested in the renovation of our house. There are numerous cracks in the cement floors and in the concrete hiding inner walls made of wattle and daub. Our neighbor to the left, Eteyé Yeshi of Tana Hotel, owns a home built fully of red bricks. Our house is the kind that people with more money than the likes of Eteyé Khadija's family, which is most people in town, would own. Eteyé Khadija's house and those to her right—all the way to Sheikh Hassan's bakery and beyond—are government-owned two-room homes with shared earthen walls. We are among a few families in the neighborhood with backyard fences sending the message that here lies a private property we do not want anyone to trespass.

This house we built with money we made as landowners is about to be renovated with money we made from selling a flour mill purchased with money from our lands. Construction has begun on our house, and my father has been hiring day laborers to help the lead builder, Abba Lemma. One of the laborers is a soldier on his way home after the disbanding of the national army. He needed money for sustenance on his way to his village. As we wait for the rebels to arrive, the number of strangers passing through town has increased. Only some of the sons of our former servants who were conscripted into the national army have returned. Others have either perished in battle or fled to another country.

The soldier asked my father to let him sleep on our veranda until the job is over. My father told him that he can stay in the old maid's room, where Little Yonas and Tariku have been sleeping. The long rainy season is near and it is getting colder at night. Little Yonas gave his bed to the soldier and moved to a mattress in my father's bedroom. The boys' room was being rented out temporarily. He was upset that he had to give up his room. My father told him that we should always host people in need because, as our forefathers would say, our homes belong to God.

I don't know why we are fixing the house at a time of such fear instead of fleeing. During the day, men stand huddled together, talking in hushed tones. People have been hiding their possessions, cleaning their old rifles for protection in case criminals decide to take advantage of the absence of real government.

This evening, there is more whispering than usual in our house. Melkamu is home. A man I have seen about town but whose name I don't know is visiting. If he were here to convert, my brothers would be praying with him. There's no prayer; they're all gathered in a corner in the living room, whispering. Weder is in the kitchen cooking doro wat. It's only made on special occasions.

I ask my cousin Tariku what's going on. He leans close to me, which always makes my skin crawl. He whispers in my ear that I am going to get circumcised tonight. He says Weder is making the chicken stew to celebrate my circumcision. That my father and brothers are waiting for me to fall asleep because that would make it easier to hold me down. The stranger is here to give them advice on how to do the cutting.

I am full of terror.

Later in the evening, the whispering continues even after the visitor is gone. Weder says the chicken stew is for tomorrow. We eat split lentil stew with cheese and injera. Coffee is over and the light has gone off. When my father tells me it's time to sleep, I feel as though I am going to faint.

I go to the girls' room and get under the sheets. I don't want to fall asleep. I don't know how to save myself from circumcision. No one would hide me; they would just bring me back home. There's so much fear out on the streets too; I don't want to get snatched by a stranger or a hyena. I hear footsteps in the hallway and pretend to be asleep. Whoever it is comes into the girls' room with a flashlight, points it at my face for a moment, and leaves. I hear him say that I have fallen asleep. It's Little Yonas. I spring up.

I am going to destroy them before they cut me.

I hear thuds and furniture being moved around hurriedly. I go to the door to take a peek down the hallway. I don't understand what I am see-ing. Melkamu and Little Yonas move the dining table to the middle of the living room, under the wide wood panel supporting our ceiling. Little Yonas climbs the table. My father hands him thin bundles of cash, which Little Yonas slides above the wood panel. My brother moves down along the panel, sliding in more and more bundles. It must be what's left of the money from the sale of the flour mill. I cannot believe that I let that Piece of Satan, Tariku, make me believe that I was getting circumcised tonight.

MY FAMILY THINKS I'm a tattletale.

Things just come out of me sometimes as if I were a radio. I once got in trouble for telling a girl at Sunday School that Little Yonas can eat five rolls of bread at once. "How dare you tell people about your brother's eating habits?" said Weder. She has been my punisher for everything. She pinches me for saying the wrong things or for interjecting when grown men debate one another. They say stupid things sometimes and I feel compelled to point it out. The day she heard that I told people about how big an eater my brother is, she pinched me on the butt, saying never to talk about our family's business to strangers. I thought the so-called secret was harmless and funny.

I don't know the rules governing the guarding of secrets. When my father brings me new clothes from Jimma or Addis Ababa, he hides it for a week. He knows people expect him to bring something new and he wants to mislead their evil eyes. When he finally gives me the clothes, he tells me not to show off. "People will say we have money," he'd say. What am I supposed to do then, not wear the fucking blouse?

They think I'm dangerous because I reveal secrets. They are right this time. Today, I told all the boys who were gathered on our front yard for football about seeing my brother hide money in the ceiling. I didn't mean to do it; it came out in the middle of a conversation about the coming rebels. Somebody said he can't wait for the tanks to get here. Someone else said he is scared of the tanks and of everybody dying. I said we are scared in my family too; that's why we're hiding money. As always, it was Tariku who reported me. I don't even know how he heard me because he's too old to play football with us, so he should not have been around. Like a proper evil spirit, he can be anywhere without being physically present. I got whipped very badly. Melkamu did it. My skin is full of bumps now. My face is caked in tears.

I'm sitting on the concrete ledge of the old storage room thinking about why I revealed the secret since I knew it was harmful to do so this time. Maybe to impress my friends. Maybe because the rules of secret keeping don't make sense to me. Or maybe I am a leaky bucket who can't contain information. I hope I get on the Foreign Radio Service someday to leak all the information I want.

THE SOLDIER STAYING with us while working on the renovation of our house is missing at morning coffee. My cousin Tariku told us that the man didn't return after leaving for the outhouse in the middle of the night.

"Did anyone look for him in the backyard?" asks my father. "Did he collapse somewhere? Was he sick?"

"He's gone," says Tariku. "He left the lantern he took with him in the barn."

"Why the barn?" asks Abba Lemma, disappointed because the soldier was his best worker.

Tariku grins and shrugs.

My father leaves the room when he sees that the other laborers are arriving. Little Yonas tells Tariku to speak up.

"He asked me to go to the outhouse with him," says Tariku. "I lit a lantern and followed."

Instead of going to the outhouse, the soldier took a turn to the barn, where he picked out one of the cows and began doing the rude thing with her. Tariku said he was too stunned to do anything about it. After finishing his deed, the soldier went back to the old maid's room to grab his jacket, his only possession. He left our house through the side door.

I do not believe it. Neither does Abba Lemma.

"This makes no sense," says Abba Lemma. "Why is that reason to run? Who doesn't fuck a cow every now and then?"

Tariku bursts out laughing.

"Don't talk like that in this house," says Little Yonas.

I suspect Tariku is the one who fucked the cow. The missing soldier is the one who felt horrified, threatening to tell on Tariku. My cousin threatened him back, saying he'll tell my father that the soldier is the one who did it. Who did the soldier think my father was going to believe, his nephew or a total stranger? That's when the soldier decided to run. If I had money, I would bet on this version of the story.

My cousin Tariku is good at blaming you for the bad things he does. He makes you fear him by always getting you in trouble. Ever since he showed me what the rude thing is, he wants to touch the button between my legs when we are alone. I refuse because I don't like him. He follows me around the house. When I threaten to tell on him, he tells me that he's going to say that I am the one who wanted it, that I like it and that I keep bothering him to do it to me. I am terrified of my siblings, especially Melkamu, discovering this. This is another case of me looking for a fish and pulling out a serpent instead.

27.

A List of Enemies

The rebels arrived right before the beginning of the long rainy season. The soldiers have been driving their tanks around for no particular reason, making cracks in our only asphalt road. Gunfire fills the night. Tariku found a grenade between the turmeric sprouts in our backyard. My father sent for a soldier who'd recently come home after the disbanding of the national army. The man examined the grenade and told us it's missing a key part that would have made it explode. We remain worried—how did the grenade get to our backyard?

Adults have been summoned to the football field at my school. Little Yonas says about four thousand people live in our town. I came with my father to see what's happening. Half the people sit on the grass, whereas the rest stand in a half circle around them. I tried counting the heads starting at the front and gave up at fifty. There are too many people here—at least several hundred.

A bearded and burly rebel soldier, the boss of all the other soldiers, stands in front of the crowd holding a megaphone. He says democracy is our right. His Amharic is a little broken. The Ethiopian People's Revolutionary Democratic Front, the most powerful party in the provisional government, is supposed to be a coalition representing multiple ethnic groups, but the soldiers that have come to our town are all Tigrayans of the Tigrayan People's Liberation Front. The FRS told us that the EPRDF is facing criticism for being dominated by the TPLF, which represents a minority ethnic group in the north and needs to pretend like it is working with representatives of much bigger ethnic groups in order to justify ruling the country.

This is a new day, says the boss soldier. We are free to elect our leaders, and today we are going to elect the head of our kebele. He wants us to raise our hands and nominate people that we trust to lead us through this transitional period. Nobody raises a hand.

"This is democracy," says the boss soldier, "the people elect their leaders in a democracy. It is not a false election like the ones that took place under the previous regime. Raise your hands and nominate. There's no getting it wrong. You are only putting names forward for the rest of the residents to consider."

A man near the front raises his hand and nominates Sheikh Hassan. That's the bakery owner, Zahara and Amina's father.

The boss soldier tells one of his men to write down the names.

"Can you tell us something about Sheikh Hassan?" asks the boss soldier. "Why are you nominating him?"

The man says Sheikh Hassan is a respected businessman, a role model.

Another resident raises his hand and nominates Getachew Fayisa, a high school history teacher. Reason for nomination: he's an educated man and would know how to administer a town.

Elias, an older classmate of Little Yonas, raises his hand and nominates Ato Asmelash Gebre Egziabher. I cover my face to keep in my laughter. I don't think anybody will vote for a former landowner who worships a foreign Jesus Christ.

"He is against giving and taking bribes," says Elias.

Then Ato Addisu and Ato Estifanos, both tailors, are nominated.

The boss soldier says that's enough nominees. It's time to elect our leader by raising hands. Sheikh Hassan, he says. Hands go up. Sheikh Hassan is a famous businessman, so I expect him to win. Forty-three hands. Teacher Getachew has the advantage of possessing a bachelor's degree. Boss soldier says sixty-two.

Asmelash Gebre Egziabher. Hands go up here and there. And there and there and there? This is too many hands. I am confused. The soldier keeps counting. I turn around to see that it's as if all hands have been raised. Many of the people raising their hands are the same ones who call us Western imports. Many who hate us for being former landowners.

The boss soldier stops counting at a hundred and twenty-three. He suggests skipping my father to vote on the other nominees. It is too many people to count.

The last two candidates have worse numbers than the first two.

The boss soldier says we have a clear winner. He asks the crowd to affirm the election of Asmelash Gebre Egziabher with an ovation. The crowd agrees.

Is this some kind of a joke?

My father has been elected the chairman of our kebele, the administrative district covering the whole town, by hundreds of votes. All because his stance against bribes appeals to the people more than Sheikh Hassan's business administration skills or teacher Getachew's bachelor's degree in history. I do not know what to say.

I know what to do.

I am going to prepare a proper list of people whose homes we are going to bulldoze for all the mean things they did to us.

———

A FEW DAYS after my father's election, all the lowly comrades of our town began flocking to our house with their gabis wrapped deferentially under their armpits the way tenant farmers used to do when they visited landlords. As soon as they see my father, they run to fall on his feet. My father has been catching them and saying, the past is gone.

I am mad.

Comrade Rectangle-Head is here. He didn't think coming here alone with his gabi wrapped under his armpit was going to be enough, so he brought three elders with him. They're all sitting by the dining table with my father, talking about how things are expensive, how they can't wait for the Peace and Stability the provisional government has been promising to materialize. They're pretending like they're not here to save comrade Sisay, who ran to hug my father's feet as soon as he came into the house.

"By God, by God, please don't," said my father, catching Rectangle-Head.

I don't understand this. Rectangle-Head is our enemy; why are we not destroying him?

I gave my list of enemies to my father:

1. Comrade Rectangle-Head, for detaining my siblings for two weeks, for arresting my parents numerous times, for watching us all the time for the purposes of meanness

2. My cousin Hirut, for reporting my father and brother to the comrades

3. Kamila Nesro, my number one bully in the neighborhood

4.   Fetiya Yasin, my number two bully in the neighborhood

5.   The Women, for making fun of me all my life and before
     I was even born, and

6.   My cousin Tariku, for being a Piece of Satan

I am sitting at a corner in the living room, watching my father forgive comrade Sisay.

"What has passed has passed," says my father. "We have all been through a lot."

No, we haven't *all* been through a lot.

"We must help each other now."

No, we will not.

My father laughed in my face when I gave him the list. As if I had told him a joke. When he saw that I was serious, his face dropped like he was looking at a sick person.

"Have I told you about the farmer in Tijji who secretly protested people like comrade Sisay when they were in power?"

My father told me about Aba Dula, a farmer who used to throw down his hat whenever he came across comrades on the street. The comrades ignored him, thinking the old man was losing his mind. Aba Dula was telling them that their power was just like a hat, a false crown that can be thrown away at any time.

"Power is not permanent," said my father. "The only permanent thing is God."

This God again. Where was He when comrade Rectangle-Head was taking everybody?

"Revenge belongs to God."

I do not think so.

I am going to go to comrade Rectangle-Head's house to end him myself.

THERE ARE POSTERS everywhere with slogans like Democracy Is Our Right! and We Want Peace and Stability! These are new phrases that came to our town with the rebels. The soldiers have turned the town's kindergarten into a temporary base. We keep hearing gunfire at night but we don't know who is firing at whom. My father, who has been letting me sleep in his bed because I am too scared to sleep alone, keeps a loaded handgun next to his bed. I am scared of guns, but I am more scared of sleeping alone.

My father won't be able to keep his handgun or the three rifles he's holding as collateral for money he lent to some farmers. The soldiers will start a disarmament campaign today. They will visit every home asking that everyone turn in their guns. Despite being the kebele chairman, my father will be treated like everyone else.

First graders have been going to school in the morning shift this semester. Today, after school, we are supposed to go home for lunch and return in the afternoon for labor education. We are going to help upperclass students clean our classrooms. I am going to comrade Rectangle-Head's house with Ribka afterward. When I asked if I could go to her house, Ribka nodded and smiled. That girl doesn't know anything.

I SIT NEXT to Ribka by the dining table at comrade Rectangle-Head's house. Her parents sit across from us. Ribka and I are eating bread with sweet tea. Her parents are probably confused as to why I have only come to their house today after almost a year of being "friends" with their daughter. They're looking at me; I look back without fear. I am a child of the town's boss now. I'm looking at comrade Rectangle-Head, trying to decide where to grab him first with my leopard claws. He's smiling, and I'm thinking, keep smiling, you son of a dog, you won't be able to very soon. I have given up on my previous plan of eating the wife and child and letting the comrade suffer. I am going to eat him. I want to see how it feels to bite him.

I am done with my bread and tea. It's getting dark outside.

"Will you stay here for dinner?" asks Eteyé Hibist.

Oh, they have dinner to spare. They must have some leftover bribe money. Not enough to flee town but enough to offer food to guests. I tell her that I won't stay for dinner. I know she's only asking because she doesn't know what to do with me. My father may have forgiven the monster but what if he only did it to appear kind in front of elders? Maybe he sent me here to spy on them.

I AM BREATHLESS when I get home. I sprinted all the way. Everyone at home is too distracted to ask where I had been, too occupied with the soldiers who have just arrived to take away our guns.

One of the four soldiers explains to my father that if he wants peace with them, he should give them all the guns he has right away. They will search our house afterward. If they find that he hid anything, they will take him to detention. My father says he understands, but he tells them he doesn't have any weapons. I know this to be a lie; there are at least three rifles in his wardrobe.

My father seems confident they won't make him open the wardrobe. He knows the soldiers like him because his last name makes him sound like a Tigrayan. A Tigrayan like them but one who doesn't speak Tigrigna because his family moved south too long ago. Not his fault. The soldiers say they want to go to the backyard. My father leads them. They all turn on their flashlights. I sit in the living room trembling. A part of me wants to go yell that there are weapons in the wardrobe and fall on the soldiers' feet to beg them not to take my father. Another part of me is afraid my father will kill me if I do that.

The soldiers return from their search. My father talks in a calm tone, being charming and friendly as usual. They ask to go into his bedroom. I get close to the door to listen.

"Please open your qum satin."

I pray to Jesus Christ and everyone else.

My father opens the wardrobe. "These aren't mine," he says coolly.

I go to a corner in the living room. I can't take being in this life anymore.

The soldiers lead my father out of the house.

Little Yonas and Tariku are in the living room with me. I feel alone in this life.

THE DAY AFTER my father's arrest, I don't want to go to school. I am ashamed of seeing Ribka Sisay. I tried and failed to eat her father last night. I tell Little Yonas that I feel sad our father has been taken. He says that's a poor excuse to miss school. After not caring about me going to school at the beginning of the year, Little Yonas has suddenly become a mean enforcer of everything school. I had begun complaining of stomachaches to leave school at recess at one point; I stopped when Little Yonas threatened to take me to the clinic to get injections.

At school, I hide outside behind our classroom door waiting for teacher Gobané. I emerge when she approaches. I explain that I need to visit my father at the detention center. Teacher Gobané wishes my father well and lets me go. I sprint across the football field into the pine tree grove at the edge of the compound. This grove is where students meet for after-school fighting appointments. It's where all the kids who want to play swing come during recess. The slope at the edge of the grove turns into mud-sliding grounds when it rains.

I find a swing and sit on it. I think about what is happening to my father at the detention center. The soldiers don't take people to the police station; they take them to their base at the kindergarten. The kindergarten has been closed, but kids have been finding excuses to go there. The soldiers give out salty crackers we have never seen in town before. I am ashamed to admit that it lifts my spirits a little to think about the free crackers I am going to get when I visit my father later.

This is going to be a long morning. I am going to write letters to each of my siblings. To Degitu even if I don't know her address. To my aunt Etabeba Haregua. To everyone I know and to others I might meet in the future.

AS SOON AS the final bell rings, I begin sprinting between the pine trees like I'm a gazelle being chased by a leopard. I don't think I am a leopard anymore. I found that out yesterday at comrade Rectangle-Head's house when I rolled my fingers like claws, twisted my face, and exposed my teeth. Rrrrrrawwwr, I kept saying, trying to get the leopard to emerge. I climbed a chair, hoping to encourage the beast somehow. Eteyé Hibist and comrade Sisay looked at each other. Ribka's eyes were wide open as if she were looking at a mad person. I kept growling, trying to get my leopard out, but nothing happened. I jumped down from the chair and ran out.

I reach our house and rush up the stair to drop off my exercise books. I can't wait to see my father and get some salty crackers.

My father is already in the house.

"What are you doing here?" I yell.

"I've been released."

He looks at me like he wants to say, what's the matter with you, you child?

My brief disappointment gives way to relief, followed by a familiar dread: the ease with which the soldiers took my father away tells me that fear has yet to be overthrown.

28

If You Want to Borrow, Come Back Tomorrow

I found Little Yonas crying, lying on a bench in the living room, surrounded by my siblings. My heart dropped. I thought the new rebel soldiers in town had done something to him. After the original rebels, the Tigrayan People's Liberation Front, left town to join the new national army, soldiers of the Oromo Liberation Front (OLF) took over our province and other provinces inhabited by the Oromo, my mother's people. They are not part of the coalition that makes up the EPRDF, but they are part of the provisional government.

The soldiers didn't attack my brother; his bad news was worse: Little Yonas didn't get the grades he needed to go to university. Zinash's youngest son, Samuel, a grade-repeater four years older than Little Yonas, got a perfect score. The town is full of rumors that Zinash bribed the exam administrators, who had stayed at her motel. The administrators, who came from Addis Ababa, asked around for who the smartest student was before switching Little Yonas's answers with Samuel's. We don't know what really happened. Everyone, especially Little Yonas's teachers, is shocked by the results. Even the Women are saying something doesn't smell right. Samuel came to our house to say good-bye the day before he left for Addis Ababa University. We entertained him as usual, said nothing about our suspicions.

We don't know what Little Yonas is going to do, but Melkamu said he should become an evangelist like him. "Maybe this is God's will," said Melkamu. "Money is of the world."

Fuck that man. Money buys food. What are we going to eat when the money from the sale of our flour mill runs out? What are we going to do if the new rebels in town turn on us?

I see the way some of the new soldiers look at us, especially at my father, like they want to send us to the land of our paternal ancestors in the north. I am learning more about my family since the new rebels arrived. Tradition says our ethnicity is determined by that of our fathers. My father carries the name Gebre Egziabher although he has never been to Gondar, where his father is from. He was born and raised in a village near the Small Town. I want to tell the soldiers that my father doesn't know of any other home, that my mother is Oromo, that I am entitled to be here like any soldier of the Oromo Liberation Front. They only see my name: Selam Asmelash Gebre Egziabher. My mother is not here to speak for us, to tell them that she is the daughter of a Galata, and a descendant of the Oromo conquerer of our home province.

The OLF soldiers have told my father that they will be dissolving his kebele government to hold new elections. My father's team of administrators had ordered a review of our kebele's accounts, finding that the majority of residents haven't paid rent on their government-owned homes for years. Rent is less than one birr a month for most people; a woman who runs a successful tej bét hasn't paid rent—thirty-seven cents per month—for fifteen years. My father and his team wanted to devise a plan for collecting those fees and using the revenue for a public project. With the dissolution of their government hanging over them, they have not been able to act.

Before the overthrow of the dictatorship, we only heard about the OLF on the radio occasionally. There are a number of liberation fronts looking to free their respective ethnic groups from our country, but the Tigrayan and Eritrean rebels of the north dominated the news. When the Tigrayan rebels came to our town, they were friendly: they gave children salty crackers, smiled at us even when they came to our homes during the disarmament campaign. They released my father after one night of detention when he was caught lying about possessing rifles.

The OLF soldiers are different. We began hearing frightening rumors about them as soon as they arrived in our town: that they have been killing and displacing people like us in other parts of the country; that in the countryside they have been piercing the bellies of thieves and criminals with spears, without trial, at public gatherings. The way they eye us on the streets, the way they never come by our homes to greet us, and the troubles they are giving my father, a democratically elected chairman of our kebele, are only reinforcing the rumors. I am terrified of them even more than I used to be of comrade Rectangle-Head, whom I don't even think about anymore. I am praying for them to lose the regional elections being held in less than a year.

IN SECOND GRADE, there are some changes at school. One of my classmates was rebuked by a teacher for bringing old Workers' Party magazines to class. The boy is the son of a prominent Workers' Party member; he would not have gotten in trouble for such a thing a year ago.

Many of my classmates from first grade, including Amir Bilal, have been left behind for failing. My neighborhood bullies, Kamila and Fetiya, also failed. Repeating a grade is embarrassing; I worry that they might do something bad to me to reassert themselves. Zahara and Amina, daughters of the baker, are also repeating first grade, the former for the second time. Ribka Sisay has passed. She wants to be my friend even after I humiliated myself in front of her parents last year.

Melkamu scolded me after learning about how I behaved at comrade Rectangle-Head's house. He had run into the comrade, who recounted the event, smiling, but clearly spooked. I am sure my brother has added this to his list of exhibits that I am possessed. I hope I manage to run away—to I don't know where—before he decides to do something about it.

MY JERRICAN OF GASOLINE has gone missing. I kept it at the back of our house, next to the chicken coop, because my father said he didn't want flammable things near the main house. Our neighbors could see into our backyard through the gaps in our fence. That's why Kamila Nesro is my number one suspect. I recently saw her strutting around her backyard wearing the missing half of my green flip-flops. It remains a mystery to me as to why she didn't steal the pair. When I told my father and Little Yonas about it, that was the very reason they cited to dismiss my sighting of the missing flip-flop: why didn't she steal the pair if she wanted to wear it around her house?

Maybe they were just using it as an excuse not to confront Kamila's parents about it. When it comes to our neighbors, my family's policy is de-escalation. My father always says, the way to survive Time and a slingshot is to keep your head down. It makes me angry. When Kamila gets into fights, her whole family comes out to go after the other kid no matter who is at fault. I thought today was going to be the same: that my family was going to keep quiet about my missing gasoline instead of helping me find it. I had spent about a year gathering nearly ten liters. Little Yonas saw me crying. He did not need evidence to believe my suspicions.

He marches to Eteyé Khadija's house. I follow him.

"Where is my sister's gasoline?"

"What?" Eteyé Khadija is bewildered. Her daughters come out of the back room.

"Where. Is. My. Sister's. Yellow. Jerrican?" he says, attacking one of the beat-up tables in the living room with his right palm. "Do you think I don't know what kind of people you are? That you hate my family, that you wish you were living in our house, that you wish you could just come over and take everything we possess? Do you want me to go to the back and find it myself? I ask you again: WHERE IS MY SISTER'S GAS-OLINE?"

I'm stunned. I want to run home and find my father.

"What are you talking about?" Eteyé Khadija plants her fists on her hips.

Little Yonas runs past Eteyé Khadija, past the sisters into the back room, and starts ransacking the place. I start crying. I follow my brother to beg him to leave. I tell him the gasoline is not worth it anymore. Let's go home. I shut my mouth when he pulls out my green flip-flop from the pile of clothes atop grain sacks in one corner of the room.

"Aha!" says Little Yonas, holding up the flip-flop, his eyes full of rage. "Do you see this?" he says to Eteyé Khadija. "Your child is a thief. Tell me where the gasoline is now."

"I did not take the gasoline," blurts out Kamila. "Examine your own house!"

"What does that mean?"

"It is your own cousin Tariku who has been taking bottles of it to Hajji Yasin's souk to sell and buy himself bread and tea at Sheikh Hassan's bakery. Everyone knows this!"

The discovery of the missing flip-flop keeps my brother and me from deflating like balloons. We walk out without apologizing.

At home, Little Yonas grabs Tariku by the collar and slaps him on both cheeks repeatedly with the front and back of his right hand. I hate Tariku but I can't look at his punishment for too long. I know those punishing hands can come for anyone. Tariku points us to the remainder of the gasoline: he had hidden it between the turmeric sprouts, half of it gone. I had avoided selling the gasoline in increments to avoid the temptation of spending the money. I regret that now.

Little Yonas tells me not to feel discouraged. That I must keep moving forward despite setbacks. He is going to get a jug of his own to help me collect more gasoline. He says in a year or two, we might collect enough gasoline to sell directly to owners of flour mills instead of shop owners who don't offer good prices. I feel exhausted thinking about all the future setbacks.

INEXPLICABLE GUNFIRE HAS continued at night. We heard a woman was shot through the foot while asleep in her house. Nobody knows who fired the bullet or why. Even at the so-called peaceful rallies in support of this or that political group, we hear guns fired into the sky.

There are rumors that war will soon break out between the Tigrayan People's Liberation Front and the Oromo Liberation Front. The two groups had agreed to share power until elections are held; they just don't trust each other to keep their respective ends of the bargain.

Children have invented a game involving bullet shells. Despite my hatred of guns—seeing them up close makes me sweat and shiver—I like this game of bullet shells. First you melt a piece of metal wire on top of a stove. You pour the molten metal into a bullet shell. You insert a nail into the liquid to make a hole in it before it cools and hardens. You tie a string to the bottom of the bullet shell, and the other end of the string to the head of a nail. You pour match powder into the metal hole inside the bullet shell before inserting the tip of the nail into the hole. You hold the middle of the string to make a half circle, and you bang the head of the nail against a hard surface—a wall or a tree trunk. If it goes BOOM, you have succeeded.

I am addicted to this game. If I am not in school, playing football, or doing homework, I am making explosions.

On my way to Sheikh Abdullah's souk to get those salty crackers the first rebels introduced to our town, I walk carefully, searching the street for any bullet shells.

I see a soldier walking by with a rifle and look away. During school break, Little Yonas and I went to visit Etabeba Haregua in the Medium Town. Two soldiers sat next to us on the back of a truck with their guns turned up. I stood next to them, looking down the barrel of one of the rifles. I wanted to move but the truck was packed. I began shaking. When my brother asked what was wrong, I pointed at the rifles. The soldier laughed and asked why I didn't tell him to turn his rifle away. I wanted to tell him that I was afraid he might shoot me.

Sheikh Abdullah has a new sign taped to the front of his counter.

IF YOU WANT TO BORROW, COME BACK TOMORROW

I read it over and over. I see what the sign is doing. It's a trick.

"Selam," says Sheikh Abdullah.

I want to go to the counter and ask for one koshoro, but I can't move. I feel like I'm being held in place by invisible hands.

"What do you want?" says the sheikh.

I can't speak. I keep staring at the sign. Something is coming to me. I don't think I want crackers anymore. I start running back to my house. I think all of me is finally learning something a part of me has known for a long time: that tomorrow is a false day. I am going home to throw away my gasoline because there is no point in saving money. No point in going to Addis Ababa. No point in anything.

Part IV

29.

Where Are Degitu's Children?

I am looking for a girl named Hadiya Abdu from fourth grade section C. Somebody told me that she has been treating Foziya Assefa, the smallest girl in my section, like her servant, scorning her in front of everyone, threatening to beat her unless she did what Hadiya wants. I'm going to her with no plan, hot and trembling. Something is driving me.

"You lice-infested girl," I say when I find her.

She just stares, stunned by the sudden hostility.

"Why are you picking on Foziya, you child of a dog? Is it because she's helpless?"

"Mn abash agebash?" she says. "It's none of your business."

"It is, you pile of rotten cabbage," I say. "Should I pull all the lice out of your hair?"

"Do you want to meet me by the pine trees at home-going time?"

"Yes," I say. "I'll show you. I'm going to break your shefafa legs."

I don't know what I am doing. I don't even like fighting. Sometimes I feel like the leopard never left me. Maybe it went quiet to trick me, to make me think that there's no beast inside me, only to jump out and eat somebody someday.

A while ago, my cousin Tariku and I went to a spring just outside town to get water along with some neighborhood kids. The government pump wasn't working. Tariku and the others began inciting one of the boys to fight me. They told him that he was useless if he's scared of a girl. I wanted one of the older women who were washing clothes nearby to interfere. The boy, who was about my age, charged me. I grabbed him with the speed and force of a much older person, locked his neck in my arm, bent him over, and started hammering his back with my free hand. I was terrified of how hard I was hitting him, but I couldn't stop, as if I were defending myself against a murderer.

Later, when school is over, Hadiya and some of our classmates will go to the pine grove to wait for me. I won't be there. I am going to find a teacher and follow them home. Hadiya and her friends will call me a coward, a bedwetter, and more. I don't care. I hate fighting.

MY FAMILY SITS around a tray of tibs, lentil stew, and collard greens, all hands reaching for cubes of beef fried in spiced butter with onions. It's my father, Little Yonas, Tariku, and me. We are back to eating meat on weekends because my father is now a coffee merchant who makes modest profits.

When the government announced that private businesses are allowed to trade coffee alongside the state-owned coffee company, which used to be a monopoly, people with capital, like my father, who had some cash left over from the sale of his old flour mill, obtained business licenses right away. The buying and selling of things is now everywhere except at state-owned stores and bakeries, which have been shuttered.

Many young men in town have become brokers who connect traveling retailers of less accessible goods to buyers in town for a percentage of the sales. In the evenings, the delalas take their commissions to Tana Hotel next door or to Zinash Hotel across the street, where they drink and dance all night before booking a room and hiring the services of one of the beautiful women who work as waitresses by day. The number of women who come from other places to work at the hotels is increasing. They don't stay for long; the new arrivals are always popular among clients, so the old ones leave in search of newness elsewhere after a few months.

The hotels are using their profits to renovate their properties, adding outdoor seating areas, hiring painters to cover the exteriors of their establishments with colorful images: a family in traditional attire gathered at a meadow beneath a blue sky, enjoying a picnic, bottles of soft drinks in hand; colobus monkeys holding up a bottle of Meta beer; and so on. The hotels have also purchased more-powerful speakers that blare out secular songs at night, so loud that sometimes I feel as though my bed is shaking. I hide and dance to those songs during the day. I repent in the evenings.

EATING MEAT IS a rare event for Little Yonas. He lives on the salary of a junior evangelist in a town some seventeen kilometers away. He is plowing into the tray before us like a bulldozer. He doesn't visit us often as there's no proper bridge over a big river leading to his town. When the river overflows during the rainy season, parts of the bridge get swept away, requiring repairs that people of the town don't have the means for. He says people sometimes cross that river walking on ropes tied to trees on the banks.

When he visits, Little Yonas asks about our gasoline collection project. After spilling my gasoline down the toilet hole the day I saw the sign about "tomorrow" at Sheikh Abdullah's souk, I had to start again from zero. Over the past two and a half years, Little Yonas and I filled four jerricans—about a hundred liters. My father forced us to sell it to keep the house from catching fire. Little Yonas had wanted to continue collecting more to sell to owners of flour mills who need fuel in large quantities. They have to pay more for transportation when they purchase it from gas stations in the Medium Town. We had the advantage of being in town, and the larger the quantity of our supply, the bigger our leverage.

The two hundred birr we made from the last sale is protected. Little Yonas decided the money is to be used for my education. Considering that I am in fourth grade, I don't know if I will ever make it to private school. I wanted to spend the money on new clothes. My brother says two hundred birr is enough to rent a room for a year in Addis Ababa. He claims he will figure out a way to move the two of us to Addis Ababa.

I am only obeying to make him happy considering how invested he is in the matter of my education. He's always wearing the same pair of faded jeans, but he buys me books. The latest is an English-to-Amharic dictionary of ten thousand words. I feel guilty I haven't been studying it daily like he wanted me to. I take it to school to show off. These days, the subject of my education is all Little Yonas talks about. He told my father that one of them has to make the sacrifice needed to rescue me from our family's cursed fate. It doesn't matter how good I am at school; if I stay in this town, someone with more money could bribe exam administrators to steal my score the same way his was stolen. What is to become of me then? An evangelist in some small town with a broken bridge? An inconsequential businessperson like Ezra, always jogging in place? A secretary in some government agency like Beza, earning little, looking a decade older than she is?

Beza came to visit us for the first time in two years during the last rainy season. She claimed she had a job at the Coffee & Tea Authority in Dembi Dollo. Her sun-damaged skin made her look as though she spent most of her time outdoors. Or somewhere perpetually hot, like near a wood-fired stove. She wore too many layers of clothing. We found out that she had long left the home of the distant relative who was employing her. When confronted about it, Beza said she was renting a room of her own. She threatened to disappear completely if we kept nagging her about her living situation, so my father ordered everyone to stop bothering her. He told her we were just glad to see her, that she should visit us anytime, no questions asked.

Sometimes I have nightmares about Beza: in one of them, a man with a very big belly—a powerful member of the new government—had defiled her. He is using her defilement to blackmail her into being a housewife. I tell her that I don't care, that I miss her jokes and her rebellions, that my father won't care about her status either. I grab her hand and tell her, let's run, let's get home fast so that, if the big-bellied man comes after us, we will have more hands to fight him. She refuses to follow me, and when I turn around to look into her eyes, I see that she really doesn't want to leave that man. The sadness was such that it choked me. I woke up with a start, struggling to breathe.

Beza's situation gives weight to Little Yonas's words about the need to get me a better education. It is another reason why I am behaving myself in regard to our money. It seems to me that, despite being an evangelist who tells people that Jesus is going to break their shackles, Little Yonas is beginning to lose hope that Jesus will ever break our curse.

"Look at Melkamu," said Little Yonas. "He stands on a pulpit every Sunday telling people what to do when all he wants to do is move to Addis Ababa and open a music studio."

Melkamu has requested a transfer to the Small Town. He told his superiors at the headquarters of our church in Addis Ababa that he would like to be based in the Small Town and continue his traveling evangelism. That some of the people who attend the church he founded in his town are mature enough in their spiritual lives to take over management of the flock. He told them he wants to help our father with the job of raising me. In truth, he wants to save money on rent and food for his music studio dreams.

Little Yonas says even Weder barely escaped the curse. She has managed to graduate with a degree in Physics despite her chronic headache. She is a teacher at a high school in a town near Addis Ababa. The bigger news, though, is that she has found a boyfriend from America. Little Yonas says Weder's escape from the curse is statistically insignificant considering all that has happened to our family. So much so that it could be an error. We have to increase the number of people who survive the curse in order to make her escape meaningful.

I WANTED TO STOP collecting gasoline at the beginning of second grade when I realized that my original plan of saving money to travel to Addis Ababa and search for my mother was futile, that I had been lied to by my family for many years, that I had readily accepted those lies despite my capacity for seeing the things that don't add up. I was raging mad the day I saw the sign:

IF YOU WANT TO BORROW, COME BACK TOMORROW

I suspect I spilled all my gasoline that day because I feared I might use it to set something on fire. I was angry at my family for weeks for making a fool out of me. I did not speak to my father for a long time. I would have asked my aunt Etabeba Haregua to take me away had she not been one of the liars. I refused to eat for two days. Little Yonas threatened to whip me. My father said he wouldn't protect me, so I began eating small amounts.

When I asked Little Yonas why my siblings lied to me about my mother's death, he said I was too young when she died, nobody knew how to tell me that she was never going to come back. "We told you she is in heaven because that is true." I demanded to know why my father led me to believe that Degitu was in the radio. He said I was the one who claimed that I heard her in the radio, that he was not going to get between me and my ears.

One morning, my father asked me to buy bread for breakfast from Sheikh Hassan's bakery. I took the money and ran. I ran past the bakery, past Sheikh Shawara's souk, past the Saturday market, past where the billboard of Marx, Lenin, and Engels used to stand before they were taken down, until I was out of town. I did not have a destination in mind. I knew my family was going to find me soon; in this town you can't go anywhere without being seen by someone. I thought about going into the forest to find a trail. I did not care about the possibility of being eaten by a big animal. My hatred of snakes was more powerful than all my other emotions, so I stuck to the main road. Sometimes it's your own weaknesses that save you from yourself. I took a break from running for a while and started again.

I stopped when I came upon the bridge over the Small River, about five kilometers from our house. I had never ventured that far away from home on my own. I stopped because walking on a bridge is another thing I hate; the thought of it alone made me feel faint. If I were brave enough to go over the bridge, I would have reached the trail that leads to Tultula's farm after another kilometer or so. He would put me on the back of a donkey and take me home immediately. I sat on a rock by the side of the road, realizing that it was too late to go home and avoid being whipped. I greeted the occasional farmer who came by, told lies about what I was doing there. They could tell that I did not belong.

My father and some men from town found me a few hours later. It was the first time ever that my father whipped me. His eyes were full of tears toward the end of the whipping. I had made him do something he had been avoiding for years, so he was doubly angry at me. He told me that he was tired. He said he had been patient with me for so long, giving me room to learn things by myself, but I had taken him for a weak man.

I was silent for a long time after that. I understood that I had betrayed my father: instead of showing the world that his parenting method was superior to that suggested by Melkamu and Weder, I failed him. I have been trying to do what I was told since then. When Little Yonas told me that I must begin collecting gasoline again, I did not argue with him. I went to school every day, I did my homework, I ate, washed myself, and slept. I passed from second grade to third and fourth, and slowly, new concerns replaced the old.

The anger of being lied to about my mother's death hasn't left me. My mistrust of people, including my father, has only increased. I am not sure the leopard is inside me anymore, but I feel that there's something, and it's angrier than the leopard ever was. Lonelier than I actually am in the world: unlike me, who speaks and writes letters, the creature inside is always silent, quietly digging deeper holes for us to hide in in the future, for we do not like what we have seen in the past and we have learned to think of the past as evidence of worse things to come.

After dinner, I take a kerosene lamp to the dining table to write letters. I have been writing to my siblings, to foreign organizations, and many unsent letters to my future friend whose nationality I do not know let alone have an address for.

I wrote to the Foreign Radio Service in Washington, D.C., asking them to reinstitute the *Eset-Ageba* debate program. My father and I miss Professor "I Worry" and Ambassador "Calm Down" very much. We have heard from the professor, who gives phone interviews to the station once in a while criticizing the Transitional Government for arresting and torturing critics. We are confused because he has been saying those things from Addis Ababa. Under the previous dictatorship, you might disappear if you said such things at a coffee ceremony, let alone on the radio.

Little Yonas taught me how to write letters in English and gave me addresses for organizations that give away Bibles and religious pamphlets.

Dear Mr. Harold:

> *Greetings in Jesus's name. How are you? I am fine, thank you.*
> *My name is Selam Asmelash and I am nine. I am from Ethiopia.*
> *Please send me your monthly newsletter Herald of His Coming.*
> *God bless you.*

Selam Asmelash

Months ago, I sent a letter to an organization in Jerusalem asking for Bibles and I received three: in Amharic, English, and Hebrew. I do not read Hebrew but I am proud of my new possession. Everybody thinks I am a big deal of a person if I can make foreign organizations send me things. I have been fantasizing a lot about all the things I can get from abroad, but mostly I just want to go there myself. I am tired of being here.

Even though the new government does not persecute Protestants, I have been whipped numerous times by my music teachers for refusing to sing secular songs. Last week, a grown man went out of his way just to pinch me on the street. Before that a teenage girl passing me on the street came close to elbow me and call me maté. My family says it is our fate to be persecuted. I tell myself that I have accepted it, but I cry every time I am attacked.

My family says things could have been worse for us if the regional government was held by the Oromo Liberation Front, who could have kicked us out of our home province. Local OLF officials dissolved my father's kebele government shortly before being dissolved themselves by the Ethiopian People's Revolutionary Democratic Front. The OLF withdrew from the Transitional Government in protest of the EPRDF's attempt to steal the regional elections that were held nearly two years ago. The two groups started fighting each other and the OLF were routed.

When soldiers of the Tigrayan People's Liberation Front, which dominates the EPRDF, came back to our town to expel the OLF, some of them used to come to our house to sit on the veranda and talk to my father. I would listen from inside the house as they boasted about how many OLF soldiers they killed in a fight on the outskirts of our town that day. It filled me with terror. The OLF were still my mother's people, and I was afraid what came for them might come for me too.

I try to stand up to bullies at school with words. I don't like physical fights; I don't want to scratch or hit people and open their skins. I fear what I might do to people if I get too angry, like that boy I beat up by the spring. I can't believe I used to think I could eat people.

I have a new school bully named Etenesh. Once, as I sat in the sun passing time during recess, she kept badgering me about being a traitor who turned my back on the Virgin Maryam.

"Maryam died and remained dead," I said. "My Lord Jesus Christ rose from the dead. Who would choose one who remained dead over one who overcame death?"

She said nothing because she was defeated by my flawless argument.

Words don't work all the time. People like Hadiya Abdu want to fight. I hope there is no fighting in those private schools Little Yonas wants me to attend. That is more reason to collect all the gasoline in the world.

TONIGHT I WILL BE writing letters to my siblings to tell them that I miss them and to ask them to send me clothes if they can. My father is too obsessed with saving the profits from his coffee business to buy me new clothes.

I even write to Weder although she's full of rigid rules and whippings when it comes to me. Her headaches have disappeared inexplicably. I suspect it might have something to do with finding a boyfriend who might take her to America. She learned that one can attend medical school in America even after completing a first degree in something else.

Weder was introduced to the man from America, Lulseged, through Teshager. The two men met when Teshager was in Azusa, California, for training at a Protestant university. Lulseged was exiled by the former regime. Teshager told him about our mother: how fierce and hardworking she was, how responsible she was for the spread of the Gospel in our hometown and beyond. Lulseged asked if Degitu had daughters who were like her. Teshager confessed to my brothers later that he felt Beza had more of Degitu's fierceness, whereas Weder was quiet and submissive. But Lulseged wanted a God-fearing wife; it had been difficult to find one in America. No one could say with confidence that Beza was God-fearing; she was probably living with a nonbeliever in Dembi Dollo.

Weder was staying at Teshager's house, helping his wife with their newborn, when Lulseged came to visit. She returned to the university shortly after meeting him to complete her final year. Lulseged is back in America. The two have been exchanging letters and talking on the phone. They are getting to know each other, praying to find out if it is God's will that they be married. My sister has become more religious since meeting Lulseged. She believes that everything, including her chronic headache and her decision to defer her graduation, happened for a reason. If she hadn't taken time off from college, she wouldn't have had the time to stay at Teshager's house helping his wife. She believes Teshager introduced her to Lulseged as gratitude for helping him in a time of need. He could have introduced him to one of the more educated and better-looking women who came to his church.

The rest of us have yet to meet Lulseged, a mechanical engineer who has a lot of money. He will be taking Weder to America if they get married, meaning her siblings might be able to follow her or at least look forward to a future of more meat, money, and clothes. I have been asking God to say that the marriage is His will.

My impression of America is that it's a land of miracles: there is democracy; I wouldn't be attacked for being a Protestant; and I could call the police on people who want to whip me. I read that in one of the new private newspapers and marveled over it for days. One can even call the police on family members. Half the people I know would be in jail in America.

That's why America is the only place I would be willing to live with Weder. When she was here over school break, she updated the daily calendar of my chores to include making beds, sweeping floors in the mornings, washing my elders' feet in the evenings. I have been making beds and sweeping floors; I refuse to wash anybody's feet.

In my letter to Weder, I wrote:

To my dear sister Weder:

How are you? I am fine, thank God. I am praying for God to reveal His will to you in regard to you and your boyfriend. I miss you. Please bring me new clothes when you visit soon.
 God bless you.

Your sister, Selam Asmelash
Ciao ciao!

I can't send my letters to Beza; no one knows her address. My father offered to help her open a hair salon in our town. She refused, saying that she never enjoyed standing up for so many hours when she was working for our distant relative. She told him to give the money to Ezra, whose shop in Addis Ababa is struggling. There is a lot more competition due to the free market and Ezra is not disciplined enough to deal with it.

Weder told Melkamu that Ezra and Teshager fight a lot, frequently threatening to end their friendship. Teshager is often upset at Ezra for wasting his family's money, for closing his shop and disappearing for days. Ezra would apologize, and according to Teshager's wife, the two men start acting like newlyweds, Ezra spending many nights at Teshager's house.

I wonder if they have continued playing the pigeon game with each other. If that's why our family remains cursed. I wonder why the rest of us have to take the blame for our brother's fault if that is the case. I wish I could ask all these questions without fear of the coalition of hard and soft tyrants ruling our house.

I AM LEARNING how to make coffee. I washed the beans in a bowl, rubbing them between my palms to remove the mucilage and dirt. I roasted the beans on a metal skillet on the stove, turning them over with a mequya. They were brown and sweaty when Weder said, enough. She came a week early for Easter and wanted to teach me how to make coffee. When she was nine years old, she already knew how to make chicken stew.

It took me almost an hour to grind the roasted beans in a mortar. I added the ground coffee to a jebena with boiling water. I removed the jebena from the stove a few times to keep the coffee from boiling over.

Most people make coffee on charcoal stoves in their living room. They do the roasting and the boiling in front of their guests. There would be an arrangement of small cups on rekebots, grass on the floor, burning frankincense on a small clay stove. My family gave up on all that long ago, except on special occasions like holidays. Even then, we no longer burn frankincense; our Christianity associates it with witchcraft. We make coffee in the kitchen and bring everything out.

As soon as I put the jebena on its base in the living room, I look up and see through the front door that a bunch of boys are playing football. I jump over the very jebena I had just put down. I sprint down our front stair and start yelling at the boys to pass me the ball. Sintayehu passes it to me; I dribble past nothing, just to show off, and pass it back to him. I run and wait for a pass back but he stops and looks toward our house. I notice that everyone else is doing the same. I follow their eyes. Weder is cutting a twig from one of the orange trees. I wonder why.

"Come back here," she says. "I'm going to give you your price!"

I don't even know who she's talking to as she runs toward us. I only realize what's happening when she starts whipping my arms. I'm very slow sometimes, and when football is involved, I forget everything.

I run back into the house. I bring out the rekebot with the cups to the living room. I sit next to the jebena sniffing, trying to suppress my tears. My father sits over there, Weder is somewhere over there and so is Tariku. I add spoonfuls of sugar into four cups. I pick up the jebena and start pouring.

"Pull your legs together," yells Weder, as if she's talking to someone in Norway. "Why are you spreading your legs like a boy? Do we need to see what's between your legs?"

New rule: a girl shall not spread her legs when pouring coffee.

The words go into my mind. The fear etches them onto my muscles. Sometimes both my mind and muscles forget the rules and the fear. Do not be surprised if in the future you see me dribbling a coffee cup.

30

Letters from FRS Listeners

TIZITA ALEBACHEW: Dear Listeners, I would like to read you a letter from a young fan of Eset-Ageba. *Her name is Selam Asmelash, she is nine years old, and lives in Ethiopia with her father. "Professor Andargachew and Deputy Ambassador Dawit were like our friends," she says.*

They did not care that we are Protestants. They explained difficult issues. They made us laugh. We know the professor is fine because he gives you interviews. We are worried about the deputy ambassador. How is he? How is his family? Has he found a job in America? I hope so.

I am writing to beg you to please bring back Eset-Ageba. *There are too many confusing things nowadays. There are many liberation fronts, for example: the Oromo Liberation Front, the Ogaden National Liberation Front, and so on. The OLF is in the jungle fighting to separate my home region from Ethiopia. I do not want my home to not be in Ethiopia. I am also afraid that if the OLF take over power, they will kick out my father and me.*

When the census workers came to collect information on my family, I was made to register as Amhara because my father, a Gondaré through his late father, was determined to be Amhara. He has never been to Gondar. My mother was Oromo and she worked harder than my father to give birth to me due to her uterine cancer. It is not fair that only my father's ethnic group gets the credit for me. If the OLF takes over my region and kicks me out, where do I go to live? To Gondar, a land I do not know? I don't want to be separated from my mother's remains, my grandmother Emama Zeritu's remains, and my Baba Gebre's remains by an international border.

I have dreams of going to America someday. Even when I go there I want to be able to say that my mother's remains are in my motherland where my umbilical cord was also buried, where my blood is mixed with the soil. My grandfather Baba Gebre Egziabher was a war hero who shed his blood in Ogaden while fighting the Italians. If the Ogaden National Liberation Front separates that land from Ethiopia, what happens to my grandfather's blood?

My father and I want to know what Professor Andargachew and Deputy Ambassador Dawit have to say about this. We loved how they made sense of events in our country from different sides. My father is a former landowner who hated the previous regime, so we were supposed to dislike the deputy ambassador. But we enjoyed his quips very much and miss him as if he were our brother. He made me realize that I love debates more than I love the news because arguments help me see more of the things that don't add up in life, saving me from becoming a fool who believes whatever she is told.

*Please tell the professor and the deputy ambassador that we wish
them well. I will also be praying for them. God bless all of you.*

With gratitude,
Selam Asmelash

*To Selam Asmelash, I hope you are listening. We here at the FRS
thank you for your letter. We have reached out to former Deputy
Ambassador Dawit Diriba, who expresses his gratitude. Unfortunately,
he has no plans to return to the debates. He is pursuing a degree in
computer science and is busy trying to provide for his family. He wishes
you well and encourages you to keep your interest in politics. As for the
professor, he says he is proud of you.*

31

Tunes of Misery

I almost fainted the day I heard my words come back to me after traveling thousands of kilometers. Besides my family members, I was only congratulated by two people—Solomon the orphan preacher and the branch manager of the Coffee & Tea Authority—after my letter was read on the FRS. We realized that most radio owners in town have stopped listening to the FRS. We don't listen to it as much as we used to either; the FRS no longer has many secrets to tell us besides claims of human rights abuses by the Transitional Government.

We hear that suspected OLF members are being tortured in prison. The government says the OLF is a terrorist group trying to break up our country. We also remember the way OLF soldiers looked at those of us who descended from northerners when they briefly held power in our province. For those reasons and because we are tired of being frightened all the time, we try not to concern ourselves with what's happening to them.

I am in fifth grade now. I share a desk with Ibrahim, the saddest boy in class. His forearms have been overtaken by scabies, so no one else wants to sit with him. The process of grade-repeating, which has made my original bullies—Kamila and Fetiya—mostly disappear from my life, has been taking away my friends. I lost Ribka Sisay, my friend and deskmate since my first day of school, to third grade. She failed after the government changed the language of instruction to Afan Oromo. When your friends repeat grades, they pass you on the streets or at school as if they have never known you. Ribka avoids me, and I do not know what to say to her. The only way I know of dealing with people who leave is punching them in the chest when they return.

Two years ago the new government said all regions are to study in their respective native languages. Many students failed to pass their grades because they belong to families that came from other regions and do not speak Afan Oromo. My father said the same thing happened to Oromos and others when former governments forced everyone to learn in Amharic. We also began learning English in third grade—too many new languages at once. I came out first in third grade; all the students who were better than me in other subjects had their fortunes turned upside down because they weren't good at languages like me. Triumph seems to come with loss right behind it; I was left with none of my close friends in fourth grade.

I am not eager to go home even if I hate school. Melkamu has come to live with us. I love my brother because I can't help it, but sometimes I feel as though I might stop breathing if I am around him for too long. All I think about is what he is going to rebuke me for next. He has taken over the boys' room, across the hallway from the girls' room, where I sleep. He has bought a guitar to practice until he goes to music school. Every evening, he spends hours attempting to play one song or another. My father and I call them tunes of misery.

At least Tariku has left us for good. He had cornered me in the living room one afternoon, thinking there was no one home, wanting to touch me places I did not want to be touched. He had not done that for a long time. Once I was old enough to go places on my own, I began making sure that I was never alone in the house with him or that I stayed close to an exit. He caught me off guard that afternoon. I cried and slapped his hands away. I was thinking to myself that I had been foolish all along: telling my father that I once allowed that rotten boy to show me the rude thing and that I allowed him to touch me again on numerous occasions because he threatened to tell on me, and facing the consequences— probably a whipping and extra Bible lessons by Melkamu—would have been less painful than always feeling afraid of being inside my own house.

Tultula appeared next to us out of nowhere on a weekday afternoon in the midst of the dry season when he should be busy harvesting coffee. He had stopped by to greet us on his way back from the veterinary clinic. I saw him look at me sobbing, hitting and pushing away Tariku. Without asking what was going on, as if he had been sent by the Holy Ghost, he picked up Tariku by the throat, his hand almost wrapping around the boy's scrawny neck. He pushed Tariku against the wall and lifted him up. I watched from my corner, stunned by the quick turn of events.

Tultula has big muscles from doing hard labor on his farm and eating as much of the milk and eggs he produces as he wants. Tariku, who is at least seventeen, didn't put up any resistance.

"I am going to kill you and turn myself in," said Tultula.

Tariku was choking, his eyes wide open like a cornered animal.

"You leave this house tomorrow morning. You mention this to no one."

Tultula withdrew his hand and Tariku dropped like a piece of cloth.

Tultula spent the night to ensure Tariku followed his orders. Tariku walked into the living room the next morning carrying his possessions in plastic bags, to tell my father, evading eye contact, that he wanted to go back to his mother. Tultula looked on, sipping coffee, like he knew nothing about the whole affair. We did not speak of what transpired at the time or after. Tultula said to me before he left for his farm that he had promised my mother to look after me, that I should tell him at once if anyone was giving me trouble because he would murder them.

I feel immense relief that Tariku has been cast out of my life. I didn't celebrate for too long. I have learned from life and from my father that the fall of one tyranny is the rise of another.

32.

Tultula

When you live by yourself in the woods, people forget to inform you of important events. After decades of eating with them on holidays, visiting them on Saturdays with offerings from my farm, Lord Asmelash didn't send anyone to tell me about the death. I found out at the market, where I had gone with sacks of onion and fruits loaded onto the back of my donkey. As I unloaded my goods, a woman with a stand next to mine said that she was sorry for my loss. What loss, I said, and as soon as she uttered Ezra's name, I felt my knees turn into water. I steadied myself against my donkey and gathered my strength.

I showed up at the green house wailing, screaming Ezra's name. I entered the tent on the front yard, and there was Ezra, sitting with the men on the veranda, covering his mouth to suppress laughter until he couldn't. My knees finally gave in and I lost myself. When I woke up, Lord Asmelash had my head cradled on his knee, holding a wet towel to my forehead.

I left the village and built myself a house in the woods to get away from all the razor-tongued women who told me that I was a man who refused to stop being a servant. I told them that Lord Asmelash and I would have been friends even if I were never his servant. They kept mocking me, calling me Tultula, a nickname I was given for being a talkative teenager.

My name is not blabbermouth.

My mother named me Ayele Gemeda. I tell people that I will not answer anyone who calls me Tultula. They laugh in my face. The women kept flaring their nostrils at the thought of me pursuing the company of the only people who call me by my name: Lord Asmelash and his family. Don't call him "lord" the village women say. He's no longer anybody's lord; nobody has a lord anymore besides the one in heaven. I want to tell them: when I visit Lord Asmelash, he says to me, Ayele, come here, Abba, sit down. He does not even call his own sons Abba. For a man who was once my master to go beyond calling me by my name, to refer to me as "father." The thought of it alone has made me cry numerous times.

As if driving me away from the village weren't enough, the village women took to calling me a medicine man. They said that I wanted to live on my own to practice witchcraft. That I talked to the leaves and herbs and trees and made concoctions that can heal any illness. That my witchcraft was behind my success as a farmer, that it was the reason I built myself a house with a corrugated tin roof instead of a thatched roof like almost everyone in the village.

The rumors began when I helped treat a few ailing people who came to me with concoctions that my mother had taught me. I am not the only one who knows how to prepare chikugn for people with stomachaches, damakase or ginger roots and feto for those who suffer from coughs. Some women brought children whose heads were full of mysterious wounds. I warmed up the jaw of a dead hedgehog on the stove and pressed it against the children's glands right under their ears. After a few more applications over two weeks, the wounds disappeared as mysteriously as they came. The village people said I was a magic man. I told them there was no magic, that they themselves could do what I did for them. They refuse to believe me, saying that I have the hands of a healer as if that were a compliment, as if they weren't going to turn around and make me out to be a fearsome creature who nurtured a secret relationship with the spirit world.

I delayed marriage at first because I didn't want any woman who didn't know of her strength until she became a widow. I wanted a warrior woman, one who could lead our household, one who could read books and teach me things, like my mistress Degitu, who taught me how to read. The problem is that those women are afraid of revealing themselves as such because people would call them a horse, a woman of poor up-bringing, or a man. Those who are brave enough to reveal themselves are too advanced to look at a minimally educated man like me.

I became like the woman who dropped what she had in her armpit while reaching for the thing in the attic. Stuck in the woods, belonging neither to the village nor to the town. Later, when I began considering that perhaps I should marry anyone, a companion for old age, I realized that most of the young women in the village would be afraid of living with a man who lives in the woods and talks to trees.

The rumors have subsided since I accepted Jesus Christ as my personal savior. People know Protestants do not engage in witchcraft. There are some eligible women at church although none who would want to be stuck in the woods with me. Lord Asmelash has been telling me that it was time to build a house in town and perhaps sell my land to open a shop or some other business there. He said I have enough money in the bank to do that. I was thinking about taking his advice until that Saturday when I walked into his house screaming the wrong son's name, making a fool of myself in front of the whole town.

"I am sorry, my son," said Lord Asmelash.

He's only thirteen or so years older than me. My mother told me she left Baba Gebre's compound right before Lord Asmelash left for school in Addis Ababa. I was born less than a year later. I have heard them say he was twelve when he went to school.

"Our lives have burst asunder again," he said. "I have to be reminded to eat let alone remember to send a messenger boy to you."

It's been weeks but I haven't been able to forgive him. Even after Lord Asmelash sent a note to me saying that he needs me by his side, that he hasn't had the time to fall apart since he has to stand up for his children, especially for the little one. Even after he said that he was not feeling well, that his high blood pressure was threatening to kill him unless he went to the regional hospital soon. I have not been able to move my legs to walk past my fence.

I am only alive by the mercy of my habits: waking up in the morning to fetch water before heading out to pick coffee or water the vegetables. I worry the woods will always be my home as they were in the beginning. That working from sunrise to sunset will be my only family.

When Lord Asmelash helped me up that day and whispered in my ear that it was the youngest boy, Baba Gebre's carbon copy, who had died a few days earlier in an accident, for a brief moment I thought I was going to lose my mind. I do not know why I had readily accepted Ezra's death; it would have been equally tragic: perhaps because that boy was always getting in trouble, making too many enemies everywhere, borrowing money and not paying it back. Little Yonas was the boy everyone thought was going places, the one who was supposed to become a doctor or a pilot and make us all proud. I fell down again groaning. Wishing I were the one who fell off a broken bridge into a raging river full of big rocks.

I returned to my home a few days later. I have been crying every day since then. Not just for the boy but because his death made everything suddenly meaningless. In this bone-deep coldness of late Tikimt, I sit by the fire every evening wrapped in my gabi, telling myself that I don't blame the village people for thinking that I am strange for living alone in the woods. The woods have always been my refuge, my truest family.

My mother left suddenly one morning when I was boy, taking two of my younger siblings with her. She was tired of all the beating and cursing. For all the herbs and leaves she knew intimately, I don't know why she didn't just poison my father. I was about seven and I had never seen my mother leave her duties at home except to go to the market, but my father often accused her of being a whore. He used to beat me up too. I don't know why my mother thought only my younger siblings needed rescuing. The beating increased after my mother's disappearance. My father called me a bastard, told me that he had no reason to feed me, that I must earn my keep. I had to cook, fetch water, and help him at the farm.

It became unbearable soon after. I ran away to the woods near a neighboring village. I did not want to alert the village people to my presence in case my father came looking for me. I stayed in the woods, sleeping on tree branches at night, eating leaves, drinking from a creek. I was malnourished, my belly bloated and my eyelashes full of lice eggs when a farmer's wife who had come to collect firewood found me. I don't know how many weeks had elapsed by then. She took me home, washed, clothed, and fed me. My father never showed up.

I became a shepherd boy for that family for a few years. The wife was like a mother to me, but her husband was harsh. They only had daughters who had been given away in marriage, so the woman was happy to have a boy. My bad luck struck again and she died of an illness. The husband made me do all the work like my father did before him. One of his sheep went missing while I was at home preparing dinner. He blamed me for it, and whipped me harshly with a rope, leaving me with lines of wounds on my back and legs.

I snuck out of the house at dawn and set off by foot for Baba Gebre's village. Every inch of my body was hurting. My mother had always told me about how Baba Gebre took in strays and fed them and gave them a place to live. Perhaps she wanted me to know because she knew she was going to leave someday. I made it from village to village despite the pain and begged for food until I reached Baba Gebre's compound.

My wounds healed in time, but the scars remain. That is another thing that worries me: the better-educated women, the sort I want for a wife, might feel frightened by the rows of scars running up and down my back and legs like ropes sewn into my skin.

33.

My One True Flower

Dear Future Friend in Jimma or Germany or America, Ghana, Lesotho, Poland, Brazil, India, Canada, Malaysia, Cuba, Jamaica, Italy, Pakistan, and all the places:

I just raised Little Yonas from the dead.

He was taken away from me suddenly several weeks ago.

We sit next to each other at the cemetery now: he, wrapped from the neck down in the cotton cloth he was buried in; I, debating whether I should free his hands because, as you know, my brother is a pincher and I can see in his eyes that he's not happy with me. He's upset because I raised him and because I accidentally did something terrible at home today. It's one of those things I do when my mind is clogged with powerful emotions. Please bear with me as I explain everything, my friend, for your understanding is important to me.

I thought a lot about how to deliver the news of my brother's death to you. In my culture, when someone's relative dies in another town, close friends deliver merdo—bad news—at dawn. Nobody I asked knows why merdo is delivered so early. It's hard to explain the source of a tradition that's become as regular as breathing after being practiced unquestioningly for too long. My father said merdo is probably delivered early to ensure the receiver is home, in a comfortable setting.

I considered delaying the delivery of this merdo by talking about other things to slowly ease you in. It felt manipulative, like when my family members hide the truth from me. I feel as though they're always keeping something from me, making a fool of me. Remember how long I waited for my mother to come back *tomorrow*? When I finally realized she wasn't returning, I lost her *and* tomorrow. I fear tomorrow now, like I fear God. I suspect the two might be the same thing.

Little Yonas's death came out of nowhere. You probably knew my mother was dying from the moment I began telling you about her. I was too slow in accepting it. I used to believe that God wouldn't bring me into the world under such bloody circumstances just to deprive me of a mother's love. I continued to believe that for years even after she was gone. Some deaths are slow enough to grant your heart the room it needs to dream of alternative stories.

In Amharic, fiction is called lib-weled—born of the heart. Stories aren't created in the head where math is done. If you made them in your head, the math department would interfere to say, two and two aren't adding up to four in this story, you must stop. That's why you make stories in the heart, far from places of precise calculations, so that you can imagine a hundred scenarios in which your dead mother continues to live. It is easy to make two and two add up to four; what's hard is imagining situations in which they add up to a different number and are true. I think that's why my people say the heart is where bravery and wisdom live. To say that a man doesn't have a heart is to call him a coward. In the tale of the donkey and the dog, the dog says that the donkey was eaten by a hyena because he didn't have a heart, for possessing a heart would have meant having the wisdom not to alert predators to his location.

Degitu's slow death gave my heart enough room to use its bravery and wisdom to create stories of survival. I know it sounds like a contradiction when I chastise my family for the story they created for me—"Degitu is coming back tomorrow"—only to turn around and appreciate my own creations. Isn't that the same thing, you must be thinking, wasn't your family giving you an alternative story to protect you from the harshness of life? That is true, my friend. But I want to be the one who forges my own instruments of survival. I want my heart to be the headquarters of my stories.

That's why I want you to hear about the death of Little Yonas in a straightforward manner and make your own decisions about how to survive it. Life doesn't always provide warnings. You deserve to experience that fundamental truth. You deserve the freedom from false hope.

Little Yonas died suddenly in the fourth week of Meskerem, over six weeks ago. I had begun writing to you the day he died, before my afternoon shift at school began. Even after I stopped writing to go to school, I continued in my head, as I often do. I stopped when I learned of his death. I have decided to include that partial letter here, along with what I was thinking while at school and on my way home, instead of duplicating my efforts.

Dear Future Friend:

I haven't seen Little Yonas in months but he is coming home today. I wish I didn't have to go to school, but I can't think of a proper excuse to give my teachers. I am going to run home at recess to see him briefly.

There's another exciting news in our house: Lulseged, the engineer from America, has decided to marry my sister Weder. I thought I was going to die from happiness when I heard about it because it means my dream of going to Washington, D.C., to get inside the radio and also get as far away as possible from all the bullies and lack of money is a step closer to coming true. My father and I went to the call center to phone Weder after we heard the news. She said that I will be the first person she will be taking to America.

More excitement followed when Little Yonas wrote to say he's taking his annual vacation to come stay with us for two months. He said his German pen pal is going to sponsor him to travel to Germany, but that, even if that falls through, he is going to hitchhike to South Africa to get a job and send money for my private education. He says he cannot stand being just an evangelist anymore. The man who used to terrorize me in the name of Jesus has been terrorized by poverty and boredom in that isolated town.

My father wrote Little Yonas and told him to be patient until Weder goes to America, but he's restless. We send our letters to Little Yonas through employees of the Coffee & Tea Authority from his town who come to the branch office in the Small Town to collect their salaries or submit reports. Little Yonas comes to town with them sometimes; he hates crossing that river alone. They ride horses or mules to the riverbank, and if the river is too full and the bridge in bad condition, they leave the animals behind and cross holding on to hanging ropes.

I'm more eager than usual to see Little Yonas. I need someone to help me improve my English fast. Weeks ago, my English and *homeroom teacher, Teshome, came into our classroom, sixth grade section A, with two boys from section B, to ask what the definition of the word "drudgery" is. Students in section B didn't know the answer. He bragged that we, his homeroom students, would know the definition. He brought witnesses with him. He stood before us, grinning with pride, sure that we would have the answer. Not a single person, not even me, knew the definition. Some of my classmates were staring at me as if to say: have you been bringing that dictionary of yours to class just to show off? Yes.*

Teshome told one of the boys he brought with him to get him a stick. We buried our faces in folded arms on the desks and offered him our backs. He didn't spare anyone.

I have been dreaming of Teshome coming into class with more words I've never heard of. Only Little Yonas can save me from this particular horror.

In social sciences period right before recess, we are listening to a distance education broadcast on the radio. I'm waiting for the bell to ring so that I can sprint to our house to see Little Yonas. I bet my deskmate can hear my heart beat. We must be halfway through the period.

Our math teacher opens the door and signals for the social sciences teacher to go to him. The two whisper to each other. The social sciences teacher walks to one of my classmates and whispers something. She goes outside. He tells me to accompany her home; something bad has happened at her house. I follow her and say not to worry: something bad must have happened at my house. That's what you are supposed to say to people who will be grieving soon— tell them everything is fine until they are in a safe place to receive the bad news. She looks away from me.

I realize something bad has indeed happened at my house when she takes a right at the main street instead of left. I see women wearing netelas upside down. I hear wailing when we reach the mosque, past the old government store.

"Who died?" I ask my classmate.

She doesn't respond.

It better not be my father because I'm going to break the planet.

The front yard of my house is chaos. All the Women are here. The ones who hate us, the ones who like us, the ones who feel nothing about us. Wailing. Flailing their arms. My child my child my child. All the Orthodox Christians who said we should go back to America. All the young Muslim men who threw stones at our house. My brother my brother. I bet even those who led the defecation campaign on our church grounds are here. Those who burned our church.

Zinash sits on the front stair crying. "My child my child, what will I tell your mother?"

Her son Samuel—the one who scored 4.0 on his school-leaving exams under suspicious circumstances—has been running her hotel. He left the university after only a week. He has been traveling to Addis Ababa frequently to fetch new prostitutes for the hotel.

"Who died, Eteyé Zinash?"

She ignores me.

I walk into the house, past the young men who cry in unison, their voices making a buzz like a thousand beetles. I look at one of them, a young Muslim man from the neighborhood. He is as black as Ezra, his beard a thick line from ear to ear. He looks away from me like everyone else. I know he went to school with Little Yonas. If

he is here crying, it can't be my aunt who's dead. It can't be my
father either because Zinash is crying, my child my child. Is it
Melkamu? Or did one of Ezra's lenders finally resort to murder?
  Shouts of wayoo wayoo are everywhere.
  What will I do without you, my child? My child my child.
  I don't see my father or Melkamu. The crowd has spilled over to
the backyard. I sit on the ledge around the old storage room. When
my mother died, they say funeral attendance was second only to
that of the member of parliament who represented our town in the
imperial government. Maybe all the people who hated my mother
just wanted to be her friend. Or they wanted to ensure she was
finally in the ground.
  The house erupts in more screams. I push past people in the
hallway and the living room to go to the veranda. Our relatives
from the Medium Town have arrived in a minibus, screaming,
wailing. Out of Etabeba Haregua's mouth, I hear the words
Yonasé, Yonasé, Yonasé, my child my child, ooou-ooou-ooou!
Somebody—I don't know who—grabs me and I yell, let me
go let me go let me go but I don't know to what country to what
place to what planet one can go to hide from God and this life
but I want to go—

I stopped writing then. I don't think I ever imagined Little Yonas's death. If I had been given a choice, I would have chosen to go before him.

The rest of my siblings and relatives arrived in the days after. We continued with grieving rituals for the next three weeks. Grown women generally walked around, wailing and flailing their arms, shouting things about the dead person. I was the only child among them doing the same.

MY BROTHER MY SHIELD

WHO WILL PROTECT ME

MY BROTHER MY FRIEND

YOU PROMISED TO VISIT

MY BROTHER MY TEACHER

WHO WILL TEACH ME ENGLISH

MY BROTHER MY CHILD

YOU SHOULDN'T GO BEFORE ME

Some women gave me bewildered looks, especially when I referred to Little Yonas as my child. They probably thought I had lost my mind. I did not care because I didn't think I should keep my mind anyway.

IN THE WEEKS after his death, I made two attempts to write to you. Not because I was ready to communicate rigorously again, but I felt an urgent need to apologize.

Dear Future Friend,

How are you? I am fine, thank you.

I am not fine fine, but that is what my brother said I should say when writing letters. You can also guess how I must be because your house, my heart, has been destroyed by grief. I have never been without shelter; I can only imagine your troubles. Maybe you were happy you didn't have to listen to me tell my story endlessly. Everyone says I am talkative. I am grateful for all the years you have been my friend when most others wouldn't.

I am sorry for the chaos in my heart. I have never been this sad in my life. I think that God creates people—or at least me—in order to tear up their hearts and see what comes out. I don't know what He found in mine, but I hope He is unhappy. I hope there was a pepper bomb in my heart that exploded in His face.

I am writing to tell you that it is going to be a while before you can get back into my heart. It is not habitable at the moment. I will write in two weeks and give you an update. I hope you find some place to survive until then.

Dear Future Friend,

It's been three weeks since we buried Little Yonas. I wanted to confess to you that I asked to be put in the grave with him. I asked politely to set myself apart from the women who often make a spectacle out of requesting to be buried with their loved ones. I wanted the men pushing soil onto my brother's coffin to know that I was sincere. I didn't ask to be buried because I didn't think you and my father and my siblings were not worth living for. I just couldn't bear the sadness.

During the funeral service at church, the preacher said we should not be mourning; we should be delighted because my brother is in a better place. I wanted to go to his daughter, who was in attendance, to choke her to death in front of everyone and ask the preacher if he was delighted.

I said to my family: Where are all those prophets who came to visit our church from Addis Ababa and told Little Yonas that God had big plans for him? That he was going to prosper and become a

refuge for the downtrodden? Where are they now? Where was their
God when a flash flood tore apart a bridge, sending my brother
flying into a river full of massive rocks? Everyone else who fell into
the river survived except for Little Yonas.

Do you know what my brother Melkamu said about that? That
Little Yonas had been taken away because he was straying from the
path God had wanted him to travel on, that he had been called to
serve but decided to leave his job as an evangelist in pursuit of
education. That God's promises for us only materialize if we obey
Him. He said this in the midst of sobbing like a little boy. No
matter how many times this God of his shatters his heart, he cannot
seem to find the courage to hold Him accountable for anything. I
say it's time we raised an army to overthrow this God person and
end His reign of terror.

The shape of my heart has been altered. I understand if you don't
want to deal with the discomfort of contorting yourself to fit in it.

SIX WEEKS AFTER we buried Little Yonas, a relative from a faraway
town arrived yesterday morning. He came into our house wailing, shouting my brother's name. My siblings, except for Melkamu, have left. Our
relatives are gone. No more sleeping on mattresses, waking up at dawn
to wail. None of us shaved our heads or wore black. Our Protestantism
discourages such practices, something my family didn't know when Degitu died.

Tayitu, my family's former maid, and her children have been an unexpected source of comfort over the past week. They moved in with us temporarily after Tayitu's husband became impossible to live with. She and

her two children have been sleeping on mattresses in my room. Her middle child, Mitike, who is about my age, sleeps with me. My father is not happy; he worries that I might get a skin disease. He doesn't even approve of me sharing beds with my cousins. He's been too ill with hypertension and gastritis, too tired from grief to argue with me about it.

The late-arriving relative walked around our living room wailing. I have stopped crying. All that remains is anger. I sat in the living room, ignoring the man, worrying about my father, who was waiting for the bus to make a long-overdue visit to the regional hospital.

"I'm burning," said my father. "I'm burning I'm burning I can't bear it anymore."

I couldn't bear it anymore either. I went to the veranda. I wished to disappear from life somehow. Or to locate God, arrest Him, and liberate everyone from His madness.

Later in the evening, Mitike and I lay in bed facing each other. Her siblings were asleep on the mattresses across the room, her mother in the scullery. I wanted to pray for my father, who was at the hospital by then, but I didn't know to whom to send my hopes and prayers anymore.

I stared at Mitike's sideburn, a tuft of soft hair reaching her left earlobe. I had only met her a few times before they moved in with us about a week ago. Their village is too far away for frequent visits.

"Do you think the curse did it?" said Mitike.

"What?"

"My mother said your family is cursed. Do you think the curse killed your brother?"

I responded by pinching her nose. I held it between my thumb and forefinger and tightened my grip. For several moments, she seemed to forget that she could breathe through her mouth. That gave me an idea: I covered her mouth with my free hand before she opened it to say that I was hurting her. Next I was on top of her, actively trying to choke her. She dug into my cheeks with both hands. Her older brother woke up because of the scuffle and her muffled moans and yelped. Tayitu ran into the room, pulled us apart, and started yelling at us. Mitike protested, saying that I was the demon who tried to kill her for no reason.

Melkamu heard the commotion and came in. Mitike gave him her side of the story; I did not protest. I stood in a corner with my bruised cheeks burning. My brother told me to sleep in my father's room. He said he was going to deal with me in the morning. I knew he was going to whip me. I wasn't afraid in that moment. I was filled with a special kind of rage.

I KEPT ROLLING from one end of my father's bed to another to exhaust myself to sleep. Normally sleep held the promise of another dawn. All I had to look forward to last night was being whipped by Melkamu. My father wasn't around to save me. He was at the regional hospital dealing with illnesses brought on by the unbearable sadness of losing his youngest and brightest son. That son died while trying to rescue me from bad education. Little Yonas was trying to fill the gap created by the death of our mother, who used to fight for her children.

Our mother died because her cancer was discovered late. She was distracted by my conception. The bearded gynecologist almost figured out she was suffering from uterine cancer. Had she not discovered immediately afterward that she was pregnant with me, she might have figured out a way to go abroad and have that cancerous uterus removed. That uterus suddenly became too precious to even think about touching because it was carrying me. After I was born, something about the process of my birth stopped the bleeding for months, tricking my mother into thinking that she had been healed. By the time the missionary doctor discovered her cancer, it had already spread into her intestine and become unstoppable.

Is this not what the Waa Himaa had said? That I was going to come in out of nowhere like a flash flood, leaving the meaning of that for my father to figure out on his own. I have never heard anybody say good things about flash floods. All I hear is that they tear down bridges and drown people. One of them just threw my brother from a poorly built bridge.

Am I supposed to believe it was a coincidence that a Waa Himaa called me a flash flood and a literal flash flood just killed my brother? What about the rest of my siblings who have been suffering because of me? We found out that Beza disappeared from our lives because she was too ashamed to tell us that she had married a nonbeliever, Yeneneh, with whom she has a child. We were too enveloped in the loss of our Little Yonas to realize that we had also been grieving all the years of Beza's life that we missed. I am sure my father has been feeling sad and responsible, driving up his blood pressure. Before I took up all his attention, Beza was my father's friend. Maybe she felt she didn't have anything left at home when she decided to disappear.

My head was spinning all night. I began frightening myself thinking that maybe the curse inside me can work with forces of nature—like the flash flood—to achieve its goals. What else is it planning? If Jesus Christ cannot break it, what will?

I TIPTOED OUT of the house shortly after the birds began chirping. I went to the outhouse where I had been keeping my gasoline to keep the house from catching fire. I peed and went to the kitchen to wash my hands and grab a match. I went back to the outhouse, which is several meters away from the chicken coop. The chicken coop is in the same detached building housing our kitchen, the old maid's room, and the old storage room, the latter two of which have tenants in them.

I started pouring gasoline around the exterior of the corrugated tin walls of the outhouse. I wasn't entirely sure that I wanted to burn myself. I also didn't care if that happened, because something had to be done to mark the death of Little Yonas. It made me angry that people thought two weeks of wailing was a sufficient response to his death. I wanted time to stop, for the sun to change colors, for the moon to turn black. None of that happened and everyone is back to being how they have always been. I do not agree with any of it, with this new living arrangement that leaves Little Yonas alone in the forest where hyenas laugh at night while I sleep in a warm bed. I disagree. I disagree. I protest. Against God. Against life.

I lit a match, threw it at a wall that's been drenched in gasoline, and went inside the outhouse. We were in the dry season, so nothing should dampen the fire, but it was taking a while to catch because of the tin walls. I stood in the outhouse thinking about the possibility of dying in that fire in a matter of minutes. I realized it had always been like that: the possibility of dying in an instant. That fire was a joke compared to all the fires that have ever burned us, all the fires that are coming to burn us in the future. Compared to the ever-raging fire that life itself is. All of us have always been standing inside a small enclosed space, waiting for that fire of life to reach us.

I thought of a time when, as a young child, I sat next to my father on one of the benches on our veranda, my legs swinging in the air because they couldn't reach the floor.

"I love you from here all the way to Addis Ababa," I said.

"That is a long way."

"It is."

"I love you from here all the way to Gondar," he said. "That's twice the distance."

"Then I love you from here to Washington, D.C."

I won.

I thought that maybe that was the point of living: to get three minutes with your father on the veranda. If you get more and more three minutes, you're winning and your father is winning. If you die, your father is not going to win. I wondered how the burning of the outhouse was going to make my father feel. How the burning of me will make him feel. I admit I didn't think that far. I was only thinking about marking my brother's death and ending the curse.

It was the chickens in the coop that pulled me out of my reverie in the end. The stupid fire, instead of coming inside the outhouse, had found it easier to catch the dry grass between the outhouse and the detached building. The space between the chicken coop and the outhouse had been overtaken by weeds and grass in the rainy season. My father usually hires Abba Lemma to clear the weeds at the end of the rainy season, but he had been distracted by grief and illness.

When I stepped out of the outhouse, I saw the fire climbing the wall of the chicken coop, which wasn't sealed with wattle and daub like the other rooms. Seeing the fire through the gaps in the wall, the chickens flew off the high wooden rails they spent the nights on, cackling loudly as if a fox had entered the room. It was only a matter of minutes before people heard the commotion and came out. I felt stupid. I had endangered my father's livelihood. The fire might go on to the main house unless it was stopped in time. I screamed and ran into the big house, fire fire fire fire.

Tayitu stepped outside, put her fingers in her ears, and screamed, ooo-ouuu ooooouuu ooouuu! Over and over. It was the alarm bell for the neighborhood. By the time people began shouting over fences asking what was going on, I was out the main door, down the front stair, across our front yard. I turned left and picked up my pace.

I BLAZED PAST ST. MARY'S, where passersby pause to bow and pay respects. I gave Mary both middle fingers. People say we are being punished because we turned our backs on her. I was so angry that I even gave the middle finger to a passing donkey.

It is written that we can heal the sick and raise the dead in Jesus's name. If that God of Israel, if that Jesus Christ of the Americans that we have suffered so much for is real, He should come down from His useless throne and do one thing to repay us for all that we have endured in His name. He must show His face to me today or I shall spend the rest of my life exposing Him for the enormous lie that He is.

I began feeling the earth rumble beneath me in a way that was familiar but I couldn't entirely recall. Our church's cemetery, like our church, is in the middle of the forest. I turned right when I reached the orphanage at the edge of town and picked up my pace even more, so everything was a blur except the birds I saw falling off trees, landing along my path. I remembered the time I saw angels falling after my mother's wailing shook heaven. Maybe that was the rumbling I was remembering. I arrived at the cemetery breathless, my rubber shoes burning my feet. I took them off and fell on my back. The earth was shaking beneath me, shaking me with it like I had a hundred cases of malaria. I pointed both middle fingers at the sky and told God it was time to come the fuck down and face me.

I heard the crunching of leaves as Little Yonas emerged from his grave.

———

MY BROTHER IS wrapped in his burial cloth. I unwrapped his head but his hands are tied up. He's been scolding me for setting our house on fire. He's also upset that I raised him from the dead. "You shouldn't have done this," he says.

I don't care what he thinks.

"You should not interfere with God's work."

"Fuck God."

He can't believe me. "Who are you? Who raised you?"

I know I am not freeing his hands now.

"Come home with me," I say.

"I can't. Someone has to be with our mother."

"Take me with you then."

"What about our father?"

I hate him so much because this is true. What about our father?

Little Yonas tries to wiggle his way out of the cloth.

I begin unwrapping the cloth. He can pinch me all he wants. One last time. I begin at his shoulders. He's naked like the day he came out of our mother. He was in her womb last before me. Maybe he left pieces of himself in there that are a part of me.

He pulls and holds me to his chest.

My heart will never be the same again, my friend. It won't be a place for someone pure. It is too crooked, too bent out of shape. If purity is what you seek, I am no longer for you.

"I have homework for you," says Little Yonas. "I need you to write my pen pal, Gisele, and tell her that I am gone." He tells me that I am the best letter writer in our family. Those are my brother's words, not mine.

"You must go home," he says.

He tells me that I should go help with putting out the fire.

"I am ashamed of myself."

I don't even care about what Melkamu is going to do to me. It is the shame that I can't bear. Having to face my father eventually.

"Go to Tultula," says Little Yonas. "He will speak for you."

I put my shoes on. I cup my brother's face in my hands and kiss his eyes, cheeks, and nose as if he were a little boy. I give him one last hug before I turn around.

TULTULA FED ME fried eggs with injera. He boiled half a kettle of milk and kept nagging me to finish drinking it. I was famished when I reached his home around noon. He was in shock that I went to him alone.

I told him everything that happened that day and begged him to keep me with him until my father returned from the hospital. He said my brother would be too worried about me, that he would call my father at the hospital and worsen his situation. Besides, he wanted to help put out the fire in case it was active.

Our house was swarmed by people of our town, who had come out with buckets full of water to put out the fire. In this town, homes are so close to each other that, unless everyone got together to stop a fire immediately, we risk losing tens of homes at once. Not enough people arrived at first, so the whole of the chicken coop and the kitchen were gone. The old maid's room, where a tenant lived, was partially damaged. Part of our backyard was full of household items removed from our tenants' rooms. The exterior walls of the outhouse had been charred. Melkamu found an empty gasoline jerrican outside and already had the idea that someone had set the fire.

I confessed upon arrival. Melkamu led me into his room and told me not to leave. He was going to come back later to start the process of exorcism. I obeyed calmly. I too want any and all evil spirits to leave me.

34

God

Turn around, little child. My face hasn't been something to look at since Cain bashed his brother's head with a stone. Here is a special kerchief to cover your nose and mouth. I am pungent.

I hear that you are on trial for being mad or possessed or defective or whatever it is that your brother says you are. I am here to pay for it in kind, to be on trial before you. Since the beginning of time, little one, the Law of Love has required me to pay for the cost of maintaining the System that makes love possible. As such, when Cain bashed Abel's head, the stone had to go into my head too. On my first-ever visit to a battlefield to comfort a wounded soldier, the only son of a blind widow, an arrow went through another soldier's neck and into mine. You can't see that arrow because of all the billions of arrows and bullets and missiles that I have had to take into my body since then. All the bombs that ever dropped are lodged right below my rib cage and let me tell you: the fire has never stopped raging; the mothers have never stopped wailing. And the stench, little child, there are no words.

I have asked myself why I made all this. I used to regret it all more often in the past. I almost flooded out the earth once. I remind myself of how it was before the beginning of time, before I invented love, when I was alone in the Dark Nothing, afflicted with a merciless thirst that would never go away or kill me. I tried to eliminate myself on numerous occasions but I always came back to the Dark Nothing with the merciless thirst. I tell myself it is worth putting one's body and soul through such unspeakable pain if it meant escape from eternal aloneness, if it meant feeling a sliver of warmth in my heart. You and the devil want to know how I became God, who gave me my power. I want you to know that I am God because I embraced the devastation that comes with making love possible.

Little child, you say that I must have lost my mother to be the cruel being that you think I am. I wish! Losing a mother would have meant that I had one at some point, that there was some love, even as tiny as a mustard seed, inside the Dark Nothing. I once sent a version of myself to earth, like an elaborate rhetorical thought balloon, or like a theatrical play. I did it upon the advice of a sage—a sort of therapist. It was supposed to be an exercise, to try to see if I remember anything about my childhood, supposing I had any. For a being who imagined light while living in the Dark Nothing, I couldn't bring myself to imagine a proper relationship with a mother. All I could see myself doing was going to the temple to challenge the rabbis as a teenager and so on. Then I was being crucified. Even in an exercise, I could only think of suffering.

I know nothing of having a mother, little child. You don't know what I would do to have somebody tell me stories about what things my mother did to save me from starvation, what crimes she committed to protect me from conscription. How my alcoholic father changed himself just for me. Do you think your father's religion is Protestantism, little one? Protestantism is merely the excuse; his real religion is you.

Let me tell you something, you girl: people think that the devil was expelled from heaven for challenging me, for questioning my power. What those people don't understand is that the freedom to question me is a core requirement of the Law of Love, by which I am bound if I am to continue living outside the Dark Nothing, enjoying the benefits of feeling and witnessing love.

You see, little child, when I invented love in order to escape the Dark Nothing, I had to create a System to facilitate love. Everything was designed to make love and its expression possible. All the mountains and rivers that you see are imitating the world inside you, the obstacles you must overcome in order to become a devoted lover. Without mountains to climb and rivers to swim across to get to the ones you love, how could you make it known to them how much they mean to you? How could you write the love poems and letters?

How long will you walk to be with the ones you love, little child?

Beyond the physical world, there was one core requirement for the successful exercise of love: freedom. The parties involved in a loving relationship must be free of duress. That is the main reason why I cannot show myself to humanity—it isn't just because I am ugly and pungent. It is because seeing me might influence their choice. That would be breaking the Law of Love. I have revealed myself to you, little child, because you have already established that your disbelief in me does not come from thinking that I do not exist, but that even if I existed, I do not deserve your respect. You have shown me that you are not afraid to tell me to jump off a cliff, and, little child, I do not know how to express the joy I feel seeing you be so free. The only thing that makes me happier than being outside the Dark Nothing is the prospect of convincing a free person to choose love.

You have been obsessed with your freedom since before the beginning of time, since you were merely an idea in my mind. You heard your father pray, saying that he wanted you to be free more than he wanted life itself. You became so obsessed with that idea that you ran across time, across millennia and centuries, screaming, amen amen amen, urging me to break the rules of time and life to introduce you to him.

Some children don't want to be born. The sight of me causes them to feel deep, unbearable sadness, and they say, we can't leave God alone like this. They are the melancholic sort; small creatures with hearts as big as the universe. Some of them return to me shortly after birth, before their memory of me fades. Millions of them gather inside my nostrils to play, mistaking my nose for a cave. If it weren't for the delicious smell of their heads, little child, the stench of burning flesh would have taken me down long ago.

You were not like those children. You were selfish, single-minded about meeting your father. I am a god who has created heaven and earth and sea and forest and all the creatures who live in them simply by saying, let there be, but I have yet to figure out the mystery of the bond between some fathers and daughters. You wouldn't give me rest: as I went from house to house to sit next to mothers nursing sick children, as I stood next to an abused wife waiting for the blow headed for her to come for me too, you ran across my mind so selfishly, yelling, amen amen to your father's prayer.

You think that I make the rain come, that I decide when the rivers swell or dry up, that I make the earth quake and the volcano erupt, but those processes were put in motion at the beginning of time. I cannot interfere with them so as to not tip the balance this and that way, breaking the Law of Love. The only thing I have control over is the Department of Rare Prayers, an office tasked with managing and responding to prayers sent by two or more people in complete agreement about what they are asking for. Oftentimes, people gather to pray about the same thing, but their hearts diverge. You've heard of the husband who prayed for rain so he could start plowing, whereas his wife prayed for sunshine so she could sun-dry her biqil. Most prayers are like that, driven by narrow desires, contradictory, or demanding interference in the System.

A Rare Prayer is in itself a manifestation of love: two or more people must join their hearts, in complete agreement over their prayer, without the slightest division between them. The prayer cannot be one that breaks the Law of Love, such as one calling for interference in the System governing the whole world. Most importantly, the prayer must be bigger than each individual's selfish desires: it must be a prayer that leads to the facilitation of more love. You and your father prayed for your freedom, the purest kind of prayer, for free people are most prepared to choose me, to choose love. The presence of free people is the basic requirement for love to exist.

Do you see, little child, why I could not have expelled the devil into the Dark Nothing because he challenged me, because he was too free? I could not have expelled him even if I wanted to; I do not have the power. It is the System, which was created to facilitate love, that automatically expels those who do not choose love. Not as punishment, but as a fulfillment of their choice not to participate in love.

The devil was expelled into the Dark Nothing because he wanted to use his freedom, his beauty and gifts, for himself alone.

There are three types of free creatures:

The first group includes those who, like the devil, want to make their gifts, including their freedom, all about themselves. They use their freedom to abandon their communities, to avoid engaging in the exercise of love, which comes with heavy costs as much as blessings. You must understand this, my little one: love and the risk of heart-shattering loss go together. The ultimate purpose of life is love. Death is the frame of love, and its unpredictability the wall upon which the whole frame hangs.

If death did not exist, love would be cheapened—it would become something you do not have to take seriously until you turn a thousand years old or never. Your lives would be empty of the tensions generated by responsibility, the tensions that keep you moving along like a story.

If, on the other hand, people came with expiration dates printed on them, they would neglect love until the end. The fear of deadlines would turn into duress.

Death, a necessary part of life, becomes a weapon because of time and space. When a person threatens to take your life, they are not threatening to do to you what life wasn't already going to do to you eventually. The real threat is about taking your time away and confining you to a grave. You counter that threat by increasing the value of the time and space already in your hands. By understanding that three minutes and a hundred years are ultimately the same thing, as are being confined to a prison cell and being free to explore the world. The question is, what will you do with that time and space: will you choose love, little child?

The existence of death is what makes the present precious enough to move people toward goodness and other expressions of love. Even then, you can see how unfocused people are, living their lives as if they have eternity, perpetually postponing their apologies, putting off the completion of their love letters, endlessly hesitating, threatening to send me over the fucking edge.

The second group of free people use freedom to break others. Unlike the devil, they do not abandon the people they are supposed to care for. They are some of the most affectionate creatures. They are so obsessed with their concern for others that they cannot see when their hugs cross the line into suffocation. They will break and mangle the people they love to make them fit some mold. Many of them oppress their children in my name, and those children might profess to choose me but their hearts are either in full rebellion or too mangled out of shape, too afraid, to even figure out what they want. That is a direct violation of the Law of Love.

The third group of free people are those who find balance between maintaining their independence and staying for those they love. Those who do not use their freedom to suppress others. Those who work for the freedom of others so as to facilitate the conditions necessary for love. Those are the people I want to multiply and fill the earth.

I feel so sad when you call me a dictator, little child. When you accuse me of not giving humans multiple gods to choose from. Isn't fear another god? Isn't indecisiveness in the face of love another god? Isn't selfishness another god? Every single day, people are given a thousand things to choose from; I, Love, am only one of them. Love requires freedom, and freedom can only be exercised where there are true alternatives to choose from.

It is not possible for me to be a dictator for I am love. I do not blame you for thinking otherwise because my words have been twisted throughout millennia. Even on those rare occasions when I am allowed to approach some people—like you—and tell them my story, the final product is either a misinterpretation or unclear. Others take those stories and twist them even further. I cannot decide the words they use to describe me. That would be breaking the Law of Love.

Take the Bible, for example, one of the books attributed to me. It says that God is love, which is the truest thing ever said about me. There are many truths in that book, but so much of it is propaganda pamphlets designed to justify the killing of kings by aspiring kings. The persecution of people in the name of sin so as to increase a priest's reach of power.

I ask you, little child, to take the truest thing about me from that book—that I am love—and scrutinize everything else in it to see if it is consistent with that. If it is consistent with the basic rule of love: where people are not free to choose, there can be no real love.

I must leave now, little child. I must go to the Department of Rare Prayers. There's a father in Argentina, praying for his unborn daughter's freedom. The child is running across my mind, yelling, amen amen, giving me no rest. I must pull the strings and push the buttons to answer their prayer. It is the only change the Law of Love allows me to make to the System, for changes made in answer to a Pure Prayer are considered an enhancement rather than interference.

Would you like to kiss me good-bye, little child? I know my face is full of arrows, unsent love letters, man-made famine, hazardous waste. You can do it from a distance; it's the thought of affection that counts. You can kiss me if you want, little child. You can kiss me anytime.

35

Exhibit Z

I t felt good to be imprisoned by my brother at first. I was no longer responsible for protecting anybody from anything. I myself needed saving from possession by evil spirits or mental illness. My brother cannot decide what my problem is. I have been in his room for three days, allowed to leave only to go to the outhouse or to wash myself. Tayitu brings me food three times a day, but only dinner for my brother, who has been fasting. I write in my exercise book when he leaves me to take a break.

I tried to describe God's face and failed spectacularly. All I can tell you is that it's the ugliest thing I have ever seen and I have seen a pile of cow dung. I didn't understand everything God said. I found some of the things He said compelling: that He's someone who once suffered from unbearable loneliness and has been suffering in a different way for trying to change His circumstances. I feel deeply sorry for Him if the thing I saw was actually God.

When my brother returns from his breaks, he commands the spirits within me to reveal their names, where they entered me, why they entered me, and so on. Neither the spirits nor I respond to this. Our silence agitates him. At one point, he forgot that he was in the midst of prayer and said to the spirits, "Your mother." I had to pinch myself to keep from bursting in laughter and irritating him even more. He hasn't shaved in days, and he keeps losing his voice.

My situation has to be resolved before my father returns from the hospital any day now. My father might put an end to the exorcism, in which case I would keep on being possessed. I suspect what Melkamu fears more than the possibility of me being possessed is the possibility of me staying unexplained. He must diagnose my illness and cure me quickly.

Tayitu tried to persuade him to end the exorcism. I heard them talking in the hallway.

"Did you think your mother was possessed?" she asked him.

"What?"

"The child is as crazy as her mother was. And her grandmother, did you not meet her?"

"None of them ever tried to burn their homes."

"That's because they had somebody to tame them a little."

Melkamu told her to stay out of our family's business.

He told Tultula the same thing: that he should know his place and go back to his house. That would have angered my father. I wrote the notes my father had been sending to Tultula, begging him to come and stay with us for a while. After Tultula came to our house screaming Ezra's name, he stayed for a few days and hurt his hand while cutting firewood: a strip of wood came flying at him and he caught it reflexively. There was a big cut on his right palm. My father brought out alcohol and gauze and sat on a stool across from Tultula. I watched my father keep Tultula's hand after cleaning and covering the wound, examining the back for several moments.

I told my sisters about it and Weder said that our father must have done that because Degitu put it in his head a long time ago. Degitu once examined Tultula's hand and became convinced that the resemblance between his nails and our father's—their distinct roundness and visible blood vessels—must have meant that Tultula is our half brother. Our parents had a fight about it: Degitu questioned our father about the timing of the departure of Tultula's mother from Baba Gebre's compound. Our father said he only remembered that it was right before he left for school in Addis Ababa. She asked him if he had any sexual relations with the woman and he became upset. He said he was only a boy of eleven or twelve at the time. She told him boys that age could produce sperm. Degitu thought our father probably had many children out there, that he neglected his family because he felt guilty about all the children he couldn't be there for.

I was thinking how I want to find all those people and make them my proper siblings as one defense against death. I used to want to reduce the number of people I love in order to protect my heart from destruction. I don't think the devastation of living will ever stop. I might as well increase my enjoyment of love.

I wrote about all this in my exercise book. Mitike, the girl I tried to suffocate, brought my exercise book and pens to me on the first day of my imprisonment. She snuck in when Melkamu wasn't around to ask what I wanted. She was sorry for me despite witnessing my insanity firsthand. She said her mother told her that I don't know how to behave properly because I didn't have a mother to shape me. Mitike asked me to tell her if I wanted anything else today. I asked her to steal money from my father's nightstand and buy me bread and tea. She said it must be true that I am insane, that I don't seem to learn anything. I told her that my father is keeping two hundred birr that belongs to me. She refused. She said she was going to ask her mother for money and bring me my favorite snack later.

I might be insane or possessed, but sometimes I accidentally do good things, such as bringing Tayitu and her children to our house. I was on my way to the market to buy onions when I saw Tayitu in her tattered work attire, sitting outside the police station staring into space, her head bleeding. Her children sat next to her on the ground. I ran up to her to ask what happened, and she said her husband had hit her. She didn't know where to go after filing a police report. I chastised her for not coming to our house. It's what I had seen older people do.

"You're family," I said. "Don't you know that?"

I dragged her and her children to our house. I could tell my father wasn't happy with what I had done. He believes that a home belongs to God and that we should host people in need for short periods. He didn't think Tayitu and her children would leave us soon. I think he has changed his mind, seeing how their presence offsets the deafening silence after all the wailing of the previous weeks. We took Tayitu to the clinic to get her bleeding head patched up.

I turn a new page in my exercise book while I wait for Mitike to bring my snack. I write a title: (Continued) Ways of Defeating Death by Making Time and Space Big.

MELKAMU IS BACK from his break. He's sitting by a table near the window reading the Bible and writing in his notebook. I feel sorry for my brother sometimes. Unlike me, who is on the opposite end of the spectrum, he never allows himself to be crazy. Maybe if Ezra was responsible or if our father was assertive about which way he wants to lead our family, Melkamu wouldn't have taken on the role of Minister of Rules and Rigidness. Maybe he would admit that he feels a little guilty for insisting that Little Yonas become an evangelist, for finding him a job in the bridgeless town.

I can't say any of these things to him because number one: I am not supposed to know better than adults; and number two: even if I weren't a child, I had just thrown away any credibility I had by setting the house on fire. That's one downside of limitless freedom no one but God would tell you about: you can't even help the people you love when they need you if you're regularly undermining your credibility.

Mitike brings me bread and sweet tea.

"God bless you," I say to her as she leaves.

Melkamu looks up from his Bible. I can sense that his struggle to figure me out has continued. It is important to the Ministry of Rules and Rigidness that everyone is reduced to a simple explanation.

I break a piece of bread and dunk it in tea. I think about Mitike's generosity. I imagine Tayitu unfurling her waist scarf to take out one birr, which is probably a tenth or so of the money she managed to escape with the day her husband hit her. I think about all the suffering she has had to walk through in order to be here giving me comfort. She caught her husband having sex with another woman in their cornfield. Instead of feeling ashamed, he became defensive and reached for his cane. She ran, but he caught up with her and struck her on the head. The husband came to my father to beg for his wife back. My father sent him away, telling him he'll call the police and report him for harassment if he came here again. My father said the drunkard has to suffer for a while before talks of reconciliation begin.

"What are you doing?" asks Melkamu.

I am chewing slowly, savoring every delicious moment. It must have confused my brother; he's used to watching me destroy bread and tea in no time.

"I am stretching time," I say.

I take a new bite and wonder how many years I can stretch this moment into.

"What does that mean?"

"Last week, I saw a woman coming out of a bus using a folding hand fan. I imagined a future in which that woman throws away the fan because it's old. I realized that we're all like that fan: ultimately throwable. There's no one out there with specific plans for each of us. Look at Little Yonas: so many prophets told him God had big plans for him but he died in a very random way."

This is a big mistake. I can see the alarm in Melkamu's eyes; I am sure he thinks it's the spirits talking. I must try to dig myself out of this hole by making sense.

"You can take a second and turn it into a year if you focus hard. You can live for three minutes or thirty years and in the end it's the same thing. The most important thing is how you spend that time. The length is not the point, the quality is. You increase the quality by maximizing every good moment. Eating bread with sweet tea is a good moment for me; I am trying to stretch it by dwelling on every bite."

I've only had such conversations with God before. I have forgotten where I am. If I say to my brother that God told me the things I am saying, I am going to get in the same trouble I did when I said God gave me money to buy candy for neighborhood children.

"Finish eating and let's pray," says Melkamu.

I agree because a little obedience is a good price to pay to avoid whippings.

I AM AWAKENED by the loud bang of the door to Melkamu's room. My brother, whom I normally wake up to find pacing the room and praying, is petrified. The door slams against a cabinet and swings back. Tultula gets in. He locks the door behind him, grabs Melkamu's right arm, twists it, and pushes him against a wall. I am too shocked to say anything. Melkamu is too tired to fight back.

"I don't want to humiliate you in front of Tayitu, so keep your voice down," says Tultula.

I am sure Tayitu and her children are already listening by the door.

"I want this child to see there's someone stronger than you who loves her," says Tultula.

I am speechless. I think Tultula went home and thought a lot about his place in this family.

"I understand that you speak to God," says Tultula. "If He is the one telling you to keep this child locked up like a criminal, tell Him to come down and speak to me."

Tultula lets go and Melkamu turns around.

"If you think locking her up is bad," says Melkamu, "wait until Abayé comes back to find out what she has done to the house. Do you know how much money it is going to take to rebuild those rooms? The tenant who lived in the old maid's room says everything she owns, her clothes, smell like smoke, and she's already talking about suing us for compensation."

"That's not a problem, I will pay for it."

"You're going to give us five thousand birr?" Melkamu smirks.

"Your father owes me at least fifteen."

My jaw drops. Melkamu's eyes want to pop out of him.

"He told me so himself," says Tultula. "We are even now."

"We will see," says Melkamu. He says my father might send me to Amanuel Hospital in Addis Ababa, where they treat people with mental illness, and that being locked up in his bedroom is nothing by comparison.

Despite all the conversations I've had with God, despite everything I have written in my exercise book about creating one's own universe out of one's confinement—which is just another form of being born with limitations—and despite all those ideas about stretching time and stretching space and defeating death, I tell myself that I will not allow myself to be locked up in a hospital for the insane. I would rather run away.

SOMETHING POSSESSED ME the moment I saw my father walk up the front stair. I ran and wrapped myself around him, almost pushing him backward. Forgiveness forgiveness forgiveness, I begged. I wanted to hug the father I love good-bye before he turned into the father who might send me to a hospital for the mentally ill.

My father sobs silently now, wiping his tears with a handkerchief, futilely because more keep coming. Tultula sits across from my father, looking away. Yesterday, after freeing me from my brother's custody, Tultula bought Coca-Cola and Abu-Walad cookies and told me we were going on a shirshir. We went to the field by the clinic and ate cookies and drank Coca-Cola. He was worried that I would be sent away, so he wanted me to enjoy my last days of freedom. We sat on the grass eating cookies and talking about his stories from the olden days. He told me that my grandfather was the kindest person he knew.

"Even more than my parents?"

"Not even to be compared."

"In what way?"

"He was selfless."

"And my mother?"

"She was selfless when it came to protecting her children, but not selfless overall."

"Why did you love her so much?"

"Because she was the sort of woman who would kill someone or give up her own life if it meant protecting her children. She would never abandon her children for anything."

I debated in my head whether I should tell him about Degitu asking the nurses for medicine that kills because she couldn't bear the pain toward the end of her life. Should I spoil her for him and set him free? I decided against it for now.

My father has stopped crying.

"Why did you set the house on fire, my child?" he asks.

"It was a mistake."

"We know that, but why?"

"Melkamu said I am possessed. He fasted and prayed for me for three days. You can pray for me more. Please don't send me to Amanuel Hospital." I have reduced myself to begging for one form of prison over another.

"But why did you do it?"

I say that I wanted to make the burning inside show on the outside because I don't think anybody understood the damage that has been done to me by the death of Little Yonas.

I start crying, my father starts crying, Tultula starts crying. Melkamu leaves the room. Tayitu walks in and starts wailing. Mitike closes the door to keep the neighbors from hearing us. To let us cry some more undisturbed.

MY FATHER TOLD Tultula that he won't be taking his money for the damage I caused and that he has saved enough to pay him back all the monies he borrowed from him over the years. He asked him to stay and contribute labor, along with some church men and neighbors who have agreed to do so. We are throwing a "dabo": a sort of party in which your neighbors come to help you harvest or build your house, and you treat them to a small feast of bread and homemade beverages.

My father told me that I have forfeited the money I had saved by selling gasoline. I did not argue with him. He told Melkamu that it would be best if he took a break for a while and went to stay with Weder. He told him that he loved all his children equally, but he felt greater responsibility for me. He promised that he will figure out a way to help him pursue his dreams of attending music school. Melkamu left a few days later.

The day he returned from the hospital, my father pulled me aside and asked if I still wanted to burn something, like the rest of the house.

"Would it make you feel better?"

I thought he was joking at first but he kept going.

"Would it make you forgive us for not telling you about your mother's death?"

I asked him if he was going to send me to Amanuel Hospital.

He said he would rather let me burn him than send me away. That if it could free me from grief, he would buy a jerrican of gasoline and let me burn down the house.

I was inconsolable for the rest of the day, partly because I did not think I deserved his forgiveness, but also because I was thinking that, someday, I am going to fly as high and far as my father dreamt for me, and my beautiful wings will be made of his bones.

36

More People to Love

We are on our way to Addis Ababa to attend Weder's wedding. The journey takes two days by bus. We arrived in Jimma last night. It's me, my father, Tultula, and Gamachu—the son of one of our former servants. There have been murmurs among the Women back in the Small Town.

"They didn't even wear black."

"Never shaved their heads."

"And now a wedding."

"It hasn't even been a year."

"Shameful business."

The Women are upset that the wedding is happening in Addis Ababa. After they grieved with us and helped us rebuild our house, it's only fair that we share our happiness with them. The problem is that my father had no part in deciding the location of the wedding. Weder's fiancé, Lulseged, is from Addis Ababa and he's paying for everything, including our accommodation and travel expenses.

We woke up at dawn to wash ourselves and return to the bus station for the last leg of our journey. We stayed at a fancy hotel in Jimma that

Lulseged booked himself. Had he sent the money instead, my father would have pocketed it and put us up in one of those rundown motels with stinky outhouses. When we went to the hotel restaurant to inquire about breakfast, they told us it was going to cost twenty-five birr per person for a plate of scrambled eggs, bread, and a cup of tea.

"Let's get out of this place," said my father. "It's the devil's house."

Tultula and Gamachu walk ahead of me carrying our luggage. My father walks behind all of us, carrying a small bag and his closed umbrella. It's a little dark.

"I hope we don't get robbed," I say.

"Why do you think I'm walking behind you?" says my father. "I am going to stab anybody who tries us in the eye with the tip of my umbrella."

"There are no thieves anymore," says Tultula. "Soldiers of the new government killed them all when they came in."

"That's true," says Gamachu. "I heard that in Mettu, one of the soldiers sat on an infamous thief and shot him seven times."

"Why waste all that bullet?" asks Tultula.

"He survived," says Gamachu.

Tultula and I are in disbelief.

Gamachu is not going to the wedding. He is a second-year medical student at Addis Ababa University and was visiting his ailing mother in a village near the Small Town for a few days. When Weder's fiancé called to ask if we had everything we needed for our trip, my father told him that he was bringing his "nephew," Gamachu, and would bless him if he paid for his bus fare. My father has become shameless about money after spending a big chunk of his savings paying back Tultula and rebuilding parts of the detached building that I set on fire. I asked him why he wasn't bothered by lying to Lulseged.

"It's not a sin if you're doing it to benefit the poor."

He's a socialist now.

"What's it to him? Not even five dollars. He has his degree, his English, and his jeans."

Ezra, the only one of us other than Weder to have met Lulseged, told us that the man does not know how many pairs of jeans he owns (shame shame—jeans to the tiller!). The rest of us have yet to meet Lulseged. Weder's engagement didn't follow tradition. Normally, the groom-to-be sends elders to the bride-to-be's parents to ask for permission to marry her. Weder was too embarrassed to have Lulseged's fancy uncles from Addis Ababa visit our hometown. She told her fiancé that my father didn't care for that sort of thing. My father likes to let us know he's modern by mocking people who spend a lot of money on wedding parties, which is everyone, saying they should use the money to build a house for the married couple instead.

Lulseged called my father from America to ask for permission to marry Weder. My father had to travel to the Medium Town; the phones in town don't take calls from abroad. He told me later that Lulseged was respectful except for "too much" mixing of English with Amharic.

"Who did he think I was? A man with a degree?"

We already knew about Lulseged's degree in engineering, but his possession of many English words rounded up our understanding of him as a well-educated man. We feel very intimidated by the prospect of meeting him.

My father tells Tultula and Gamachu to stop near the gates of the bus station. He wants to buy us breakfast from the women with stands along the station fence. A giant square of deep-dish bread and a cup of tea cost only one birr.

"You see," says my father. "They were trying to rob us at the hotel."

Gamachu and Tultula compete for who can eat the fastest. My heart breaks a little when I remember how Little Yonas used to bulldoze our dinner trays.

My father insists on more bread and tea for the two men. They say they are full; he tells them that's nonsense, they're young and can take more. Here, he can afford to play a big man.

Weeks ago, my father told me that he is going to make Tultula my legal brother. He wanted to know what I thought, and I said I supported it 1,000 percent. I asked him if he thought Tultula was his biological child. He said Tultula has been like a son to him all these years and that was all that mattered. He is going to tell my siblings when we all meet in Addis Ababa.

Tultula cried the day my father told him. I hugged him and cried with him. My father sat over there trying to suppress his tears but he didn't succeed. We are a family of criers.

WE HAVE GATHERED at the front porch of a bakery on our first morning in Addis Ababa, piles of cake and glasses of milk with coffee before us. Melkamu is paying; I think he wants to be my friend, but I need to calculate how many cakes are enough to erase four days of imprisonment. We spent the night at a house Lulseged rented for us. Weder stayed behind making final wedding preparations with her bridesmaids: Teshager's wife and other friends she made at university. Beza is a bridesmaid but has yet to arrive from Dembi Dollo. The wedding feast is being prepared at a hotel and has already been paid for. Such is the nature of modern weddings.

We are waiting for Ezra before we head to the bus station to receive

Beza and spend the afternoon shopping. My father has promised to buy me new clothes and shoes. The excitement has diminished my appetite; I can't eat more than half a slice of cake. I keep staring at a donkey across the street, who is sifting through trash, knocking about a stray wicker basket with his nose. I had imagined Addis Ababa as a very clean, square, and unnatural place.

My father claims the city was immaculate in the days of His Imperial Majesty Haile Selassie I. Streets so clean you could eat off them. When his favorite son died, the emperor walked barefoot behind the hearse all the way to church. The streets were clean enough for his feet. I think my father secretly worships our last emperor, although he's not as bad as the people who were shocked to learn after the revolution that the emperor had a toilet, that he pooped like mortals.

My father said it was the dictator, Hailemariam, who "took a shit" on the city and on our country. I don't know who to believe. Professor "I Worry" and others on the radio have said that the revolution was necessary, that our country couldn't go on allowing a few landowners to take advantage of the masses. I agree, but I also wish the dictator hadn't taken a shit on our country.

Professor "I Worry" has returned to America after being imprisoned for a few months. He has yet to appear on the FRS to tell us the details of his arrest. He was critical of the ruling party, EPRDF, for harassing and arresting opposition members in the run-up to the national elections about a year ago. We wouldn't know if that was true because, in the Small Town, the parliamentary candidate for the EPRDF ran unopposed. My father was once again elected by a big majority to run our kebele. He accepted the appointment even though he did not submit his name for consideration—he was nominated. He was planning to resurrect his old project of collecting back rent on government houses before local ruling party officials began pressuring him to join the party. He did not want to join the party but he also did not want to defy them, so he resigned.

The new government is good at keeping the threshold of harassment low enough for most of us who are so tired of being afraid all the time to justify staying quiet. It is going to be a while before we become as demanding of more rights as Professor "I Worry."

THE STREET IN FRONT of the bakery is buzzing with people and cars. The loudness of market days in the Small Town is no match for the endless honking of car horns here.

Out of the stream of passersby emerges a familiar face. It's Ezra. He's with a man I have never seen before. "Who's the man with Ezra?" I ask Melkamu. "He's so beautiful."

"If you read your Bible," Melkamu whispers, "you'd know the devil was beautiful too."

I wrap myself around Ezra and kiss his cheeks. His friend shakes our hands. His name is Haile. He tells us he is an evangelist; Ezra adds that he's also a prophet.

"Praise be to God," says my father.

Melkamu is unmoved.

Ezra asks if I was going to eat all that cake. I push my plate to him. I cannot believe myself; this was once my definition of heaven: cake upon cake upon cake in Addis Ababa.

I almost didn't come on this trip. I missed too many days of school in the first semester—because of the grieving and my imprisonment by Melkamu. At the end of the semester, I lied about being done with finals and missed my general science exam, worth 60 percent of my grade. I didn't feel like going anywhere that day—I faked a stomachache and slept all day. For the first time since I began school, I was in danger of repeating a grade, which would disappoint Little Yonas. I decided to apply myself in the second semester. I have been studying, getting perfect scores in all subjects except music. I am even getting perfect scores in handicrafts, using my mother's old spinning wheel to make yarn out of cotton. Most students make embroideries or crochet tablecloths, so my classmates have been making fun of me, saying that I look like an old lady when I spin yarn.

I was afraid that missing a week for the wedding might hurt my grades. Weder said she'd never recover from the heartbreak if I were to miss her wedding. I was finally convinced when Beza agreed to bring her son to Addis Ababa to meet everyone.

Beza had promised to bring her son to us for Christmas. She canceled her trip when the time came. My father had had enough, so we both went to the call center. He began sobbing as soon as he got on the phone, telling her that he felt abandoned by her after our mother died, that he didn't know what he did wrong, that he thought she loved him when she was little. Both my father and Beza knew the operators always listened to our phone conversations, and yet my father was too sad to hold back. She must have felt the same way.

"What is wrong with a cleft lip?" he said. "What gave you the idea that I would ever be embarrassed by my own grandson just because he has a cleft lip? Who raised you, my child? Did I or your mother ever give you this idea?"

I myself have been thinking about those questions—*Who raised you, my child? Did I or your mother ever give you this idea?*—in trying to figure out who gave me some of my fears.

Beza told my father that she didn't want people of our church to see her son at this time. We found out later that she believed God punished her son with a cleft lip because she was living in sin. She and Yeneneh got married after the child was born, and the husband has converted to Protestantism. We made a compromise with Beza in the end: she will bring her son to Addis Ababa where she will also be able to consult a surgeon to fix the cleft lip.

I wish my sister could see how desperate my father and I have been for more people to love.

IT DIDN'T SURPRISE me to learn that Beza had been keeping big secrets from us. I myself don't tell my family about the pages and pages of secret letters I have written to my future friend as well as several pages of monologue by God. If Melkamu discovers my stash, he will take it up as the ultimate evidence of my undiagnosed madness or possession. I wonder how many secrets the future will give me, how many of them I will keep from my father and siblings, how far those secrets will drive us apart. I think about Ezra's love of sucking Teshager's mouth. I learned recently that sucking someone else's mouth is called dhungoo in Afan Oromo. It is what married couples do to each other. My father hasn't been told that Ezra does that with Teshager.

I wish we could all tell each other everything, declaring the end of secrets in our family. The distances forming between us are only helping death, which is going to come for us one by one. All of us will be together later for the first time since the death of Little Yonas. I wish I could stand up and say: the only way to defeat death and the sadness it brings is to steal time by making the sweet present very big, but we can neither achieve sweetness nor be present if we continue to be divided by secrets and fear. I would be accused of being crazy if I did that.

Since my encounter with God or whoever was purporting to be Him, I sometimes have a strange experience in which I feel as though I have stepped out of life to look back and everything seems like a fake arrangement, so I tell myself, stop stop stop, to snap back to life. Solomon the orphan preacher came to sit next to me on the veranda once and asked what I thought the purpose of life was. I turned to him and said, do you want to go mad? He was bewildered. Don't ask yourself such questions unless you want to go mad. He laughed, but in a knowing way.

BEZA'S SON, HENOK, looks like a freshly baked deep-dish bread. I want to take a bite out of his cheeks. He has been sitting on my father's lap since we arrived at the rental house from the bus station. I want to take him but my father is being selfish.

"You seem to think everyone is beautiful," says Melkamu.

That's because I have seen God, I want to say.

I wish I could open my chest, put Henok in it, and disappear to a place where there is no death. "I want to eat you," I say to him.

"You demon child," says Beza, "stay away from my son."

"I'm no fool," I say. "I'm going to wait till you leave the room."

"I will do the cooking," says Tultula.

"I will bring the salt," says my father.

"Those three are definitely related," says Beza.

Later, after Tultula steps out with Melkamu to fetch a crate of Coca-

Cola for lunch, Beza asks my father if he thinks Tultula is his biological son, if that's why he wants to adopt him. Weder suggests doing a
blood test.

"I oppose this!" I say, springing from my seat.

"Calm down," says Weder.

"If we are going to share our inheritance with him, we should know
the truth," says Ezra.

"What inheritance?" says my father, laughing. "He's richer than all of
us combined."

Everyone looks at my father.

"He has a hundred and thirty-two thousand birr in the bank."

All the jaws are on the floor.

"What is he going to do with all that money?" asks Ezra.

"That is for him to decide. I want him to build a house in town, sell his
farm, maybe open a business." My father says he doesn't want Tultula to
live alone in the woods anymore, that we must help him find a wife.

"He should invest his money," says Ezra.

"Stay away from him," says my father.

"Yes," I say, "stay away."

"What is wrong with you?" asks Beza. "Why don't you want a
blood test?"

"I don't want to find out he's not my blood brother."

The little man of the house, Henok, comes to me and says, his toddler's
enunciation made even sweeter by his cleft lip, "Ashishte." My aunty. I'm
in shock. I start quizzing him to see if he knows any English words, but
nothing.

"What are you teaching him?" I ask Beza.

I grab the boy's hand and take him to the room I'll be sharing with my sisters tonight. "It's learning time," I say to Henok. I am going to teach him everything Little Yonas taught me.

Tomorrow, more people will be sharing this bedroom with us as my aunt Etabeba Haregua and her daughters arrive. The rest of our extended family isn't coming because a trip to Addis Ababa is too expensive for them. Lulseged and Weder have promised to visit us in the Small Town in a few weeks for him to meet everyone. My father is expected to throw a mels party.

IT WASN'T A TYPICAL WEDDING. This Monday, a day after the wedding, instead of gathering at the front porch of that same bakery eating breakfast, we should have been at the house waiting for the bridesmaids and groomsmen to bring us a handkerchief tainted by Weder's hymen. They should have walked around the room singing and dancing, showing us the handkerchief and collecting gifts, rewards for the bride.

My father and brothers, including Tultula, looked handsome in their brand-new suits at the wedding. Melkamu played the guitar for the man who sang during the ceremony at church. It was not an unpleasant experience. My father has told Melkamu that he will use our house as collateral to borrow money from the bank and give it to him. I asked my father if Melkamu's pursuit of a career in music was a wise investment. He said that was up to Melkamu to find out, that we do not want him to resent us for the rest of his life for not helping him try.

I was a flower girl. I looked like a small bride in my white dress and white shoes. Beza did my hair with a curling iron and put a tiara on me. I walked before the bride and groom tossing petals and confetti. Weder's husband is as tall as Melkamu but balding. He has a hearty laugh that reveals almost all his teeth. I couldn't recognize Weder at first. The makeup had disappeared the half-star-shaped scar between her eyebrows. She got it as a child when she slipped and fell on broken glass while ducking to evade a pumpkin Beza had thrown at her. It is the story of all our lives: getting into more trouble while trying to run away from another trouble.

I SIT ON MY FATHER'S lap at the bakery. The waiters connected three tables to accommodate our party. There're not enough seats. Teshager and his family are here as are my aunt Etabeba and her daughters. Ezra's prophet friend is missing.

"I hear you are a wealthy man," Teshager says to Tultula.

Teshager is about to leave his job at church to start a large vegetable farm. He says the new government is creating opportunities for businesses and he feels he should take advantage to be able to provide for his growing family. He is working on raising funds. He tells my father that he should advise Tultula to invest in his venture. My father says they will discuss it later.

"How is your coffee business doing?" asks Teshager.

My father explains that profits are always decreasing because more and more people are entering the field. He cannot go into wholesale; one can't succeed without giving bribes. "All those quality-control officials at the Ministry of Agriculture are very rich now."

"One of them is my customer," says Etabeba Haregua. "He was a nobody under the Dergue. He just bought a hotel for fifty thousand birr."

The quality-control officials are the people who decide if your shipment of coffee is good enough to be sent to Addis Ababa for export. You don't want to buy truckloads of coffee only for them to say your coffee is bad.

"Are you going to stay poor because your crazy religion says not to give bribes?" asks Etabeba Haregua.

I look across the street in search of my donkey friend from the other day but he's not around. The wicker basket is still there. I see a goat approaching the trash site. It reminds me of Sheikh Hassan's goat, the leaf thief. I cannot believe this but I miss the Small Town.

On Saturday, my brothers took me to a tall building where I got in a lift for the first time. I ate cotton candy, which I was afraid to put in my mouth at first. At the fancy house Lulseged rented for us, there's a kind of toilet you can sit on, and hot water comes out of the faucets. I estimate the bathtub could fit a barrel of water. I thought about the number of trips I make to the water pump back home in order to fill a barrel.

The goat across the street has trapped his neck in the wicker basket's handle and can't get it off. Look, I say to my father.

I keep leaning forward on my father's lap to make him pull me back. Church elders have been saying that he needs to get married. He has asked a farmer friend of his to introduce him to suitable women. Most of the single women at our church are too young, even though our membership has nearly tripled after the overthrow of the dictatorship. My father cannot marry someone who isn't a Protestant, especially since he is expected to lead by example as a senior member of the elders' council responsible for overseeing church operations.

Mamitu tried to rope my father back into her life recently. She's old and ailing and has no children or close family members to care for her. People in those circumstances enter into a legal agreement with someone willing to care for them in exchange for inheriting their properties upon their death. She offered it to my father but he refused. He introduced her to a willing candidate: the owner of a new private clinic in town. Ezra believes my father is punishing Mamitu on behalf of Degitu, who is gone forever, unreachable, and cannot tell him that she has forgiven him.

I wish you could see that goat across the street right now. A group of boys has gathered around him to laugh, instead of helping him separate from that wicker basket. The poor goat was too curious to find out what was inside the basket to pay attention to the handle. I say to Tultula, let's go help that goat. He takes my hand and we walk across the street.

I can't wait to go back to the Small Town, partly to show off my new dresses—one is made of rose satin with white embroidery on the chest—and my knockoff Adidas sneakers. More importantly, I cannot wait to get back to playing football with Sintayehu, Atinkut, Jamal, and the others. A few girls have begun playing with us. Their parents say, that game is not for girls, you're going to lose your virginity jumping up and down, come back here, you girl. It is too late; once you become possessed by the spirit of football, there is not an army that can turn you back because of the dizzying cocktail of chemicals that washes over your brain and makes you feel invincible.

I can see us gathered at our front yard at sunset. The parents will chase us with sticks in hand. Come back here or I'll break you, they'll say. Stop screaming, it's getting late, they'll say. We will ignore them and keep running around for we know in our hearts that the whipping and the scolding that await us are the frame of our joy. Amidst our stick-bearing parents, amidst uncertainty over the rule of a new government, amidst the history of mutual antagonisms between our families that might flare up in violence somewhere down the road, amidst the possibility of illnesses and accidents and deaths, amidst a fragile world, PASS ME THE BALL, PASS ME THE BALL, we shall shout. We will pass the ball to one another, sometimes between one another's legs, dribbling out of necessity or just to make something beautiful. Amidst all the madness, we will make our own world.

Our bliss won't be limitless; our joy will be checked by the goals we score against one another. But we will also score goals for one another. I have decided that I am going to break the record for the most goals scored in my neighborhood, which is currently held by Atinkut the Spice. I am going to score a goal for Little Yonas. I am going to score a goal for my father, my number one friend. I shall score one for Degitu, the big tree that shielded her children for as long as she could; for grandmother Zeritu Saeed, the terrorist; for my grandfather Baba Gebre, the war hero; and for my aunt Etabeba Haregua, our living shield. I am going to score a goal for each of my siblings, even for Melkamu. I shall score a goal each for Professor "I Worry" and for Deputy Ambassador "Calm Down." I will score a goal for Ribka Sisay, whom I haven't seen in a long time, and for her father, who has lost a lot of weight. I am also going to score a goal for you, my future friend. I will even score a goal for God, the madman who created so much chaos while desperate to escape aloneness. I am going to score a goal each for my country, for the Sudan, for Somalia, and even for Egypt. I am going to score a goal against sadness—

ACKNOWLEDGMENTS

My heartfelt gratitude goes to my beloved mother, Mulatwa Ayele Raré, who left me stories of hard work and relentlessness before she went to heaven. Come on, I told myself numerous times during the development of this novel when I felt depleted, you are your mother's child, you can do this! To my late father, Melesse Sibhat Zeleke, my first friend, for teaching me the importance of debate, of independence, of wasting time, of sitting on the veranda to daydream and talk to oneself for hours. To my dear sister, Tewabech, for her everlasting cheerfulness, for the stories about my childhood. To my late brothers, Tedla and Dawit: to Tedla, for teaching me how to read and write; and to Dawit, for teaching me how to love outside the lines, which is a lot like defying familial expectations to become a fiction writer instead of a lawyer or a doctor responsible for rescuing her relatives out of poverty. To my late cousin Aster Bekele, who told me the most stories about my mother. To all members of my immediate and extended family as well as family friends in Yayo, Ilubabor, who told me stories about the olden days.

Love and gratitude to my best friend Mengesha Fekade, for always debating me, for being my rock, my chosen family. To Bill and Desiree Bohning, for giving me a home when I was drafting the earliest version of this book. To all friends who were there from the beginning and to those who joined along the way, offering encouragement and much needed comfort through their persistent presence in my life, especially: Meti Bekele, Lauren Demers, Bonnie Frieden, Alemayehu Gemeda, Nebiyou Girma, Salem Gugsa, Edom Kassaye, Andrea Love, Tehetena Mesganaw, Soleyana Shimeles, Redate Solomon, Ghion Wubeshet, and Betty Yimenu.

While attending the University of Minnesota's MFA program in creative writing, I was a recipient of fellowships and grants that allowed me to devote myself to researching and writing this novel: the DOVE fellowship, the Beverly & Richard

Fink Summer Fellowship, the Walter H. Judd Fellowship, and a generous travel grant from the College of Liberal Arts. I am grateful to my thesis advisors at UMN: V. V. Ganeshananthan and Julie Schumacher, who read my messy early drafts with generosity and enthusiasm, and provided critical feedback and encouragement. To Patricia Hampl, whose "Reading as Writers" course changed my life. To my MFA colleagues, who read early drafts and asked important questions that helped me see the project more clearly, especially Jennifer Carter, Theodosia Henney, Leslie Hodgkins, Kelsey Reynolds, Connor Stratton, and Alexis Zanghi.

Special thanks to Gao Yer Gonza Vang for her friendship, kindness, and writerly insights. To Mae Rice for her friendship, insights, money, and life-sustaining weird humor. To Holly Vanderhaar for being my source of continuity through persistent kindness during the bumpy phases of the MFA.

I would like to thank the Minnesota State Arts Board for the Artist Initiative grant that enabled me to devote several months to completing and revising the novel.

Many thanks to the archivists at Deutsche Welle in Bonn, Germany, especially Dr. Cordia Baumann, for their extraordinary hospitality during my two weeks of research at their facilities in the winter of 2018. To all those at the National Archives and Library of Ethiopia who were kind and patient with me as I pestered them for weeks, demanding issue after issue of old newspapers.

I want to thank my agent, Ayesha Pande, for all the labor and wisdom she poured into finding a home for my messy novel. To my genius editor at Viking, Allison Lorentzen, for the incredible notes, for giving my novel its wings. To Camille LeBlanc and everyone else at Viking involved in the rigorous process of preparing this book to go out to the world. To Charlotte Humphery, formerly of Chatto & Windus in the UK, for her kind notes.

Last but not least, my love and immense gratitude to my friend Dr. Wendy Laura Belcher of Princeton University, who also doubles as my guardian angel, mentor, worrier, and sponsor. This book would not have been possible without Wendy's extraordinary generosity, without her advocacy on my behalf at every stage of my writing career, and without the year of room and board she provided me, allowing me to devote my time to completing and revising the novel. May all the motherless children of the world find a Wendy.